SO-AQC-907

PAT WARREN

NOWHERE TO RUN

ZEBRA BOOKS
KENSINGTON PUBLISHING CORP.

ZEBRA BOOKS

are published by

Kensington Publishing Corp.
475 Park Avenue South
New York, NY 10016

First Printing: April, 1993

Printed in the United States of America

FOUR AND A HALF STARS!

IF SHE COULD ONLY GET TO THE GUN . . .

Carly's hand gripped the scissors tightly as she stepped closer to the kitchen. She thought the gun was in the first drawer past the doorway. Quickly, she eased around the corner and fumbled for the drawer knob. It was then she sensed something or someone behind her. Whirling, she raised the scissors high.

A dark shadow separated from the kitchen side wall and came toward her. She heard the ugly laugh she now recognized from the phone calls. Her throat closed, and she couldn't scream — could only think to run. His hand shot out to grab her, but she angled out of reach and tore back into the living room, nearly stumbling over a chair.

He was right behind her. She could smell an unwashed body and bad breath, could hear his labored breathing as he again reached for her. Dodging the furniture, she brought down her arm, the scissors poised to do harm. But he easily knocked the weapon from her hand and lunged for her . . .

Prepare Yourself for

PATRICIA WALLACE

LULLABYE   (2917, $3.95/$4.95)
Eight-year-old Bronwyn knew she wasn't like other girls. She didn't
have a mother. At least, not a real one. Her mother had been in a
coma at the hospital for as long as Bronwyn could remember. She
couldn't feel any pain, her father said. But when Bronwyn sat with
her mother, she knew her mother was angry—angry at the nurses and
doctors, and her own helplessness. Soon, she would show them all the
true meaning of suffering . . .

MONDAY'S CHILD   (2760, $3.95/$4.95)
Jill Baker was such a pretty little girl, with long, honey-blond hair
and haunting gray-green eyes. Just one look at her angelic features
could dispel all the nasty rumors that had been spreading around
town. There were all those terrible accidents that had begun to plague
the community, too. But the fact that each accident occurred after
little Jill had been angered had to be coincidence . . .

SEE NO EVIL   (2429, $3.95/$4.95)
For young Caryn Dearborn, the cornea operation enabled her to see
more than light and shadow for the first time. For Todd Reynolds, it
was his chance to run and play like other little boys. For these two
children, the sudden death of another child had been the miracle they
had been waiting for. But with their eyesight came another kind of
vision—of evil, horror, destruction. They could see into other
people's minds, their worst fears and deepest terrors. And they could
see the gruesome deaths that awaited the unwary . . .

THRILL   (3142, $4.50/$5.50)
It was an amusement park like no other in the world. A tri-level mar-
vel of modern technology enhanced by the special effects wizardry of
holograms, lasers, and advanced robotics. Nothing could go wrong—
until it did. As the crowds swarmed through the gates on Opening
Day, they were unprepared for the disaster about to strike. Rich and
poor, young and old would be taken for the ride of their lives, trapped
in a game of epic proportions where only the winners survived . . .

*Available wherever paperbacks are sold, or order direct from the
Publisher. Send cover price plus 50¢ per copy for mailing and
handling to Zebra Books, Dept. 4132, 475 Park Avenue South,
New York, N.Y. 10016. Residents of New York and Tennessee
must include sales tax. DO NOT SEND CASH. For a free Zebra/
Pinnacle catalog please write to the above address.*

*To Marilyn Becker because old friends
are the best friends.*

Chapter One

Detective Sam English popped the tab on a can of Bud, kicked off his shoes, and plopped his stockinged feet onto a brown tweed hassock. Watching Monday night football was one of his favorite pastimes. The Lions weren't doing too well this year, as usual, but Detroit fans were a loyal bunch. Sam leaned his head back, taking a long swallow as the team captains lined up for the toss of the coin.

He watched the kickoff, then reached for the bag of burgers he'd picked up on his way home. Sam tried not to eat too much fast-food, but he'd put in a killer of a day and he hadn't felt like cooking tonight. He had the first sandwich in his hand when the phone rang.

"Shit!" Sam reached for the phone and answered none too pleasantly.

He listened, twelve years as a cop bringing him instantly alert. "What makes the wife so sure it's not a suicide?" he asked the sergeant on duty.

"Bruise marks on the guy's throat. Coroner backs her up."

Hard to argue with the pros. "Doc's already on the scene?"

"Yeah. Captain Renwick wants you over there pronto. Says for you to pick up Vargas on the way since it's in his neighborhood."

Setting down his sandwich, Sam found the pen in his shirt pocket and scribbled the address on the white burger bag. "Got it. Call Ray and tell him I'm on my way." He hung up the phone and stared for a moment at the television screen as he shoved his feet back into his shoes. Detroit fumbled. He flipped off the set and stood. His team would probably lose anyway.

It was a rare day in Motown when no dead bodies were reported found. The locals weren't too thrilled to have their city dubbed the murder capital of the country. But facts were facts, and the guys working out of Homicide were used to dealing in realities. And nobody was kept busier than the half-dozen or so investigative teams from the Main Precinct on downtown's Beaubien Street. Sam knew that the Captain put him and his partner, Ray Vargas, high at the top of his best list. That still didn't make it any easier to get going after the ten hours he'd already put in today.

Picking up his jacket from the chair where he'd tossed it barely ten minutes ago, he shrugged into it. He bent to peer through the window of his twelfth-floor co-op at the murky Detroit River separating the city from the Canadian border and saw that it was still raining. Swell. Grabbing the sack containing his dinner, he made for the door, resigned to the fact that he'd have to eat in his car.

It wouldn't be the first time — or the last.

Fifteen minutes later, Sam took the Moross exit off the Edsel Ford Expressway, turned onto Chandler Park Drive and pulled to the curb in front of the fifth house on the right. Detective Ray Vargas slammed his front door, hurried down the steps and into Sam's black Trans Am.

Neat was the word that best described his partner, Sam had decided a long time ago, with his precise haircut and well-trimmed mustache. Tall and slim,

Ray dressed more like a college professor than a cop, leaning toward tweed jackets and neatly pressed slacks. Which was in direct contrast to Sam, who preferred jeans, button-down Oxford shirts, and well-broken-in corduroy sport coats. Ray even wore a tie much of the time. Sam only owned two, which he wore mostly for court appearances.

Squinting through the rain, Sam saw Ray's Great Dane staring out the window, his front paws braced on the couch-back. "I see Hamlet's training at obedience school really paid off."

"Yeah," Ray agreed as the Trans Am shot forward. "Now he only gets on the furniture when I'm not around, which is most of the time." Ray braced himself with a hand on the dash as Sam made a U-turn back onto Moross and headed toward Mack Avenue. Stretching his legs, he bumped his knee on the underside of the glove compartment and swore softly. Several inches taller than Sam's six feet, he never seemed to have enough room in Sam's ancient car. "When you going to trade this heap in, put your Smokey-and-the-Bandit days behind you, and get a real car?"

It was an old discussion, one they had every time Sam drove, which was why they usually took Ray's wagon. "When they give me a raise." Which wasn't exactly true. He'd gotten the Trans Am the year he'd joined the force, and he was attached to it. With the rebuilt engine he'd installed himself recently, he could get her up to 85 mph in seconds. That sort of thing came in handy if you were a cop.

Ray squirmed uncomfortably. "I'll be too old to care by the time that happens." He took a small notebook out of his pocket and flipped it open. "What've we got? Dispatch said you'd brief me."

Sam cruised to a stop at the light, stuck behind a city bus. He'd finished the lukewarm burgers just before reaching Ray's. Now the craving for that after-dinner cigarette clawed at him. He fumbled in his

9

pocket for his roll of mints. Six weeks and two days, yet the need for nicotine had hardly abated. He'd tried lemon drops, gum, and now peppermints. Crunching down on one, he brought his mind back to Ray's question. "Caucasian, male, forty-five. Wife found him dead in his car in the garage, motor still running."

Ray clicked his pen and began to take notes. "Suicide?"

Sam was grateful that Ray was the detail man, while his strength was as a tough interrogator. They balanced one another well, often assuming the roles of good cop, bad cop instinctively with the ease of long familiarity. "Doc says no. Finger-marks on the neck." The light changed, and traffic began to move. He made a right, then another quick one onto Hillcrest.

Ray glanced up as they approached the house, frowning at the scene. Despite the rain still coming down, there were several small clusters of people huddled together, an ambulance with its red light turning eerily, a black-and-white parked at an angle, and a television truck from Channel 7. "Who the hell called the press? Was this guy a big shot?"

Sam stopped behind the ambulance. "Attorney by the name of Homer Gentry. I never heard of him." Getting out, he glanced up at the night sky, wishing the damn rain would quit.

"That makes two of us." Ray pocketed his notebook and got out, sticking his unlit pipe in the corner of his mouth.

Hillcrest looked to be a decent place to live, Sam thought as he glanced around. Mostly brick ranches, a couple of colonials, neat yards, a sense of neighborhood pride. It was only a couple of blocks long at this end, but across Mack Avenue, on the Grosse Pointe side, the street angled all the way to Lakeshore Drive and the river. Murder didn't discriminate, visiting good areas and bad with increasing regularity, a fact that never ceased to frustrate him.

Sam frowned at the newsmen setting up their cameras, turning on their lights. Another circus in the making. Murder anywhere was always news. While Ray stopped to get the report from the two uniforms who'd been first on the scene, Sam made his way to the back.

As he walked, he glanced toward the add-on family room with windows on three sides. The back door was propped open, and he could see a heavy-set woman in a rocker and two young girls huddled together on a couch as well as several women hovering nearby. There was the sound of weeping and female voices attempting to comfort. The victim at least was out of his misery, but the family might never get over his murder. Sam brushed rain out of his hair and entered the garage just as the police photographer finished, nodding as he left.

Alongside the Buick, the coroner had his clipboard propped on the front fender jotting down notes. Dr. Lester Freemont looked up, then smiled wearily. He'd known Sam English for years, had met him over more bodies than he cared to count. "No rest for the wicked, right, Sam?"

"So it seems." The Buick's door on the driver's side was open. Sam leaned in for a look. Homer had been a slight man with thin, sandy hair. He had on a rumpled white shirt, sleeves rolled up on his freckled arms, and navy suit-pants. Thick horn-rimmed glasses rested halfway down his sharp nose, and his hands were grease-stained. "What'd you find out, Les?"

Dr. Freemont moved to the door. He'd made only a peripheral exam, of course, until the detective assigned to the case gave him permission to move the body. "Strangulation," he said as Sam straightened.

"I see the bruises. Are you sure he wasn't injured

11

earlier, then came out here and turned on the engine?"

"I'll know more when I get him downtown, but I'd be willing to bet his lungs will be clear. There's always the possibility he was propped in here to make it look like suicide." Leaning into the car, he used his pen to point to the victim's throat. "See right here? His Adam's apple's crushed. Looks like two large thumbs squashed it in. And these marks along here, they were likely made by the killer's other fingers. Look at the wide hand span." He spread his own hand out, holding it right over the prints. "Much larger than mine. I'd say you're looking for a big guy with huge hands."

Sam thought of the woman in the rocker, perhaps the victim's wife. "Or a hefty woman?"·

Doc shrugged, then shook his head. "Doubtful. We have to assume our victim didn't hold still while he was being strangled. He could have been surprised while working in the garage, though I don't see signs of a scuffle. Maybe he'd just climbed in his car, about to go somewhere. At any rate, it would take two mighty strong hands to crush the cartilage of the larynx, cut off his air supply, and hold on till he died. And while he was probably fighting to stay alive."

Doubtful it was a woman, but Sam wouldn't rule it out until he checked it out. He'd run across women who'd been angry and, with adrenaline flowing, had temporarily been stronger than many men.

"What do you suppose that shiny stuff on his neck is?" Sam asked.

"I'm not sure," Dr. Freemont answered. With the end of his pen, he touched a small section of skin, then brought the tip to his nose. "Odorless. Colorless. Looks like some kind of ointment. I'll check it out and let you know."

Sam nodded, then glanced down at Gentry's grease-stained hands. "Let me know what you find under his fingernails. Maybe he scratched the guy enough to get us some skin, some blood even."

"Sure thing. Can I tell the boys to take him?"

Hearing footsteps, Sam looked up. "Here comes the fingerprint crew. Let's let them see if they can pick up anything first." He glanced back at the man behind the wheel, at the dark bruises. "Maybe we can get a print off his neck." It would be difficult with that ointment on him, but there was no harm in trying. He'd read of a case where the FBI had lifted a print off a victim's eyelid once. Turning to the technicians, he gave them his instructions.

Leaving the garage, Sam walked over to join Ray who was standing outside the open door to the back room. The Channel 7 television interviewer was inside holding a mike up to the chubby woman as a technician beamed lighting on both of them. "The victim's wife?" Sam asked.

"Yeah. I asked her to hold off talking to the press until after we spoke with her, but she doesn't listen well." Just then, Lois Gentry let out a wailing sound and a fresh batch of tears trailed down her plump cheeks. "This may be her fifteen minutes of fame."

Sam couldn't criticize Ray's cynical remark. He'd seen it too many times himself, the survivors embracing the news media and ignoring the police who were trying to help not exploit.

Finishing inside, the cameraman shifted his focus to the two detectives, then to the body being placed on the gurney.

Sam stepped aside and shoved his hands into his jeans pockets. It was going to be a long night.

The man sat in the worn chair in his motel room with his eyes fastened on the television set, scarcely aware of his shabby surroundings as he drew deeply on his cigarette. Here it was, finally, and the lead story yet.

There were murders daily in Detroit and he'd won-

13

dered if this one might be shuffled over, ignored in light of bigger news. Must be a slow night. Thanks to the man, that stupid Homer Gentry was getting more attention in death than he had in life. Certainly more than he deserved.

Channel 7's well-known anchorman, Bill Bonds, was frowning and serious. He led into the story, his voice registering a weary frustration. Probably the newsman was tired of reporting still another killing. There would be more to come, the man thought.

The picture shifted to an overweight blonde dabbing at her eyes as two gangly girls held on to her. The wife and kiddies, undoubtedly, the man thought. Now they'd know how his family had felt when his father had been taken from them.

Bonds continued talking as they switched to the scene in the garage, the body being wheeled out on a gurney and then quickly shoved into the waiting ambulance. Several neighbors were standing around looking nervous and frightened.

Pleased, the man nodded as he put out his cigarette, then reached for his forgotten beer. He leaned his head back for a long swallow, then set down the bottle. Reaching into his shirt pocket, he removed a folded paper and picked up his pen. Slowly, with great satisfaction, he crossed off the first name on the list.

One down, four more to go. "An eye for an eye and a tooth for a tooth," according to the Bible his mother had so often read to him. So be it.

He snapped off the set and finished his beer. Yes, soon they'd all know. Cracking the knuckles on his big tobacco-stained hands, he settled his head back and closed his eyes.

". . . Happy birthday, dear Dad, happy birthday to you."

Will Weston smiled at his daughter as she finished her slightly off-key good wishes. "Thank you, Carly."

14

He reached for his wife's hand, including Isabel Weston as always. "And you, too, my dear."

"It's your favorite, Dad," Carly said as she set the pineapple cake with whipped-cream frosting on the low coffee table in the Weston family room. "I made it myself, and you know what a labor of love *anything* I bake is."

Her mother smiled, long ago having accepted that her daughter's dexterity in the kitchen left a lot to be desired. "You have so many other talents, dear, that we don't mind if you're not Julia Childs." She handed Carly a dessert plate then looked up at her husband. "I know you love this cake, Will, but I think you should have only a small piece. Dr. Alberts would have apoplexy if he saw you ingesting all that cholesterol."

Will Weston moved back to his easy chair, sat down, and placed his feet on the ottoman. "It was only a mild heart attack, Isabel, and it was nearly a year ago."

"Mom, lighten up," Carly said as she cut her father a medium piece. "It's Dad's birthday."

Isabel poured tea into a pale blue Wedgewood cup. "All right, but just this once." She smiled lovingly at the man she'd been married to for thirty years. "You *are* healthy now and I'd like you to stay that way."

Accepting the cake from Carly, Will winked at her. "Fifty-seven isn't exactly ancient, Isabel. I believe I've got a few more good years left in me." With relish, he dug into his dessert. On the one hand, it was nice to be fussed over occasionally, he thought. But the two women in his life seemed to take turns doing so, which could be annoying as hell.

Carly slipped off her heels and curled up in the corner of the couch, arranging her full skirt about her legs before tasting the cake. Not bad, she thought, considering how much she hated to bake. Or cook. Or even grocery shop.

Growing up, she'd never bothered to learn and now, on her own, she preferred to eat out or buy fast-food, most of which she'd been forbidden to eat while living with her parents. If her mother would drop in to visit Carly's apartment on any given day and check out the contents of her cupboards and refrigerator, she'd be appalled. Of course, Isabel Weston was far too well mannered to just drop in, even on her own daughter.

"I think you've got a *lot* of good years left in you, Dad," Carly said, always one to side with her father.

"Thanks, sweetheart," Will said, sending her a smile.

"Mmm," Isabel murmured, sipping her tea. "But I'd still feel better if you'd retire, Will. The prosecutor's office isn't what it was when you took over fifteen years ago. The stress of dealing with all those criminals . . ." She sighed worriedly. "I know that's what caused that heart attack."

"Nonsense," Will said, savoring his cake as one can only the forbidden. "It wasn't my job, and it wasn't even cholesterol. I've had a heart murmur since my childhood. It certainly doesn't mean I can't work."

She hadn't meant to start this, but since they had, Isabel decided to shore up her argument. "You *have* worked, for years. It's time to let one of your assistant prosecutors take over. You could retire. We have plenty of money and—"

"I want to see the eleven o'clock news." Will Weston clicked on the television, effectively ending the discussion. He loved his wife dearly and denied her little, but this was one subject on which he remained adamant.

Isabel had come from a wealthy family, her father and grandfather having amassed a fortune in the tile business. But Will had never been comfortable melding her inherited money with his hard-earned dollars. Nor could he retire and do so. His wife was wonder-

16

ful, but she'd never understood his feelings about that.

Isabel sent Carly a frustrated glance and sighed. Will could be so stubborn.

Carly set down her plate and patted her mother's slender shoulder. "You worry too much, Mom," she said in a low tone. "Dad's fine, and he loves his work."

Her mother made a face as she leaned closer. "And I hate his work. You know the kind of people he deals with daily, Carly. He talks to you about his cases. The absolute dregs of society. Who wouldn't worry?"

"He's a pro, Mom, and he's careful." She rushed to change the subject. "How many are we having for Thanksgiving dinner this year? It's next week, you know."

With difficulty, Isabel let herself be steered. "The usual twelve to fourteen. I've asked the Garettes and Toni, of course. Nathan and Emily Rogers. Stephen Sanders and . . ."

"Stephanie and Luke?" She'd grown up with Stephanie Sanders and had seen far too little of her since her friend had married an undercover detective last year after a messy divorce.

"Mmm, but they're not certain they can make it. Stephanie's baby's due soon." Leaning back, she studied her daughter. On the surface, Carly appeared happy enough. Yet through a mother's eyes, Isabel could see a restlessness, a discontent. There seemed to be a lingering sadness in the blue eyes so like her father's and dark smudges beneath, carefully disguised by clever makeup. Was Carly still upset over that scoundrel she'd broken up with months ago? "Will you be bringing a guest?" she dared ask.

Carly brushed a stray strand of hair off her cheek and shook her head. "Nope. Just little old me. I'd offer to help you with dinner, but we both know what a disaster that would be. Why don't you let me pick

17

up the pies? That little bakery on The Hill does a wonderful job." The exclusive shopping section of Grosse Pointe known as The Hill had a variety of specialty shops that Carly and her mother had frequented for as long as she could remember.

"Thank you, dear, but you needn't. Mabel and I will handle things." Almost daily, Isabel thanked her lucky stars for the housekeeper who'd been with the family well over twenty years.

"Is Dad going hunting on the Friday after?"

Isabel frowned. She'd never approved of her husband's fondness for that sport or for his love of guns. At least she'd convinced him to keep his collection at his hunting cabin up in Owendale, an area of northern Michigan locals referred to as *the Thumb* since it was located in the thumb part of the mitten-shaped state. "You know he wouldn't miss that weekend for the world." Will and three of his oldest friends had hunted together for years.

"Well, I'll be damned," Will Weston said, sitting forward and turning up the volume. "Someone's killed Homer Gentry."

The two women on the couch turned to the screen. "Who's Homer Gentry?" Carly asked.

"An attorney. My staff and I have prosecuted loads of cases with him. Quiet sort of man, kind of a plodder, but a straight arrow."

Isabel watched as the camera moved in close on a rumpled-looking woman weeping copiously and listened for several minutes. "The poor thing. Do they know yet who killed her husband?"

Will listened intently for a moment. "Apparently not. His wife found him seated in his car, strangled."

"Dear God," Isabel whispered.

Will watched the TV camera scan the Gentrys' backyard. "Ah, there's Sam English, the fellow with his hands in his pockets, and his partner, Ray Vargas, the one with the mustache. First-rate detectives, both

18

of them. They'll find the killer." Wearily, he sat back, wondering who in the world would want to kill a mild-mannered, unassuming lawyer like Homer Gentry.

Carly studied the faces of the bystanders, then the two detectives her father had mentioned. They looked impatient and annoyed at the television crew's intrusion. She couldn't blame them. Grief should be a private matter, not a three-ring circus. She couldn't imagine anything worse than crying in front of a camera for the whole world to witness.

Isabel rose to clear their dessert dishes. "I don't know what kind of a world this is becoming. Murder almost daily."

Carly carried the remaining cake into the kitchen. "We're relatively safe here in Grosse Pointe, Mom. Most of that takes place in Detroit. I'll bet we don't have five killings a year around here." Although she no longer lived there, Carly felt that the elite suburbs consisting of the five Grosse Pointes were as safe as Westchester County or Palm Springs.

"Don't kid yourself," Will said, following them in. "It's a violent society we live in. Random killings can occur anywhere. Family disputes erupt into murderous rages in every neighborhood. You saw the area where Homer Gentry lived, near St. John's Hospital, not five miles from here. I imagine he thought it was a safe place."

"Oh, my," Isabel commented. "That close? Do you think someone in his own family killed this lawyer?"

"I don't know. The point is, we aren't immune from danger, even here. Which brings me to another favorite topic." He slipped his arm around his daughter's waist. "That carriage house you rent is in a changing neighborhood, Carly, and not the best area for a woman to live in, especially alone."

"Amen," Isabel added.

"Dad, don't start. You know as well as I that Indian Village's been renovated recently with lots of young families and single professionals moving back in." Her frown took in both her parents. "You two are professional worriers." She glanced at the kitchen clock, then kissed her father's cheek. "I have to be going. Again, happy birthday."

Isabel walked her to the door. "We'll see you Thanksgiving then, about five?"

"I'll be here." Carly hugged her mother, picked up her jacket, and opened the door. "Still raining."

"It's so dreary out there," Will said as he joined them. "Why don't you stay the night?"

Carly repressed an exasperated sigh. "It's only a little rain. I'll be fine."

"Then give us two rings when you get home," Isabel insisted.

Carly laughed and shook her head, feeling as if she were a teenager again. "All right." She hurried down the steps and into her car. In moments, her red Porsche 911 was humming. Swinging out of the circular drive, she headed for Lakeshore Boulevard.

Arm-in-arm, her parents watched her taillights disappear in the gloomy night. "I worry about her," Isabel confessed, which she knew came as no surprise to Will. "She tries to hide it from us, but she's so restless. I don't think she's over that banker."

Will frowned. Pierce Nelson. How he'd love to rearrange the man's handsome face. Pierce had deceived Carly and she'd found him out, then walked away from him. But it had cost her. Will disagreed with his wife, believing that Carly was over Pierce. Yet, he was aware, she seemed a little unfocused.

Carly had worked in a law office as a paralegal for a while after college and become bored with that. Then she'd teamed up with a friend and done some interior decorating, but that had ended two years ago. Now she was fiddling around with some photography. Perhaps the problem was that she really didn't *have* to

20

work, thanks to a healthy trust fund left her by Isabel's father. Maybe if there were need, Carly would zero in on something. As it was, she served on the symphony committee, arranged charity luncheons, and drifted along. It wasn't a healthy life for a young woman of twenty-eight. Will fervently hoped Carly would find some purpose and soon.

"She'll be all right," he told his wife with more conviction than he felt.

Slowly, Isabel closed and locked the front door. "At her age, I'd been married three years and had a child."

Will Weston drew his wife close and kissed her cheek. "She'll be all right," he repeated.

Chapter Two

Carly kept a careful foot on the gas pedal as she drove her powerful little car south on Lakeshore Drive which wound along the Detroit River. The windshield wipers easily kept up with the light rainfall. Few cars were on the road as midnight approached, but the yellowish glow of the old-fashioned street lamps kept the darkness at bay. Shivering, she wished she'd brought along her raincoat as she switched on the heat.

The eastside area known as Indian Village, where Carly lived, was only about ten miles from her parents' home, yet they always made it seem light-years away. Hard to let go of only children, she supposed, even though she'd moved out years ago. The Westons' large, pillared colonial house was lovely, but she preferred the older residences in her neighborhood.

Nearly all of the huge three-and-four-story mansions that few single families could afford alone had been sectioned off into rental apartments. Her own living quarters were over a three-car garage that undoubtedly had housed a family chauffeur back when the exclusive community had been occupied by the very wealthy. The new occupants had pitched in, painted and pruned, decorated and trimmed. Carly loved the sprawling lots, the huge trees, and the charm of a bygone era. And she loved her privacy.

The quiet boulevard street ended, turning into a

four-lane thoroughfare as she left Grosse Pointe and entered Detroit. Stately homes still dotted the side streets for a ways before Lakeshore changed into Jefferson Avenue and commercial buildings replaced residential. The traffic was heavier here, the crime rate higher, the lights brighter. Stopping for a red light, Carly looked neither to the left nor right.

If someone had told her that she gave the impression of cool and unapproachable, perhaps even snobbish, she'd have protested loudly. It was simply a manner she'd developed through the years, a self-sufficient and independent demeanor that discouraged familiarity from those she didn't know. And those she didn't want to know.

The light changed to green, and Carly started forward, aware that she was most comfortable with her own set of friends, the people she'd lived among and grown up with. She'd attended Liggett, a rather exclusive prep school, then gone on to the University of Detroit along with most everyone she knew. Grosse Pointers tended to stay within their own group, to marry within their own circle, to go to work for the friends of their parents. It wasn't superiority as much as a preference for the familiar. Most people hated to stray out of their comfort zone.

Even now, her best friend was Toni Garette, whose parents lived on the same block as the Westons and owned an upscale restaurant called The Glass Door. She'd almost married a young man with whom she'd gone from kindergarten through college. When she realized she'd said yes to Brett more as a reaction to having stood up in too many friends' weddings rather than from a deep love, she'd broken it off. Fortunately, Brett had come to the same conclusion and they remained friends.

And, after trying a variety of jobs, she was currently working with another old college friend, Jim Tyson. Jim had recently opened a photographic studio and had persuaded Carly to let him teach her about cameras. She was having fun learning about lighting and lenses, angles and contrasts, colors and textures. He was a patient teacher, creative and talented, and had won several awards for his work. He'd apparently seen a glimmer of aptitude in her and wanted to mold her into his assistant, but she was uncertain yet that photography was her goal.

Of course, Carly admitted with a resigned sigh, she didn't seem able to settle on a goal.

Turning right off Jefferson onto Seminole Avenue, she slowed to a residential crawl. Almost to her place, she spotted a familiar figure and cruised to the curb, hitting the button to lower the passenger window. One of her neighbors from across the street, Mark Lane, was out walking his Irish setter. "Great night for a stroll," Carly called out as Mark hunched his shoulders against the rain and stopped to lean down to her.

"Yeah, that's what I tried to tell this mutt. You out for a midnight ride?" Mark reeled in the leash against the straining dog.

"My father's birthday dinner."

"Ah, yes, the duty visit. They still after you to move out of this wicked neighborhood?" Mark ran a freckled hand through his hair, shaking off the rain.

Carly ran occasionally on clear mornings, and her path had crossed Mark's—which was how they'd learned a little about one another. Mark was thirty, an only child fighting a father who wanted him to join the family brokerage firm and move back home. Instead, he'd done as much job jumping as Carly, having tried real estate, insurance and, currently, a stint at an auto dealership.

She nodded at him, knowing he'd understand. "They never let up."

"I know what you mean." The Irish setter had wrapped the leash around Mark's feet in his anxiety to get going. Stepping free, Mark spoke over his shoulder. "Want to meet me for a run in the morning about seven? Weather should clear up by then."

"I'll see. If I'm not out front, go on without me." She gave him a wave as she raised her window. Moving on, she turned into her drive and followed it to the back of the lot. Although the garage could accommodate three cars, the renters of the front house had beaten her to the punch. A definite drawback on nights like this, she thought as she pulled close to the outside stairs that led to her apartment. Quickly, she dashed up and went inside.

Her mantel clock was chiming the witching hour as Carly turned on a lamp. Noticing that the light on her telephone answering machine was blinking, she walked to it and hit the play button.

The first message was from Jim, reminding her she was to be at his studio at ten for her first lesson in the darkroom, developing the black and white snapshots she'd taken last week. Impatiently, Carly waited for the second message.

Only there was no voice after the beep. It sounded as if the caller had dialed the wrong number and been too embarrassed to say anything. She couldn't exactly hear breathing, but there was definitely someone on the line. Finally, there came the click of the hang-up. How odd.

The third one played, and Carly forgot the strange call as her friend Toni's voice came on asking her to be at The Glass Door at noon. They'd have lunch and finalize the plans for the wedding shower they were giving early next month for another friend, Amanda Stone. "Be there, on time," Toni's voice commanded.

Carly rewound the tape and slipped off her jacket. Like a dutiful daughter, she called her mother to let her know she'd arrived home safely. Flipping on the stereo, she punched in the CD player and waited for Michael Bolton to begin telling her he wanted to be her soul provider. In the bedroom, she turned on

25

more lights, then stopped to glance into the mirror, running her hands through her long, thick hair.

Maybe she should get a trim. That's what she'd do, get her hair cut, then meet Toni at noon. And there was that new boutique that had opened on The Hill that she'd been meaning to visit. Probably Toni could get away, and they'd go together. A fun day after all the rain and gloom today.

Carly heard a sound and went to the window, peering out. The trees, nearly bare of all their leaves, swayed in a wet wind, scratching at the glass eerily. Out by the curb under the street light, she saw a man wearing a cap standing in the rain. She couldn't tell if it was Mark and couldn't see the setter anywhere. Now why would someone stand there at this hour getting soaking wet? Downright silly. She pulled the blinds and drew the drapes, then remembered Jim's message.

It wasn't as if she really worked for him, not yet anyway. She'd call him and reschedule. She liked studying with Jim, but only when she didn't have more important things to do. And Toni was counting on her to help with Amanda's shower.

That settled in her mind, Carly went into the bathroom to undress, her thoughts returning to her parents. Her mother would undoubtedly have read something sinister into that curiously silent message on her answering machine. And her father would have said that the man by the lamp post looked suspicious. Slipping on her long nightgown, Carly shook back her heavy hair. Life was simply too short to dwell on every little thing, she decided.

Homicide in Police Headquarters downtown on Beaubien Street was on the first floor in the back. Sam's desk faced Ray's in the far corner under a section of windows that never looked clean. Sam looked up from his paperwork as Ray made his way through the squad room, stopping to talk to a couple of the guys. He lingered longer at Sergeant Mary Margaret O'Malley's cubicle, admiring the three pink carnations in a small vase on her desk.

Megs, as she was known, was the only female officer in their division and took a lot of good-natured ribbing for the flowers she brought in summer and winter in an effort to add some cheer to the room. She was a damn fine officer, one Sam would rather have covering his back than most anyone except Ray. The carnations were probably from her husband, Dennis, who worked out of a west-side precinct.

Finally, Ray sat down in his creaky swivel chair. "Did you get the report?" Sam asked.

It was the Tuesday after the Thursday that Homer Gentry's body had been found. Sam figured that Dr. Freemont had had enough time to complete his findings.

"Yeah." Ray withdrew a folded sheet from his inside jacket pocket and tossed it over to Sam. "Not much there. The stains on the victim's hands were from working under the hood. Nothing foreign on his clothes, no hairs that weren't his. They did come up with two small brown fibers under his nails—the kind found in cheap jackets or pants. Gentry was wearing navy slacks and a white shirt, no jacket. Could be something, then again maybe not."

Sam scanned the brief summary. "We should check out his closet to see if he owns something brown that would match. I wondered that night why this guy was working on his car in a dress shirt and slacks. And why he wasn't wearing some kind of jacket since it was evening and cold out."

Ray shrugged. "I figure he was one of those guys who doesn't change clothes after work. Or maybe he was in a hurry to install new points in his car, which is what his wife said he was doing when she left him. Or could be he was just plain hot blooded."

27

"There's another odd thing," Sam went on, still studying the report, "the only fingerprints on the ignition and key were the victim's. So the killer didn't strangle him and then turn on the engine to make it appear like a suicide. Gentry himself must have turned on the car in an enclosed garage. Pretty stupid."

"Maybe he just turned it on for a minute to check his work," Ray threw out.

This is how he and Ray worked best, Sam thought, playing devil's advocate back and forth until they came up with something. "And during that minute, our killer just happened to arrive? Pretty coincidental." Sam didn't believe in coincidence.

"Stranger things have happened." Ray reached to point something out on the report. "Check that out. The shiny stuff on the victim's neck is petroleum jelly. That's a new one on me."

It was new to Sam, too. "We'd better ask Mrs. Gentry if Homer used the stuff for whatever reason. If not, it had to come from the killer's hands." He returned to the medical examiner's report. "Did you see this? The span from forefinger to thumb measures ten inches, so wide that the killer's fingers overlapped at the back of the victim's neck as he squeezed? Doc pointed that out to me at the scene."

Ray nodded. "We're looking for a guy with hands like Wilt Chamberlain. 'Course, Homer had a small neck, wore a fourteen-and-a-half collar."

Sam pulled out another report from a stack of papers on his desk. "Due to the ointment, no prints could be lifted from Gentry's neck, and there were none aside from family members on the car or anywhere. They dusted that whole garage and the house."

"Maybe he wore gloves."

"Possible. They found only the victim's prints on the car door, but on the garage door handle, they picked up Gentry's prints and his wife's plus traces of

28

the petroleum jelly. That would indicate the killer had the stuff on his hands or gloves."

"Or Gentry had the jelly on his neck and the killer got some on his hands when he squeezed the life from him. Here's another thought. Do you think the killer maybe smeared his hands with petroleum jelly so his prints would appear smudged on anything he touched?"

"Yeah, could be." Sam placed the two reports in a file folder he'd already labeled with the victim's name. "Wet footprints on the cement in the garage couldn't be distinguished because the wife and those two girls had run in and out by the time our guys got there. No muddy footprints outside." He leaned back in his chair. "I hate to say it, but nothing on the scene's going to help us, except we know this creep's got big, strong hands."

Ray's methodical mind set the scene as he toyed with his pen. "So let's see what we've got. According to his wife, Gentry was working on his car while she and the kids went shopping. He's got the garage door down 'cause it's cold and raining. He finishes and, for some reason known to him alone, he sits down behind the wheel and turns on the motor. Maybe even the radio, though it wasn't on when the wife found him. At any rate, he doesn't hear our killer slide up the garage door. He's probably left the driver's door open. The killer walks in, lunges for Gentry's throat, and finishes him off. No sound, no struggle that anyone hears. Then he pulls down the garage door, since that's how Mrs. Gentry found it, and calmly walks away without a soul seeing him."

Sam let out a frustrated whoosh of air. They'd spent two days combing Gentry's neighborhood, talking with adults, teens, kids. Disappointing legwork that had gotten them nowhere. "Apparently no one saw anything unusual. No strangers around, no questionable cars, nothing."

"The shadow strikes again. Unbelievable." Ray pulled his pipe from his jacket pocket.

Sam shared his partner's frustration. With all the technology at their fingertips, there were still far too many killings where not a clue could be found. "Mrs. Gentry said nothing was stolen or missing from either house or garage, so the strangler wasn't after something, as far as we can determine. I think we can dismiss the thought that it was a random killing. I hardly think some maniac with big hands was just passing by and decided to open Gentry's garage door and off him because he had the urge to kill right then."

"Right, so it probably was someone he knew. Which is why Gentry didn't yell out."

"Okay, so we go with that angle." They'd already interviewed Lois Gentry and the two girls, Homer's widowed sister who lived across town, and a handful of the attorney's friends. "Best bet would be Gentry's cases, past and present." Most homicides were committed by someone known to the victim. And a lot of people held grudges against lawyers.

Ray pulled out his notebook and flipped it open. "His office is on Morang. He started in private practice five years ago and worked alone. Secretary's name is Madeline Brown. Been with him from the start and doubles as a legal assistant. I called her earlier. Said she'd be there all day."

Sam pushed back his chair and stood, grabbing his jacket as he heard his stomach rumble. "Let's go. First we stop for lunch. I haven't eaten all day." And the half-a-dozen cups of coffee he'd poured down his throat had him feeling wired.

"You buying?" Ray asked, rising.

"Only if we have a real meal. I'm tired of greasy hamburgers and fries."

"You and me both." Ray followed Sam out of the squad room.

* * *

"You two picked a bad day for lunch," Toni Garette said as she sat down at the window table where Carly and her mother were seated. "The day after Thanksgiving's the busiest shopping day of the season." And The Glass Door was located near a mall where Santa Claus had arrived via helicopter that morning.

Carly watched two young mothers at the next table trying to contain the excitement of their toddlers long enough to order. "I think you're right. But Mom was at loose ends with Dad gone hunting, so I thought we'd come see you. Have you got time to have a bite with us?"

"Just a cup of coffee, I think." Unobtrusively, she signaled the waiter, who hurried over and took their orders. Toni shook back her long blond hair and turned to Carly's mother. "I've just got to tell you again, Mrs. Weston. The dinner yesterday was wonderful. Nobody can beat your pumpkin pie. You wouldn't consider giving me the recipe, would you?"

Isabel Weston smiled her pleasure. "So you could put it on the menu here, you mean? I don't believe you need any help from me, Toni. Your selections are all delicious."

"Thanks." She waited while the waiter returned to pour their coffee before handing her friend a sheet of paper. "Here are the two menus I came up with for Amanda's shower. Why don't you look them over later and let me know which one you think we should go with?"

"Sure." Carly scanned the menus briefly before slipping the paper into her shoulder bag.

Isabel tasted her coffee, deciding she'd have only one cup. She'd had plenty yesterday, and the caffeine had kept her up half the night. "Who is Amanda marrying again? I know you told me, Carly, but I've forgotten."

"His name's Bob Prentiss, and he's not very memorable," Carly commented drily.

31

"Oh, come on," Toni protested. "He's not *that* bad."

"What does the young man do?" Isabel wanted to know.

Carly all but rolled her eyes. "He manages a gas station. *But* he has plans to own the station one day."

Toni crossed her arms and leaned forward. "What's wrong with that?"

In answer, Carly *did* roll her eyes.

Toni laughed. "All right, but maybe he's good in bed."

Carly made a face. "Would you want those grease-stained hands on you?"

As both young women laughed, Isabel shook her head. "Honestly, you two. He could be a perfectly nice young man."

Obviously, she wasn't getting through to her mother, Carly decided. "I'm sure he is, but that's not the point. Amanda and Bob have so little in common that if they make a go of this marriage, it'll be a miracle. Attraction's not as important in the long run as liking the same things, sharing the same background."

"Whoa, you just lost me," Toni said with a grin. "I'm all for a good healthy attraction. It can get you over the rough spots like nothing else." Toni had had a few serious affairs, but was currently unattached. She watched approvingly as the waiter served Carly's reuben sandwich and potato salad with a flourish. "I wish I could eat like you and not gain an ounce," she told her friend enviously.

"Metabolism," Carly said smugly.

Isabel let the waiter place her seafood salad in front of her before returning to the subject. "I'm surprised at you, Carly. You and Brett had everything in common, yet you broke up because there was no spark between you. Or so you said."

"That's true," Carly conceded, "but don't you think

32

that most attractions simmer down after a while? Then, when he wants to go bowling and she'd rather attend the symphony or she's used to vacationing in the Bahamas while he prefers camping out, Amanda and Bob are going to have some serious problems."

"I had no idea you were such a cynic, darling," Isabel said with genuine surprise.

"I'm a realist, Mom, not a cynic." After what Pierce Nelson had put her through, she was more than ever a realist, Carly thought.

Toni sipped her coffee. "Actually, what I think, dear friend, is that you've never felt an attraction so strong that all else be damned. Am I right?" Her bright blue eyes challenged her friend.

Carly toyed with her potato salad thoughtfully. "Maybe. But I can't imagine being so caught up in someone that I wouldn't consider the practical side of a lifelong relationship."

"What about Stephanie Sanders?" Isabel reminded her.

"Yes, exactly," Toni chimed in. "Stephanie's crazy about Luke Varner, and they're as different as night and day. She moved from a Grosse Pointe estate to live on a houseboat with him, for heaven's sake."

Carly knew a losing battle when she heard one. "All right, so Stephanie's the exception. Luke may be an undercover cop who's lived in a different world than Stephanie was brought up in, but I have to admit, there's something about that man that makes a woman stop and wonder."

"Aha!" Toni said gleefully. "There's hope for you yet, Carly." From the corner of her eye, she caught the maitre d's urgent look. "Uh oh. A problem. Will you excuse me? I'll catch you before you leave."

"Certainly, dear." Isabel set down her fork. "I'm not very hungry. I think I ate too much yesterday."

"Did Dad leave early this morning for Owendale?"

"Oh, yes. About eight." Patting her mouth with

the heavy linen napkin, she sighed. "I hope he's careful. He's been so distracted lately. And he looks tired."

"Then relaxing with old friends is probably just what he needs." Carly savored the sharp bite of the mustard on her corned beef.

Isabel took out her compact to check her makeup. A natural redhead, she'd gradually shifted the color of her hair to more of a warm auburn when she'd entered her fifties. Which made it nearly the same color as her daughter's, though Carly's hair was so much thicker. His two redheads, Will always called them. She wished he were here with her now. "Dad plans to be home by Sunday afternoon. He wants us to attend the funeral services for that attorney who was killed last week."

Finishing nearly her whole sandwich, Carly pushed her plate aside and reached for her coffee. "I see by the papers that the police haven't a clue who killed the poor man."

"A terrible thing." From under her lashes, Isabel studied her daughter. Carly had some peculiar views on men and marriage. Perhaps that was why she hadn't settled down yet. If only she could find someone who would share a love with her like she and Will had. But young women today didn't seem to want the same things that women in her day had wanted. More's the pity. Putting her lipstick away, Isabel Weston wondered if she were indeed getting old.

Her mother was moving into one of her brooding silences, Carly thought. Isabel had always been a worrier, and, lately, she was getting worse. Perhaps she could distract her. "Do you have time to help me with Amanda's shower, Mom? It's too crowded to go shopping at the mall, but we could go to the stationer's and order the invitations."

Yes, anything to delay going home to that house, so empty without Will. "I'd be happy to help."

"Great." Smiling, her spirits rising, Carly signaled for the check.

It was colder in the northern Thumb area of Michigan than when they'd driven up Friday morning, Will Weston thought as he trudged up a small incline. But at least the snow had held off and the sun was shining. Yesterday it had been cloudy and quite windy.

Not one of them had bagged anything, though they'd spent some three hours tromping about in the woods after arriving. Today, they'd split up, determined to at least get one good-sized buck. Will gazed upward and calculated by the position of the sun that it was nearing noon. They'd all four set out about ten, which meant that he'd been wandering around a couple of hours.

He wasn't really tired, he told himself. It was just that trying to walk quietly so as not to spook a deer was a strain. And he had on so damn many clothes. With the butt of his shotgun under one arm and the barrel resting on his wrist, he began to unbutton his red hunting jacket. He'd worked up a sweat under his sweater and flannel shirt.

At the top of the hill, Will paused and looked around. He didn't spot any of his red-jacketed friends, nor could he see signs of wildlife anywhere. He knew the deer were around. Last year they'd gotten three and had to have them butchered and delivered later. Surely this season they'd get at least one. Mabel and Isabel both were good at making venison taste like the most succulent beef.

Hearing a sound somewhere to his right, Will looked around, wondering if one of his friends were in the area. They'd be easy enough to spot through the bare trees in their red jackets. But he saw no one and decided he'd imagined the noise.

Starting down the incline, Will found himself huff-ing a bit, his boots pounding heavily on the dried leaves underfoot. There was an uncomfortable hitch in his side and his chest felt tight. Damn, he didn't need this right now.

By the time he reached the wooded area where the land leveled, he was breathing hard and his face was damp. He decided he'd better stop to rest a bit. Slowly, he went into the woods aways until he came to a big old white pine. He lowered himself carefully to the ground and leaned back against the rough bark, releasing a weary breath. He'd never want to admit it to Isabel, but he really didn't have the energy he used to have.

Will opened his jacket all the way, loosened his collar, then lay his shotgun across his lap as he stretched out his long legs. A sound—like the snapping of a small twig—caught his attention, and he turned his head, looking all around. Only a small animal, he decided as he leaned his head back and closed his eyes.

The air smelled so good up here, clean and rich with that scent of pine. Maybe he *should* give some thought to retiring soon. He could build on to the cabin, do whatever Isabel wanted done. Ah, but she'd probably hate it up here year round. She rarely came with him even to visit, though in the winter, the area was so peaceful and lovely.

Carly used to come with him when she was younger. He'd taught her to shoot a rifle, and she was damn good, though she'd never hunted. Then Isabel had found out and had a fit, so, for a while, they'd both stopped coming. His closest friend, Nathan, liked to hunt, so he'd convinced Will to resume the yearly trek; and their other two old friends had joined them. They'd been at it about twelve years now, always on the Thanksgiving weekend.

Feeling a little better, Will opened his eyes. And almost jumped out of his skin to see a burly man wearing a cap and dark clothes standing over him. Too

36

startled to speak, Will stared, his eyes widening and his heart picking up its pace.

"Don't you remember me?" the man's gruff voice inquired.

"Can't say I do." Bracing a hand on the ground, Will attempted to stand while the fingers of his other hand crept toward the shotgun's trigger. But the stranger jabbed a thick fist into his chest, pushing him back. Unnerved, Will grew angry. "What's the matter with you? What do you want?"

The man's face turned stormy. "I want you to know what it feels like to lose everything." Suddenly, his huge, hands shot out and closed around Will Weston's throat.

Stunned, Will tried to make a sound, but the thick fingers wouldn't let him. His free hand flew up to grab at the man's arm, trying desperately to break his grip. The hard fingers on his neck tightened, squeezing harder. Helplessly, Will struggled, but already, his air supply was gone.

As his eyes widened, Will Weston's last thought was that he did indeed recognize the man.

He held on a few moments longer, then the man relaxed his hands and straightened. Involuntarily, Weston's body jerked and his fingers tightened on the trigger. The shotgun discharged, the bullet going wild, the sound echoing through the still woods. Slowly, Will slumped against the tree trunk, his eyes forever open.

"Number two," the man whispered, stepping back. *Vengeance is mine, saith the Lord.* Sometimes, the Lord needed a little assistance.

He stared at his handiwork a moment longer, then cautiously made his way through the woods, his dark clothes blending in with the decaying colors of fallen branches and bare trees.

Chapter Three

Sam leaned back into the cushions of his comfortable couch, stretched his feet onto the low oak table, and rolled his shoulders to try to get rid of the kinks. It seemed like he'd been sitting here for hours going over the same damn reports, notes, and interview sheets. The results were that he'd become bleary-eyed and had yet to come up with anything new.

He shifted his tired eyes to the wall of windows looking out on the cold November afternoon. Nothing much out there to cheer him either. He crossed his feet, clad in fur-lined slippers, one atop the other, adjusted his Detroit Lions sweatshirt, and crossed his arms over his chest. No matter how many times he reviewed the past week's pile of paperwork, he kept coming up with the same answer. Which was that they were no closer to finding Homer Gentry's killer than they had been the rainy night they'd first leaned over his dead body.

Disgusted, he leaned forward, bracing his elbows on the knees of his worn jeans, dangling his hands, and lowering his head thoughtfully. Sam was a firm believer that every murderer left at least one clue, no matter how small. All a detective had to do was find it. He brushed a weary hand across his unshaven face. Where the hell was it?

Rising, he went into his small kitchen, opened the

fridge and looked at the pitiful contents. He hadn't had a chance to get to the grocery store in quite a while, and it showed. Saturday afternoon, and the markets were probably jammed. Maybe he'd just scramble some eggs and go tomorrow. He picked up the quart of milk, opened it, and held it to his nose. Too late. Turning, he poured the pale liquid down the drain.

Moving automatically, he put on a pot of coffee. Something hot to take the chill off the gloomy day. After plugging in the pot, he walked to stand gazing out the window. Dreary. It'd be better if it snowed. At least, it would be white and clean-looking. The river below was gray, gusty winds churning the water and slamming it onto both Canadian and American shores. Jamming his hands into his back pockets, he turned away, wandering back to watch the pot drip.

By all rights, he should be dressing to go out with some smashing woman on this late Saturday afternoon. Take her to dinner, maybe a movie, then back to her place and . . . and let nature take its course. It had been too damn long, his tightening body reminded him. Remembering the pile of papers spread out on his table, the killer still out there somewhere thumbing his nose at the police, and the other cases he and Ray had to juggle as well, Sam acknowledged that it might be some time before his itch was scratched.

The coffeepot light was on when he went in to check. He grabbed a mug and poured just as the phone rang. Back in the living room, Sam caught it on the second ring. "English here." Easing down on the couch, he sipped the hot brew and listened. "Yeah, I got it." Slowly, he hung up.

Prosecuting Attorney William Weston had been found dead in Owendale, seemingly strangled by the same huge hands as Homer Gentry, the second victim in nine days.

Crunching down on the peppermint in his mouth, Sam listened to the assistant medical examiner read from his notes as he and Ray stood over the remains of Will Weston in the morgue.

"As you can see, no marks on the body aside from the throat. The larynx has been crushed, and there are deep bruises, apparently made by strong fingers, on the back of the neck." The young man pushed his rimless glasses back up onto his nose as he set aside his report. "Any questions?"

The room was cool, sterile, chilling. Sam swallowed his mint. He had less trouble viewing bodies on the crime scene than in this antiseptic atmosphere. There was a forlorn anonymity here that always bothered him. "Has forensics checked him out yet?" he asked.

"Yes. The body arrived late last night, and Dr. Freemont did his preliminary work-up then, after the photographer and forensics finished."

Sam leaned down to study the prosecutor's neck, shiny in the overhead light. "Do you happen to know what that is on his neck?"

"According to Doc, it's petroleum jelly, the same type found on the other strangulation victim." The assistant pulled the sheet back to cover the victim. "Doc called earlier to say he'll be in after church if you want to talk with him."

Ray scribbled in his note pad. "Who brought him in?"

"State police. I understand, because Mr. Weston was Detroit's Prosecuting Attorney and because a similar killing occurred within our jurisdiction last week, that Owendale will cooperate and let us take the lead on this one. Is that right?"

"So we were told," Sam answered. "Has the family been in to identify the body?"

The assistant said he remembered the daughter vividly. "Thick auburn hair, back ramrod straight, trem-

40

bling hands. She identified her father late last night. She took it hard."

Who wouldn't take something like this hard? Sam asked himself. He thought of his own father, who oddly resembled Will Weston more in death than in life, and ground his teeth. And he thought of someone out there with big hands and an urge to kill. First a small-time attorney and now the P.A. There had to be a connection somewhere. They'd find it, in time.

He looked at the nametag on the man's white coat. "Thanks, Ted. Ask Doc to send over his findings as soon as he can, will you?"

"Sure thing."

Out in the deserted corridor, Sam drew in a deep breath and started walking. It was never pleasant, checking out bodies, investigating murders. But it was far worse if you knew the guy, even casually.

Will Weston had been a man Sam had admired since coming on the force. Will treated cops like equals, realizing that both he and they had dirty jobs to do and respecting that. On the stand, he'd never tried to discredit or downgrade an officer, always appearing supportive and unbiased. He'd had a dozen or more assistants, and yet Sam had never heard that even one of them had been treated unfairly by Will. That alone said a lot about the man.

Hurrying to keep up with Sam, Ray pocketed his note pad. "He'd just turned fifty-seven last week. Only the good die young, isn't that what they say?" Ray, too, had respected Weston.

Sam hit the crossbar on the glass door, shoved it open, and blinked as he walked out into a bright noonday sun. Quite a contrast to yesterday's overcast day. But the improved weather did little to cheer him. "We've got to get that sonofabitch off the streets."

Ray opened the driver's door of his Ford wagon. On the way over, they'd discussed that the strangler probably knew both Gentry and Weston. "We need to take another look at Gentry's caseload and see if we can match up a name with guys Weston prosecuted." Getting behind the wheel, he paused to look at his partner climbing in beside him. "That ointment seems to tie it to the other victim. You think this guy's on a roll, that he'll kill again?"

"Your guess is as good as mine. If we could find the connection, we'd at least have some names he might be going after next." Sam slammed his door as Ray started the car. "Go north on Jefferson. We need to pay a visit to Will's widow."

Ray backed out of the space, then swung out of the parking lot carefully. Unlike Sam, he was a cautious driver who rarely exceeded the speed limit unless absolutely necessary. Rushing to the scene of a murder didn't make sense. The dead weren't going anywhere. "How do you think she can help us?"

Frowning at the classical music drifting from the radio, Sam flipped the off button. "How can you listen to that day in and day out?"

"Violins are calming. You ought to give it a try."

Sam grunted, then returned to Ray's question. "The Westons have been married a long time. Maybe Will talked to her about some of his cases. It's worth a try. Besides . . ."

"Besides, you'd kind of like to tell her you thought a lot of her husband, right?"

"Yeah, that, too." Ray knew him well. But even he didn't know everything about Sam's background. Only two men in the department did, Captain Renwick and Luke Varner. It was no one else's business, he thought.

Searching in his pockets, he found his roll of mints and popped one. Damn, he'd kill for a cigarette, just one. Some days were worse than others. His thoughts shifted to Isabel Weston. He'd met her years ago, but she probably wouldn't remember him. A classy lady, like so many others he'd known back then.

He pictured the Weston house tucked away on a winding street in Grosse Pointe Shores. Secluded, protected, inviolate. Only someone had sought Will Weston out away from his isolated haven and violated him anyhow. Nowhere could anyone be really safe from maniacs, though Will's neighbors probably felt secure surrounded by their wealth and power. He'd often argued that point with his father. And gotten nowhere.

They were creeping along in the far right lane behind a junk heap with a cracked back window and a missing tail light. "Damn, Ray, you drive like a little old lady out for a Sunday outing. Will you pass this jerk and get moving?"

Ray checked both side and rear mirrors, then switched to the faster left lane. "Speed limit's thirty here. An impatient nature can bring on an ulcer, you know."

"A complacent nature can annoy the hell out of your friends, you know."

Unaffected, Ray crawled along in the left lane, unconcerned about the cars zooming around him as they left the city limits of Detroit. The river was calmer today, the breezes light. A few hardy joggers could be seen following the path on the right. He seldom got out this way though he'd grown up only a few miles from here. "The Westons's street shouldn't be too much farther. Woodland Shores, isn't it?"

"Take the next left, circle around the median strip and then hang a right."

"Sounds like you've been here before," Ray commented as he switched on his left blinker.

Yeah, he had. He'd known these streets like the back of his hand a hundred years ago. Or so it seemed. Returning always bothered him, bringing back the guilt. Freud would have a field day with his head, Sam thought as they turned onto Woodland

43

Shores. "Up there, just around the curve, the one with the pillars."

Ray parked in the circular drive behind a red Porsche convertible. Somewhere in the distance, church bells were chiming. Stepping out, Ray frowned at the double doors of the huge house, bracing himself. This was the part he hated most, questioning the grieving family. "Some days I hate this job."

Sam closed the car door. "Yeah, me, too." Taking a deep breath, he stepped onto the porch.

A nightmare, Carly thought. She was smack dab in the middle of a nightmare. As bereft as she felt, her heart ached more for her mother. Gently she pulled the afghan crocheted in shades of blue over Isabel Weston as she lay on the leather sofa in the den. Finally the sedative that Dr. Alberts had insisted Isabel take was working. Or perhaps it hurt too much to be awake and her body had just closed down so her mind could rest.

Sinking into her father's favorite easy chair, Carly watched her mother sleep and rubbed at the spot between her eyes where a tension headache had taken up residence. The call had come yesterday afternoon from a nearly hysterical Mabel. The housekeeper had choked out the news while, in the background, Carly could hear her mother's anguished sobbing. Like a wild woman, she'd driven over and been here ever since, except when she'd left to identify her father's body.

Carly swallowed around a lump that refused to go away as she glanced around Will Weston's favorite room. Even now, she could hardly believe that he would never walk through that door again or sit behind his desk and peer at her over his glasses. Never hug her again, or smile at her in that gentle way he had, never . . .

44

She held a clenched fist to her mouth to keep from crying out. She hadn't been able to weep like her mother. There could be relief in tears, she knew, but somehow, they wouldn't come. Perhaps because she was so filled with anger at the injustice of it all. Why had this happened to such a good, kind man? How would her mother get through her remaining years without the man who'd been so long at her side? Who would Carly go to when she wanted to mull over a problem or share a funny incident? She loved both her parents, but she'd always been especially close to her father. Where was the madman who'd done this unbearable thing, and why hadn't the police found him?

Carly ran a shaky hand through her hair and leaned her head back, closing her eyes. Their friends, so many good people, had drifted over last night as the news had spread, to comfort, to try to help. Dazed, in shock, she'd let them. Only an hour ago, she'd sent Mabel home, knowing the poor woman had scarcely closed her eyes all night. And Toni, who'd been a pillar of strength. She'd sent them all home so her mother could rest and she could be alone with her grief.

Ultimately, everyone had to handle grief alone and in their own way, Carly thought. No one could prepare you for it, nor truly share it with you. They lived in a violent society, Dad had said just last Sunday as they'd eaten birthday cake. She'd dismissed his warning as the hovering concern of a parent. She no longer would.

At first, her father's friends had thought Will had suffered a heart attack. Uncle Nathan had knelt beside him, preparing to administer CPR while one of the others had hurried back to the cabin to phone 911. That was when they'd noticed the bruises. Strangulation. What a terrible death. His three friends had been deeply shocked.

As was everyone else, which was why the phone

hadn't stopped ringing. Her father's staff, members of the Bar, co-workers, the police, judges, acquaintances, and friends — all expressing outrage and offering sympathy. Then the press had invaded, reporters at the door, television crews filming outside despite the fact that she wouldn't allow them in. She'd grown angrier with each passing hour at the intrusion, at their insensitivity. Anger was so much easier to handle than gut-wrenching grief.

She heard the doorbell then and leaped to her feet, not wanting her mother awakened. She'd unplugged the phone, but there was that damn door chime. Hurriedly, she went out to the marble foyer, pulling the door to behind her. She would get rid of whoever it was in no uncertain terms. Before they could ring again, she put on her frostiest look and yanked open the door.

Sam nodded politely to the woman standing in the doorway. "Good afternoon. We've come to see Mrs. Weston. I'm . . ."

"Mrs. Weston isn't receiving guests just now. Goodbye." Carly had the door nearly closed when a large masculine hand stopped it.

Not receiving guests? Who was this babe with her to-the-manor-born attitude? Sam cleared his throat. "This isn't altogether a social call, ma'am."

Carly tipped up her chin, her exasperated gaze flitting over the men. If these two were from a TV station, she would call the station manager and lodge a complaint just as soon as she sent them packing. Enough was enough. "Who *are* you?"

She had an imperious manner that had Sam gritting his teeth even as he recognized her. Will's only offspring. Spoiled, patronizing, aloof. She obviously thought herself superior to most, certainly to the two lowly public servants on her doorstep. Sam tried to remember he'd really liked her father.

Noticing that Sam had balled his hands into fists,

46

Ray stepped forward with a gentle smile and flipped out his I.D. "I'm Detective Vargas, and this is Detective Sergeant English. We'd both like to offer our condolences to Mrs. Weston and the family. I know this is a bad time, but we have to ask her a couple of questions."

Carly felt like shrieking, like collapsing. Instead, she straightened her spine and narrowed her eyes. "Now? Well, you can't. My mother's lying down."

Sam tried to forgive her since she was protecting her mother. And perhaps her pompous actions were a cover-up for her own grief. "Then perhaps we could step in and ask you a few questions?"

Carly's headache, the one she'd been struggling with all day, was beginning to pound with a vengeance. "I don't see how anything I have to say could possibly help. Why don't you leave us alone and go find the lowlife who killed my father?"

Despite his acquired prejudice against women like the one in front of him, Sam admired the elegance. From that carefully tamed reddish-brown hair past the pale gray sweater and matching skirt to the expensive leather pumps, she looked like class. She also looked like trouble. "We're working on it," he told her, his tone as cool as hers. "If you could just spare us a few minutes . . ."

The tall, lean one was at least dressed well, Carly thought. This one looked like a TV version of an undercover cop. Burt Reynolds playing Dan August in a rumpled corduroy jacket worn over jeans, curly black hair and dark, assessing eyes. The last thing she needed was to talk to an arrogant detective. "I don't think so."

"Carly, dear, who is it?" Isabel Weston walked surely, if a bit more slowly than usual, across the white marble floor.

Sam caught the daughter's muffled "damn" before Mrs. Weston appeared in the doorway. He moved in,

47

reaching to shake the older woman's hand, introducing the two of them, offering their sympathies.

"That's very kind of you." Years of training paid off for Isabel. She'd been taught dignity even in grief, and she held on to that familiar comfort. She hadn't slept very soundly, had heard the voices, and had to rise. She'd cried most of the night and knew that tears only left her feeling worse. She disliked the fuzzy feeling drugs left her with and planned to tell Dr. Alberts she would take no more. Everyone was well intentioned, but she didn't want oblivion. She wanted Will back.

Since she couldn't have that, she could at least remain composed in public. She owed that much and more to Will's memory. She drew in a deep, steadying breath. Her control was fragile, but definitely in place. "Please come in."

"Mom, you don't have to see them now," Carly protested even as her mother swung wide the door.

"Sam English," Isabel Weston repeated as she looked up at the detective. "You seem familiar. Have we met?"

He'd underestimated her memory—and her strength. But she was a reminder of another time, and he hated strolls down memory lane. He decided to finesse her question. "I admired your husband very much," he said, following her into the off-white and pale blue living room with its large brick fireplace.

"Thank you." Isabel waved them to the sofa and took the gold wingback for herself. Looking up, she noticed Carly frowning her disapproval from the archway. "I'm fine, dear." She knew her eyes were red-rimmed and swollen, but perhaps on this day, she could be forgiven that. Otherwise, she was neatly groomed, as always. Carly didn't understand that it was important for her to go on as usual, that it was the only way she would survive.

Sliding her hands into her skirt pockets, Carly went to stand by the mantel. Only someone very close to her would know that her haughty demeanor was a camouflage of her concern for her mother and her own pain. She turned to face the dark-haired detective. "Are we suspects? Is that why this couldn't wait?"

"Carly, I hardly think so." Isabel shared her daughter's frustration and grief, but not her anger. "These gentlemen are just doing their job."

Trying to suffuse a tense situation, Ray jumped in. "That's right, ma'am. For starters, if you could supply us with a list of your husband's relatives and friends so we could check them out?"

Isabel seemed suddenly less certain. "Oh, my. Will that be necessary?"

Ray went on to explain. "Nearly eighty percent of homicides are committed by someone the victim knows." He had a feeling this wouldn't be the case with Will Weston, that the killer was most likely connected with the prosecutor's work. But they had to start somewhere, to eliminate all possibilities.

"That's preposterous," Carly said vehemently. "I will not have you grilling our family and friends as if they were common criminals."

"Carly, please." Isabel raised a shaky hand to her throat, then turned to the two men seated on the couch. "You have to understand. My daughter's just had a terrible shock."

"Mother, are you apologizing for me?" Carly felt on the verge of explosion and didn't care who knew it. *"They* should be apologizing for bullying their way in here at a time like this." She turned her fury on Sam, since he was the closest to her. "I want the name of your superior officer."

He faced her calmly, trying to decide if she were having a delayed reaction to grief or if she were just a spoiled brat. Right now, he opted for the latter choice.

49

"Captain Renwick. R-e-n-w-i-c-k. Would you like the phone number?"

She studied his dark eyes and saw that he wasn't as composed as he would like her to think. She saw the temper, the challenge, and something else. A disdain that infuriated her all the more. Who the hell did this two-bit detective think he was? But she wouldn't allow herself to get into a screaming match with him and upset her mother further. "Just leave your card on the table." She turned to Isabel. "I'll be in the den if you need me." Head held high, her lower lip caught between her teeth, she left the room.

Definitely a spoiled brat, Sam thought as he listened to Mrs. Weston apologize again for her daughter. "We understand completely," he told her as Ray flipped open his note pad. "Mrs. Weston, did your husband ever discuss any of his cases with you, perhaps a difficult one or two, mentioning names?"

Isabel shook her head. "Rarely. I listened when he did, of course, but I didn't take note of any names." She glanced worriedly through the arch leading to the foyer. "Will talked to Carly about many of his trials, sometimes for hours. He often said she had a quick mind and amazing insight." Wearily, she looked at them, blinking back a fresh rush of tears. "Perhaps later, when she's more herself, you can talk with Carly."

The day hell freezes over, Sam thought. They would solve Will Weston's murder without help from his pampered daughter, thank you very much.

The tall priest's thinning brown hair blew about in a stiff November wind as he stood at the graveside and opened his black book. Will Weston's bronze casket, draped with the American flag at one end and a blanket of flowers at the other, was at the center under the canopy. Off to one side stood the family, supported by closest friends. Others gathered all around, num-

50

bering several hundred, most silent with heads bowed as the priest began.

Sam stood back, his eyes watchful, his stance seemingly relaxed. He saw Ray just over the priest's right shoulder and half-a-dozen other plainclothesmen mingling with the crowd. Of course, given Will Weston's status within the legal and police community, there were officials, judges, lawyers, all the way down to bailiffs and law clerks present as well.

His eyes scanned the area slowly. The ground underfoot was crunchy with frost, the air cold and clear. Will's final resting place was on a small incline with few grave markers in this newer section as yet. There were several large trees, bare of leaves at this time of year, strategically planted, and a fountain over the next rise that in warm weather undoubtedly added a certain charm. Sam shivered. Cemeteries were not his favorite places.

He saw no one unusual around, though he was well aware that many killers returned to the scene of the crime, sometimes flaunting their ability to get away with something right under a cop's nose. Of course, in this gathering, it would take one hell of a clever fellow to go undetected.

Unless the killer was someone in a dark suit with head bent in prayer alongside the casket, pretending to be the friend he never had been.

Turning up the collar of his black raincoat, Sam stepped closer, shifting his gaze from face to face, trying to memorize each for possible future reference. Isabel Weston looked vague and a little fragile, though he doubted that she was. Clutching her arm on one side was a woman about her age, obviously a close friend. On her other sided stood Carly Weston.

Damn if she didn't look good, even in grief, Sam thought. Her heavy auburn hair was pulled back from her pale face and fastened with a gold clip at her nape. She wore little makeup. She didn't need it. The slim black coat emphasized her slender frame, the high heels showing off a pair of great legs. But she didn't impress him.

Beautiful on the outside, shallow on the inside. Foot-stomping, temperamental, snobbish. If he hadn't known other women like Carly Weston personally and intimately, he'd have perhaps been drawn to her looks. If he hadn't seen for himself what a spitfire she was, he'd think she looked vulnerable today, her defenses down.

Then her eyes met his. He saw the flash of annoyance, almost of contempt, then the deliberate snub as she turned from him. He almost laughed. She was so damn obvious, so true to form.

As the priest ended the service and invited the mourners to a reception back at the Weston house, Sam raised a brow toward Ray. They hadn't thought about that. He nodded in his partner's direction, indicating they should go. Maybe they'd get lucky mingling among people there. Unobtrusively listening, they might catch a name carelessly dropped, a reference made in a relaxed moment, an incriminating comment.

Sam glanced at his watch. It wasn't exactly what he'd planned for his afternoon, but he thought it important enough to adjust his schedule. Hands in his pockets, he watched the group straggle off in clusters toward their cars. Quite a few lined up to file past the casket for a final farewell, then to stop for a word with Mrs. Weston and Carly. Several of the women dabbed at tears, but Will's widow and daughter, both wearing dark glasses, appeared dry-eyed and in control.

The rich were amazing, Sam thought, not for the first time.

The man stared at himself in the dingy motel-room mirror. If he had one outstanding trait, it surely had to be that he could easily blend into many backgrounds, probably because he looked like everyman. Of medium height with brown hair worn average length and brown eyes, the only notable thing about him was his muscular arms and chest, easily camouflaged by loose clothing. And, of course, his big, working-man's hands. He removed his brown work jacket and tossed it onto a chair, then lit a cigarette.

He'd gone to the cemetery to see Weston buried. Carrying a winter rake, pruning shears, and a large trash bag, he'd taken on the role of a groundskeeper. And no one had even glanced his way. He'd always known he was smarter than those dumb cops.

More than any one of the others, Weston was to blame. Not once, but twice, he'd betrayed him. Weston had recognized him finally at the end. The man felt good knowing his face was the last one Weston saw before dying.

After his thumbs had sunk into the flesh of Weston's neck, the prosecuting attorney's gun had accidentally fired. But the man had hurried off, blending into his surroundings, escaping undetected. Because the Fates were with him. Because he had a mission to accomplish and there were still others needing punishment.

Taking a deep drag, the man sat down on the sagging bed and leaned over to untie his shoes. The Weston women had looked pale and in shock. He laughed out loud. He'd only begun to make the Westons pay. He slipped off his shoes and rubbed his big hands together in anticipation.

The woman's death would take more care, more planning. She'd had it easy all her life, too easy. But all that was about to end. Killing her wasn't enough. He wanted her to worry and wonder a long while, to lie awake nights in fear, to look over her shoulder constantly, to puzzle over who was stalking her and why. He'd already begun staking her out, but it was too soon to make his move. He would play with her until he was ready to reveal himself to her, until he was ready for her to know exactly who he was and why he had to kill her.

Yawning, the man snubbed out the cigarette in a glass ashtray, then stretched to remove something from his pants pocket. He placed the tube of petroleum jelly on the rickety night stand and lay down, paying no attention to the squeaking of the cheap bed springs. A short nap, and he'd awaken refreshed. Then he'd figure out his next move in his plan to send Carly Weston to join her father in hell.

Chapter Four

Ray Vargas wished his memory was as good as Sam's. But it wasn't, which was why he took notes constantly. The problem was it was difficult to scribble in his notepad inconspicuously as he wandered among the Westons' guests trying to overhear conversations without seeming to eavesdrop. Which was why he kept drifting to corners and turning aside to jot down things.

The pages were filling rapidly. The Westons had very little family on either side, but he'd met several nieces, nephews, and cousins. He had a list of their neighbors and now was able to put faces to the names as he listened carefully on the fringes of small groups. He'd noted that Judge Nathan Rogers appeared to have been Will Weston's closest friend and that Jane Garette, who along with her husband, John, owned The Glass Door, was probably Isabel Weston's best friend. Ray had spoken with both, and they'd seemed honest and genuine.

His eyes moved to a tall young man someone had pointed out as Brett Stevens, a neighbor Carly Weston had known forever and been engaged to at one time. Attentive and protective, Brett hovered around Carly, offering her coffee, giving her the occasional comforting hug. Also Ray had spoken for a few minutes with the bearded fellow who was helping himself to a huge plateful of lunch. His name was Jim Tyson, and he owned a photo studio where Carly helped out occasionally. A nice guy who seemed genuinely fond of her.

Another friend, Toni Garette, was by Carly's side almost constantly. Toni was a knockout, Ray thought, watching her toss back her blond hair as she steered her friend over to the buffet table. He couldn't help wishing he'd met Toni under other circumstances.

It wasn't wise to mix business with pleasure, Ray had decided some time ago. Besides, it would be foolish of him to approach an obviously monied and sophisticated woman like Toni Garette with anything other than police matters on his mind. Of course, the fact that he was a Harvard grad, knew the right fork to use, and had traveled extensively wasn't obvious to most. Toni was likely prejudiced, thinking that both he and Sam were merely "dumb cops." Knowing that wasn't so, Ray could handle people's preconceived notions.

Unlike Sam, Ray thought, as he gazed across the room and found Sam studying Carly Weston. Sam had a real thing about the wealthy, a disdain that was as obvious as it was so far unexplained. Ray hadn't bothered to question this quirk of his partner's, realizing that every man had a few idiosyncrasies.

As Ray watched from the sidelines, Carly excused herself and headed for the kitchen. He saw Sam follow her moments later. Those two were like oil and water, Ray thought, inching his way through the crowd in the dining room. Perhaps he'd better be within hearing range in case they got into it again. It wouldn't do for one of Detroit's finest to get into a verbal battle with the victim's grieving daughter on her home turf.

In the kitchen, Carly found Mabel overseeing the

56

caterers, who were busily refilling platters and bowls, putting on fresh coffee, opening more wine. "You're doing a wonderful job," she said, giving the small woman a quick hug. "I don't know what we'd do without you, Mabel."

"Thank you, dear." Mabel wiped her damp brow with the back of her hand. "How's your mother holding up?"

"Better than I'd dared hope. She's sitting down with the Garettes just now, having a bite to eat."

"Oh, good. And have you eaten?"

Carly turned aside, pressing a hand to her stomach where the burning seemed to center. "I will, later." Rising on tiptoe, she searched for the bottle she'd last seen on the top shelf of the far cupboard. There it was, behind the steak sauce.

Someone dragged Mabel away, and Carly was grateful. She didn't want anyone to see and start fussing over her. Pulling open two drawers, she couldn't locate a clean spoon. Frustrated, she spotted a clean juice glass on the counter, poured in a generous serving, and downed the liquid quickly. Making a face, she placed the glass in the sink and returned the bottle to the cupboard just as a hand touched her shoulder. Rearranging her expression, she turned.

"Stephanie, hello." Carly opened her arms and hugged her very pregnant friend. "It's so good to see you."

Drawing back, Stephanie's blue eyes filled with sympathy. "I'm *so* sorry about your father. He was such a decent man."

Carly nodded her thanks. She and Stephanie had grown up blocks apart, gone to school together and, though she hadn't seen much of her lately, Carly considered Stephanie a good friend. She'd married Zane Westover awhile back, which had turned out to be a grave mistake. Zane had not only turned out to be a criminal, but he'd tried to kill his wife. Stephanie had staged her own disappearance and had been on the run when an undercover cop hired by her father had found her in Florida. That cop had been Luke Varner, who'd married Stephanie after her very messy divorce from Zane.

"I'm sorry you couldn't make it over for Thanksgiving." It had been the last day she'd seen her father alive.

"Me, too. I wasn't feeling very well, and Luke was away on special assignment."

"Is Luke here now?" Carly asked.

"No, he's still away. I don't see much of him these days." Stephanie patted her rounded belly. "But I'm not alone."

Carly smiled for the first time that day. Stephanie had miscarried Zane's baby and been devastated. Carly knew how much she and Luke wanted this child. "When are you due?"

"Any day, which is why I wish Luke was back. But he will be soon, I know." Absently, she rubbed at her lower back as she shifted her weight from one foot to the other. "My father asked me to convey his sympathies, too."

"How is he?" Stephen Sanders had suffered a stroke last year, his second.

"Much improved. His speech is still a little slurred, but he's walking better. He doesn't go out much yet."

Carly saw a movement out of the corner of her eye and noticed the dark-eyed detective, Sam English, leaning against the kitchen doorway, calmly watching her. She felt her spine stiffen at the sight of him. What was there about that man that caused her blood pressure to rise?

"I hope, when things settle down, you'll make time to come visit," Stephanie was saying. "It's been forever since we've had a long talk."

"I'll make it a point to do that," Carly promised. The Varners lived on a houseboat on Lake St. Clair. "I want to see if you've put lace curtains and flowered slipcovers on Luke's masculine retreat."

Stephanie laughed. "Not quite, but I have made a few changes." She thought of the plants she'd brought, a few paintings for the bare walls, print tablecloths and napkins, toss pillows in bright colors. Feminine touches all, but Luke seemed happy with her additions, especially the bassinet draped in white eyelet. She glanced at her watch. "I have to leave. The doctor's scheduled to probe and poke at me in an hour. Take care, Carly."

"Thanks, I will. See you soon." Carly watched her old friend move through the arch, stopping to speak with Sam English. Stephanie probably knew him through Luke. Carly wished she'd have thought to ask her what she thought of the big jerk. As Stephanie left, Carly saw Sam weaving through the caterers toward her. Her hands clenched automatically as she braced herself.

Believing that the best defense was an offense, Carly met his eyes as he stopped in front of her. "Handcuffed any of our guests in the living room yet, Detective English?"

Sunday she'd been furious with him; at the cemetery she'd been scornful; and now she was dishing out sarcasm. He'd promised himself he'd keep his own temper under control, that he'd kill her with kindness. "Not yet, but I do have a couple of my men keeping count of the silverware."

"It's such a comfort having you look after us. I wonder how we managed before. Of course, if you and your men had kept a closer eye on my father, perhaps he'd be alive today."

He caught the anger, and something else. He heard the pain and understood her a little better. He had a tendency to cover up his feelings with gruffness, too. "We didn't know the killer would strike again, or who he'd be going after, Carly."

59

She didn't like the familiar way he said her name. And she didn't like the way his tone had softened. She much preferred him when he was primed to do battle. Much safer that way. Sam English made her uneasy, though she wasn't quite sure why. "Then you do believe the same person killed both my father and that Detroit attorney who was strangled?"

Sam shrugged, not wanting to admit to anything that she might later throw back at him. "That's what I read in the newspapers." Her dress was black, high-necked, long-sleeved. How could something so simple look so damn sexy on her?

"Do you believe everything you read in the papers?" Because she needed something to do with her hands, she turned to the counter and poured a cup of coffee she didn't want and probably shouldn't drink, given the state of her stomach.

"Yeah, that's me, a true believer." He leaned against the kitchen counter, crossing his feet at the ankles.

He declined the coffee she offered, so she sipped it herself, as she studied him from under lowered lashes. At least today, he had on a jacket with matching pants and a pale blue shirt with button-down collar. No tie, of course. She doubted that he owned one, although she remembered her father mentioning that department regulations called for plainclothes detectives to wear them. Sam English appeared to have a disregard for regulations.

Her eyes drifted upward, and she noticed that his nose had a slight bump, as if he'd broken it playing some sport years ago. Or, more likely, in a fight. Carefully, she set down the cup. "Who *do* you believe killed my father?"

"If I knew that, I'd have him in custody. Real life isn't quite the way the detective shows on television would have you believe. You can't wrap up a case conveniently in sixty minutes."

Did he think her so gullible? Or so stupid? Carly raised her chin a fraction. "Maybe you could quit quizzing our friends and go out there and find him."

"Maybe you could help me."

She frowned. "How, exactly?"

"Your mother mentioned that Will often talked about his cases with you." He hadn't intended to interview her, but something had him changing his mind.

"He did. Do you think someone he sent to prison killed him?"

"Possibly. Or someone's relative who feels Will didn't give him a fair shake. Or someone on his staff, passed over for promotions, carrying a grudge. Or someone he'd fired, someone jealous of his success. Or just some looney tunes with a fixation. Take your pick."

Carly let out a sigh. "Some choices."

"Either that or someone wandering around this house right now who's laughing up his sleeve and getting away with murder."

That suggestion brought her temper back. "There's no one here who would harm my family."

"Are you so sure?" From her quick flareups of temper, Sam thought there was a good deal of passion in her despite those cool looks she threw his way. He couldn't help wondering if she displayed that same passion in bed.

Carly opened her mouth, ready to let go with a scathing answer, then thought better of it. Instead, she looked him calmly in the eye. "Is it just *my* family, *my* friends, that you distrust, or do you suspect everyone you run across as having sinister agendas?"

"Are you so naive that you believe just because someone has megabucks they're lily-white and innocent?"

Perhaps it was the past few hellish days she'd endured, or maybe just the obnoxious man before her.

61

Carly didn't know which, but she did know she was close to losing her temper. Again. She wouldn't give him the satisfaction. "I am not naive. But I am fresh out of patience. Why don't you go play cops-and-robbers somewhere else?" Turning, she walked away from him before she popped him a good one.

Sam watched her go, then turned to look in the sink. He'd seen her toss back a drink earlier, and he'd wondered what it was. Was she sneaking belts of booze at noon to help her get through the day? He picked up the glass. It was coated with a white, chalky residue. He leaned down to smell it. A liquid antacid. So she was more a bundle of jumpy nerves than even he had suspected. Interesting contrast to her aloof act.

Carly Weston was a royal pain in the ass, but he'd give her this much: she definitely wasn't boring.

Slowly, Carly raised the shotgun to eye level, her hands slippery with perspiration. Taking careful aim, she zeroed in on her target. The figure in the viewfinder was hazy, the features blurred, yet she could tell someone was there. A man, and he was smiling. She closed her eyes a long moment.

He began to laugh, and she opened her eyes. The gun she'd been holding was gone, and now she was looking into the barrel of a rifle aimed at her head. "No!" she screamed.

"Run," her father's voice commanded.

Carly began running, stumbling in her haste to get away, then falling to the hard ground. Her heart pounding, she looked back over her shoulder. The shadowy figure had dropped the gun and was now reaching out to her, long arms stretching forward. His hands—those huge, powerful hands—were coming closer, closer. Then they closed around her throat, and she screamed . . .

Carly sat up in bed, her pulse racing, her eyes flying open. Panting in labored breaths, she tried to calm down. The dream had been so real, so frightening. Her face was clammy, her hands trembling. Shoving off the covers, she swung her legs over the side and gazed out the window. The sun was up, but just barely.

The second nightmare this week. Rising, she walked to the bathroom, stripped off her damp gown and tossed it into the hamper. Turning on the shower, she waited until the water warmed, then stepped under the spray.

Afterward, wearing yellow sweatpants and shirt, she went into the kitchen in her bare feet. Maybe the old childhood remedy would relax her. She poured milk into a saucepan to heat.

Later, sitting in her living room sipping warm milk and watching a winter sun slowly light up the sky, Carly wondered if she'd ever feel good again. She'd never been a person easily depressed, but since they'd buried her father a week ago, she just couldn't shake her gloomy mood.

Even her mother seemed to be coping better. Of course, Isabel had her routine—a standing appointment at the beauty shop twice a week, bridge on Tuesdays at Lochmoor Club, lunch Saturdays with three old friends. Carly was sure that adhering to that routine helped Isabel get through the days, although she knew how desolate her mother's nights must be. And she, who'd been used to being alone, was finding her days long, lonely and restless, and her nights impossible.

She'd read endlessly, answered the huge pile of sympathy cards and notes, and spent time with her mother. And still, she was fidgety, restive, bored—which was why she'd called Jim last night, thanked him for his patience, and asked if she could come back to work in his photo studio again. Like the good friend he was, Jim had seemed delighted. She only hoped she could concentrate.

She badly needed something to fill her hours, some purpose, a reason to get up mornings and get going. Carly was aware she'd felt like that before Will's death, but much more so now. She needed to feel involved, excited, useful. Finishing her milk, she rose to go into the kitchen to fix a cup of instant decaf coffee.

It was nearly nine. She'd finish dressing, have just one cup of decaf — maybe getting off caffeine would help her sleep better — and be on her way to Jim's studio. If she kept busy, worked hard and tired herself, perhaps tonight she'd be able to sleep. And not dream.

At precisely ten, Carly slipped on her down jacket, grabbed her camera case, and skipped down the wooden outside steps. She was nearly to the bottom when she stopped, gasping in shock. Slowly, she descended all the way to the ground and stared in horror.

Her beautiful red Porsche 911, not yet six months old, had every window smashed in, even the heavy plastic rear window. Stunned, she walked around the car, her mouth open in disbelief. Who could have done this, and why? Tomorrow was the first of December and Halloween was long gone. Neighborhood kids pulling a prank? She'd lived here five years, parking in the same spot always, and there'd never been an act of vandalism before in this block, none that she'd heard of.

It was as she stepped back that she noticed that her front tire was slashed. Anxiously now, she circled the car again and found all four tires had been ripped with some sharp object. She felt like sitting down and crying. She loved that car, the first one she'd picked out alone without her father's help.

Her father. The chilling thought crept in unbidden.

Backing to the steps, Carly looked around the yard like a suddenly frightened animal. No one in sight, nothing amiss. Precious few places for someone to hide now that the trees had shed all their leaves, though many of the trunks were thick. She knew that all of the renters in the main house worked and had probably left hours ago. They'd had no reason to look over at her car, parked some distance around the corner from the entrance to the garage.

Still, why hadn't anyone heard something? Why hadn't she, light sleeper that she was? It would be literally impossible to smash in a car's side windows and the entire front windshield without making some noise. Out on the street, she heard a sound, then saw a car drive past. She didn't recognize it, but that wasn't unusual. It was a long block.

Confused, she looked back at the Porsche, uncertain what to do. Call the garage, her insurance company, the police? Would they laugh at her if she inferred a connection to her father's murder? Sam English most likely would. No, she couldn't stand that.

Perhaps she was over-reacting.

Marching back upstairs, she decided she'd have to call Jim and tell him about her problem. But once inside, she had second thoughts. What if someone were watching her place, trying to give her a warning? She wasn't stupid enough to let her pride get in the way of her safety. She'd ask for that other detective, Ray Something. Shedding her coat, she picked up the phone and dialed.

Sam caught the phone in mid-ring. "English here."

The desk sergeant's voice informed him that a Carly Weston was on the line asking for Ray Vargas. But Ray was checked out.

"Do want to take the call?"

"Yeah, put her through." Sam leaned back in his

chair and waited, wondering what she wanted. He hadn't seen or heard from her since the reception at her mother's home. He heard the hesitancy shaded with annoyance when she came on. "Is something wrong, Carly?" he asked.

Torn between anxiety and embarrassment, she gripped the receiver. "Yes, but I'm not sure you're the one I should talk with about it."

"Ray's out. You're stuck with me. What is it?"

His voice sounded lazy, like he was already finding it amusing that she called. Damn, but she didn't want to do this. "It's my car," she began. "The windows are smashed in."

Sam sat up straighter. "What do you mean, smashed in?"

"As in with a ballbat or something. All of them. And all four tires have been slashed as well."

"Where are you?"

"In my apartment. I found it like that about five minutes ago."

"Stay there. I'll be right over."

She felt a wave of relief. He wasn't laughing after all. "My address is . . ."

"I know where you live. Give me fifteen minutes." He hung up.

So did she. Of course, he'd know where she lived. He was a cop. Maybe she had done the right thing in calling him.

Carly walked to the kitchen to put on a pot of strong coffee. She might as well drink caffeine. After this incident, she probably wouldn't be able to sleep tonight anyway.

Sam paced up and down the paved driveway, growing angrier with each step. Where the hell was she? He'd told her to wait right here.

He'd arrived minutes ago, checked out the car and the area, then gone upstairs to knock on her door. No

66

answer. He'd peeked in the one window he could reach. No sign of anyone. He'd seriously considered breaking in, but decided to hold off. Instead, he'd walked out to the street and looked both ways, seeing no sign of Carly Weston anywhere.

She couldn't have gone far on foot. He'd rung the bell at the front house, and no one had been home there either. Had she tired of waiting for him and called someone to come get her? His encounters with her had shown him she wasn't the patient kind. He'd told her fifteen minutes, but they'd radioed him in his car and he'd had to take a detour on the way over to talk with someone on another case, someone he'd been trying to reach for days. The traffic on the way over had been unbelievably heavy.

So he'd been a little late. Who but a spoiled, impatient heiress-type would take off when the police were on their way, the police that *she* had called?

He'd just about decided to go back up and pick her lock to make certain the person who'd trashed her car hadn't grabbed her and locked her in her own bathroom when he heard footsteps behind him. Turning, he saw Carly jogging toward him wearing bright yellow, her ponytail bouncing behind her. He wanted to throttle her.

Panting, Carly slowed, then stopped near him. "You took your sweet time getting here," she said in puffy spurts.

Sam wished he could spare the time to count to ten. "Where the hell have you been? I told you to wait here."

"I did, for half an hour. By then, I'd decided that if you didn't consider this a big deal, neither should I. So I went for a run." She bent over, doing her cooling down exercises, stretching and flexing her legs.

"I was delayed on police business." He looked her over from top to bottom, his face moving into a frown. "What is that?"

67

Puzzled, Carly glanced down the front of her clothes. "What is what?"

"That outfit you're wearing."

"A jogging suit."

"No kidding? Imported, I imagine. French or Italian. You'd be better off in something from K-Mart. Wears better."

"Wears better," she repeated, dumbfounded at this ridiculous conversation they were having alongside her smashed car. "I'll keep that in mind."

"You shouldn't have gone off like that." He pointed to her car. "Suppose the person who did that were still around and he'd come after you?"

Carly sighed, praying for patience. Why hadn't Ray Vargas been available? "I ran down the center of a residential street. Do you really think someone's going to snatch me and shove me into his car in broad daylight?"

"It's possible. Next time, when I tell you to stay put, I want you to stay put."

She saw red. "Just who do you think you are, giving me orders?"

"Right now, I'm the cop who's watching over you so you don't wind up . . . so nothing happens to you."

That shut her up. Her mind finished his sentence. *So you don't wind up dead like your father.* Carly felt the fight drain out of her as she silently stared up at him.

Again, Sam pointed to her car, glad to see he was finally getting through to her. "This doesn't look like teenage vandalism to me. The guy who did this appears to mean business. You might also keep that in mind."

That thought, which had been buzzing around in her brain, was the reason she'd gone for a run. Sitting and fretting didn't seem to work. Carly felt a sudden chill and shivered. "Look, I'm going in before I catch cold. If you need me to answer any questions, come

68

on up." She ran upstairs and unlocked her door.

Sam followed, closing the door behind them and looked around as she left to grab a towel. He'd never been in one of these carriage houses and found he was impressed. It was larger than he'd thought, with lots of windows, including a skylight in the ceiling of the small, serviceable kitchen.

He'd expected the *House-Beautiful* perfection of her mother's place and was pleasantly surprised to find it cozy and inviting instead. Carly had chosen soft colors, ivory and pale green, and large, comfortable furniture. There were lush plants everywhere, a red brick fireplace in one corner, big pillows carelessly tossed onto the floor, and an overflowing bookcase. Looking up, he saw something interesting and moved to the far wall.

The framed photo, large and very lifelike, was of a huge tiger caught in mid-stride as he paced his cage. At first glance, the animal appeared to be gazing almost lazily over his shoulder. But on closer examination, you could see the rippling readiness of his powerful muscles and the dangerous glint of his eyes. Sam wouldn't have guessed that the suppressed violence depicted in the photo would have appealed to Carly Weston.

He walked to the windows and looked out through the bare treetops. An older woman in a raincoat and headscarf strolled past carrying a brown bag of groceries. Across the street, a tow truck was jump-starting a Camaro while a young mother pushed a baby carriage along. A quiet, pleasant neighborhood. Yet somewhere out there was the creep who'd violated Carly's Porsche.

Was it a coincidence that this happened right after Will's murder? Or was there a connection? Who would know Gentry, Will, and Carly? An odd three-some at best.

He heard a sound and turned. She'd changed into a

blue cableknit sweater and jeans. The ponytail was gone and her hair hung down past her shoulders. He had the damndest urge to touch it. Clearing his throat, Sam began to pace, shifting his mind to the reason he was here. "I radioed in for a fingerprint crew, though I doubt we'll pick up anything. They should be here soon. I checked the area while I was waiting for you and couldn't find anything resembling a weapon."

Carly tucked her feet under her in the corner of her couch, wondering why Sam English appeared a shade nervous. Oddly, that fact calmed her. "Several neighborhood kids play ball in the street after school nearly every day. One of them could have left a bat out there. Or he could have found a piece of wood. There're a lot of trees around here."

Feeling warm, he slipped off the leather jacket he was wearing and sat down at the opposite end of the couch. "Do you have any idea who might have done this?" He watched her face, saw the quick flash of fear in her eyes before she dropped her gaze and shook her head. She hadn't looked quite so vulnerable even at her father's funeral. "We'll get him, you know." He wasn't sure he was reassuring her or himself.

Her eyes when she met his were filled with doubt. "Will you?"

"With your cooperation. I know you're going to fight me on this, but I need a list of your friends."

"I won't fight you."

A minor victory. "And your ex-friends. Any boyfriends you've jilted, or jealous girlfriends, or people you've angered, intentionally or otherwise." He bent one knee and angled his body so he was facing her. "Can you think of anyone you've pissed off lately?" Oh, damn. "Uh, sorry."

She smiled. He was almost blushing at his slip. A

hard man to figure. He had on a white vee-neck sweater and jeans that fit snug and smooth. She could smell a hint of peppermint. "I've heard the word before," she told him.

"Have you?"

"Even said it a couple of times."

He raised a questioning brow. "Hard to believe, a classy Grosse Pointer like you."

Carly propped an elbow on the couchback and leaned her head into her hand. "You don't have a very high opinion of me, or people in general who live in the Pointes, do you, Detective English? A smug, self-satisfied, superior lot, prudish and proper, is that what you think of us?"

He shrugged. "Some are all right. And the name's Sam."

She studied him, though he'd averted his gaze. "Someone hurt you, a woman, I imagine. A Grosse Pointe woman, so it follows that all of us are the same."

He hid behind a half-smile. "Did you major in psychology?"

"No. I would have thought you'd guess that I'd majored in something really useful, like napkin art or flower arranging."

There was a catch in her voice instead of the mocking humor he'd expected. It had him wondering. "What *did* you major in?"

She blinked, feeling oddly vulnerable suddenly, and turned to look out the window. "It doesn't matter. Your men have just arrived. You'd better go down and meet them."

He wanted to say more, to say something to bring back her feistiness. It seemed to suit her more. But he couldn't think of the right words. Standing, he picked up his jacket. "About that list of names . . ."

"Yes, I'll get it to you."

Sam put his hand on the knob as he glanced again

at the tiger in his cage. "I'm surprised you chose that photo."

"Are you? It serves to remind me of something a woman shouldn't forget."

"What's that?"

"That while it's easy to be attracted to a dangerous male animal, it's best to keep him caged where he can't hurt you."

As he left, Sam frowned, knowing full well that they weren't really discussing the tiger.

Chapter Five

Jim Tyson turned off the amber light in his dark-room and opened the door that led out into his studio. "You're very good, Carly," he said over his shoulder, "and you know I'm not just saying that. I could get half-a-dozen apprentices to work with me. But you've got a special feel for photography."

Trailing behind him, Carly walked to the stool by the window and eased herself onto it. She wanted to believe him, but had been afraid to hear his opinion. Yet just now, as they'd developed her last three rolls, she knew they were better than anything she'd done so far. But just how good was that?

"Good enough for what, Jim?" she asked, looking up at her tall friend. "I mean, where do I go with this tiny talent you've discovered in me? Studio photographer, apply to the Grosse Pointe *News* to snap pictures for their society page, do a collection for a coffeetable book? What would you suggest?"

Jim moved a backdrop out of the way and took the stool on the opposite side of his worktable. "Sure, you could do any of those you wanted to, with a bit more training. But I'd like you to try something else with me."

"And what would that be?" Carly asked as she re-fastened the clip holding back her hair. They'd worked in Jim's darkroom for over two hours gauging temperature, adding chemicals, working out the timing as they agitated the sensitive paper in the solution, then pinning up the prints to dry. She'd scarcely noticed the time, so absorbed had she been in seeing the pictures she'd taken gradually take shape.

He handed her a phone message his receptionist had given him earlier. "This is a call I have to return, from Anders Gifford. Do you know him?"

"I know Anders slightly through my father."

"Then you're probably aware he's the editor of *Inside Detroit*."

"Yes. They did an article on Dad last year. Not bad, as I recall."

"Right." Jim ran a hand along his bearded chin. "It's mostly a pictorial magazine, though they do some good pieces. Anders talked with me last month about doing a photo essay on Detroit from the standpoint of a city evolving. From racial violence in the sixties, through urban renewal projects, the effect the auto industry upheaval has had on residents, the Detroiters who refuse to relocate to the suburbs."

"He wants you to take the photographs and he'll write the piece?"

"More than that. He wants two perspectives, the emotional and the dispassionate. The personal and the general. The intimate faces of the people and the public view of the city. From what I've seen of your work, we'd be a good balance for each other."

Carly was stunned. "You want *me* to work on this project with you?"

"Yes." Jim leaned forward, wrapping his long legs around the rungs of the stool. "I'm good at zeroing in on the pulse of a town, of showing what differentiates one community from another and makes it unique. You remember when I did that spread on Ann Arbor as a college town back when we were in school?"

"Sure, and I agree you're very good. But I'm brand new at this."

"That's all the better. You have a fresh outlook, not

jaded or influenced by the work of others. And you tend to get involved with your subjects, to get that special cooperation from a person you connect with that makes your pictures emotional. Like that woman you captured haggling over the price of a pumpkin with that farmer last month. Anyone looking at that print could see her determination to get a bargain and the farmer's almost comical resignation to her persistence."

Carly smiled. She had been pleased at the way that one had turned out. "Thanks, but that's only one shot out of three rolls and—"

"Carly, every photographer goes through literally hundreds of snaps to get just a few worth printing. But those few are the ones that separate the talented from the mediocre. I believe you've got that quality."

It had been so long since anyone had praised anything she'd done that Jim's words warmed her, yet also filled her with doubt. Had those special pictures just been flukes, accidents and not likely to be repeated? Carly'd often been complimented on her looks, her wardrobe, her sense of humor, her poise, wit, and intelligence. But rarely on an accomplishment that would fill her with pride in an achievement. She longed to believe, yet she was hesitant. "I appreciate your faith, but I don't know, Jim. It sounds like a very important project. What if I let you down?"

Jim smiled as he shook his head. "You won't. Listen, you can do this, Carly, and who knows where it will lead? I'll get the particulars from Anders, and he'll pay for the film, of course. I'll outline some ideas I have, and we can discuss any you come up with. And I'll be around if you need my input."

She was warming to the idea, actually getting excited about it. "You mean I'd just go off with my camera and film, wander around taking pictures of people and scenes that appeal to me, then come back here and develop them?"

"Right. I'll be doing the same, only from another angle. As I've told you before, no two photographers would ever view a scene the same, nor take the identical picture. Then together, we'll choose the ones we'll submit to Anders. And he'll arrange them to accompany the text he'll write." Noticing her growing interest, Jim's voice turned persuasive. "Come on, Carly. You told me earlier you felt out of sorts. This project could be just the ticket, involve you, and make you forget your problems."

And adjust to the shock of her father's death. He didn't need to say the last sentence out loud. It was clear enough to Carly. Perhaps Jim was right. She could at least give it a try. "All right, if you're sure you think I'm good enough to work with you."

Jim grinned. "Absolutely." He reached for his phone. "Let me call Anders and get the particulars."

As he dialed, Carly sighed. She hoped she was making the right decision. She had to do something. Most of her friends were involved in careers or marriage and babies. Lately, she seemed to have lost interest in merely lunching with one of the crowd or shopping endlessly. She had too much time on her hands—time to dwell on missing her father, to pace and worry about who had trashed her car, to wonder if that someone were after her.

The Porsche was being repaired, and she was driving a loaner, a daily reminder of the unsettling incident. She never left her apartment these days without her stomach jumping nervously as she checked her surroundings, without looking over her shoulder a dozen times as she drove or walked. She was a victim of her own imagination, of her fear. Perhaps focusing on doing something worthwhile would force her concentration in another direction.

As Jim hung up, she returned her attention to him.

"Anders is glad you'll be the other half of the team and wished us both luck."

"You'll probably need it, working with this amateur."

"Every pro starts out as an amateur, Carly. Don't sell yourself short." Untangling his legs, Jim stood, rising to his full six-foot-five height. "Come on, let's go over our strategy."

By five in the evening, it was dark along the Detroit streets. Carly drove the Olds loaner carefully along Jefferson through light traffic, her nerves jumpy. She couldn't get over the feeling of being watched.

Abruptly, she changed lanes, cruised half-a-block, then darted in front of a slow-moving station wagon. Her eyes fastened on the rear-view mirror, she saw a gray Volkswagen speed up and stay just behind her in the far left lane. Was that the car she'd noticed when she'd swung out of Jim's parking lot? Probably not, she told herself as she wiped a damp hand on the pantleg of her jeans.

She almost missed stopping for a light, so absorbed was she in looking behind instead of ahead. Bouncing to a halt, she saw the Volkswagen idling two cars behind. She'd never noticed just how many of those little Bugs were around until today. Even though the street lights were on, the interior of the car was shaded, and she couldn't make out who was driving it.

The blare of the horn from behind jolted her, and she quickly stepped on the gas. She was less than three miles from her street. She was over-reacting again, she told herself. When would this feeling of being pursued end? she wondered.

Finally, Carly saw that she was nearly to Seminole, put on her blinker, and turned left. She'd only gone half-a-block when she saw the gray Volkswagen following about two car-lengths behind. Oh, God!

Heart pounding, she tried to formulate a plan.

77

She'd turn into her drive, and if he followed, she'd lean on the horn. Some of her neighbors had to be home by now. Quickly, she checked to make sure both car doors were locked. She simply wouldn't step out until he'd either gone away long enough for her to run upstairs or until someone came out at the sound of her horn.

At the drive, she slowed, then turned right. Almost creeping, she kept her eyes on the mirror and one hand on the horn, ready to blast away. The Volkswagen reached her drive, went one house farther and turned into the drive across the street. As Carly watched, the Bug's lights went off. Then a woman climbed out from behind the wheel, followed by two small children. Limp with relief, she let out a trembling breath.

She was driving herself crazy, Carly decided as she parked the car, grabbed her camera case and purse, and ran upstairs. Locking the door safely behind her, she sagged against it.

Much more of this, and she would go stark, raving mad. Tossing her coat and things onto a chair, she quickly turned on several lights, then closed the blinds on every window. She was chilled to the bone and moved to turn up the heat. She noticed that her hands were shaking.

In the kitchen, she opened the fridge and found a bottle of white wine. To hell with the stigma of drinking alone. Tonight, she definitely needed the warmth and perhaps the oblivion of alcohol.

Ray Vargas sat at his desk, toying with his empty pipe as he often did when he was thoughtful. And frustrated. It was seven in the evening, and they'd been at it for hours. Days, actually. "I give up," he said with an uncharacteristic sigh of defeat. "I've gone over every file in Gentry's office and checked out each client he represented. Not one seems to have had motive and opportunity, to be without a strong alibi or resemble our admittedly sketchy profile of the killer with huge hands."

Across their two desks in the squad room, Sam leaned back wearily and rubbed his tired eyes. "I've done the same with Will Weston's client list going back the same five years. No matches."

"Maybe we need to go back further," Ray said, then clamped the pipe's stem between his teeth. He'd quit smoking two years ago, yet still enjoyed the smell and feel of a pipe in his mouth.

"And I suppose we have to consider checking all of Weston's assistants' cases in the remote possibility that one of them handled a name that cross-checks with one of Gentry's clients." The numbers could be staggering in a city the size of Detroit, with each prosecutor handling hundreds per year.

Ray glanced at another bulging file on his desk. "I didn't get anywhere interviewing relatives and friends of Gentry. No one suspicious there. How'd you make out with Weston's?"

Sam shook his head. "Weston hung around with pillars-of-the-community types. Judges, council members, lawyers, high muckie mucks of business. To hear them tell it, everyone loved the man."

"Someone didn't," Ray reminded him.

"Yeah." Sam ran a hand over his chin, feeling the scratch of his unshaven face. It had been a long day and wasn't over yet. He picked up the fingerprint report on Carly's car. The only clear ones had been hers. Of course, you wouldn't have to touch a car to smash in its windows with a heavy object. "I wonder if there's a connection between Will's death and his daughter's car being vandalized," he pondered aloud.

"I can't see that there would be," Ray said. "She's never worked for him or even with him. And if it were the same guy, why would he trash her car? Why not

79

kill her like the other two, especially since it wouldn't be so hard to do, living as she does in that isolated carriage house?"

Carly's secluded living quarters had been bothering Sam, too. The woman ruffled his feathers, but he'd sure as hell hate to see anything happen to her. He remembered the way she'd looked the last time he'd seen her—at her place, while they'd waited for his men to arrive to dust her car. She'd been subdued, vulnerable, almost sad.

She'd been right on the money when she'd guessed he wasn't crazy about suburban types like her and her friends. But she'd been way off on the reason. He'd hated to leave her looking so lost and alone, then had wondered ever since why that bothered him. Carly Weston was nothing to him except a possible puzzle piece in a complicated murder mystery he was trying to solve.

Yet he found his thoughts drifting to her at odd moments.

"How'd Carly Weston's friends check out?" Ray asked.

"I don't know. She hasn't given me the list yet." Checking his watch, Sam picked up the phone and dialed her number. After eight rings, he hung up. He hated hounding people, yet it seemed the only way to get information from some.

"Hey, Sam, how's it going?" The man walking over and pulling up a chair was lean and hard-looking, his hair short and sprinkled with gray, his face habitually guarded. "Hi, Ray."

"Luke," Sam said, reaching to shake Varner's hand. "When'd you get back?"

"Finished the stakeout a couple hours ago. We were up north in the Thumb. Colder than hell up there."

"But you got your man?" Ray asked, knowing Luke wouldn't have returned until he did.

"Sure did. Just dropped off the paper work." He

leaned the chair back on its rear legs and turned to Sam. "I hear you two wound up with the Weston case. Will was a good man."

"Yeah, he was." Sam indicated the files on his desk. "And a busy one. We've been combing through hundreds of cases. Nothing yet." He remembered the funeral reception, running into Luke's wife. "I understand Stephanie grew up with Carly Weston. What do you think of her?"

"Carly?" Luke shrugged. "Nice enough. Heard she was nuts about some guy a while back, then broke it off."

Sam's interest picked up. "How long ago?"

"Last year, I think."

Ray flipped open his notepad. "Name's Pierce Nelson. Banker type. Smooth operator from what I gathered from Carly's friend, Toni Garette."

"Why'd they break up?" Sam wanted to know.

Luke's front chair legs hit the floor. "The guy neglected to mention a wife back in New York is the way I heard it. Don't quote me though or Stephanie will hit the roof that I told you."

"You think Will found out about the wife and Nelson didn't like the interference so he went after her daddy?" Ray suggested, then quickly shook his head. "Nah. Where would Gentry fit in?"

"How's Carly involved in your investigation?" Luke asked.

Sam told him about the Porsche.

"Did you set up police surveillance on her place?" Luke knew the secluded area where Carly Weston lived.

"Yeah, we did," Ray went on to explain, "but it's hard for a cruiser to pick up on anything on the back of that wooded lot. They go by, but . . ." He shrugged.

"Maybe there's no connection," Luke added. "Could be a totally unrelated incident." He stood, rolling his tired shoulders. He needed a hot meal, a hot shower, and Stephanie, not necessarily in that order. "Maybe you could suggest that Carly go live with her mother until you catch this guy."

Sam shot him a pained look. "Have you tried giving suggestions to these Grosse Pointe women?"

Luke smiled despite his fatigue. "I hear you. They don't listen well."

Sam nodded knowingly. "You got that right. That baby of yours here yet?"

A father-to-be at forty-one. The thought still sent a glow of pleasure through Luke. "Not as of an hour ago." He yawned tiredly. "He'll probably make an appearance tonight when I feel as if I could sleep a week." He sent them a wave. "See you guys later."

Sam watched him go, thinking about their conversation. Then he picked up the phone and dialed Carly's number again. Still no answer. He thought he'd noticed an answering machine the day he'd been in her place. Frowning, he hung up.

"Did you see this message?" Ray held out a pink slip.

Sam glanced at it, then groaned aloud. "Clio McIntyre? The psychic? What does she want with us?"

"The usual. She read that we were on the Gentry-Weston case. She's had a vision."

"I'll bet she has. I don't have time to waste with her." Sam stood, reaching for his jacket. "It's nearly eight, and I'm calling it a night. See you tomorrow."

"Right." His pipe clamped between his teeth, Ray sat back contemplatively. He'd bet a week's pay that Sam would head for home by way of Carly Weston's place. And it was nowhere close to his usual route. Good police work or something more? It would be interesting to watch those two, Ray thought.

Her rental car was parked where her Porsche usually was, and the lights in her apartment were all ablaze. Sam eased his Trans Am to a stop near the foot of the stairs and got out. Did she just get home, was she not answering her phone, or was her phone out of order? he wondered as he climbed up.

He knocked several times, waited, and knocked again. No sound of movement from inside and no music or television detectable. She could be taking a shower, he supposed. A damn long shower. Impatiently, he waited, glancing around the yard full of trees.

He could spot half-a-dozen hiding places from up here. If their killer were interested in Carly, he would have little difficulty offing her here. He'd already done his dirty work in a lighted garage in early evening and in broad daylight with an assortment of hunters wandering about. This would be a piece of cake. How could he convince this stubborn woman to move in with her mother for the time being? Turning, he pounded on the door again.

Some minutes later, as he was reaching into his pocket for the tool kit he always carried, he heard a small voice from the other side of the door ask who was there. "Carly, it's me, Sam English. Open the door."

There was a pause. "How do I know it's really you?"

For Christ's sake. "Look out your window." He stepped over and leaned in. Finally, the blinds parted ever so slightly, then closed again. He heard the chain being pushed back, and the door opened. "What do you want?" she asked.

She stood there wrapped in a white terrycloth robe when he'd have guessed she'd choose silk or satin. Her hair was loose and mussed, hanging past her shoulders. She blinked owlishly in the bright light, as if she'd just awakened. "I've been calling and there's been no answer. I came to see if you were all right."

"I'm fine." But she let go of the door and staggered

back, almost losing her footing.

He stepped in, studying her. No, not sleepy. Damned if she wasn't smashed. "You've been drinking," he said, surprise making him blunt.

Standing a bit unsteadily, Carly tightened the belt of her robe around her slender frame. "A little. What's it to you?" Carefully, she made her way back to the couch and plopped into the corner.

Sam closed the door and walked over to stand looking down at her. "Is something wrong? Did something happen?"

"No, no." She waved a hand vaguely. "Everything's just dandy. Life's a bowl of cherries, didn't you know, Defective English? Whoops." She giggled. "That's a good one. Defective. Sort of fits." Leaning forward, she picked up the wine bottle and topped off her glass. "If you want to join me, you'll have to go into the kitchen and get your own glass."

He glanced over at the table against the far wall and saw that she'd disconnected her telephone answering machine. Turning back, he slipped off his jacket and sat down, half-amused, half-worried. "I think I'll pass. How long have you been drowning your sorrows all alone here?"

Carly cocked her head, closed one eye, and measured the amount of liquid left in the bottle. " 'Bout as long as it takes to drink that much wine."

Only about a third remained. Sam had the feeling she wasn't ordinarily much of a drinker. Leaning back, he stretched one arm along the couchback. "Have you eaten anything lately?"

"Not hungry." She took a sip of wine, then set the glass on the end table with exaggerated care.

"Why are you doing this to yourself?"

She shrugged, her hands curling around the folds of the robe's collar. "Why not? In wine, there is escape, isn't that what the old saying is? *In vino veritas.*" Her words were slurred and slow in coming.

84

"I believe that means in wine there is truth." He moved closer, almost within touching distance. "What's the truth about you, Carly?"

She let out a small, bitter laugh. "The truth is I'm scared, Mr. Policeman. He's out there; I can feel it. I got away today, but he'll be back. He's very patient." She sipped more wine.

Sam came to attention. "Who's out there, Carly? Was someone following you?"

She gave him a wobbly nod. "A gray Volkswagen. All the way home from Jim's place." She giggled then. "Turned out to be my neighbor and her two kids." Sobering, she shook her head in confusion. "Can't be. I *know* he was there. He won't give up."

Delusions or reality? In her particular state, it was difficult to determine how much was real and how much of her conversation was wine-influenced. "Did you see someone, Carly?"

"Man in a cap. Stands out there under the lamp post watching me. Even in the rain. Very patient man. He'll be back, I know."

She was getting more specific. "What did he look like?"

"Wore a cap pulled down low over his face."

"Where did you see him and when?"

She picked up her glass and took in a big gulp. "Out by the street, couple weeks ago."

A couple of weeks ago? Will hadn't even been killed back then? She wasn't making sense. Still, he'd have to question her about this again when she was sober. He reached to take the wine glass from her as she nearly missed setting it on the table edge. "I think you've had enough of this for now. How about if I make you some coffee?"

He was close to her, close enough that Carly could smell peppermints on his breath and the cool outdoors on his skin. She liked his hair, black and curly, a little long. He needed a shave, but she didn't mind.

Trying to focus, she looked into his eyes. "You know the worst part, Sam? I can't go to my father and tell him about it. He's gone, Sam." There was a catch in her voice, and she tried swallowing around it. "Oh, God, I miss him so much."

"I know you do." Awkwardly, feeling a bit out of his depth, he took her in his arms.

Her cheek rested against the rough knit of his sweater. His arms felt so good, so strong holding her. Like Dad's had felt. Only she'd never feel her father's arms around her again. He'd never again be able to make the world seem less harsh for her.

The tears came then, tears she'd been unable to shed since that fateful phone call. She held on to Sam, weeping for her father, for her poor mother, and for herself. Wrenching sobs tore at her as she hiccuped, sucking in air, then gave in to the deep wailing again.

Sam had never considered himself a tender-hearted man. Yet her grief moved him. True, she was the darling daughter of a man who'd spoiled her rotten. But she was very much a woman mourning just now; and, somehow, it felt right being here with her while she let it all out.

If she remembered later when she sobered up, she'd likely be embarrassed — or perhaps she'd pretend this never happened. But he was glad it had. For the first time, Carly Weston seemed human to him.

He wasn't sure how long she wept on his shoulder. He held her lightly, occasionally making reassuring sounds to her, letting her set the pace. After a while, he felt her calming, then felt her breathing even out as she drifted to sleep.

Almost reluctantly, he picked her up, took her into her bedroom, and lay her down on her bed. Taking a blanket from a chair, he covered her, then stood looking down at her for a long moment.

Even the rich had their troubles, their demons, Sam

86

thought.

Quietly, he let himself out, locking the door behind him.

The man got into his car and sighed. Every time he visited his brother, Pete, in Lapeer, it left him depressed. Pete wasn't as severely mentally retarded as some of the other residents in the home. Yet he was incapable of living on his own. The man wished he could stay with Pete, but he had some things to take care of first.

If things hadn't happened to tear apart his family, if his father hadn't been sent to prison, and if his ashamed and despondent mother hadn't committed suicide, Pete would have had the care he needed at home. And the man would have been able to go on to college, to become somebody. Somebody like Carly Weston.

She'd grown up with everything—a loving family, money, a fine education, privileges. All that the man had missed out on. But she'd pay soon. Just as the others had. And then he'd go get Pete and the two of them would move somewhere quiet. He'd get a job and take care of Pete. Sweet, innocent Pete. *Blessed are the meek for they shall inherit the earth.* Amen.

The man cracked his large knuckles, then started the ancient motor and shifted gears. Soon, it would all be over and his parents could rest in peace.

Pulling his cap down low over his forehead, the man drove the Volkswagen out of the parking lot.

Chapter Six

Carly heard the clock on her mantel striking the hour. Four chimes. She dared open an eye. The room was standing still, thank God. Slowly, she pushed back the afghan and sat up. The pounding in her head had ceased as well. She might just live.

She shoved both hands into her hair, leaned against the couchback, and let out a deep sigh. It had been a horrendous night, and she had no one to blame but herself. Three in the afternoon, and she finally felt almost human again.

She remembered only vague snatches of her flirtation with alcohol as an escape. She'd done some drinking in college, which had seemed the thing to do at the time. She'd even gotten pretty tipsy a time or two. But she'd never set out to seek oblivion in drinking before. And after this experience, she was certain she never wanted to do it again.

Her stomach made a noise, and Carly pressed a hand to the spot, wondering if a piece of toast would stay down. Better not risk it just yet. She'd been pretty sick most of the night.

She recalled the phone ringing several times during the evening, but she'd ignored it as she'd sipped on the wine and let her frightened mind wander. Then there'd been the pounding at the door and Sam sitting with her. She'd babbled at him, then she'd begun sobbing. And he'd held her, just held her. Carly moaned aloud at what he must think of her now.

He hadn't thought much of her before; she could well imagine how disgusted he'd been with her last night. She couldn't recall going to sleep, but suddenly she'd awakened in her own bed and had barely made it to the bathroom in time. That had been the first of many such runs during the interminable night.

Around nine in the morning, she'd taken a shower, then several aspirin, drunk lots of water, and curled up here on the couch. How could heavy drinkers go through this regularly? she wondered as she got to her feet somewhat testily. Perhaps if she took another shower and got dressed, she'd begin to feel like herself again.

An hour later, she sat at her small kitchen table sipping hot tea with lemon and gazing out the window. It was snowing and had been for some time, though very little was sticking to the ground as yet. She'd been chilled and had put on her tan corduroy slacks and a matching sweater with a cowl collar that nestled around her neck, warming her. The day was cold, but she really should venture out a little. The frosty air might complete the job of clearing her head.

She drank more tea, relieved that her stomach was accepting it. Carly thought she should at least return her messages, yet she felt too comfy to move right now. Her mother had phoned, as well as Jim and Toni. The man from the garage, saying her car would be ready tomorrow. And a short message from Sam asking her to call when she had time.

No mention of her intemperance. So civilized of him. Carly pushed back her hair as embarrassment flooded her. She had no cause to be angry with Sam. It wasn't his fault she'd decided to test her endurance, only to find it woefully lacking. Why had she opened the damn door? Why hadn't she just let him get tired of knocking and leave?

Because he wouldn't have. The man was nothing if not persistent, because of his job, because of his personal makeup. He'd have kept pounding away until the door had crashed in before he'd have walked away. She was surprised he hadn't jimmied the lock or come in through the window.

Finishing her tea, she rose to set the cup in the sink and was on her way to the phone when she heard a knock at the door. Who now? she wondered with a frown as she walked to peer out the window. Oh, Lord. She couldn't quite see the person standing in front of her door, but she recognized the Trans Am parked below. Detective Sam English undoubtedly here to see if she'd survived. And to give her one of his long, disapproving looks.

Bracing herself, Carly opened the door.

He wasn't smiling, nor did he look critical or condemning. That helped. She took a deep breath before he could say anything. "Yes, I'm okay, and yes, I owe you an apology. I'm sorry I sobbed all over you. Chalk it up to . . . to . . ."

"A delayed reaction, probably."

She could accept that. "Probably." He looked too good standing there in a weak afternoon sun with snowflakes on the shoulders of his leather jacket. Healthy and together, which, at the moment, she envied. "Was there anything else?" she asked, hoping he'd run along now that he'd checked on her.

"Matter of fact, there is. Mind if I come in?"

Wordlessly, she stepped back and walked to the couch. It had been wishful thinking to hope he'd go away.

He took the bentwood rocker opposite her, thinking she looked better than she had a right to after pouring two thirds of a bottle of wine down her throat last night. She didn't want to talk about that, he was certain. He did, but he'd wait and ease into asking her about her drunken mutterings. "Do you know a man named Kerry Logan?" he began.

Carly frowned thoughtfully. "The name doesn't ring a bell. Who is he?"

"So far, it's the only name we've been able to tie in with both your father and Homer Gentry. He was a law student who worked in the prosecuting attorney's office for a while; then, on Will's recommendation, Gentry hired him on as a legal aide when he first opened his own law practice. Tall guy, blond All-American type." The kind of man he figured she'd go for—probably handsome and charming. "He'd be about thirty now. Could you have dated him, say four or five years ago?"

"No, I don't recall someone like that."

"Are you sure?" It was the first lead they'd come up with, and he needed to know if the tie-in was three-way.

"Pretty sure. I don't usually forget the names of men I've dated, though I could have met him at a party back then and not seen him again. As for his working for Dad, that's entirely possible. A lot of law students did."

"Did you date a lot, Carly?"

The question seemed a bit personal. "Is that the detective asking, or the man?" And why would he care one way or the other?

Sam shifted in the chair, wishing he'd rephrased the question. "We can't rule out that one of your old boyfriends might be behind all this." Of course, there was nothing to indicate that one was.

He made it sound as if there were hundreds to haul in and interrogate. "Did you question this Kerry, and he mentioned me?"

"We haven't found him yet, but we will. We ran a routine check on him, as we're doing with a lot of other names, and learned he got kicked out of law school, used a couple of aliases, and had a juvenile record."

Sam English seemed more relaxed today, Carly thought. He had on a blue sweater over faded jeans. She could see curly black hair at the V-neckline, could remember her head pressed against that firm chest last night. Was he more at ease because he'd seen her at her worst last night? "I'm sorry I can't help you, but I don't know a Kerry Logan."

The sun was sinking outside the window. Sam watched her turn on the tableside lamp. "You haven't given me that list of names," he reminded her.

"I know. I will." The phone rang, startling them both. She didn't move. "The answering machine will pick it up." She didn't feel like talking with anyone right now or explaining to the caller that Sam was with her.

Across the room, the machine clicked in after the fourth ring as they listened in silence. Carly's voice asked the caller to leave a message after the beep. But no one spoke, yet no one hung up either. The moments stretched on as the tape kept recording. Carly felt a shiver race up her spine.

Frowning, Sam rose to stand looking down at the machine, cocking his head to listen more closely. Someone was still on the line, but not speaking. He couldn't hear breathing, yet there'd been no disconnect. Finally, the caller hung up and the machine clicked off, the red message light beginning to flash. He walked over to join her on the couch. "You get many prolonged hang-ups like that?"

Carly tried to keep the concern out of her voice. She remembered the other times very clearly. "That's the third."

"When was the first?"

"The night that attorney died. I remember because it was my father's birthday and I'd just returned from having dinner with my parents." Surely a coincidence. Everyone got hang-ups, especially on answering machines. Some of her friends never left messages, explaining they hated talking to machines.

"And the second?"

"Last night."

"Is that why you disconnected your answering machine?" And proceeded to get smashed.

"Yes."

This caller hadn't been on the line long enough to track, even if they'd had a tracer on her phone, Sam knew. Could have been an indecisive caller realizing that he had the wrong number after hearing Carly's voice. But three times? That bothered him. "Tell me about Pierce Nelson," he said, watching her face, remembering how she'd confessed last night that she felt someone watching her, someone who'd stood outside in the rain several weeks ago.

Carly raised a brow. "Why?"

He saw surprise and then that flash of annoyance in her eyes. "Because he's a part of your recent past, because things between you two ended badly, and he could be nursing a grudge."

"Who told you that?" She was getting tired of his probing into her life, past and present.

Ray had found out from Toni Garette, but Sam thought it best not to reveal that. "What difference does it make? Tell me about him."

She supposed she had little choice since, if she refused, he'd find out from another source. "Nothing much to tell. We met, we dated a while, we broke up. End of story." Which was stretching the truth, but he already knew far more about her than she was comfortable with.

"And you didn't know he had a wife back in New York?"

She should have realized he'd have run a check on everyone she'd ever nodded to by now. "Hardly. I

93

know you don't think much of me, but I don't knowingly date married men."

He leaned an elbow on the couchback. "That's not true, Carly."

She met his gaze, her eyes flashing. "It most certainly is. I *never* would have gotten involved with Pierce if I'd known he was married."

"I mean about my not thinking much of you." To his surprise, he found he meant it. Sam knew he had preconceived opinions about women like Carly, and some of what he suspected was true. She'd been spoiled, over-protected, pampered. But last night he'd discovered she was also sad, frightened, and trying to cope the best she could with her loss. And with being thrust into a possibly dangerous situation totally out of the realm of her experience. He found himself reaching to touch her hair. "I think you're handling all this better than most people I know might."

His sudden shift in attitude unnerved her. Her emotions too close to the surface, she felt her eyes fill and quickly looked away. "I . . . thanks."

She had a quiet kind of style that had him admiring her despite his personal prejudices. Her hair was soft, fragrant. He wanted to bury his face in it.

He was touching only her hair, yet it felt like a caress. Though she could remember little of his visit last night, something had shifted in their relationship when he'd held her as she'd wept. She didn't want to think about just what it was. Her stomach rumbled, reminding her she hadn't eaten in a very long while.

Sam heard it and smiled, drawing back. "There's a great little place not far from here. Italian food like you've never eaten. Come to dinner with me."

His invitation surprised her. "I don't know. I have some things I should do." She'd slept away the whole day. Yet even as she said the words, she knew she wanted to go. With him, she'd be safe. She wouldn't have to look over her shoulder or spend another evening here alone, waiting for the next hang-up or watching for the next stranger smashing in her car windows.

"You like spaghetti?" Sam asked, rising. "I know the owners. Rosa's sauce is almost better than sex."

She raised a brow at him. "How can I resist that recommendation?" She went to get her jacket.

Buckled into the passenger seat of the Trans Am, Carly watched the early evening traffic as Sam headed for downtown. She'd been right to come. She felt more relaxed already. And safe with Sam beside her. Absently, she listened to his police radio interrupt in periodic spurts, the volume low.

"Are you warm enough?" Sam asked, adjusting the heater.

"Mmm." Carly watched the snow drift down, then melt on contact, keeping the streets damp. They sped down Jefferson, and she wondered what his car could do out on the highway if he really opened her up. Mildly curious, she gazed at the storefronts as they neared the center of town. "Are we close?"

Before he could answer, his radio crackled loudly, then the dispatcher's voice came on. "Unit four-ten. Do you read me?"

Sam flipped the switch, raising the volume. "Four-ten here. Go ahead."

"Unit nine-oh just reported in, Sam. Ran across a rape in progress in an alley on Congress near Brush. One officer chasing the perp. Victim got a good look at him. Sounds like the guy you and Ray've been tracking."

Sam swore under his breath. He didn't have time to take Carly home, and the neighborhood wasn't one he would drop her off in. "Roger," he said, then clicked off. Rolling down his window, he activated his flashing light and shoved it atop the roof, then executed a

95

right turn off Jefferson with tires squealing. "Sorry about this, but we have to take a little detour here."

Intrigued, she studied him closely. His face suddenly looked like a stranger's, hard and distracted. "You're working on a rape case?"

He nodded grimly. "He's quick and brutal. Usually, when he's through with his victim, he leaves them a little souvenir. A knife slash across a cheek. Once, he cut her throat."

Involuntarily, Carly shuddered. "Did she . . . die?"

"Yes." Arriving at Congress, he did a quick left and saw the black-and-white angle-parked ahead at the alley. "Don't know if this is him, but I've got to check." Screeching to a stop behind the police car, he opened his door as he shoved it into park and pushed down the locks. "Wait right here, and don't step outside." This wasn't the wisest thing he'd ever done, take a civilian to a crime in progress. Hurrying to the alley, he hoped Carly would do as he'd instructed for a change.

Within the safety of the car, Carly looked around with interest. This was an area of town she'd rarely driven through, even in broad daylight: a row of somewhat shabby office buildings, nearly deserted at this hour; a sleep-cheap motel down a block, its garish sign blinking; the neon lights of a movie house across the street; and a nearby bar where two women in skimpy skirts lingered in the doorway. The swirling snow danced in the car's headlights and the overhead street lamps as she peered into the alley.

The woman was seated on a cardboard box gripping a full-length coat about her thin body as Sam listened to the uniformed officer's update. In the dim light, Carly noticed something on her cheek which could be blood. Lowering her head, the woman started to cry. Sam gave her his handkerchief and briefly touched her shoulder, then turned aside, as if embarrassed by the gesture. Carly had been aware of his concern for her last night, but hadn't thought it

96

would spill over into his professional dealings. A hard-nosed cop with a soft spot for victims. More interesting by the minute.

She saw the other officer return, out of breath and alone. Apparently, he'd chased the rapist and lost him. Carly dared roll down her window a fraction, unabashedly trying to eavesdrop. She couldn't quite make out the words, but she caught Sam's tone. She heard frustration that they'd missed catching the guy and praise for both officers for their quick action.

Lord, what a way to make a living, she thought. To have to deal daily with fatalities and helpless targets, with violent men and misfits of society, with the troubled and the troublesome. Small wonder Sam and other cops like him were a suspicious lot, hard edged and quick tempered.

An ambulance with siren screaming drew up behind the Trans Am, skirted it, and parked in the center of the street. The two hookers across the way barely glanced toward the commotion as a man carrying a briefcase walked past them. One of them approached him, but the man walked on, shaking his head. The white-jacketed driver jumped from the ambulance and hurried to the alley.

Carly watched the first police officer pocket his notepad, then lean down to talk to the woman. Moments later, Sam took hold of her arm and helped her to her feet. Her knees nearly buckled, but he supported her weight until the second officer took her other arm. Walking slowly, they led her to the waiting ambulance. Sam protected her head as she ducked to step aboard, and the second EMS attendant helped her onto the stretcher. After exchanging a few more words with the uniformed men, Sam walked back to the Trans Am.

Before sliding behind the wheel, he reached into his pocket and found a mint, popping it into his mouth as he sat down and released a tense rush of air.

97

Carly's mind was on the trembling victim as the ambulance doors were closed. "How is she? Did he . . ."

"The guys got here in time. She'll be all right." Her cheek would heal. But inside . . .

She could smell the snow in his hair mingling with mint, could sense the futility he felt. "But the rapist got away."

So close, yet they'd missed nabbing the guy. "Yeah, this time. But the victim gave us a good description." Which matched the last victim's report. Remembering the young woman's frightened eyes and bloodied face, Sam's hands itched to spend ten minutes alone with the sonofabitch who'd almost completed his assault.

"What was she doing walking alone in this neighborhood?"

Sam sighed, realizing Carly Weston would never understand this other world. "Walking to catch a bus, working overtime in that office building, saving up to buy a car. She's only twenty-three and the bastard nearly ruined her life." Angrily, he started the car and shot down the street.

She watched him peripherally, realizing instinctively that he needed time to adjust before returning to the cool cop demeanor he hid behind most of the time. She'd seen another part of Sam English revealed tonight. He wasn't jaded nor nearly as unaffected as he tried to pretend. All this got to him. It *really* got to him. Knowing he could relate to victims gave her a different perspective of the man.

Sam drove half-a-dozen blocks in the wrong direction before he realized it. Making a U-turn, he headed back toward Petrini's. Forcing his hands on the wheel to relax, he glanced over at Carly. "I'm sorry."

The apology encompassed a multitude of things. She understood. "Don't be. You're entitled. You have a rough job, and you do it well."

He heard a new note of respect in her voice and

wished it didn't please him. With effort, he shoved the past half-hour to the back of his mind. "How does spaghetti, homemade bread, and a bottle of red wine sound to you?"

Carly winced. "If you don't mind, I'll skip the wine."

Feeling better, Sam laughed as he pulled into the parking lot of the small Italian eatery.

In the far corner of the dimly lighted restaurant, Rosa Petrini herself served two plates of steaming spaghetti to her favorite cop and his new woman. Snapping her fingers to her nephew, the busboy, to re-fill the basket of crusty bread, she watched Sam take his first bite, then close his eyes in appreciation.

"Perfection, Rosa, as always," he told her.

Rosa beamed her thanks in a wide smile. "You're a sweet-talker, Sam English." Shifting her speculative gaze to the woman, she narrowed her dark brown eyes. She'd known Sam ten years easy, and she could count on the fingers of one hand the number of women he'd brought to her place. Idly, she wondered if this skinny one with the *bellisimo* hair would last. "Your lady friend, she could use a little meat on her bones."

Carly found herself wanting to explain. "I eat a lot, but nothing sticks."

Rosa's rich laugh rolled from her. "I should be so lucky. *Mangiare con gusto,*" she said, rushing back to the kitchen.

"Which means eat heartily," Sam translated as he twirled pasta around his fork tines.

She hadn't been sure she could eat after the uncomfortable night she'd spent and the unsettling scene she'd just witnessed. But after a cautious taste, Carly found she was famished and dug in. "This is wonderful."

Sam waved to Nick, Rosa's husband, as he came

99

out of the kitchen and took his place at the counter behind the cash register. "Glad you like it. I eat here a lot."

Carly lathered butter on warm bread. "I'm not a real whiz in the kitchen."

"I like to cook, when I have a free evening."

"Which you rarely do, I take it. Are you always on call?"

Sam took a sip of his red wine and shook his head. "Right now, we're backed up and short-handed." Which was the case most of the time.

She studied him through the flickering candlelight. He had a strong chin and nice hands. His hair was curly and thick, the kind that made a woman want to reach out and touch. She felt the tug of attraction and made an effort to ignore it. "What made you go into police work, Sam?"

He finished chewing slowly, wondering how to answer her. "It seemed like the thing to do."

Carly swirled spaghetti. "An evasive answer."

It would seem she saw through him. "All right, you want a better one. I wanted to do something altogether different from what my family was involved in."

"What are they involved in?"

He gave her the rehearsed answer he gave everyone, the one no one in Detroit questioned. It was based in truth, just not all of it. "The auto industry. Isn't everyone?"

Was that why he had this thing about upscale Grosse Pointers, because his family were auto-factory workers? "You like your work, don't you?"

"Some days." He spooned more grated cheese on his pasta. "Other days it really sucks." Since she was in a chatty mood, he'd take advantage. "Why'd you break your engagement to Brett Stevens?"

Her fork in mid-air, she turned to stare at him. "Is there anything you *don't* know about me?"

100

Oh, yeah. A hell of a lot. He didn't know how it would feel to tangle his fingers into all that red hair or what her generous mouth would feel like under his. "Not much," he answered noncommittally.

She didn't know whether she felt amusement or irritation. "Do I get equal time to ask about all the women in your life?"

With a sigh of satisfaction, Sam pushed his empty plate aside and wiped his mouth before answering. "I'm not the one in danger, Carly. The one who feels someone watching, following, standing outside in the rain. Or the one who has hang-ups on the phone." He saw her look down at her plate and knew he'd hit home. "Do you remember telling me those things last night?"

She did and now regretted it. "Yes, but I want you to know that Brett has nothing to do with any of that. He's a nice guy and a good friend who wants only the best for me."

He touched her hand. "So am I, Carly." Feeling her suddenly thoughtful gaze on him, he signaled for the check.

Back at her apartment, she felt a little silly standing just inside her dark living room while Sam, gun in hand, checked out every room. Yet she also felt relieved. Perhaps he thought she was taking all this lightly, but Carly knew she wasn't. The main reason she'd gotten blitzed last night was that the fear had gotten to her.

Sam returned and bent to snap on the lamp. "All clear. The blinds are closed, the drapes drawn." He walked over to where she was still standing by the door and shoved it closed. "You could go to your mother's and stay with her until we catch this guy." He'd suggested that once already on their drive here.

"We've been over this. I won't be forced out of my home. Besides, it could be weeks, months."

"Thanks. Your faith in me is encouraging."

"I didn't mean it like that." His back was to the lamp, his face in shadow, yet Carly could see his dark eyes studying her in that unsettling way he had. She felt a jolt and recognized it as that male-female awareness that precedes a rush of passion, that indefinable something that is as difficult to describe as it is to fake. She hadn't felt such a strong ripple in a long while and wasn't thrilled to be feeling it now. Not with this man. Yet she could tell that he felt it, too. "Thank you for dinner," she said and took a step backward only to find the door directly behind her.

She was the wrong woman to want, Sam reminded himself. He'd known it from the day he'd first laid eyes on her. For him, she was from the wrong side of the tracks, a monied woman who'd undoubtedly grown up with fussing nannies and finishing schools, with debutante parties and dancing lessons. He was, by choice, inner city, beer and bowling, down and dirty. He'd watched people die up close, and would again. She'd covered it well tonight, but she'd been shocked watching what went on in that grimy alley. No, it was all wrong.

Then why was his hand trembling as he raised it to touch her hair?

"Sam," she protested, "I don't think . . ."

"Good move. Don't think." Before she could say more, his mouth closed over hers. He felt her stiffen for a long moment, resisting him or herself, he wasn't certain which, then suddenly relaxing, opening to him.

He'd expected a chilly response at best, thinking she'd revert to her cool upbringing. He'd been wrong. He felt the heat bubble up from within her and spread through him. His arms wound around her, drawing her closer. She smelled so good and tasted even better. His head spinning, Sam deepened the kiss as desire slammed into him.

102

She'd thought his mouth at times seemed hard, almost cruel, yet Carly found his lips incredibly soft as they moved over hers. His hands were roaming her back, his solid chest crushing her breasts. She didn't mind. It had been so long since she'd been held, been desired. Senses reeling, she forgot everything but the way he made her feel, and she kissed him back.

When she felt his fingers slip under the hem of her sweater, she drew back. Breathing hard, she touched a hand to his chest to put some distance between them while she waited for her brain to clear. The intensity, the quick surge of unexpected need, had her stunned and worried.

Her track record with men wasn't the best. She raised her eyes and saw him staring at her, an unexpected look of confusion on his face.

"I didn't plan that, but I'm not going to apologize for it," Sam said.

Carly nodded her understanding. "I have this incredibly bad habit of falling for the wrong men." She tipped up her chin just a fraction. "I'm not going to do that with you, Sam."

He let go of her. "That's a good plan, Carly." Stepping around her, he opened the door. "Put the chain lock on."

She did, then listened to his footsteps going down. Leaning against the door, she couldn't help but think that she was way out of her depth with that man.

Toying with her was maybe the best part, the man thought as he sat on a downtown bench near the waterfront watching Carly Weston snapping pictures. She'd been at it for some time now, zeroing in on two young children bundled up against a chilly breeze as they chased each other under the watchful eyes of a parent strolling nearby.

Earlier, he'd parked along Jefferson near her corner, thinking she'd probably go somewhere on this sunny Saturday. In no time, he'd spotted her red Porsche turning off her street and followed her, carefully staying back several car lengths. She'd stopped at several stores, obviously running errands and buying things, then wound up here about an hour ago. He was certain she was unaware of his presence.

The man pulled up his collar and took a drag on his cigarette, wishing he'd worn his cap. He studied Carly from this safe distance as she finished putting new film in her camera. Next, she moved over to two old men playing checkers on a bench. She spoke to them briefly as they looked up at her with interest. Then they nodded and she stepped back, lining up her shots. Silly thing for a grown woman to do, run around taking pictures of strangers.

'Course she probably had nothing better to do. Money coming out of her ears, she could afford to waste her time. Not having to work hard the way he'd had to day in and day out. At least he'd saved the money he'd made during the years he'd spent in that hellhole. It wasn't much, but enough for a while. Until his mission was completed and he could move away with Pete.

It was taking longer than he'd thought. The fourth man on the list was down in Florida, he'd learned recently, and due home soon. But victim number three would be back tomorrow and be sent to his eternal reward next. Meantime, the man was enjoying hounding Carly. Even now, as she walked to the railing along the Detroit River, he saw her glance anxiously over her shoulder as she walked.

But he was too clever for her, he thought, as he casually turned the pages of his newspaper. No one would suspect a working man catching the sun and reading his paper on a public bench. For a few moments longer, he watched the woman with her red hair tied back with a piece of yarn. Then he rose, tossed away his cigarette butt and sauntered out of sight, moving to the side street where she'd parked her car.

He smiled to himself as he reached for his ring of keys hanging from his belt. He wished he could see her face when she discovered what he had planned for her. It would make her skin crawl, make her scared to leave the safety of her home.

Which was exactly how the man wanted her to feel.

Chapter Seven

It had been a good day, Carly thought as she turned onto her street. She'd been out since mid-morning in the crisp, cold air, grateful to have her own car back. She'd stopped at Jim's studio and picked up some of her better prints to study at home, done a little shopping, bought a cup of coffee from a street vendor, and then spent the rest of the afternoon doing what she was beginning to enjoy more and more: taking pictures.

As she turned into her drive, she thought of the little towhead down by the waterfront. He couldn't have been more than three, and he kept pulling off his cap and tossing it aside as if he loved the feel of the breeze in his hair. His mother had tied the string of a red balloon to his wrist, and it had bobbed about as he'd run circles around her. Carly had caught him jumping up as if he could hug the balloon, on his face a look reflecting a child's innocent pleasure at simply being alive. The Detroit skyline had been in the background. She'd taken several she thought might be good; but that would be the exceptional one, she was certain.

Parking the Porsche, Carly scanned the backyard. Not yet six, and already getting dark. The small spotlights hidden beneath the shrubs of the front house were on, gently illuminating the regal old Tudor home. She dreaded the long winter stretching ahead with its short days and long nights. She'd just have to keep busy, that's all. Quickly, she gathered up her packages, camera case, and shoulder bag, then eased out of the car.

Arms full, she turned and was about to start up when she saw a dark shadow separate itself from the side of the carriage house. Her heart started thudding as she backed up nervously. He was coming toward her. *Oh, God.*

"Carly?" Sam stepped out from under the shadowed eaves.

She sagged against the stair railing, nearly dropping her packages as she recognized him. "You scared me half to death," she finally managed.

Moving to her, he took the heavy camera case from her and a large cardboard box. "I'm sorry." He glanced toward the dark woods behind them. "It's pretty dark already. Aren't you afraid to be out alone?"

Yes, she was, and awfully tired of being afraid. But she didn't want to let him see how she felt. "Life's a risk, Detective English. Where's your car?"

"Parked along the far side. I've been strolling around the area, just checking things out."

Her eyes widened. "Why? Is something wrong?"

"No, nothing new." He'd gone in to the station and found Ray poring over mug shots. They'd spent several days and a lot of man-hours going back even further, through ten years of case files from Gentry and Weston. Finally, they'd come up with over a dozen names of men who'd had something to do with both victims. He'd gathered the mug shots in a manila envelope and called Carly, thinking she might recognize a face or a name her father had mentioned. He'd gotten only her answering machine, so, by the end of the day, he'd decided to check up on her.

Was it business, or was it an excuse to see her

again? Damned if he knew.

He'd felt a little better when he'd seen that her car was gone. At least she wasn't inside drinking. This concern for a woman was something new to him, and he wasn't altogether comfortable with it. He found himself feeling a need to protect Carly Weston one minute and wanting to bed her the next.

Standing in front of her now, he felt a little foolish as he held out a manila envelope. "I've got some mug shots here I'd like you to look at. I took a chance you might be home."

She started up the stairs. "That's my dinner in that box — pizza with the works — so carry it carefully." Juggling her packages, she unlocked the door and led the way inside. She dumped everything on a chair, removed her jacket, and turned to take the pizza box from him.

She searched his eyes, wondering if she should invite him to eat with her. The kiss they'd shared several days ago was locked in her memory, escaping occasionally to warm her. Now, studying him, she decided the mug shots weren't the only reason he'd shown up so unexpectedly. "Hungry? Want a beer?"

Sam raised a brow. "I wouldn't have pegged you as a beer drinker," he said, following her into the kitchen.

"Thought I was white wine or champagne?" She smiled at him as she took two bottles out of the fridge. "Even though I hit the wine a little heavy the other night, beer goes better with pizza." She slid several pieces on a large plate, then popped the dish in the micro. "It's cold tonight. Why don't you go in and light the fire while I heat these?"

Later, sitting on the floor in front of the crackling fire and leaning on an overstuffed pillow, Sam watched her devour her second piece. "There must be an Italian in your background."

Carly swallowed contentedly. "You don't have to be

108

Italian to love pizza. Actually, I'm crazy about any and all junkfood." She saw him look surprised and smiled. "Did I shatter another of your preconceived notions about the snobbish circle I grew up in?"

"Yeah. I thought you'd learned at your mother's knee how to make everything from truffles to trifles, and that you always ate things like caviar and quiche."

"Not so. When I lived at home, my mother and our housekeeper made these painstakingly nutritious meals including something from all of the food groups. You know the kind—leafy spinach, whole-wheat bread, five fruits a day. I wasn't permitted to eat anything as common as a hot dog because no one ever knew what it contained." She laughed. "I sneaked them, of course, and a whole lot of other forbidden foods. The day I left home, I stopped eating healthy and went for the gusto."

Sam took a long swallow of his cold beer. "Don't you worry about cholesterol and fat and all that?"

She shook her head. "I ate right my first twenty-two years. I figure I've got a few more binge years left before I have to start watching it."

A log shifted in the grate and Sam turned to watch the flames spiral upward. He felt relaxed, comfortable, and was more than a little surprised to find he did.

He was a man who worked in a rough, violent world, peopled mostly with other men and the kind of women it was best to stay away from. The few women he'd known on a more than casual basis he hadn't felt contented enough with to want to share long, cozy chats. He hadn't lingered with many, feeling the need to be on his way after the loving. The fact that he didn't feel in a rush to leave now, but rather was thinking up reasons to see Carly, to stay longer with her, puzzled him.

Carly contemplated a third piece, then decided to

wait a while. Puffing up her pillow, she leaned an elbow into it and stretched her legs toward the fire. She was separated from Sam by the food and dishes between them, yet it wasn't a tense or deliberate distance. Since the night they'd detoured to the rape scene, had dinner together, and he'd held her, kissing her breathless, she'd been thinking a great deal about him.

And something didn't add up.

"Sam, where did you grow up, in what part of the city?" she asked, hoping she sounded casual and not nosy.

The question, so out of the blue, threw him. Setting aside his plate, he rearranged the pillow at his back, needing a moment to come up with an answer. "Not far from here."

He was staring into the fire, not looking at her. "In Detroit?"

Showdown time. Had he made a slip, or was she just too damn smart? He had a choice, to continue to evade her inquiries and hope she wouldn't see through him or to invite her to step closer. Slowly, he turned to look at her. "No. Grosse Pointe."

Her intuition had been right on target, Carly thought. He wasn't scornful of people he perceived as privileged because he'd grown up poor, but rather because he'd grown up among them. And probably because, as she'd originally guessed, one of them had hurt him. Most likely a female.

Silently, he watched her expressive face register a variety of emotions. And questions.

She sat up, tucking her feet under her, cross-legged. "Where in Grosse Pointe?" There were five Pointes north of Detroit, several bordering the river.

In a way, it was a relief to tell her. He wasn't comfortable with subterfuge, but he'd had his reasons. "The Shores, about four blocks from your parents' home."

110

Carly screwed up her face thoughtfully. "I don't re-call a family named English. My mother knows just about everyone."

Sam sighed. "How about Kingsley? Raymond and Priscilla Kingsley."

The name clicked immediately. "Kingsley Cadillac? That's your family?" Raymond, Sr. had started the dealership years ago, and now they had at least four auto showrooms. Her mother knew Priscilla Kingsley, though not well.

"You got it. English is my mother's maiden name."

He'd brought up more questions than he'd answered. "But why, Sam? Are you estranged from your parents?"

"Not exactly." He sat up, toying with his empty beer bottle, his eyes on it instead of her. "It's a long story."

"I'm not going anywhere." She shifted the plates to the side and inched a bit closer. "Tell me."

Oddly, he felt he wanted to. "We never saw eye-to-eye, my father and I. I always managed to disappoint him. He wanted my brother and me to be just like him. To attend his alma mater, to follow into the family business, to marry a *suitable* girl from an *acceptable* family. To be goddamn clones. It's a privilege to be a Kingsley, my father used to say. I couldn't hack it."

Carly heard the bitterness, the repressed anger, the hurt. "So, did you just walk away?"

"More or less. I spent two years at U. of M. in Ann Arbor studying business administration. I didn't do badly, but I hated every minute of it. Summers at home, Dad had me working at the dealership. I didn't fit in there either. I was beginning to question the whole scene, the way of life. I found it stifling. I took up running because no one I knew did it. It got rid of a lot of frustrated energy." And introduced him to Marcy who'd eventually led him to a deeper frustra-tion. But that was another story, one he rarely let him-

111

self remember, much less discuss.

"That's why I took up running, too. My parents thought it was gauche. Do you have any brothers or sisters?"

"One. My brother Ray is two years younger and is just like my dad. Gung ho on the business, joined the right clubs, married the daughter of my mother's best friend. Ann's a female clone. Their lives are all mapped out from birth to death. Predictable, safe, boring."

Sam studied their twined fingers, wondering when he'd reached for her hand. He was also wondering how his story was sitting with her. He was basically saying he hated the lifestyle she, too, had inherited. Or chosen. "So I quit college and knocked around a couple of years. Then I met Luke Varner."

She'd guessed that he knew Luke, but not that they were old friends. "That long ago?"

"Yeah. I knew Luke way before he met Stephanie. Even before he married his first wife." Luke had almost lost his grip back then. But he'd turned himself around, with Stephanie's help. Theirs seemed to be one of the few relationships Sam had ever observed that seemed solid. "I liked what I saw in Luke and decided to try the Police Academy. I've never been sorry."

Carly decided that she'd been wrong. Apparently it hadn't been a woman who'd disappointed Sam English, but his whole family. "Your folks don't approve of your work? Is that why you don't use their name?"

He gave a short, bitter laugh. "You could say that. My father still thinks I'll outgrow playing policeman. Besides, if I get into a tight spot, I'd rather some low-life wouldn't be able to make a move on my family."

So he still cared about them, deep down. "You're the Kingsley black sheep then."

"No, the *dumb* sheep, according to my father. He thinks I'm crazy to risk my neck daily when I could

112

live the cushy life."

She tightened her hand in his. "I don't know why some parents want to take round pegs and shove them into square holes."

"Yours never tried to influence you?"

She shrugged. "A little, I suppose. My father got me a job working in a law office for a while, but I didn't like it. Actually, I've never been much of a rebel, except in small ways. I went to the same college my mother attended, the one all my friends went to also, and got engaged to the boy down the block I'd grown up with."

"But you woke up, broke the engagement, and moved out of the family home. Will couldn't have been pleased with those choices."

"No, he was always warning me of the dangers. Ironically, though he lived in what is considered a protected neighborhood, violence found him anyway." She glanced out the window and realized she hadn't closed the drapes. She hadn't felt the need with Sam here. "I never felt uneasy here until lately."

"If there is someone out there trying to scare you, Carly, it wouldn't matter where you lived. But I hope you know that we're working to find him, that we're watching you."

"Watching me? Is that why you're here, to check on me?"

He could have said more, but he'd already said too much. "The mug shots." He reached for the manila envelope he'd left on the table, slid out the pictures. "See if anyone here looks familiar, if a name rings a bell."

Feeling oddly disappointed, Carly studied each photo in turn and read the accompanying descriptions.

Firelight brought out the red in her hair, Sam thought as he kept his eyes on her bent head. He wanted to untie the piece of blue yarn, to watch her hair tumble free. He wanted to do a whole lot more, which was probably an indication he'd better get the hell out of here. After unexpectedly playing true confessions, he was feeling uncharacteristically exposed.

Finally, she handed back the pictures, shaking her head. "Sorry."

"It was a long shot." Picking up their plates, Sam stood. "I guess I'd better get going." He waited while she took the dishes into the kitchen. As he put on his jacket, he noticed the light on her answering machine blinking. "You want to play that while I'm here?"

She did. It turned out to be Sam's earlier call, asking if he could bring the mug shots over. Wordlessly, she walked with him to the door, wanting him to stay, yet afraid to say the words out loud. "Thanks for telling me about your family. It explains why I had the feeling that you disliked me for some vague reason I couldn't pinpoint."

"It wasn't you, although you were pretty obnoxious. A spoiled brat." The consequences be damned, he stepped closer. She smelled like something expensive, like jasmine, like Carly.

"You were pretty arrogant. The macho cop." Her heart picked up its pace, and a knot she hadn't known was there deep inside tightened.

He touched her hair, then took her face into his hands and tipped her head up. "I don't want to want you."

Her fluttering hands settled at his waist. "I don't want to want you either. I'm on shaky ground with all that's happened lately. You only confuse me further."

"We'd be lousy together."

"Definitely."

What a crock, Sam thought as he bent to kiss her.

Oh, God, she wanted this, wanted him, Carly thought. She'd occasionally longed for the forbidden, for what was wrong for her, though she'd seldom acted on those yearnings. With Sam, she wanted to reach out and touch the fire.

He kissed like a thirsty man who'd staggered in from the desert, drinking deeply from her. Then he changed the angle, his arms going around her, and kissed her again. He could feel her nipples harden through her light sweater, rubbing against his chest as he buried his face in her hair. Why was he putting himself through this?

Sam pulled back, then stepped away. Aware that his hands weren't quite steady, he shoved them in his pockets. "My turn to thank you for dinner," he said.

She wasn't quite recovered, was wondering if she would, but she would fake it. "Anytime," she said, even managing a smile.

He opened the door. "I'll be in touch."

"Fine." She watched him go, then returned to the kitchen to clean up. She wouldn't think about the kiss, Carly decided as she finished and gathered up her packages. It was just a kiss, anyway, she told herself. Only fools made a big thing out of a little kiss.

Only fools lied to themselves, she thought with a sigh.

Absently, she set aside the prints she'd collected to study later. Then she picked up the box containing the blouse she'd ordered two weeks ago from the new boutique, anxious to try it on. It was silk, long-sleeved, in an unusual shade of green she'd been searching for to go with a plaid skirt she'd purchased awhile back. Even the clerk had admired the cut and the fabric as she'd boxed it this morning.

Carly opened the box, shoved aside the tissue paper, and lifted out the blouse—and gasped out loud.

Shredded, the beautiful garment had been slashed with long jagged tears through the front, back, and both sleeves. Her pulse racing, she lay it on her bed, trying to deal with her frantic mind and runaway thoughts, trying to recap her day.

She'd stopped at two shops on The Hill and at Jim's

studio before driving downtown and parking on a side street, then walking to the riverfront to take her pictures. She'd locked her car each time, she was certain. On the way home, she'd stopped for gas and then for the pizza.

The blouse had been whole when she'd picked it up. Who could have gotten into her locked car and ruined it? And why? Her hands suddenly shaky, Carly hurried to close the window blinds. Peering out, she saw no one, nothing unusual. Still, a shiver skittered up her spine.

Back in the bedroom, she wondered if she should call Sam. What could he do except come back and look at the blouse? Then he'd insist that she go stay with her mother. Or worse yet, that he stay here and watch over her.

No, she'd mention it another time. She was bound to see him again soon. Trembling, Carly packed the tattered blouse back in its box and set it on her closet shelf. Walking to the bathroom, she turned on the water in the tub. Years ago she'd gotten into the habit of taking a long, hot bath when she was upset or worried and unable to relax.

The water would relax her body, she thought. But what would it take to ease her mind?

"Guess what?" Ray asked as he flung himself into his desk chair opposite Sam. "I finally located Kerry Logan."

Sam turned from the typewriter he was using to fill out still another form. "Great. Did you question him?"

Ray shook his head. "No need. He's been in Jackson Prison for three months. Logan's not his real name either, which is why I had trouble finding him."

"Guess we can cross him off."

Ray scrounged around in his desk for a piece of gum. "Did Carly recognize any of the mug shots or the names?"

"Nope. Looks like we're going to have to run down each one."

"Terrific." Ray came up empty handed and slammed his drawer closed.

"Have a mint." Sam tossed him the roll. "What about Brett Stevens?"

"Nah, he's squeaky clean. Church-going stock-broker, coaches Little League, family goes back almost to the Mayflower." Making a face, he tried a mint. "Did you check out the other guy?"

"Pierce Nelson? Yeah." Sam dug around and found his notes. "Works for the Detroit Bank, main branch, loan division. Separated from his wife back in New York, but hasn't filed for divorce. Currently romancing the daughter of one of his bank's vice presidents. Not exactly the salt of the earth, but I doubt he's a killer. His alibis for both murders check out."

"Damn. I was hoping one of them would pan out so we wouldn't have to go searching for all those cons and ex-cons. Ten years. Some could have disappeared, but good."

Sam agreed. "Or died. Or still be behind bars. I don't like it either. Got any better ideas?" He returned to his typing.

"No." Ray studied the list of names, then set it aside. "You getting along any better with Carly Weston?"

A loaded question. "Yeah, some." Sam concentrated on filling in the blanks. "On the Wilson case, you take a deposition from his ex?"

Apparently he wanted to change the subject, Ray thought. He'd play along. But his partner was acting mighty antsy these past few days. And he'd bet a dollar to a doughnut Carly was the reason why. "Yeah, yesterday. Why?"

"Captain wants to see it."

Ray found the file in his drawer, removed the sheet,

and got up. It was Sunday and he didn't feel like hanging around all day. "Want to come over later, watch the Lions get tromped? I could pick up some Chinese. Or maybe pizza and beer."

Pizza and beer. He'd had that last night, with Carly. It would be too obvious if he dropped in to see her again. And too dangerous. Maybe he'd just finish up here and sort of drive by her place. Just to make sure she was all right, of course. "Not today, but thanks," he said to Ray.

"Okay, see you later." Ray dropped the report on the captain's desk and left the nearly deserted squad room.

Sam leaned back in his chair. He should have gone with Ray. It was dead around here. And Carly probably wouldn't be home. Even if she were, he shouldn't be looking her up unless he had official business to discuss with her.

The problem was, he'd always hated Sundays. Too much free time made him restless. Hunching over the typewriter, he went back to work.

Carly turned her Porsche into her mother's circular drive and pulled to a stop by the door. "I'm stuffed. They really do serve a nice brunch at Lochmoor. That new chef's a big improvement over the last couple."

Isabel Weston smiled. "I'm so glad you invited me, dear. I haven't seen enough of you."

Actually, Carly thought, she'd never been fond of the Lochmoor Club, probably because she'd didn't golf and had never bothered to get to know very many of the members. But she knew how much her mother enjoyed going there, which was why she'd called to invite her to Sunday brunch. She also had been feeling guilty about not seeing more of Isabel. "Maybe we can go shopping one day this coming week."

"That would be nice." Isabel opened the door,

wishing Carly would buy a decent car. Leaving this one was like trying to climb out of a ride at an amusement park. "Come in a minute, will you? I got you that bedspread you admired last month at Jacobson's."

"Mother, how nice of you." Carly turned off the engine and got out.

Isabel found her keys and opened the door. "Well, you're the only daughter I have to spoil so . . . oh, my God!" Stepping into the foyer, she raised a hand to her throat in shock.

"What is it?" Carly eased around her mother, who'd stopped in her tracks. What she saw had her eyes widening.

Through the open door to her father's study, she saw papers scattered all over the floor, his desk drawers open, the contents tossed carelessly aside. Books yanked off the shelves were everywhere. In the living room opposite the study, artifacts from the mantel had been shoved to the carpet and a lamp shade hung crookedly. "You've been robbed!" Carly whispered.

Isabel slowly moved forward. "Do you think so? Or just vandalized?"

"Mom, people don't vandalize homes like this. They break in to steal." Noticing she was shaky, she led her mother to the chair alongside the hall table, then glanced about uneasily. Surely he wasn't still here. Could she be wrong? Had someone broken in looking for something? Was there a connection here to her father's murder? Or was she getting paranoid?

"Sit right here, Mom. I'm going to call Sam." She picked up the phone and dialed the number she'd already memorized. First her father, then her car and the blouse, now her mother's home.

When was all this going to end?

"You're sure you've checked all the rooms and this is a list of everything that's missing?" Sam asked Isabel Weston.

"Yes, Detective English, I believe so."

Carly sat down beside her mother in the breakfast nook. "Would you like more tea, Mom?"

"No, dear, I'm fine." She looked through the arch at her housekeeper as she busied herself in the kitchen. "Mabel, I can't thank you enough for rushing right over on your day off."

Mabel paused in the act of hand-washing a delicate vase that had been knocked to the floor, then dusted for prints. "I shouldn't have left at all, Mrs. Weston. And I'm not going to from now on. I'm going to stay in the guest room until they catch the person who's doing these terrible things to this family." She sniffed, more upset than her employer.

"That really won't be necessary," Isabel protested.

But Mabel wasn't having any. "Yes, ma'am, I'm staying." She'd already served them cold cuts and fruit. "I'm going to finish straightening up. Why don't you take yourself a little nap."

"You're a wonder, Mabel," Carly said approvingly, then turned to touch her mother's hand. "Mom, let her stay. I'll feel better." She looked at Sam. "Mabel's worked for the family for twenty years."

"Twenty-two," Isabel corrected, then drew in a deep breath. "I suppose it'll be all right. Such a nasty business."

Yeah, it was, Sam thought. And puzzling. The value of the missing items—jewelry, some cash, and several expensive artifacts—was costly, but not staggering. The thief had left behind a valuable coin collection, an antique gun, priceless paintings, items easily hocked like VCR's and TV's. Which indicated he was working alone, probably without a van.

There'd been no forced entry, and the burglar alarm had been carefully deactivated. Was this connected to Will's murder, or was it a random robbery? Sam had had his fingerprint experts here for two hours, but he doubted anything would show up. Thieves today were clever and wore gloves. So far, they'd found no traces of petroleum jelly. He'd already questioned the neighbors, and no one had seen anyone suspicious. The thief had slipped in and out totally undetected in broad daylight.

Just like the man who'd killed Homer Gentry and Will Weston.

Sam put the list in his jacket pocket and stood. It was already late and dark out. "Carly, I'll follow you home."

Carly rose. "You needn't. I drive that route often."

"I'll follow you home," he said, slowly enunciating each word.

Isabel nodded her agreement. "Yes, please do. And, Carly, you call me when you get inside."

Giving in, giving up, Carly hugged her mother, then Mabel, and went outside. As she opened her car door, she glanced over at Sam's older Trans Am parked behind her. "I could leave you in my dust, you know."

"Think so?" He grinned at her. "I'd hate to have some cop arrest you for speeding."

She grinned back and climbed in.

It was beginning to feel like a familiar scene, Carly thought as she stood just inside her dark doorway while Sam, his weapon in hand, quietly checked all of her rooms. However, with this upsetting day, she had to admit she was grateful he was with her, even if she'd given him a hard time about following her home.

"All clear," he said, returning his .38 to his shoulder holster as he walked to Carly. Moonlight drifted in, falling across her face. She looked worried and a little tired. He slid his hands along her arms. "Are you all

121

right?"

She nodded. "Just concerned. I hate having my mother upset. She's been through enough."

"Maybe there's no connection. I'll know more in a day or two." He stood looking at her, just looking at her. She had on a suede dress in rust and simple pearls, her hair worn up in some sort of a twist. She looked distant, unapproachable, untouchable.

Maybe that was why he wanted her so desperately.

She should have turned on the light, Carly thought. It was dangerous standing in moonlight with Sam English, with his eyes probing hers. Dangerous and foolish. "Why don't I make us some coffee?"

He waited a long moment, finally coming to a decision. "I can go, or I can stay. Your choice. But if I stay, it won't be to have coffee."

Carly felt her heart lurch and the room tilt a bit. He was leaving it up to her. Her father had always told her to take the time to make sure something feels right, then simply go for it. This felt right.

"Stay," she whispered.

Chapter Eight

That one soft word was all Sam needed. He bent to her, his mouth taking hers greedily. She responded, as by now he'd known she would, hungrily. Her arms were around him, her hands diving into his hair. She moved against him, and he thought he'd explode.

He couldn't wait, not this first time. He couldn't kiss her deep enough, couldn't hold her close enough. He was struggling with a sharp, urgent need that threatened to overcome him. His hands were everywhere, trailing along her ribcage, moving to the front, and fumbling with the row of buttons. His mouth never left hers as he all but shoved the dress from her while she stepped out of her heels.

Passion rose in Carly like a tidal wave. She was as feverish as he, pushing Sam's jacket from his broad shoulders, then jolting when her hand touched his gun holster. She heard him swear softly against her lips as he worked his way out of the harness and tossed it aside. "The bedroom," she murmured, groping along the opening of his shirt, the need to touch his flesh overwhelming.

"Too far," Sam muttered, knowing he'd never have the patience to make it. Shedding his clothes and hers, he drew her over to the open, carpeted area in front of the fireplace. His hands thrust into her hair, the blunt fingers scattering the pins every which way. His knees weakened, so he shifted her to the floor and followed her down, thinking the couch too narrow.

Carly moaned low in her throat as her hands caressed the hair of his chest, then moved to encircle, to stroke his back. She felt him tug off her pantyhose, then arched as his lips claimed first one breast, then the other, drawing on her flesh deeply. Mind spinning, she pressed his head closer while her hips shifted restlessly.

There was only a hint of illumination drifting in through the slatted blinds, but Sam's eyes had adjusted to the dimness. He thought she looked beautiful wearing only moonlight, her hair spread out on the carpeting, her eyes darkening as her arousal deepened. He'd wanted to go slowly, to treat her like the lady he knew she was, but needs hammered at him. When her clever hands roamed lower and closed around him, he almost lost it.

"God, Carly, I want you so much," he whispered close to her ear, his voice hoarse. "I don't think I can wait."

Carly wanted no lazy loving either. "Don't wait. I want you, too." Desire had her squirming beneath him, had her aching. As she felt Sam's fingers slip inside her, she closed her eyes and let the incredible feeling take her.

This was what she'd needed, this mindless retreat from herself. The outside world was kept at bay for this small measure of time. She felt wanted, loved, safe, if only temporarily. This was the only reality in a world gone mad.

She felt his hard body tremble as he hovered over her, his dark eyes shimmering with passion. Could any woman resist being wanted this wildly? she asked herself. Then he was on her and in her, his thrusts deep and sure. The climb was faster than she'd ever known, more frantic. In moments, her body rippled with pleasure and her mind went blank as she absorbed the waves.

Long minutes later, she lay quietly listening to Sam's harsh breathing slow, holding him still locked within her. She was a little dazed at how easily he'd managed to send her flying. She wasn't frigid, but she'd always had such trouble getting there. Men, she'd come to realize, rarely did. She'd about decided she'd never find the patient lover she apparently needed. Yet with Sam, she'd exploded almost violently moments after contact.

It had been more like an episode of hot, reckless sex than tender lovemaking. It had been the single best experience she'd ever had.

She'd surprised him, Sam decided. Gone was the reserved, aloof, unapproachable lady, replaced by an intensely passionate woman who gave as good as she got. Carly was a woman a man made love *with* not *to,* a greedy participant who'd shattered his control far more easily than he was comfortable acknowledging. She'd made him forget everything but her and his helpless attraction to her.

Which might present a problem.

Rising on one elbow, he gazed down at her. Her eyes were soft, her mouth slightly swollen from his. "How do you feel?"

"Stunned."

That made two of them. He wondered if such unbridled passion, such a feverish need for completion, was something new to her. Or if she'd been used to more tender encounters, candlelit bedrooms, champagne, and sweet preliminaries. "I guess, on a romantic scale, that didn't even make it to a five."

"Maybe." She raised a hand to touch his cheek. "But on a sensual scale, it shot off the chart."

125

He smiled at that, then sobered quickly. "I didn't use anything," he confessed. This hadn't happened to him since his teens, this craving that had overruled good sense and all reason.

"I know." Carly raised a hand to brush back her hair. "I'm not usually so . . . so . . ."

"Careless?"

She'd been thinking foolhardy enough to grapple on the floor with a man she barely knew. But what they'd done hadn't been as much imprudent as inevitable. "I wasn't prepared for . . . it's never happened for me like that before. So blindly, so fiercely. I couldn't think."

Sam didn't want to admit that it never had happened quite that way for him either. Rolling to the side, he took her with him, keeping their lower bodies locked together. He struggled with a belated self-anger at his stupid haste, his careless loss of control. Unwilling to let her see, he braced himself for a very important question. "Do we have a problem, or are you on the pill?"

"We're okay." But he hadn't known that when he'd maneuvered her down, hadn't stopped to ask or to think, like she herself. Frowning, she wondered how they could have both lost control so easily.

Through his relief, Sam noticed the frown and trailed his thumb down her cheek, then along the fullness of her lower lip. He felt too good to completely withdraw as small afterwave tremors from her teased at him. "Are you sorry now?"

With just that light, gentle touch of his finger, he had her full attention again. Though his eyes were on hers, his other hand closed over one breast, the movement a caress. Deep inside, she felt him growing, hardening with renewed desire, and felt her own astonishing response, as fierce as the first time.

Fragments of a conversation she'd had with Toni

126

at lunch a while ago came back to her. Her friend had commented that she didn't think Carly had ever felt an attraction so strong that all else be damned. Toni had been right. But, lying here naked on her living room rug with Sam English buried deep within her, she felt it now. "Sorry?" Carly shook her head. "How could I be sorry? No one's ever made me feel the way you do."

He didn't say anything, but she saw the tension leave his face just before he gathered her closer to kiss her deeply. This time, he explored her mouth unhurriedly, then shifted to explore her body with his hands as he watched her reaction to his touch. Leisurely, he investigated every curve and hollow, searching out all her sensitive spots as she felt her breathing go shallow. He was throbbing within her now, and she was no longer able to lie still. She reached for him and . . .

The phone rang, shattering the silence. Tensing, Carly cocked an ear to listen to the machine pick it up, play her recorded voice, then the sound of the beep.

"Carly, this is Mom." Isabel sounded worried, frightened. "I can't believe you're not home yet. Where are you? Did you decide to stop off somewhere? Please, please call me the moment you walk in the door." The phone clicked off.

Carly relaxed, a smile forming. She'd gotten a wee bit distracted. "I guess I forgot to call. My poor mother."

Sam shifted her until she was on top of him, then thrust upward, letting her know he was growing impatient. "She can wait a few more minutes, can't she?"

She closed her eyes on a shiver of pleasure. "Definitely."

"I have to show you something," Carly said as she sat across from Sam at her kitchen table. It was ten in the evening, and they'd just finished eating. Sex, it would seem, made one ravenous.

Sam leaned closer and trailed a hand along the opening of her white terrycloth robe, his fingers slipping inside to caress the soft swelling of her breasts. "I've already seen it, but you can show me again."

She felt her face flush. Good sex, it would also seem, made one mellow and a little foolish. She'd called her mother back after the second time they'd made love, hoping she didn't sound the total idiot as she'd answered Isabel's questions somewhat vaguely. Sam had taken her hand and coaxed her to her bed then, saying the floor was getting a bit hard.

Afterward, both starving, they'd wandered to the kitchen and she'd watched Sam fix a mouth-watering cheese and mushroom omelette while she'd made toast. In the afterglow of passion, they'd eaten and talked and, to Carly's relief, found they were comfortable with one another even after that stunning sexual bout.

But just now, as a cold December wind whipped the bare branches of a backyard tree against the kitchen window drawing her attention to the gloomy night, Carly felt herself drawn back into harsh reality. And remembering something she knew she ought to show Sam.

She stood, shaking her head. "No, that's not it. Come with me." She led him to the bedroom, took down the box from her closet shelf, and showed him the ripped blouse. When she told him the story of what had happened, he planted his fists on his lean hips covered only by his jeans and frowned at her. "Why didn't you call me about this when you first discovered it?"

Carly made a dismissive gesture. "It was late last

128

night. What could you have done at that hour?"

Sam ran a hand through his hair, feeling a rush of impotent anger. "Not a hell of a lot, I suppose, but you should have called me anyway. You're sure you locked your car doors at each stop?"

"Pretty sure. It's something I do so automatically that I don't even think about it."

And there'd been no forced entry into her mother's house either. The same man, perhaps someone who'd once been a locksmith? Shit! He was grasping at straws, looking for a needle in a damn haystack.

Sam looked at the shredded blouse, then looked at Carly as she stood quietly watching him. Almost roughly, he pulled her into his arms. Someone was out there, someone who was sending out warning signals. What if that someone got tired of playing games and hurt her? He held on tighter, the thought making his stomach muscles clench.

She felt his anxiety and leaned back. "What is it?"

"I feel so damn helpless." It wasn't an easy confession for a cop. "I want so badly to catch this guy, yet I feel as if we're chasing our own tail." He reached up to smooth back her hair. "I don't want you to stay here alone at night anymore."

"Now, look, Sam, I . . ."

His hand moved to squeeze her shoulder. "I mean it." He'd thought originally that she'd be better off at her mother's house, but not after the robbery today. Had it been a robbery or just made to look like one to frighten, to warn? Even the alarm system hadn't kept out the intruder. No, he wanted Carly really safe. "Either you come to my place or I'll stay here nights." And he'd still worry about her. "And during the day, I want to know where you are and that you're not alone."

"Sam, I can't report my every move to you. I . . ."

Angrily, he picked up the blouse and waved it at her. "Look at this goddamn blouse! You think this guy's fooling around? You're in danger. Why won't you believe me?"

She took a step back, tying the belt of her robe more tightly. "You're scaring me."

"I certainly hope so." He'd meant to, yet he was sorry he had to. "Come here." He reached for her, holding her close, as if the very act could keep her safe.

Feeling his frustration mount, Sam leaned his cheek against her hair, inhaling her scent. What the hell was happening here? He'd wanted to take her to bed, and he had. And it had been terrific. Usually by now, he'd be out the door and on his way, whistling happily about a nice shared interlude. Yet here he was, not wanting to leave her. Wanting instead to protect her.

Leaning back, he looked into her eyes and saw the worry he'd put there. "I just don't want anything to happen to you."

"Neither do I."

"Then let me—" He heard a sound and turned, bending to retrieve his jacket.

"What was that?"

"My beeper just went off." He hit the button on the black gadget, turning it off. "I have to call the station." This late, it couldn't be good news. He walked to the living room and dialed in.

Carly trailed after him, curling up on the couch. His comments after seeing the blouse frightened her. It was evident that he thought she was taking all this too lightly. She really wasn't. She was scared half out of her mind. But what could she do, barricade herself in her apartment with a shotgun and stay put until they caught this maniac? Shaking back her hair, she glanced over at Sam.

He was turned away from her, talking in a low voice. The skin of his back was tan and smooth, his jeans riding low on his slim hips, his feet bare. He was tall and strong and so very male. Sorry? No, she wasn't at all sorry she'd taken him to her bed. She would do it again.

Sam hung up the phone and swore ripely, then turned to face Carly. "There's been another strangling."

Ray flipped open his notebook and checked his information before briefing Sam. "His name's Doug Anderson. He's got a rap sheet long as your arm. Petty stuff. Couple of B&E's, car theft, purse snatchings. And convenience-store robberies. He likes to hit the all-night ones about three a.m."

The man on the ground was slight, no more than five-six, with a small, wiry frame. He was dressed in cheap but flashy clothes and had on a fake Rolex watch. There was a fairly recent jagged scar on his left cheek near his temple. He looked up at them, unseeing, with a bug-eyed stare. His neck had been neatly broken, the bones crushed. And again, there was a residue of shiny ointment on the man's throat. Undoubtedly petroleum jelly.

Sam dropped the edge of the blanket back over the victim's face and scowled into the cold night sky. They were in a dingy section of Woodward Avenue at the mouth of an alley that backed up to a string of cheap bars, topless restaurants, and abandoned store fronts. The air was ripe with the smell of garbage from nearby cans. Neon signs winked garishly across the street and the steady thrum of rock music drifted from an open doorway. "How'd you get here so fast?" he asked his partner. The way Ray drove meant that Sam usually beat him to the crime scene.

"I was at Donna's, all snuggled down with her, watching some sappy movie that had her crying. When I got the call, *I* felt like crying." Ray pulled up the collar of his coat as a chilly wind whipped around the corner, wishing he were back in his friend's apartment. "I hate cold weather."

"Yeah, me, too." Sam walked out to talk with the first officer on the scene. Several bar patrons stood on the fringes gawking, their curiosity evident as they whispered among themselves. "Did you find him?" he asked the short, stocky policeman.

"No. That guy over there with the mustache and apron is the bartender at the joint across the street. Says some wino came in 'bout an hour ago, shaking and scared to death. He'd wandered into the alley to take a leak and found the victim. He ran into the bar needing a drink and told the bartender about the body. He called us."

"Where's the wino?" Sam asked.

The cop shrugged. "Gone by the time we got here."

"Swell."

"I think the guy was on the level." He removed his cap and brushed back thick blond hair. "We had a briefing just last week on the strangler. Did you check out this guy's neck? Adam's apple crushed, skin all marked up."

"Yeah, I saw it." Sam stuck his hands into his pockets. What possible connection could a petty thief have to Homer Gentry and the Prosecuting Attorney?

The young officer shifted his feet uncertainly. "Hope I did the right thing by asking the desk to call you."

"Yeah, you did."

"Think it's the same guy that did those other two?"

"Appears to be." With a brief nod, Sam walked over where the police ambulance was parked. The attendant lounged against the open door smoking. "Okay, he's yours, Paulie."

Paulie threw down his butt and stepped on it. "Is it a rush job? You want me to get Doc on him right away?"

Sam shook his head. "Morning'll be soon enough." He strolled back to Ray. "What do you think? Is this Anderson one of the punks Gentry represented?"

"Name doesn't ring a bell, and I've gone through Gentry's client list over and over. Could be we've got *two* guys with big hands running loose."

Sam thought that possibility unlikely. They'd kept a lid on the news media about the strangler's hands and the crushing of the larynx, hoping to head off any copycat murders. Far as he knew, that information hadn't been leaked. And their ace-in-the-hole, the ointment, so far no one outside the department knew of it. "Let's see what else we can dig up on Anderson in the morning."

Ray glanced at his watch. Midnight. "Well, this pretty well shoots my plans for tonight." He thought of Donna, probably asleep by now in her big four-poster bed. "Might as well go home."

Sam noticed the disappointment on Ray's face, and the frustration. "Why don't you marry Donna? You know you're nuts about her."

Ray thought of his ex-wife, of how the marriage he'd had such high hopes for had crumbled after two years because she couldn't stomach his job or get used to his hours. "No, thanks. I've been down that road once already, and it's full of potholes."

The ambulance pulled away, and the two uniformed officers dispersed the few stragglers still hanging around. Ray fell in step with Sam as they

133

walked toward their cars. At the Trans Am, Ray stopped, staring inside. "What's Carly doing here?"

"I was at her place when they paged me." He hadn't wanted to bring her, not to this place. But he'd been even more reluctant to leave her alone. He'd insisted and, surprisingly, she hadn't argued, agreeing to stay inside his locked car until he returned.

"I see."

Sam wasn't quite sure why, but he suddenly felt defensive. "No, you don't." He told Ray about the break-in at the Weston house and Carly's ripped blouse. "I don't want her alone, especially at night."

"Maybe you should step up surveillance on her."

Sam was anxious to get going, anxious to avoid more questions. He could see the suspicious glint in his partner's eyes. He'd always hated anyone probing into his personal life, questioning. Yet, he reminded himself, Ray had every right to ask about Carly Weston since she was a part of the case. "Probably, but that carriage house she lives in is damn hard to keep an eye on."

"So take her to your place."

Sam stared at Ray for a moment, then walked around to the driver's side. "See you in the morning."

The man shut off the TV. Nothing on the late-night news either. The only reference to Anderson's death had been on page twenty of the *Detroit News.* Doug would be pissed if he knew he was so unimportant in the overall scheme of things. The little shit had always thought he was something special.

He'd found out just how special. The man cracked his large knuckles as he remembered the look on Doug's face when he'd glanced up from the beer he'd been nursing and seen him. He'd damn near fallen off the bar stool in his haste to get away. But it hadn't worked. The man had found him cowering in that filthy alley like the yellowbelly turncoat he was.

The man had seen in his nearly paralyzed gaze that Doug had known exactly why he was about to die. It had pleased him to hear the wily snake beg for his life.

Picking up his list, he crossed off the third name. Two more to go. The fourth still wasn't back from vacation. The man hoped he was enjoying his trip. It would be his last.

As to the woman, she was undoubtedly scared shitless by now. He smiled lazily, picturing her well-bred face registering fear. He was enjoying playing with her. Did she think that having that cop hanging around would keep her from having to pay? The man almost laughed aloud.

Two more, and then he'd go get Pete, make a new life for the two of them. And the stupid cops who thought they were so smart hadn't a clue.

Soon. It would all be over soon.

Captain Renwick was not a pacer. Sam knew that his superior officer used to walk a beat years ago and had trouble with his feet. That was one reason he felt uneasy watching Renwick striding the width of his small office, then turning and retracing his steps, his expression unreadable. The other reason was that it was barely eight in the morning and he'd been called in for a chat, something the captain rarely did before noon.

Slouched in the chair opposite Renwick's desk, Sam looked relaxed, almost lazy, but his mind was alert and racing. He knew he was good at what he did and had the citations to prove it. But he also bent the rules now and then, causing him to be called on the carpet occasionally and being reminded that police work was a team effort and maverick officers weren't looked upon with favor. However, he couldn't think of anything he'd done lately to warrant this unexpected meeting. Patiently, he waited for the man to get to the point.

Running a hand over his thinning hair, Captain Renwick stopped behind his chair and braced both hands on the back as he swung his eyes to Sam. "I went to a fundraiser at Cobo Hall yesterday. Black-tie dinner honoring Michigan police officers killed in the line of duty. Proceeds go to the widows and children. A good cause, but I hate those dress-up affairs."

He was sure coming in the back door on this one, Sam thought. "Yeah, me, too."

Renwick sat down, leaning his elbows on his desk pad. "I was taken aside by the mayor. He told me he's not happy about this strangler still on the loose. Then I come in this morning and find this." He picked up the newspaper on his desk, unfolded it and tossed it to Sam.

The headline in the *Detroit Free Press* read: Serial Killer Strikes Again. The story below detailed the finding of Doug Anderson's body, the article anything but flattering to the Police Department. Sam swore under his breath.

Renwick scowled. "Why wasn't I told we'd had another strangling?"

Sam realized the captain was getting pressure from the top. It didn't make his job any easier either. "I was called out about ten last night," he began.

"Go on."

"I just got in to type up the report. Same M.O. as the other two, although this victim doesn't seem to correlate with Gentry and Weston. A two-bit punk with a sheet going back to his teens. Ray's over re-checking Gentry's case files to see if he was ever Homer's client, but the name doesn't ring a bell from what we've already seen."

"Maybe there *is* no connection."

"Possible, I suppose, but I stopped in to the morgue earlier and Doc says that in all probability the killer's the same man, the same unusual spread of fingers, the crushing of the larynx, the petroleum jelly on the neck. It all matches."

"How'd the papers get it so quick?"

Sam shrugged. "He was found in a sleazy section of Woodward, but I suppose some reporter could have been in the bar across from the alley. Or one might have been hanging around the morgue when they brought him in."

Renwick leaned back in his chair thoughtfully. "Three men strangled, and the killer's left not one clue nor been seen by a single person. What the hell's going down here, Sam?" He tapped a finger on the newspaper Sam had set down. "I hate bad press."

Sam shifted in his chair. Renwick's voice, he knew, grew softer as he grew angrier. It was very low right now. "I'd like to be able to give you something positive, Captain. We're cross-checking case files from Gentry and Weston, we've interviewed family and friends, neighbors, co-workers. And we'll start today to take apart Anderson's life. So far, we can't make a connection, so we have no idea where he'll strike next or even *if* he will. We simply don't have anything solid yet."

"I understand that the prosecutor's daughter called in about her car being vandalized. Is that connected?"

Wondering who had told the Captain about that, Sam shrugged. "I don't honestly know if it is." He didn't especially want to get into Carly with Renwick, yet since he knew about her car, perhaps he should tell him the rest. "She's had some mysterious things happen. Hang-ups, seeing a guy standing out on the street at night, loitering under her lamp post. And a blouse she'd picked up from a shop was slashed into pieces when she opened the box at home. Could be him, though as far as we know, he didn't stalk the other victims, just moved in for the kill. Or it could be some other creep."

Renwick frowned. "Did you take the blouse in to the lab?"

Sam nodded. "This morning."

The captain had been in Sam's shoes years ago, trying to break a high-profile case with little to go on. That was the only reason he was keeping a lid on his temper, which was more than the mayor had done with him yesterday. Politicians always wanted answers *now*, and they didn't much care how they got them. "You question her? Put her under surveillance?"

"Yeah. We've talked with just about everyone the whole Weston family knows and cleared them all."

"Maybe you should assign someone to her. Weston was a good friend of the mayor. If something happened to his daughter, he'd have my ass and yours, too."

"I do have a cop on her." He wasn't about to mention that he was that cop.

Renwick leaned forward again. "All right. Let me know if you learn anything. I mean *anything*. I want to be kept posted on this daily, you hear?"

Sam stood. "I want to get this guy as much as you do. Maybe more."

Sticking a fresh cigar in his mouth, the captain regarded his detective. "If you were me, what would you tell the mayor?"

138

His hand on the doorknob, Sam swung back. "That we're doing the best we can with what we've got to work with."

Renwick reached for his matches. "Do better."

Oscar Hammer pressed the tip of his stubby pencil to his tongue, then bent to write down the measurements he'd just taken. Thoughtfully, he rewound his metal tape measure.

"So, what do you think?" Carly asked. "Can you do the job?"

"Yeah, sure," Oscar said, hitching up his work pants.

She was relieved. She was anxious to get this large closet off the kitchen turned into a darkroom so she could develop her own prints. She'd gotten her landlord's permission, but getting Sam's had taken longer.

He hadn't allowed her to invite someone over for an estimate until he'd personally checked the man out. Oscar had a little business going called *The Happy Hammer,* operating out of his van and advertising with flyers delivered to homes in a variety of eastside neighborhoods. He'd been at it for twelve years, a balding middle-aged man who had trouble keeping his pants up over a potbelly he'd yet to acknowledge enough to buy clothes a size larger. Carly had hoped he would prove acceptable so she wouldn't have to start hunting again.

"Like my card says, no job too big or too small," Oscar went on. "But it's going to cost you."

Carly crossed her arms over her chest. "How much?"

Oscar bent to his clipboard, did a bit more figuring, then ripped off the top sheet and handed it to her. "All my work comes with a thirty-day warranty."

Checking over the numbers quickly, Carly nodded. About what she'd expected. "Fine. When can you start?"

"Tomorrow probably. Provided I can pick up the lumber later today. Gotta take a few more measurements."

"Terrific." Carly smiled her approval, then turned to the archway as she heard a knock at her front door. "You go ahead while I see who that is." She walked through the living room feeling a shade nervous. Sam had warned her not to open the door without checking, and she had no intention of not listening to his cautious directives. Of course, Oscar was in the next room, but she had her misgivings as to how effective the portly little carpenter would be against a killer who had managed to strangle three men and walk away undetected.

Peering through the blinds, she saw a young man holding a long white florist's box waiting impatiently. She opened the door, leaving the chain on. "Yes?"

"Delivery for Carly Weston," the man said, reading from the order sheet attached to the box.

Carly held out her hands. "Just slide the box through the opening, please."

The deliveryman raised a questioning brow, but did as she asked, then held out his clipboard. "Sign for it on Line 24, please."

She did, then gave back his clipboard, thanked him and closed the door. Moving to the couch, Carly smiled in anticipation. Flowers from Sam. She hadn't thought of him as being romantic, but perhaps he had a hidden side she'd yet to discover. She slid the ribbon off and lifted the lid, pulling back the tissue paper.

Carly gasped audibly, nearly dropping the box from her lap. Nestled in the tissue was one blood-

140

red rose, its petals ripped off and lying scattered throughout. With trembling fingers, she reached for the small white envelope and removed the card.

Roses are red, violets are blue. Nowhere to run, I'm watching you.

The cry that came from deep in her throat was half whimper, half sob. Closing her eyes, she struggled to breathe, fear rippling through her. Too much. It was all too much.

Quickly, she set down the box and went to the phone to call Sam.

Chapter Nine

Carly used her light meter to get a reading, then calculated her exposure. Checking the angle, she framed the picture in her mind, then peered through the viewfinder at her subject.

The little girl was about five, with dark curly hair and wide brown eyes. She sat on Santa's broad, red lap looking a little hesitant. Carly saw Santa ask a question and watched the child solemnly nod yes. Her hands steady, she waited for the right moment. Then suddenly, there it was, the little girl looking up at the big, bearded man with hope written clearly on her young face and the sure knowledge that Santa would deliver. Carly clicked the shutter.

Pausing, she stepped back, shifting angles, adjusted the depth of field, then took several more. Satisfied, she relaxed and found Sam studying her thoughtfully.

He'd been watching her for well over an hour, had lost track of the number of rolls of film she'd gone through. They'd driven to the enclosed shopping center at Eight Mile and Kelly Road known as Eastland Mall in mid-afternoon and made their way through the crowds of shoppers. Carly had insisted she was going to take pictures, and he'd insisted she wait until he could accompany her. She hadn't liked cooling her heels until he picked her up, but nonetheless she'd waited.

Since arriving, she'd snapped Santa settling his bulk on his throne-like chair, his elf-helpers lining up the rows of excited children, the weary parents forgetting their tired feet when it was their child's turn to climb up and run through the wish list. And the little ones. She'd stooped and knelt and craned her neck to get the shots she wanted. He found himself looking forward to seeing the results.

Sam knew he'd become cynical through the years, not quite buying into the magic of Christmas, seeing instead a holiday orchestrated by merchants greedy for the almighty dollar. Yet, watching Carly, he tried to see things through her eyes.

Her approach was personal and unabashedly sentimental. She didn't just see things, but sought to understand the emotion behind the scene and then capture it. He'd glimpsed a few of her snapshots at her place and knew that the photos she'd taken today would prove to be even better. In the beginning, he'd thought her shallow and superficial. Sam wasn't sure if she'd changed or his view of her had.

He watched her hand out red-reindeer balloons to the kids, her way of thanking her small subjects, he supposed. She was carelessly generous, naturally so, with all of them. Next, she had the parents sign the necessary release forms before returning to him.

"I'll be ready to leave in a couple of minutes," she told him, intent on finishing the final roll. Scooting past him, she zeroed in on a toddler, barely two, who'd squirmed through the ropes and was petting a life-like replica of Bambi. She set the aperture and clicked.

"Take your time," he told her, shoving his hands in his pockets, never straying more than a few feet from her. Christmas carols drifted through the loudspeakers and the steamy indoor air was heavy with the fragrance of cinnamon buns from a nearby

143

shop. As he waited, Sam's eyes moved through the crowd, checking and rechecking the faces.

He'd had to do some major rescheduling to become Carly's self-appointed bodyguard. Ray had been understanding, even helpful, in scrambling their workload around so Sam could have more time away from the station. Evenings, while Carly planned the next day's shoot and sorted her photos, he caught up on his paperwork at her kitchen table.

He followed Carly to a pet store around the corner, where she quickly changed lenses and began snapping a little redheaded boy who'd flattened his face against the window as a brown puppy, up on his hind legs, whined at him excitedly from the other side. What had he gotten himself into with this case? Sam asked himself as he watched her. Or, more correctly, with this woman?

Years ago, he'd learned that a cop had to stay detached. Involvement with someone he was protecting would make him vulnerable and could get him killed, to say nothing of his subject. It weakened a cop's defenses to even know the people on his case very well. Decisions would be based on emotion rather than clear, intelligent thinking. He couldn't let that happen.

He was already there.

The day she'd received the mutilated rose and the note, Sam had rushed to her side, held her to him, taken on her trembling fears. She'd clung to him, this woman who wasn't a clinger, and told him she was frightened. So very frightened. He'd wanted to smash something. Without asking himself the whys and wherefores, he knew two things: he wanted Carly safe and he wanted to get the sonofabitch who was doing this.

Yet there was only so much he could do, even as a detective. Surveillance had been doubled, and he'd seen to it that Carly was rarely alone. He'd gotten her a car-phone and a gun, shown her how to use both. Her father had introduced her to guns at an early age, so she wasn't a novice. The neat little .38 Smith & Wesson made her nervous, but she'd accepted it silently. As she'd accepted his being with her perhaps more than both of them were comfortable with.

Meantime, the search went on. He'd gone in person to Eastside Flowers, the florist who'd delivered the rose, and been able to learn very little. They were awfully busy with Christmas floral arrangements, poinsettia orders, and holiday corsages, the officious little owner had told them. The floral arranger in the backroom remembered that he'd personally put the single red rose in the box intact. The two harassed women behind the counter answered his questions vaguely, sounding distracted. The shorter one recalled only that the purchaser had been a man who'd paid in cash. And, oh yes, he'd worn a cap pulled down low over his forehead.

They'd gotten nowhere in tracing the blouse, nor had they discovered anything unusual in tracking Carly's whereabouts the day it had been ruined. And, so far, they hadn't been able to tie Doug Anderson to either of the other two strangulation victims. Feeling the frustration mount, Sam knew they badly needed a break.

Rewinding her film, Carly walked over to Sam. "Sorry I took so long," she said. She hated this clocking in and clocking out. Yet she hated even more the thought of being alone with some maniac possibly watching her every move.

"It's okay." Sam threw an arm around her shoulders casually. "How about we wander down thataway and find something to eat?"

"Mmm, food. A man after my own heart." Carefully, Carly placed the camera and film into her bag and zipped it closed.

Sam sent her a sharp look she didn't notice. After her heart. Was he? Good God, was he even considering it? He shook his head as if to clear it. "Are you having a Big Mac attack, or do you want to go south of the border to Taco Bell?"

Carly raised a suspicious brow. "You, actually choosing junk food?"

"Yeah. See what you've done to me? I used to eat broiled fish and salads and drink milk. Aren't you ashamed?"

"Real men don't eat that healthy garbage," she teased.

He moved his lips close to her ear. "Maybe we should skip dinner and go home so I can show you what real men do."

She laughed up at him. "Maybe we'd better eat first. I might need to revitalize my energy supply for later."

"Good idea." He led her toward the mall's food-court.

Sam pulled the sheet out of the typewriter and lay it on top of the stack beside the machine. Damn paperwork, he thought, shoving back the kitchen chair, standing and stretching. How he hated all the reports and forms he had to fill out daily. He snapped the cover back on Carly's portable and set it aside. Done for the day.

He wandered into Carly's living room and saw that the fire he'd laid earlier was still going but needed stirring. He also saw that Carly had fallen asleep, curled up in a corner of the couch, a book open on her lap. A Ludlum mystery, he noted. He might have known she'd be drawn to the complex plot. Bending, Sam opened the mesh curtain and tossed in another small log then turned to study her.

She was wearing that same oversize white terrycloth robe after her bath, and she looked younger than her years. Yet, even in sleep, an occasional quick frown skittered across her features, and he knew she wasn't resting well. Neither was he, nor would he until they caught the strangler.

Hearing a sharp noise from just outside, Sam looked up quickly. It had sounded as if someone had hit the front of the building with a board or blunt object. He moved to the window and peered through the blinds.

"What is it?" Carly asked from the couch, sitting up.

Sam's keen eyes scanned the yard, but he could see nothing unusual. "I'm not sure."

Carly tamped down a quick rush of fear. Sam was here with her. There was no reason to panic. "Do you see anything?"

"No." Even as he said it, the noise sounded again, louder and more insistent. Sam reached for the jacket he'd tossed on a chair and put it on, then took his gun out of its harness. "I'm going to go check it out."

"Sam, wait." She heard the strain in her own voice as she rose. "Do you think you should?" The man had killed three times already, with his bare hands. Would even a gun stop him?

"This is what I do for a living, remember? Stay here and stay back from the window." He opened the door slowly, looked carefully both ways, and stepped outside.

Carly sank back onto the couch, holding a fist to her mouth to keep from calling out to him. She'd been a hair away from begging him not to go, not to expose himself to possible danger. She didn't know

147

whether to pray that the man responsible for this nightmare would be out there so Sam could get him or to pray he wasn't for fear he'd somehow over-power Sam.

Idiot, she told herself. He was a cop, experienced, streetwise. But her pounding heart knew only fear, fear for her lover. Noticing that her hands were shaking, she thrust them into the pockets of her robe and waited.

It seemed a very long time later, yet had probably been merely ten minutes, when the door opened and Sam came in, along with a blast of cold night air. "A loose shutter," he told her. "I secured it the best I could, but the restraining hook's broken." He locked the door, sliding the dead bolt home.

Carly released a shaky breath. How long could they live like this without going mad? "You look cold. Come warm up."

Sam shook a light snow from his hair, lay his jacket and gun harness on a chair, and came to rub his hands together in front of the fire before sitting down with her. Just as he did, the phone rang. "Let the machine take it," he told her. "If it's someone you know, you can pick it up."

Instantly Carly recognized the voice that began speaking after the beep, though she hadn't heard it in months. "Carly, this is Pierce. I saw Toni recently and asked her to have you call me. But I guess you've been busy. I wanted to tell you that I'm really sorry about your father. I know you two were close. And I wanted to let you know that I'm legally sepa-rated from my wife now. I . . . I was hoping we could see each other again. Maybe have dinner one night. Like old times. . . . I miss you, Carly. Call me, please."

The phone machine clicked off. Sam turned to look at Carly, who was staring into the fire, her expression unreadable. "We checked him out, and he's clean." He felt she should know, but she didn't respond. "Are you going to call him back?"

"No."

"Are you still in love with him?"

She sighed, shoving back her hair and leaning her head on the couchback. "I never was, not really. I fell in love with the person I thought he was."

Sam wondered why her answer pleased him. He stretched his legs toward the fire's warmth. "Sounds like his feelings run a little deeper."

"I doubt it. Pierce is a user. But even so, it takes two." She shifted her head so she could see him. "Have you ever been in love?"

Her image popped into his mind so easily, even after all these years. Small, blond, wide-eyed with innocence. "Like you, I fell in love with all that I thought she was." He gave a dismissive shrug. "It was a long time ago."

Carly let the silence go on for several minutes before diving in. "Is it so hard to talk about all that?"

He didn't want to lie to her, but he wasn't comfortable delving deeply into the past. So, he asked himself, who said a man could always be comfortable? "I'm not sure I know how," he answered on a long sigh.

"Just take your time." They'd had only one conversation about his past. Carly found she wanted to know more. "When you were in college?"

Sam could picture the young man he'd been, caught in an impossible situation, needing a friendly ear. "I'd just finished my sophomore year, and I was home for the summer, working at the dealership, unhappy with my life and dreading my future."

"She worked at the dealership, too?"

He stared at the dancing flames, seeing another time and place. "No. Her name was Marcy Nolan,

149

and she'd been hired as a baby sitter for a neighboring family on our street. The lady of the house was very social, very busy, so Marcy took care of her kids all day. Two little boys, three and five. I met her one day while I was out for a run and struck up a conversation."

"And you began dating?"

"We began sneaking around. Marcy's employer didn't want her dating while she lived at their place. So Marcy would tell her she was going for a walk after she put the kids to bed. And we'd meet down by the river or at the park. Nothing like a clandestine rendezvous when you're young and stupid to get the juices flowing."

He surely couldn't still be carrying a torch, Carly thought, not after so many years. Yet his voice sounded strained. "How old was she?"

"Almost eighteen, and I was a hotshot twenty. I fell for her like a ton of bricks. I was naive enough to believe that our future would be bright and assured. But I'd failed to take into consideration two small facts: Marcy was from the wrong side of the tracks, and I was the heir apparent to the Kingsley dynasty, the oldest son."

"Your family didn't accept her." It wasn't a question.

His laugh was a bitter grunt. "Yeah, you *could* say that. After two months of meeting on the sly, I got tired of hiding and took Marcy to meet my family. Marched right up to dear old Dad, holding Marcy by the hand, and told him we were in love." He shook his head, seemingly puzzled at how he could have been so gullible as to not have guessed the outcome.

"He was upset?"

"Upset?" The laugh was deeper now, tinged with anger. "He exploded. But not in front of Marcy. Polite as always, he asked her to wait in the living room and took me into his study. Good manners prevailed in our house no matter what we felt. Dad shut the door and told me that I could romance the young lady for the balance of the summer because, after all, boys would be boys and he, too, had sown a few wild oats in his day. I must be very careful not to get her pregnant, of course. Then I could bid her a fond *adieu* and get on with my education in the fall. But marriage? To *someone like that?* Don't even think of it. Marcy was not *our* kind of people. She came from an undisciplined, dysfunctional family. What a laugh since the Kingsleys are a classic example of dysfunctional."

Carly put a hand on his arm because she saw he was hurting, even after all this time. "I'm sorry, Sam." What else could she say? She couldn't really relate, because his experiences were foreign to her upbringing. "My family has money, especially on my mother's side. But they're not class conscious. My great-grandfather used to lay tile in his native Italy." She watched Sam rub at a spot over his eyes. "What did you do?"

"I took Marcy home and told her I'd figure out a way. Well, here I was, twenty years old with a small savings account and no job experience except working for my dad. Finally, I thought I had things worked out. We talked it over, and I kept on seeing Marcy, because my father didn't object to that part, and I began saving my money. The plan was that, come September, I'd leave for school as if everything were okay, but instead of starting classes, I'd sell a bunch of my stuff—the furniture in my apartment in Ann Arbor, some jewelry I'd been given over the years, a couple of bonds I had—and we'd set out for parts unknown and get married. I was still reaching for that happily-ever-after malarkey that I hoped I

151

could find with Marcy because I sure as hell hadn't found it at home."

"So what happened?"

Sam let out a disgusted huff of air. "If I hadn't been so young and stupid, I'd have probably seen the signs from Marcy that she was less than thrilled to be running off with a disinherited son to live on a shoestring God-knows-where. She thought of a better plan. She went to my father behind my back and told him I was nuts about her and that I was about to blow my future and run off with her. However, if he'd hand over twenty thousand dollars, she'd be persuaded to forget she ever met me."

"My God," Carly said softly. "At seventeen, this girl was that shrewd?"

Sam gave a bitter laugh. "Oh, yeah. And, much to my surprise, my father paid her off."

"That goes to show you that he does care for you, that the money meant less to him than you do."

"On the surface, you'd think so. But not really. You have to know my father. Twenty grand didn't mean a whole lot to him. Having me in his control did. He gave her the money, then called me in and told me all the hurtful details. And then he launched into a long lecture about how piss-poor my judgment was and how I'd better let him make my decisions for me for years to come because obviously I fell for one of the oldest tricks in the book."

Carly linked her fingers with his, trying to assess his tension, even after all these years. "I hope you didn't believe him."

"For a while I did. He was big and powerful and knew all the right buttons to push. And the first woman I'd ever cared about had betrayed me badly. I went back to school, hating the money that enabled my father to jerk me around, hating Marcy for loving money instead of me."

"Is that about the time you left college?"

"Yeah. I stayed about two weeks, then walked away from all of it. All of them." He sent her a sardonic look. "So, yeah, I've sampled being in love. And for my money, they can keep it. Do you blame me for feeling that way?"

Carly kept her eyes on the dancing flames. "Oh, I don't know. That happened about fifteen years ago, right? All this time later, you're still blaming everyone who has money for the actions of one misguided man—your father. Not all affluent men are unfeeling, I assure you, and I know quite a few. And secondly, not all women love money more than a particular man."

"I haven't seen a hell of a lot of women choose a poor man over a cushy life some rich guy can give them."

"Maybe you don't run with the right crowd. My friend Amanda comes from pots of money, and she's marrying a fellow who works in a gas station. I imagine her life will change dramatically. The point here is that it isn't whether the woman has money or doesn't that matters. It's what's inside her that counts. And what's inside the man, as well." She, too, had shifted her opinions lately, Carly noted. Yet she believed every word she'd just said.

Sam studied her a moment, then gave her a slow smile. "How'd you get to be so smart?" Or was she just terribly naive?

Carly shrugged. "Sometimes you can see the whole picture better when you're not posing for the photo."

"Maybe you're right. Maybe I just haven't met that many women of strong character."

"Speaking of women, where was your mother through all that?"

Sam shrugged. "My mother goes along with my

153

father—on everything. In her eyes, he can do no wrong. So, the heir apparent flew the coop and they concentrated on number two son, who did not disappoint them. He's just like my father, and he's probably turning *his* son into another clone. Which is a damn shame, but there you have it."

"Do you ever see them?"

"Rarely. My mother had surgery a couple of years ago. My brother called me. I went to the hospital, and she seemed glad to see me. But when my father arrived, I left."

"Has he ever apologized or said he'd made a mistake?" She wanted to ask if perhaps his father had tried; but Sam hadn't let him, still nursing his wounds, but decided not to.

Sam shook his head. "You know what Henry Ford the Second said: Never explain, never complain. That sums up Raymond Kingsley's philosophy, too."

"Maybe one day . . ."

"I doubt it. Let's change the subject." He shifted to face her, slipping his arm around her. "Want to run away with me, somewhere no one can find us, far from this crazy world?"

The thought held much appeal these days. "Yes. We could put on disguises, pretend to be lovers from another time. Rhett and Scarlet. Napoleon and Josephine."

"Fred and Wilma."

"Who?"

"Fred and Wilma Flintstone. And one day we'd have a little tyke named Pebbles."

"And Dino instead of Fido."

He grinned at her. "Now you've got it." Another sound came from outside, and he felt Carly jerk in startled reaction. "Easy. It's just the wind on that loose shutter. I'll fix it tomorrow."

Carly moved closer, slipping her hands up under his sweater, touching the warm skin of his back. She was tired of talking and wanted action, the kind that would take her mind off the wind whistling outside and the stranger out there somewhere who was frazzling her nerves. "I want to make love with you, right now. I want to forget everything but here and now. I want to be a little crazy, to lose all control."

"Aren't you a little afraid to totally lose control?"

She made a face at him. "You're supposed to lose control when you make love. That's what it's all about."

"Is it?" His mouth was a breath away from hers. "Show me."

Smiling, she bent to her task.

"The guy's smart. I'll give him that." Ray sat down at his neat desk across from Sam's cluttered one and unzipped his jacket. "I just came from the lab. He must have worn rubber gloves without his usual smear of petroleum jelly. The boys couldn't pick up a thing from either Carly's blouse or that rose."

Sam set aside the report he'd been reading and leaned back in his chair. "Why doesn't this surprise me? Sure he's smart, or he wouldn't have walked away from three murders without even one witness catching a glimpse of him. Or maybe just lucky." Luck had to run out sooner or later.

"The note in the flower box was written on the florist's card with an ordinary blue ballpoint pen." Ray rubbed his face wearily. It was more than frustrating to have a guy kill three in a row and not leave them a clue to go on. It was getting embarrassing. The media was demanding action. It would be only a matter of time before the mayor gave the captain another nudge and really put on the pressure. Some days he wished he were in another line of work — *any* other line.

"At least we can rule out one thing." Leaning forward, Sam picked up the report and held it out to Ray. "The boys lifted one good solid print at the Weston house after that break-in. It belongs to Harold Formes, the housekeeper's estranged husband. His prints were on file 'cause he's served time for B&E. And he's a former electrician who'd know how to disengage the alarm system."

"Well, that's some progress, I guess. I frankly didn't think the strangler had broken in there. It's not his style. He likes to kill."

Sam nodded grimly. "I sent two blues to Formes's last known address to pick him up. His ex-wife says he's an alcoholic, so he probably fenced the stuff and holed up with the booze it bought."

"Mrs. Weston must be relieved." Ray unwrapped a piece of gum and stuck it into his mouth. "She's a classy lady. Like her daughter. Class will always tell, don't you think?"

Ray was trying to bait him, but it wasn't going to work. He had no intention of discussing Carly with his partner, or anyone else. Mostly because he wasn't certain of his own feelings when it came to the classy Miss Carly Weston. "If you say so."

Megs approached their desk area, a holly sprig stuck into her red hair in honor of the coming season. It didn't seem out of place on her. "How's it going, Megs?"

"Can't complain. But you might. Captain wants to see you two." She glanced over her shoulder at Captain Renwick's glassed-in office. "I was just in there. He's getting some heat about the strangler."

Sam swore under his breath. "I knew it was coming." Resigned, Sam stood, checking his watch. It was only four, but the sky outside was gloomy with snow clouds hovering. Carly was at her place, working in her newly completed darkroom. He'd warned her not to leave without notifying him, without lining up someone to go with her. Her own fear had her cooperating quite meekly of late. But the strangler had outwitted them too often for Sam's peace of mind. He'd go to Carly's right after the captain chewed them out. "Let's get it over with, Ray."

"It's a waste of time, Captain." Sam paced the small office, chewing on a mint with vicious displeasure. "They're a bunch of phoney baloneys, and we all know it."

Captain Renwick clamped down on the unlit cigar stuck between his teeth and longed to light it. But the doctor had warned him to cut down to four a day since they'd discovered his irregular heartbeat. He glanced at the clock. Two more hours till the next match. He pulled his attention back to Sam English. "I don't like the idea any more than you do. But this woman's a relative of someone on the city council."

"When was the last time a psychic helped solve one of our cases, Captain?" Ray asked. His tone was polite, but hinted at his disdain for resorting to such measures to solve crimes.

Renwick switched the cigar to the other side of his mouth. "Only one I know of was six or seven years ago. That woman from the west side who told us where that kidnapped little boy would be found after we gave her his shoe."

"That was a fluke," Sam insisted. "And besides, that's not *this* woman." He stopped striding long enough to glance at the piece of paper he'd been given. "Clio McIntyre. Sounds like a damn country-

157

western singer. Jesus!" He just loved it when the politicians looking for headlines got involved. They'd already had six weirdos who'd 'confessed' to being the strangler. This much news coverage always brought out the nuts.

"Simmer down, Sam," the captain said quietly. He'd never been a shouter. His men often had to listen hard to his raspy voice. But they listened. "You got any better ideas? Just one good lead, and I'll tell that councilman to go stuff it."

Sam ran a hand through his hair. "I wish to hell we did."

Ray read the paper Sam had tossed back onto the desk. "She wants us to collect a personal item of clothing from each of the victims so she can . . ." He glanced up at both men before reading the rest out loud. ". . . absorb the essence of the individual." He, too, dropped the paper. "We're sure going to look like clowns explaining that to the families."

Renwick agreed, but he had a few people to answer to himself. "We've got Anderson's clothes down in the morgue. No relatives have claimed anything. I'm sure Mrs. Weston will cooperate. And Gentry's wife called just the other day, wanting to know what was happening, so she'll give you what you need."

Sam's head snapped up. "Why'd she call you and not one of us?"

The Captain looked him right in the eye. "Because she's getting impatient."

"Aren't we all?" Sam yanked open the office door and left.

Ray noticed the Captain watching Sam's hasty departure thoughtfully and moved in with a quick explanation. "We've both been putting in a lot of hours on this. Sam's a little touchy, but he's fine."

Renwick shifted his gaze to Ray. "You keeping anything from me, anything I should know?"

Shaking his head, Ray got to his feet. "Frustration makes a cop edgy. You remember, Captain." He certainly wasn't going to be the one to mention Sam's interest in Carly Weston. If Renwick even suspected personal involvement, he'd yank Sam right off the case. Which would probably send his partner right over the edge. Pocketing the psychic's phone number, Ray moved to the door. "I'll get on this right away."

Renwick stared at the closed door for several minutes. Then he reached into his pocket for a match, struck it, and held the flame to the tip of his cigar.

There were times when a man had to bend the rules.

Chapter Ten

Carly hung up the last strip of negatives to dry, then moved to the stainless-steel sink to clean up the trays containing the developing chemicals. She was used to the deep amber light of her darkroom now, and she worked with quiet efficiency. This aspect of photography was every bit as exciting as taking the pictures because this is where she could begin to see the results. The next step would be the proofs, and then she'd print the best to show to Jim.

Finishing, she looked around to make sure everything was in order as he'd taught her then flipped on the overhead light. She felt comfortably tired and enormously pleased that she'd had the darkroom built. She'd spent quite a bit on equipment, including an enlarger. With her camera, attachments, assorted lenses, and now her darkroom, she could do something creative alone and without assistance, an outlet she'd apparently been needing, for it gave her great satisfaction.

Leaving the darkroom, she walked through the kitchen and into the living room, snapping on lights. Not yet five and already darkening outside. Winter was definitely here. Peering through the window, she saw that one of her neighbors had strung Christmas lights along the roofline of his house. The gay colors winked on and off in the twilight gloom, reminding Carly that the holiday was fast approaching.

She yawned, then stretched, rolling her shoulders. Her first Christmas without her father, a depressing thought. She'd have to plan to spend more time with her mother, who, despite her many close friends, would undoubtedly be sad. On the brighter side, it would be her first Christmas with Sam.

Sam English. Or Sam Kingsley. Two disparate men sharing the same body. His story about his first love the other evening had touched her, but more importantly, it had explained a lot about what had made him into the man he was today.

His distrust of and disdain for the wealthy and powerful had come from his manipulative father and his ineffectual mother. Sam had decided a long time ago that all affluent men used their money to get their way and that their wives were wimpy creatures who followed their men blindly. A narrow view, but she could understand how he'd formed it. She couldn't help wondering if he'd ever really change that outlook.

Her parents weren't anything like his, Carly decided as she flopped down on the couch with a lazy sigh. Her mother had been born into wealth, yet had married her father when he'd been a law student. Will Weston had worked long and hard to get somewhere, and Isabel had run their home, raised their daughter, and been involved in a number of fundraisers that had helped hundreds.

Isabel had started a scholarship program, begun a literacy effort through the local library, and her most recent passion centered around the homeless. She had chaired many a luncheon, tea, and fashion show, raising funds for suitable housing for people down on their luck. The Weston family, always aware of the fortunate hand fate had dealt them, had tried hard to give back to the community.

She'd been the one who hadn't contributed much.

Searching for what she wanted to do with her life, she'd mostly floated along somewhat aimlessly. She could understand why Sam had thought her an unproductive, spoiled brat when they'd first met. She had been. But lately, Carly found her priorities shifting, undoubtedly triggered by her father's death and the events since.

All her life, she'd felt protected, safe, almost sacrosanct in the close-knit community where she lived. But violence had crossed even that nebulous boundary line. Here was a situation that neither her family's influence nor money could stop. For the first time, she was facing a wall she couldn't climb or even go crashing through. She was at risk and learning to cope with the constant threat of danger. It had changed her.

She'd become more aware of small pleasures, perhaps because she was so afraid they'd suddenly be taken from her. She'd become more tolerant, more giving, more open. Sam had commented on the changes he saw in her just last night, and she'd taken his words as a compliment. Though she still felt that two people from opposite ends of the economic structure would likely not last together in a permanent arrangement, she was beginning to weaken on that point as well.

Because of Sam. Alone here on her couch, she could admit to herself that she'd been attracted to Sam from the start. Despite his arrogance, his contempt for all he'd thought she was, and the fact that she'd been sure he was ghetto born and bred. Maybe because of it.

She'd known that opposites did attract and believed it with a certainty now. But could that attraction last? Of course, Sam had been raised very much as she had—with most anything money could buy and an opportunity for the best education. But he'd turned his back on all that to the extreme. Yet there'd been one screaming difference in their childhoods. She'd been raised with unconditional love and, from what Sam had told her, he hadn't known much love at all—only control.

So it was love that made the difference.

Was she falling in love with Sam English? At twenty-eight, Carly didn't consider herself jaded. But cautious, very cautious, and distrustful. Certainly she wasn't the kind of woman who'd ordinarily consider a serious relationship after knowing a man only a few weeks. Still, she had to admit, Sam excited her like no man she'd ever known.

The phone rang, and she quickly rose to her feet. Sam had fallen into the habit of calling every couple of hours when she was home alone and then again just before he was ready to leave the station. She answered with a smile in her voice.

"Carly?"

The voice was unfamiliar. Definitely male, low and kind of raspy. "Yes," she answered hesitantly.

He started to laugh then, deep and throaty. Not an amused sound, but a sinister cackle.

Shivering in reaction, Carly dropped the receiver into its cradle and stood staring at the instrument in horror. Had that been the strangler, the man who'd killed her father and those two others? Was he the same one she'd seen outside that night in the rain by the lamp post with a cap pulled low on his face? Oh, God, did he know where she lived? Did he follow her that Saturday, jimmy the lock of her car, and shred her blouse? How did he get her unlisted phone number? What did he want with her?

Heart racing, she picked up the phone and quickly dialed Sam.

* * *

163

"We should have installed this after those hang-ups you had," Sam told Carly as they watched the Michigan Bell technician attach the device to her phone.

"How does it work?" she asked.

"Every time the phone rings, the caller's number is digitally displayed on that box. If it's a number you recognize, obviously we have no problem. If it isn't, you write it down immediately, then answer and try to keep the person on the line."

Carly remembered the eerie laugh. "Do I have to? Isn't the number enough?"

Sam shook his head. "I got approval to put on a tracer. I wouldn't think a man who's been able to evade us so far would be dumb enough to call you from his home phone, do you? So most likely, we'll get a string of numbers from phone booths. But we'll be able to pinpoint a neighborhood at least."

"By the time you learn the location of the phone booth, he'll be long gone," she offered.

"Sure, but there might be a pattern. I can't see him going way out of his district to make his calls, especially late at night. Besides, he might make a mistake, and we might get lucky."

"If you have the number, why do I have to keep him on the line?"

"Because of the tracer."

"I doubt that'll work. Don't you have to keep the person on the phone quite a while? He couldn't have stayed on more than a few seconds."

"You said you hung up on him. Maybe if you hadn't, he'd have said more."

She shuddered and leaned into him, dreading the thought of listening to that madman breathing on the other end of a phone. "All right, but I'm not nuts about this plan."

The technician finished and gathered up his equipment. "You're all set."

Sam saw him to the door, then turned back to take Carly into his arms.

"Do you really think this will work?" she asked, holding on to the solid strength of him.

"It's worth a shot."

She closed her eyes. "God, I wish this were over."

Sam lay his cheek on her bowed head. "So do I, honey."

Quietly, Sam closed the door to the interrogation room behind him and sat down in one of three orange plastic chairs around a scarred wooden table. Seated across from him was a heavy-set woman who looked to be somewhere in her forties, wearing a gauzy floral-print dress that hung limply down to her ankles. Her jet black hair was piled into some kind of a knot atop her head, her heavy eyelids were dusted with deep purple, and she wore three rings on each hand.

"Clio McIntyre, this is Detective Sergeant Sam English," Ray said by way of introduction from his seat to the right of Sam.

Clio studied the unsmiling officer. "You don't have much use for psychometry, do you, Detective English?" she asked in a whisky voice that carried a hint of the South.

Sam raised a brow. "Psychometry?"

Her scarlet lips smiled. "Yes. Psychometry is the mental relating of an object and its owner through a medium's contact with that object."

"And you're the medium?" Sam asked.

"Yes. Sensations and impressions come to me after touching an object owned by a certain person." She saw that he still looked skeptical and sighed

165

heavily. "I suppose I'll have to prove myself to you. May I hold your watch a moment, please?" When Sam hesitated, she frowned at him. "I'm hardly going to steal it from you here in the police station."

"We're wasting time," Sam said. He nodded toward the items on the table, each belonging to one of the victims. "You should be concentrating on those, not on convincing me."

"If I don't convince you, whatever I say about those will be of no value." Her red lips parted showing very white teeth.

Sam handed the watch to her, a look of impatience on his face. Maybe if she didn't look like a damn gypsy about to tell his fortune, he'd have less trouble believing her.

Holding it in one hand, she fingered the watch with the other as she closed her eyes. "Yes," Clio said after a moment, "it's coming through. You have a mole on your left cheek. Not the cheek of your face, that is, but your buttocks. Your right foot is a quarter-inch shorter than your left, you once got sick drinking gin and haven't had a swallow of it since, and you're trying to give up smoking. This is the third time, and you'll finally make it." Clio opened her eyes and sent him a questioning look. "Am I close, Detective?"

Sam's expression didn't change, but he was certain she could tell in his eyes that she'd been right on the money. "Let's get on with this, shall we?"

To her credit, Clio refrained from looking smug and picked up a battered cotton hat that Homer Gentry's wife had given them. It had been his favorite. Again, the psychic held the hat between her two hands, rubbing the material gently as her eyes closed.

She was silent so long that Sam shifted in his chair restlessly. "Well, do you pick up on anything?"

He still wasn't sure he bought all this crap. If catching criminals were this simple, they wouldn't need cops at all, just keep a few of these nuts stashed away in the back room of stations across the country.

"It's raining," Clio's low voice drawled, "and he's in some kind of a small building like a shed where there are tools hanging on the walls. He's just fixed something, and he's tired, sits down. His mind's on dinner with his family. He's a real family man." Suddenly her hands clenched in the folds of the hat. "But someone is there. He can't see who it is because he doesn't have his glasses on. They're thick, with dark frames. He puts them on and . . . and now he knows who it is. And he knows he's going to die." With a jerk, Clio's head dropped to her chest, and she let out a sob.

Despite his misgivings, Sam leaned forward. "What does the assailant look like?"

It took her a moment, but she raised her head slowly, and her face looked pained, her eyes tightly closed still. "A big man. No, not big. Solid. Wearing work clothes. His voice is scratchy, like he smokes a lot. He turns and strolls down the driveway in the rain."

Ray wanted to know more. "Is he short or tall, dark or fair? What color are his eyes, his hair?"

"He's walking away. I can't tell."

Ray shot Sam a look that seemed to question what they'd both witnessed. Experienced cops, they'd seen it all and knew that a lot of information had been in the papers as well. People read the facts, then their imaginations took over.

"Okay, Clio," Ray told her calmly, "try this." He took Gentry's hat from her and handed her Will Weston's sweater, the one he'd been wearing the day he'd died.

167

She held the sweater to her chest, rubbing the wool between her fingers. Under her purple-shadowed lids, they could see her eyes moving back and forth. Finally she spoke. "We're in the woods now, and it's all shadows and shade. Sit down under a tree and rest. Pain in the left side. Mustn't overdo. Heart condition. Close the eyes for a minute. Put the rifle down. There."

Just when Sam thought she'd drifted off, her head swiveled around and she sat up taller.

"There's a face very close. Open the eyes and see him. After all these years, what could he want? Try to get up, but a big hand shoves into the chest. Then the fingers around the throat, squeezing, tighter. No! Someone's laughing, an ugly, evil sound." She slumped back in her chair as if exhausted.

"Clio, what can you tell us about the man, the one with the hands on the victim's throat?" Sam asked.

"Blurry," she muttered. "Can't see clearly. Wearing a cap, pulled low on his forehead. Thick, heavy work shoes. Slowly walking away through the trees, snow crunching underfoot."

"What do you make of it?" Ray mouthed to Sam, and saw his partner shrug. The next item was Doug Anderson's fake Rolex watch. Ray put it in Clio's hand and waited.

Her eyes opened, and she stared at the watch. Her voice changed, became contemptuous. "Cheap, like its owner. Ex-con, always living on the edge. Young, not yet thirty. Would club his own mother for a buck. In the bar, dark and noisy, looking for a hustle, nursing a beer." She looked up and stared ahead, her eyes on a scene they couldn't see.

"An old buddy walking in. Not good news. Gotta get outta here." Clio started breathing hard, as if running. "Can't get away. He's so strong. Hands

168

around the throat, can't breathe. No, no. I didn't mean it, buddy."

"Didn't mean what?" Ray demanded. "Did the owner of the watch do something to a buddy?"

"A rat. He thinks I'm a rat."

Ray exchanged a dubious look with Sam. "What's the buddy look like?"

"Dark clothes. Black jacket. No, brown. Yes, brown. And I see keys, lots of keys."

"Keys? Where are the keys?" Ray asked.

"On a ring, hanging from his belt loop. They jingle as he walks out of the alley. I see him getting in his car and . . ."

"What kind of a car is it?" Sam interjected.

"Small, compact, imported. Driving to a motel. Rooms by the week. Inside, get the list. Cross off the name."

"Jesus," Ray whispered.

"Are there any more names on the list?" Sam wanted to know.

She frowned, hesitating. "Two. Two more."

"Can you read the names?"

"No, not clear." Her eyes closed, then flew open. "Wait. A man and a woman. Two more names."

A woman. Sam felt his blood run cold, then grew annoyed with himself. What was he doing believing some crazy psychic who got her kicks jerking cops around. Then again, how the hell could she have known some of this stuff? He reached behind him for the box on the table, pulled out Carly's ripped blouse. "See if you can pick up anything from this."

Clio set down the Rolex and held the tattered blouse carefully. Her eyes were on the far wall as she fondled the silky material. Suddenly, they grew wide with fear. "She's in danger. He's after her. He's watching her."

169

Sam felt his throat tighten. "The same man, the strangler?"

She nodded distractedly. "He follows her sometimes. He wants her the most of all. He's been fantasizing about her for years."

Years? That was ridiculous, Sam thought. They'd checked out Carly's past, every man she'd ever dated or been close to. No one even mildly suspicious. Clio was losing him again. He pushed back his chair and stood. "Thanks for coming in, Ms. McIntyre."

Clio took a deep breath as if coming back to herself. She looked at Ray and saw the suspicion in his eyes, then glanced up at Sam. Detective English was worried and covering it with annoyance. "Anytime," she said, heaving her bulk out of the chair. "I hope I've been of some help." She shuffled to the door, then turned back to Sam. "English is your middle name, isn't it, Detective?" With a soft smile, she left the room.

"What'd she mean by that?" Ray asked.

"How the hell should I know?" Sam answered, frowning after her.

Most cops hate Christmas. Whatever they feel about the occasion personally, professionally they hate dealing with the crazies who inevitably surface with greater frequency during such a sentimental holiday. Sam was no exception.

Wearily, he ran a hand over his unshaven chin, then yanked the report out of his old Underwood typewriter. He'd put in a grueling day. Early this morning, he and Ray had been called to the area of Grand Circus Park in the center of downtown Detroit, where another rape victim had been left, cut and bleeding. They'd gone with her to the hospital and questioned her about her assailant, but she'd been in shock and unable to give much information.

But the rapist they'd been after for months had left his by now familiar calling card: a jagged knife wound along her left cheek.

They'd been back at the station by noon for a briefing, then had headed out to Jackson Prison, where they'd pored through the file on Doug Anderson, hoping to make a connection. Doug had served time twice since he'd left juvenile jurisdiction and gotten off on a couple of other counts.

They'd gotten the names and records of his cellmates, both free now, to track them down, thinking that Doug may have had a loose tongue and confided something worthwhile to someone. *I didn't mean it, buddy,* the psychic had told them Doug had said when he'd seen his killer. If they were to believe her, the words seemed to indicate that Doug had ratted on a buddy, perhaps while in prison, maybe gotten the man in trouble. When he'd been released, perhaps the man had come after Doug and killed him. Maybe it didn't happen that way, but since the possibility existed, they had to check it out.

Lord knows they didn't have many other leads to work on.

Ray was out hunting down Jack Malloy, Doug's last cellmate, and Sam had just returned from talking with Henry Kowalski, the other ex-con who'd lived with Doug awhile. Checking over the report he'd typed up, he knew there wasn't much there. Henry either knew nothing or was damn good at answering questions without revealing a thing.

Sam glanced out the window and saw that it was snowing. He wasn't crazy about driving in snow, but at least a clean white blanket on the grim streets around the station made the area look better than it was. The main precinct was in the heart of a district known as Greektown, an ethnic community that attracted a lot of visitors, both locals and out-oftowners. And a photographer he knew intimately.

Carly had insisted she'd be safe with Jim Tyson along, and Sam had reluctantly given his permission for her to wander about Greektown to take pictures yesterday. He knew he couldn't lock her away, yet Clio McIntyre's chilling words haunted him. *He's following her. He wants her most of all.* And the most puzzling statement of all: *He's been fantasizing about her for years.*

Sam separated the NCR forms he'd finished typing, put one in his out-box and the other in his file folder. He could certainly understand a man fantasizing about Carly. He did his fair share of that himself. But what man from her past had known her well enough to carry a torch for years?

Based on his inquiries, it had to be someone who knew her only peripherally, for they'd checked out all the men in her life going back to high school. Someone, perhaps, whom she'd refused to date, and the guy had turned that rejection into a resentful obsession. Some might dismiss that as a real long shot. But not a cop. Sickos often became fixated on a certain unattainable individual. The fatal attraction phenomenon. It happened to celebrities regularly. It could happen just as easily to a non-celebrity who caught the wrong man's interest.

But if that were the case, Sam pondered, what possible connection could that kind of man have with Homer Gentry and Will Weston? They'd already investigated huge stacks of files that Homer had represented or Will had prosecuted. Sam sighed as he stood. If Ray didn't come up with something solid from questioning Jack Malloy, they'd have to delve into Gentry and Weston's cases going back even further.

An enormous task, but they simply had no other choice.

172

Sam glanced at his watch as he picked up the phone. Five o'clock. He'd check with Carly, who was probably finished working in her darkroom by now, and maybe pick up some Chinese for dinner on his way to her apartment.

And he'd make a detour to a place he'd passed today for a surprise for her.

"It's a beautiful tree," Carly said for the second time that evening. "Thank you." Rising on tiptoe, she kissed Sam.

It was odd, Sam thought, how pleased she was at a small gift, one that had cost him a mere forty bucks. He had the feeling when she'd been dating guys like Brett Stevens and Pierce Nelson, she'd probably received hunks of jewelry and imported perfumes. He didn't want to even try to compete with monied men.

By now, he'd figured out that Carly was not only sentimental, but a romantic at heart, despite her insistent stand on independence. He knew she'd be facing a difficult holiday, the first one without her father. And the first one where a maniac was stalking her. Perhaps they could both use a little Christmas cheer.

As he'd guessed, she had loads of decorations stored in a back room. He'd braced the tree in its stand; they'd eaten their Chinese dinner, then they'd decorated the tree together while carols played on the stereo. Now, standing back to admire the results of their efforts, his arm around Carly's waist, Sam couldn't remember the last time he'd felt quite this relaxed.

"Yeah, we did a pretty good job if I do say so myself," he told her, then kissed the top of her head. "I haven't decorated a tree since I was maybe ten years old."

She angled to look up at him. "Didn't you do it as a family?" Her own memories of holiday preparation were many and warm. Though she'd been an only child, her mother and father had seen to it that all three of them shared all the festivities. From early on, Carly had helped decorate the house, bake cookies, wrap presents. Perhaps that was why she had such good feelings about the whole celebration. Apparently, Sam had missed out on yet another childhood pleasure.

"We didn't do a hell of a lot as a family. Dad was always working late, and my mother liked to hire things done. The housekeeper decorated the tree. It was an artificial one, white with red balls and gold bows. Picture perfect, like something out of *House and Garden*. My mother didn't want a real tree messing up her immaculate house, her flawless living room. The result held all the warmth of a hotel lobby." He smiled down at her and inhaled the piney fragrance of the Douglas fir. "Now that's a *real* tree."

"And here I thought you'd think I was corny to put up all those sentimental ornaments, the ones we've picked up on trips, some I made way back in grade school. And stringing popcorn to weave through the branches."

A few weeks ago, he might have, if he'd have even bothered to give Christmas trees a thought. Sam was aware that he'd deliberately avoided thinking about all that since it would kick in memories of his lonely, unfulfilled Christmases past. "Not corny. Nice. Really nice."

Her arm around him tightened. Reading between the lines of the little he'd revealed, Carly was beginning to realize just how emotionally deprived he'd been growing up in that sterile household. "I suppose you and your brother received a lot of gifts though," she ventured, hoping to hit on at least one good memory.

"Oh, sure. Mom ordered them from catalogs sent to the house from the best of stores, and the housekeeper wrapped them. Perfect packages under our perfect tree. Mom was too busy to do it herself. There was a Christmas ball to chair, a luncheon to host for Dad's employees from all the dealerships, teas to attend. Socialites have a crowded schedule during the holidays. Hard to slip in the needs of two little boys who'd been taught not to complain." He turned, knowing he needed to change the subject before he got himself down in the dumps. "So, how was your day, Miss Photographer? Did you print any pictures you'd like to show me?"

Carly felt herself tense. They were moving into her vulnerable zone, an area where she felt totally uncertain. "A few," she said carefully, stepping back. "I don't want to bore you with all that. Tell me about *your* day."

That he was certain he didn't want to do. She was worried enough about the man somewhere out there. Tonight was all about trying to make her forget him, if only for a little while. "Stop avoiding this. Let me see some of the pictures you've taken for that magazine project. I'm not a judge in a contest, you know."

No, but she was still uneasy, afraid she'd see in his eyes that her efforts were pitiful. And then she'd have to watch him struggle to cover up his real opinion. "I don't know."

"Come on, Carly. Just a couple?"

She gave in, preparing herself for the worst. Hesitantly, she went to her darkroom. It took her a long while but finally, she picked out three and reluctantly handed them to him, chewing on her lower lip as she did so.

175

Sam snapped on the table lamp. The first one had been taken at Eastern Market where farmers gathered twice a week early in the morning to sell their wares. She'd zeroed in on an older woman wearing a big apron over a fur-lined jacket, her hair tied back with a plaid scarf. Her face was lined, weathered from the sun and wrinkled by her years, but it was a face with character. In her work-roughened hands, she held an assortment of vegetables — chunky potatoes, pale round onions, and long carrots with bushy tops — produce that she'd undoubtedly raised herself, her dark eyes filled with quiet pride.

Carly had caught the dignity of a simple woman, marked by her years of hard work, yet secure in her self-esteem, in a job well done. He shifted to the second photo.

This one had been taken in the inner city, a cement basketball court in a park setting. It had been a windy day with snow swirling through a grayish sky. A young boy of perhaps twelve was caught in motion leaping up to lay the ball in a blowing basket, on his face a look of utter concentration as he strained to jump high enough. The ball was in midair, heading for the rim, yet it was impossible to tell whether he made it or not. But that wasn't important. What was important was the boy's effort, his attention centered on his goal for that moment in time, the hope clearly etched on his features.

The last photo had been taken with a zoom lens focusing in on two hands hovering over a chessboard. One hand was freckled and deeply veined, probably belonging to a grandfatherly old man. The thick fingers were slightly curled, seemingly vacillating, as if the owner had been having a hard time making a decision. The other hand was that of a youngster, boy or girl, perhaps ten, smooth-skinned with short, blunt nails. It seemed to have just been

176

raised from a second white rook now challenging the black king which was in a vulnerable position, one where a check could not be averted. Studying the print, Sam could almost hear the young voice preparing to shout out, "check and checkmate."

Sam fanned out the three five-by-seven black-and-whites and studied them again, trying to determine what made them quite unique. One was a little underexposed, and he didn't know enough about photography to know if Carly had done that on purpose for effect or if she'd miscalculated. So it wasn't her technique that was outstanding. After a moment, he realized what it was and turned to see her watching him, her eyes hesitant.

"They tell a story," he said. "Each one of them tells a story."

"Do you think so?"

"I know so. It's not just looking at a picture. You grab the viewer and drag him into the scene." He set the photos down on the table. "I wonder if you know how good you are."

Carly brushed back her hair with an unsteady hand. She hadn't known how much his opinion mattered to her until she heard it. "Oh, I have a long, long way to go. I'm just learning. You should see Jim's display. He blends, taking a person from one frame and shifting them to another. He blurs the background in such a way that the foreground focus is so sharp it almost leaps off the paper at you."

"Those are techniques anyone can learn, Carly," Sam told her, moving closer, wanting to touch her. "You have an eye for a scene that makes it personal. You see something others would pass up as ordinary, and you make it extraordinary. That's talent."

To her embarrassment, she found herself flushing. "Thank you." She kissed him lightly. She'd needed this, needed to feel pride in something she'd done on her own. She wondered if he knew what a gift he'd given her. Still, it left her feeling oddly uncomfortable, as if she were receiving praise long before she'd paid her dues and had earned it. She searched for a change of subject. "How about a movie?" She glanced at the mantel clock. "Just in time. I'm a big fan of oldies, and one of Hitchcock's best is on TV tonight. Remember *Rear Window?*"

"Sure." Sam set aside the prints, deciding to allow her to shift the focus. Perhaps in time she'd believe in herself the way he already did. "Jimmy Stewart's a photographer stuck in a wheelchair with a broken leg and sees a murder outside his back window, right?" He settled back on the couch while she adjusted the television.

"That's the one. Sure you want to watch it?"

"On two conditions."

Carly curled up alongside him as the movie credits began to roll. "What conditions?"

"First, that you get us a bowl of the leftover popcorn. And second that we turn out the lights and pretend we're in a balcony or a drive-in so we can neck."

She laughed. "Since when did you need a perfect setting to neck? I seem to remember a night not so long ago when you threw me down on that hard floor over there without so much as a pillow for my wee little head."

Sam gathered her to him. "You're right. Let's bypass the preliminaries and move right into the main event." He slid his mouth to her ear and began to explore the sensitive folds.

Carly felt a delicious shiver take her. "Hey, what about the film, the popcorn?" She peered over his shoulder. "Look, there's Grace Kelly. Wasn't she gorgeous?"

Sam gave her an exaggerated sigh. "All right, we'll

watch the movie. Hold that thought though, and we'll come back to it."

She smiled at him as she settled into his arms. "I'm counting on it."

"That was a pretty neat ending, don't you think?" Carly asked, stifling a yawn. When Sam didn't respond, she sat up and looked at him. "Hey, you didn't sleep through the big finish, did you?"

Sam set aside the empty bowl he'd been holding. " 'Course not. You can't eat popcorn while you sleep." He shifted off his spine and stretched, then yawned expansively. It had been a long day.

Carly reached to smooth back his hair. "You look tired. Time to hit the hay?"

"Yeah, probably. Trouble is, I feel drowsy out here, then I get into bed and I can't sleep." And probably it would be like that until he could put the man he was seeking behind bars.

"I have the same problem, so I picked something up the other day to help us both." She reached for her oversize purse that she'd left on the end table.

"What is it?"

"I got these pills at a health food store where Jim and I stopped when we were in Greektown shooting. They're called tryptophane. All natural ingredients. It's supposed to be the same as drinking a glass of warm milk before bedtime."

"Why not just drink the milk?"

"Because milk is fattening and this little pill isn't," she explained with perfect female logic.

"You're worried about a glass of milk when you pack away two thousand calories in one of those fast-food burgers?"

Carly frowned as she rummaged inside her purse, trying to locate the small bottle. "I don't *always* eat fast-food. Oh, nuts, where is it?" Scooting back, she began to dump the contents onto the couch seat between them. Her makeup case, her wallet, sunglasses, keys and . . . and a folded white sheet of paper.

Watching her eyes widen, Sam followed her gaze. "Is that yours?"

Carly felt a shudder of apprehension. "I don't remember putting a piece of paper in my purse." She watched him pick it up by the corners and unfold it. Curiosity had her leaning closer to read over his shoulder.

The question: Who needs to learn the lesson, judge not that ye be not judged? The answer: the godfather.

Chapter Eleven

"You wanted to see me?" Luke Varner asked as he pulled up a chair alongside Sam's cluttered desk and dropped his lanky frame into it.

"Yeah. Thanks for stopping by. I know you've been putting in a lot of hours on the Simpson case." Sam pulled out his bottom drawer and searched through for a file.

"You can say that again." Luke ran a tired hand over eyes that felt bloodshot and grainy. "What's up?"

"You've worked on several serial killings, and I wanted your opinion." Quickly, he briefed the senior detective on the strangler's victims and updated him on their findings so far, then handed him the most recent note. "I was hoping you could tell me something about this guy that I've overlooked."

"No fingerprints, I take it?" Luke asked as he took the note.

"None. He must have handled the paper with rubber gloves. The bastard smears his hands with petroleum jelly before he strangles his victims so his prints are always smudged."

"That's an old trick. Sounds like he's been around, maybe served time. That's where a guy's apt to pick up something like that." For several minutes, Luke studied the words on the page. "The riddle means nothing to anyone on the case?"

181

Sam shook his head. "It was somehow put in Carly Weston's purse, and damned if we can figure out how it got there. She never goes anywhere alone, and I'm with her every night at her apartment. Couple of days ago, she went with this photographer, Jim Tyson, wandering through Greektown on a photo shoot. He swears she was never out of his sight. She always keeps her car doors locked." He mentioned the blouse incident as well.

"Who has a key to her place?"

"I had the locks changed last week. She and I have the only keys." Sam knew the frustration he felt was in his voice, but he was helpless to hide it. And the fear. Hadn't he been warned a hundred times that personal involvement with a victim or possible victim would interfere with the objectivity so important to good police work? But even Ray was stymied. That's why Sam had decided to ask his old friend to see if Luke could give them some fresh insight.

"Nobody's tampered with the locks?"

"Not that I can tell."

"Could be he's a locksmith. Maybe, if he's an ex-con, he learned the trade in prison."

Sam had to admit he hadn't thought of that. The psychic had said the man she'd envisioned had keys dangling from a belt loop. He made a note to check eastside locksmiths.

Luke read the note one more time. "Could be a religious freak with this Bible quotation, I suppose. He's fairly literate. I'd guess he's printing to keep you from analyzing his handwriting and learning more than he wants you to know."

"Yeah, I kind of figured that, too."

Luke tossed down the note. "It's been my experience that serial killers come in two categories. The

182

most common is the random killer who usually kills with sexual overtones. That includes the guys who get visions or hear voices telling them to kill. Or the guy who's snuffing all short, blond women because he was jilted by one years ago. That sort of thing."

"I don't think this fellow fits into that category."

"Right. The other one is the revenge killer. A member of a certain family wronged him, in his twisted opinion, so he sets out to kill them all to get even. Or it could be job related. A guy gets fired from a company, so he mows down everyone in that department, his immediate superior, and anyone else unlucky enough to be around when he decides to make his move."

Sam leaned back in his chair thoughtfully. Revenge was a more likely motivation. "That sounds more like it."

"I'm sure you're aware that strangulation's the classic method of killing to shut someone up. But, since this joker's got such big hands, it may be simply that he enjoys snuffing someone. He gets off on it."

Sam nodded, aware that many murderers enjoyed killing.

"We need some new laws to handle these guys," Luke went on. "Some states already have anti-stalking laws in force, and a couple have them pending. They've even started a new division in some police departments called the threat unit, men trained to follow and capture stalkers. But, until we have it here, all we've got to work with are restraining orders and surveillance teams."

"But in this case, the problem is we can keep a watch on Carly under the assumption that she may be his next victim. But we can't put a team on him since we don't know who the hell he is."

"Yeah, I know."

Sam thought he'd take a chance and mention another long shot. "Now, don't laugh, but we had this psychic in here last week. Clio McIntyre. I don't know how much credence to put into her thoughts, but when she was discussing the last strangling, she said that the victim recognized the killer and said something like, I didn't mean it, buddy."

Luke ran a hand through his short brown hair liberally sprinkled with gray. "Hell, I don't know if you can believe the things a clairvoyant claims to see either. But that's probably what this guy is doing: getting even. He kills a lawyer, a prosecuting attorney, and a punk with a record. I'd guess the lawyer didn't get him off, so he became a target. The P.A. is obvious. Maybe the punk was in jail with him and ratted on him for something. These guys are pretty delusional, you know."

Toying with his pen, Sam looked up. "This McIntyre woman said something else, something that really bothers me. She pictured the killer—kind of hazy-like—at his motel room crossing names off a list. There were two more on it, a man and a woman, but she couldn't make them out. When I gave her Carly's blouse, she said that he's after her, been fantasizing about her for years."

Luke frowned. "That's not good. I suppose you've checked everyone she's ever dated or been close to?"

"Checked and rechecked."

"These guys can carry grudges for years. Maybe somebody who worked on the Weston yard and she didn't give him a tumble when she was a teenager. Some guy in high school she turned down for the prom. Her dentist who developed a crush. Could be anyone."

"Thanks, that helps a lot. All I have to do is sort

184

through the entire population of the Pointes and half of Detroit." Sam threw down his pen so hard it bounced off his desk and onto the floor. "Damn!"

Luke stood, then looked down at his friend. "I see you've gone and done it, old buddy."

"Done what?" Sam asked testily.

"Fallen for her. Believe me, I know all the signs. Maybe you should take yourself off the case."

Sam thought that over, but not for long, knowing the idea didn't sit well with him. "Would you?"

Luke shook his head. "No. I was in your shoes, and I didn't. I just stuck to her like glue. But I've got to warn you."

"What?"

"He almost got her anyhow."

Sam's jaw clenched, remembering all that Luke had been through last year, then recalling his wedding to Stephanie. "How's Stephanie and that brand-new baby boy?"

Luke smiled, and the fatigue seemed to drop from him. "They're fine. Say, I've got an idea. Why don't you and the lady in question stop over tonight? I know Stephanie'd like to see Carly." And maybe he'd learn more about this puzzling case.

Sam thought of how unnerved Carly had been by the note they'd found, of how tense she'd been since. "We just might do that."

"Great. Got to run. See you, say around eight."

"Thanks, Luke. I appreciate it." Sam watched Luke leave the squad room, then swung back to his desk and picked up the note again, staring at the crudely scrawled letters. "Where are you, you son-ofabitch?"

The snow crunched under the Trans Am's tires as

185

Sam pulled to a stop alongside Luke's van and turned toward Carly in the bucket seat beside him. "You're awfully quiet. Was this a bad idea, coming out here to visit Luke and Stephanie?" She'd hardly said six words during the drive out to the private marina where the Varners's houseboat was dry-docked for winter.

Carly sat up straighter, grabbing the box that nearly slid off her lap. "No, it was a good idea, and I'm eager to see the baby." Sam had called her earlier, mentioning the invitation, and she'd been delighted. Her pleasure had been short-lived when he'd forbidden her to go shopping for a baby gift until he could accompany her. While she understood the necessity for his vigilance, this constant need for protection was getting her down.

Despite her words, Sam was aware of her lack of enthusiasm and guessed at the cause. "I'm sorry if I was short with you about shopping alone. You know I—"

"You were doing it for my own good. I know." Carly felt as weary as she knew she sounded. She turned to Sam, her eyes filling. "I'm sorry I'm such a pain to be with these days. It's just so hard to be policed constantly."

He took her hand across the gearshift lever and squeezed it. "I understand. I wish it wasn't necessary."

"Me, too." Carly sighed. "I've been trying to figure out what that note meant, and I can't come up with a thing. I feel so damn frustrated."

Sam opened his door. "Let's let it go for tonight and just enjoy ourselves. Not think about things for a couple of hours, okay?"

Carly nodded her agreement, then waited for Sam to come around and help her out. They walked

186

along the path, hard-packed with snow. Holding his hand, she stepped onto the dock leading to the houseboat, watching for slippery patches. "Have you been here before?"

"Yeah, a couple of times, but not since Stephanie moved in. I imagine she's made a difference in Luke's bachelor pad. And now, there's the baby. Hard to picture old Luke as a domesticated father."

"It can happen to the best of men," Carly said, wondering what Sam would make of that comment.

"Isn't that the truth. A man drops his guard for a minute, and some lecherous woman throws a lasso over his poor, unsuspecting head and, panting lustily, lures him in. Next thing you know, he's married, there are ruffles and bows on everything, and a baby in the next room."

Carly stopped in mid-stride at the bottom of the stairs leading up to the boat braced in its moored frame. In the dim lamplight by the railing, she frowned up at Sam. "Lecherous woman? Panting lustily?"

"Damn right." Sam averted his head so she couldn't see his lips twitch. "Remember that night not so long ago when you threw me onto your living room floor and ravished me? Remember how you wouldn't let me up even when your poor, worried mother phoned to see if you were all right? Remember how you carried me into your bedroom finally and held me captive there for hours?" He ducked a well-aimed elbow. "If that isn't lustful behavior, I don't know what is."

"You want lusty behavior, I'll give you some." Laughing, she wound her arm around him, her fist pounding his back with mock seriousness.

Sam grabbed her arm and pulled her close, the package getting slightly mangled between their

187

bodies. "Don't hurt me," he pleaded with a grin. Holding both her hands and the box captive between them, he lowered his head to press his mouth to hers.

Smiling around the kiss, Carly eased back and looked into his eyes. "You know what's the very best thing about you?" she asked.

Sam's brows rose and fell in an exaggerated response. "My bedside manner? My soulful eyes? My magnificent body?"

Her gaze locked with his, she shook her head. "No matter how down I am, you can always make me laugh."

He knew he wasn't really a funny guy, far from it. Yet he so hated seeing her down that he found himself trying to find ways to bring up her spirits, to bring about that slow, crooked smile. "Did you know that Charley Chaplin said that a day without laughter is a day wasted?"

"I believe that's true, but there're so many humorless people in the world. Thank goodness I've found one who isn't." Rising on tiptoe, she reached for his kiss.

Arms wrapped around each other, they barely noticed when the door at the top of the stairs swung open and Luke Varner stepped out. "Hey, no necking on my dock."

Feeling too good to be embarrassed, Sam grinned up at him. "You going to call the cops on us?" His arm around Carly, he started them up the steps.

"Not a bad idea." Luke held the door open as Carly and Luke greeted him, then followed them down into the houseboat's living room. "Let me have your coats. I have a fire going, although you two don't look as if you need to warm up." He winked at Carly as she eased out of her jacket.

Oddly, she found herself blushing, unable to think of a time even in her teenage years when she'd been caught necking. To give herself a moment, she turned to warm her hands by the fire. "So where's that little guy? I'm dying to see him."

"Stephanie's nursing him in the bedroom. She told me to tell you to go on in." Luke hung the coats on the rack and turned to Sam. "How about a drink? Scotch all right, or are you on call?"

Sam followed his friend into the compact galley. "I'm off for the night, and scotch sounds fine." Hands in his pockets, he looked around.

The houseboat had been Luke's retreat at a time in his life when he'd needed to heal after the death of his first wife. It had been sparsely furnished, unabashedly masculine, and a shade messy back then, as Sam remembered. In the year since Stephanie had married Luke, they'd added a large inviting couch in deep blue, low oak tables, and warm gray carpeting. A bookcase was on the far wall, stuffed to overflowing; there were several large striped pillows tossed about, and the kitchen table sported a floral cloth. There was a cozy feeling that had been missing before. "The place looks good," he commented, taking the glass from Luke.

"You should see the bedroom. Curtains on the window, a baby bassinet. Even a spread on the bed." Luke shook his head. "Women." He took a long pull on his drink.

"Yeah, you look like you're suffering, all right."

Luke led the way into the living room and lowered his lean frame into his favorite plaid rocker. He stared at the door to the bedroom, where his wife was feeding their son, for a long moment. "She was worth waiting for, Sam."

Sam dropped into the far end of the couch. "I figured." Hearing a sound, he glanced toward the corner where a beige cat with yellow streaks stared back at him from a cardboard box. Several mewing sounds and shuffling noises followed. "Don't tell me Benjamin's done it again?" Luke's *male* cat had turned out to be anything but.

Sipping his drink, Luke sent the cat box a tolerant look. "Damn nuisance. Second litter this year. I wish I knew where that tomcat's hiding out."

"Looks like everyone's reproducing around here."

"Yeah. Speaking of such things, from what I saw out on the dock, I'd say I hit it on the head about your feelings for Carly, right?" Luke watched Sam stare into his glass without answering. "Unless it's just hormonal."

Sam sighed. "I wish that's all it was. You know how I feel about men in our line of work trying for permanent relationships. Damn few work out. Ray's divorced, and I could name half-a-dozen other cops in the same boat. You and Stephanie are lucky."

"Yeah, but it took me two go-arounds."

Sam ran a hand across his face as he glanced toward the closed door where Carly had disappeared. "Since meeting her, some days I feel as if I'm losing control, you know?"

Luke nodded, understanding. "That's what happens when a man wants a woman real bad. He loses control. And for a cop, that can be fatal." He well remembered nearly killing a man with his bare hands just after rescuing Stephanie from him.

"So what do you suggest?"

"Catch the bastard who's after her first. Then, find out if you want Carly badly enough to compromise." Luke picked up a pale blue receiving blanket that had been folded and left on the table alongside

190

his chair. "Because she will change your life, old buddy. They all do."

Sam twirled the glass in his fingers and stared at the door.

On the other side of the bedroom door, Carly sat at the foot of the kingsize bed and watched little Max go at his dinner, his tiny hand curled on his mother's swollen breast. She'd never seen a baby nurse up close and was surprised to find her throat clogging with a rush of emotion. "He's beautiful," she whispered.

Stephanie's eyes caressed her son. "He is, isn't he?"

"You look very happy." Was that a twinge of envy she felt?

"I am." Stephanie looked up. "During those hellish years married to Zane, I'd wondered if I'd ever be happy again."

"I know it was horrifying, having Zane go after you. I only wish I knew who's hounding me and why."

Stephanie disengaged her son and carefully placed him over her shoulder, gently patting his back. "Luke told me tonight about the ripped blouse and the note you found in your purse. Does any of it make any sense to you?"

Carly shook her head. "I've racked my brain trying to come up with someone who might have had a grudge against my father and me. Plus those two other men, neither of whom I knew. I'm totally in the dark. I find myself wavering between frustrated and scared half to death."

"I remember." Stephanie shook back her long blond hair. "If it hadn't been for Luke, if he hadn't found me, I probably wouldn't have made it."

191

"The only time I feel really safe is when Sam's with me. I hate feeling so dependent."

The baby burped, and Stephanie settled him in her lap, then adjusted her clothes. "How do you feel about Sam English?"

Carly shrugged. "Ambivalent."

"It's all right. You don't have to tell me if you don't want to. It's just that I heard he's moved in with you, and I wondered about that."

"You think I'm trying to avoid an honest answer?"

Stephanie raised a brow. "Are you?"

"Probably." Carly brushed back a lock of hair from her face. "Okay, I care about him. Quite a bit. But I don't know if it's because of this mess I find myself in where I'm so damn *needy* or whether I'd feel the same if we'd met, say, at your wedding."

Stephanie smiled. "Funny thing is that you were both at our wedding and didn't even nod at one another. That's a hard one to call. I guess you'll have to wait it out."

Carly leaned forward, propping an arm on her bent knee. "What's it like being married to a cop?"

"Lonely at times. Frightening when he's on a stake-out and unable to call. But Luke loves what he does and he's good at it. And I love Luke. I'd love him no matter what job he had."

Carly decided that was about the bottom line, so she smiled. "Can I hold Max?"

"Absolutely." Rising, Stephanie picked up her son and placed him into Carly's waiting arms. For a long moment, she watched her friend smile down at the sleeping infant, noticing how her features had softened as she spoke to the baby. "Come on. Let's join the guys."

Stephanie opened the door, anxious to see Sam's face when he first spotted Carly holding Max. She saw what she'd hoped to see before the hard-boiled cop masked his feelings. Moving to Luke, she took his hand. He, too, had been hard-boiled not so long ago. Time and love had changed Luke Varner.

She turned to look back at her friend and sent her a silent message. *Go for it, Carly. You won't be sorry.*

The following morning, Sam lined up a second large pile of folders on his desk. The P.A.'s office had been most cooperative and sent over a file on every case Will Weston had been involved with going all the way back. He'd gone through about half of them so far, making note of names that were possibilities.

Over at Homer Gentry's office, Ray was doing the same thing, going back to the very beginning when the lawyer had first set up practice doing public defending and court-appointed cases. There had to be a name there that would cross-check with a name in this stack, Sam thought. There had to be a connection somewhere.

If the psychic could be believed, each man who'd died had recognized the killer. Maybe Luke's scenario had been right. It was one Sam and Ray had considered also, the thin thread that connected the killer to the three victims. It was a more positive approach than trying to find some guy that Carly had inadvertently pissed off as a teenager.

They badly needed a break on this. After the last note, Carly's nerves were frayed. His own weren't faring much better. He was short tempered, snarling at nearly everyone, his sense of humor all but gone.

Sam admitted to himself that he was reluctant to delve into his feelings too much just now. Yet he knew that Carly had a grip on him. He didn't know if it was because she was so vulnerable at the present, or if it was something deeper.

He'd had other lovers, though not a long string of them. He was too wrapped up in his work to get totally wrapped up in a woman. And he wasn't wrapped up in Carly Weston. But he did feel for her, he did care. He just didn't want to put a label on those feelings and ruin a good thing.

You've gone and done it, fallen for her, Luke had said. *That's what happens when a man wants a woman real bad. He loses control. And for a cop, that can be fatal.* He simply couldn't allow his feelings for Carly to cloud his professional judgment.

Meanwhile, the natives were getting restless. The captain had a great deal of pressure on him from the mayor and even more from the news media. Sam glanced at his watch. The press conference was set for four o'clock. He wasn't thrilled that Renwick had told him in no uncertain terms to be there as a backup in case he didn't have the answers to reporters' questions after he read his prepared statement.

How could he reply to questions when he had no answers himself? The other thing was he felt a detective's need to withhold some information from the press so he wouldn't tip their hand. Like the business about the petroleum jelly. So far, they'd managed to keep that little clue under wraps despite the media hounding. Around the precinct, he was known as a cop who could talk convincingly to reporters without revealing much. But this case was different. This case he was personally interested in, and he wanted to stay in the background in the event some alert newsman picked up on that.

Sam went back to work on the list of names.

When Ray returned, they'd compare and, hopefully, they'd hit on one or more that matched. Then there'd be the job of tying that man in with Doug Anderson. Maybe then, they'd have the name of their strangler. He had an hour before the press conference. Sam picked up the next file.

Sitting in the back row, Sam watched the captain seated at the table near the front, several microphones in front of him, the hot television lights beaming forth. Renwick had read the statement and was now answering a couple of questions from the reporters seated on folding chairs facing him. The TV field-man was directing the questioning while the newspaper people sat scribbling in their notebooks. Sam scowled at the way they'd labeled the killer as the eastside serial strangler.

Not that it didn't fit, but he always felt that tag names gave a killer more distinction than he deserved, and he knew some murderers got off on that. Too many cold-blooded killers had become almost folk heroes due to the press giving them a persona of sorts. He could picture this solidly-built creep in a cap with his huge, working-man's hands, sitting in the motel room as Clio McIntyre had envisioned, watching himself on the six o'clock news and laughing as he had when he'd phoned Carly. The thought sickened Sam.

The back door to the room opened, and a uniformed officer headed for Sam. Silently, he handed him a note.

Sam read it, then got to his feet and hurried out. He'd wanted out of this news briefing, but not this way.

The strangler had struck again.

* * *

Judge Nathan Rogers had been sitting on the bench for over twenty years and had a reputation for honesty and fairness. His wife had spent the afternoon at a local mall taking their grandson to see Santa Claus. The judge's case had ended early today, and he'd come home and gone down to his basement workroom to putter around. When she'd returned, his wife had found his body.

Standing beside Ray, Sam thought that at first glance it would seem that Judge Rogers had been cleaning his hunting rifles when one had accidentally discharged and shot him in the stomach, causing him to bleed to death before help arrived. However, the police Mrs. Rogers had summoned had notified the medical examiner who had a different opinion.

Dr. Lester Freemont straightened from examining the body. "I had them call you guys because of what I found," the doctor said. "His windpipe's been crushed. See the marks on his neck? Big, broad finger-marks. Same as the other strangulation victims."

"What about the gunshot wound?" Ray asked.

Freemont shrugged. "The gun either discharged accidentally during or after, or the killer himself inflicted the shot after strangling him."

Ray frowned. "Why would he do that?"

The M.E. scratched his head. "Damned if I know. Who can figure how an insane man thinks?"

"You think he's insane?"

The doctor raised a questioning brow. "Does a sane man methodically strangle four men?"

"Don't let a defense attorney hear you say that," Ray said. "We'll take the rifle in and check it for prints."

"The rifle's probably smudged with petroleum

196

jelly just like the victim's neck if our guy touched it," Sam added disgustedly. He continued to stare at the man on the floor, wondering why he looked faintly familiar. Maybe he'd testified in his courtroom. "How long's the judge been dead, Doc?"

"Mrs. Rogers said she found him a little after three. I'd say he was strangled at least an hour before that. I'll know better after I get him on my table."

Ray looked puzzled. "There's no sign of a forced entry. You think Rogers let this guy in, then they came down here?"

Sam shook his head. "Doubtful. You can almost see the shock and fear on the judge's face. Like the others, he probably knew him, but he wouldn't have trusted him enough to let him into his home." The premise that the strangler knew something about locks was making more sense. And again, he'd walked away in broad daylight. They hadn't yet questioned the neighbors, but he'd be willing to bet no one saw anyone unusual. This guy had the uncanny ability to blend into any background, it seemed. "Let's check the doorknobs for traces of the ointment, too."

"Right. Mrs. Rogers told us she didn't think anything down here's been disturbed. You think we should still have the area dusted?"

"Yeah, we better not take a chance. He's got to make a mistake sometime." Sam glanced at the coroner as he headed for the stairs. "Thanks, Doc." He spoke to Ray as they climbed. "I hope the judge's wife is up to answering a few questions."

Emily Rogers had short, dark hair with an attractive silver streak falling just onto her forehead. Her blue eyes were red from weeping and her face pale

197

with shock, but she held herself with a calm dignity that impressed Sam. He sat back on the comfortable sofa in the judge's den where citations, awards, and photos lined the paneled walls. "We hate to bother you with questions at a time like this."

She waved a manicured hand. "Don't apologize. I understand. I want to do everything, *anything* I can to help you capture whoever did this to Nathan. He was such a fine man. He didn't deserve to die, much less so horribly." In her hand, she worried a fine linen handkerchief. "We'd just returned from a Florida vacation." Her voice drifted off.

Ray sent her a sympathetic look. "Naturally, we wouldn't know if Judge Rogers spoke with you much about his cases. But if he did, could you recall one, not necessarily recent, that particularly bothered him?"

"They *all* worried him." Emily removed her glasses and carefully dabbed at her eyes. "I can't recall any one that caused him more concern than the others." She squinted thoughtfully. "There *was* this one custody case, about two years ago. Dreadful mess. Right in Nathan's courtroom, the father shot his wife. He'd apparently smuggled in a gun. She didn't die, but the boy, who was only ten, witnessed the whole thing. Awful. It was after that that they set up metal detectors in the courthouse, you may recall."

Nodding, Ray took out his notebook. "Anything else?"

"There was another one some years ago. Nathan had sentenced the man to prison after the jury had found him guilty of some white-collar crime. Embezzlement, I think. Later, he learned that his wife couldn't cope and committed suicide, leaving two small boys, one of them mentally retarded. Nathan always agonized so over the children."

"Do you recall any names?" Sam asked.

"No, not offhand. But I think Nathan's assistant might, if you talk to him. Nice young man. Clark Abbott."

Ray jotted the information in his notebook to check out later.

Sam leaned forward. "I know it's difficult for a judge not to acquire some enemies. Can you think of any your husband may have had?"

"Not really. Nathan was so kind. Everyone thought so."

The bereaved widow speaking, almost defensively. He should have expected as much. Mrs. Rogers could be right, of course. But most people, those in law enforcement especially, had a whole string of enemies. A majority of them never did anything about their animosities. Some, unfortunately, did. Obviously, he'd have to get information about the judge's life from another source. Still, he'd give it one more try.

"Do you know of any arguments the judge has had, lately or some time back, perhaps with someone who worked for him or with him?"

Emily shook her head. "Truly, he was a man everyone liked."

They would get nothing but more of the same here. Sam stood, and Ray followed. "We won't take up any more of your time."

Emily rose with them. "I remember when Isabel went through this. I went over that afternoon and stayed with her. Little did I dream I'd soon be going through the same thing. I must call her." Her eyes filled.

Sam sent her a sharp look. "Isabel?"

Mrs. Rogers sniffed into her handkerchief, then recovered. "Yes. Isabel Weston. She's one of my

199

closest friends. You're aware that her husband, Will, was killed recently, I'm sure."

That was it. Sam almost swore aloud. When he'd first looked at the message about Judge Nathan's death, he'd tried to remember why the name seemed vaguely familiar. And downstairs, his face had rung a bell. "And your husbands were close friends also?"

"Oh, my, yes. Nathan was up north hunting with Will when that monster killed him."

Something else was clicking in. "You and your husband were at the Weston home after Mr. Weston's funeral, right?"

"Yes, indeed. Isabel held up so well. And poor Carly. She was such a comfort to her mother. But then, she's always been stronger than most people thought. We're her godparents, you know. A lovely girl."

Sam's eyes met Ray's as they both thought of the note at the same time. *Who needs to learn the lesson, judge not that ye be not judged? The godfather.* "Was that information in one of the papers?" Sam asked Ray.

"I can't remember, but I'll check it out."

"Did I say something helpful?" Emily Rogers asked, looking from one to the other.

"Possibly." Sam held out his hand and shook hers. "Again, thanks for talking with us." He looked around the quietly elegant Grosse Pointe home as they walked to the door. A huge real Christmas tree decorated by a loving hand stood in the marble foyer, a reminder of the forthcoming holiday that would now be empty for Emily Rogers. "Is someone here with you?"

"Yes, our son, Alan, and his wife. They're upstairs with my grandson. I didn't want him to . . . to see all the policemen. He's only four." She opened the door just in time to see her husband's draped body being rolled on a gurney to the waiting police ambulance. She gasped out loud and held the handkerchief to her mouth.

Sam touched her arm. "Shall I get your son? Will you be all right?"

Emily squared her shoulders and shook her head. "I'll be fine. Thank you."

Walking to his car, Sam popped a mint and acknowledged a reluctant admiration for the dignified way both Isabel Weston and Emily Rogers handled tragedy. Their upbringing, or their faith, or just their strong personalities helped them keep going like troupers. He wondered fleetingly how his mother would behave under similar circumstances. The same, most likely, only more so. She'd have a catered reception arranged by nightfall.

Realizing he was being uncharitable at best and unfair at worst, he opened the door of his Trans Am. "I'm going to head for Carly's. Where are you off to?"

Ray shrugged as he pulled his collar up against a chilly evening wind. "I'm going to hang around long enough to check with the two uniforms to see if they learned anything in questioning the neighbors. Then I'm going to the station for a while. I've got several files with me from Gentry's place and half-a-dozen names that are possibles. I want to cross-check them with yours."

"I put my notes on Weston's files in my top left drawer. There are only a dozen or so I didn't get to before I had to go to the press conference."

"How'd that go?"

Sam made a face. "The usual bullshit. I left before it was over to come here. Tomorrow, we'll need to get into Judge Rogers's office and get a list of his cases. And he goes back a good twenty years."

"Jesus, that's a lot of names to cross-check."

"Yeah. Listen, when you get in, would you look up the newspaper article on Weston's funeral and call me at Carly's? I want to know if the fact that Judge Rogers was her godfather was reported anywhere."

"Will do." Ray headed for his car. "Say hi to your redheaded lady for me."

"She's not my lady."

"Yeah, right." Ray strolled off.

Sam started the engine. That was twice in one day that someone had commented on his relationship with Carly. Why was he even bothering to deny it?

Face it, English, you're mooning over a babe, and it's become noticeable. Despite the grim scene he'd just witnessed, he felt better as he thought of Carly waiting for him, Carly welcoming him, Carly hot and wild beneath him in front of a blazing fire. He'd called her before leaving the station to say he'd be late. Now he'd be arriving with bad news, that of her godfather's death.

He needed to soften the blow. She'd had too damn much on her plate lately. He'd take a quick detour and pick up a few things. A good bottle of wine. Her favorite food. Flowers maybe. And candles. He'd never tried it on her, but he'd be willing to wager that Carly would go for romance. He'd never been big on it himself. But there were times . . .

Sam shot out of the drive and raced toward Indian Village.

She'd been crying, and she didn't bother to hide the fact as she opened the door to Sam and pulled him inside. She helped him dump his bundles in a

202

nearby chair, opened his jacket, and burrowed into him. She badly needed to be held.

"I hate crying, hate this helpless feeling." Her voice was one she barely recognized. Filled with anxiety and pain. And it was becoming all too common. "Who is doing this to us, Sam? Why is he killing the people I love? Why is he after me?"

He held her, knowing she had to get it out, knowing he had too few answers for her. No stoic acceptance for Carly, but an honest, heartfelt grieving. She was too in touch with her feelings to hide them most of the time, much more so since he'd known her. He smoothed her wild hair and pressed her damp cheek to his heart. "Who told you?"

"My mother. She's devastated. Our families have been close all my life. I grew up with Alan Rogers, stood up in his wedding. I called Judge Rogers Uncle Nathan even though we're not actually related." She sucked in a hiccuping breath. "Poor Aunt Emily. When's it going to end, Sam?"

"I wish I knew, honey." He felt the impotent rage every cop feels too damn often.

Carly shifted to look up at him, her lashes spiky from her tears. "It's the same killer, isn't it? The strangler?"

"We think so." What more could he say? What reassurance could he offer her? "We'll get him, Carly. I just wish I could tell you when."

"How many people is he going to kill before you do? What about my mother? Or Aunt Emily? What if he goes after one of them?" She hated the need to ask him. She didn't mean to blame him. But who else could she ask?

He remembered the psychic's vision, the list with two remaining names, a man and a woman. Had Judge Rogers been the man? And the woman, was she in fact Carly and not her mother or her god-mother? Sam tightened his arms about her, the fear becoming a huge lump in his throat. "I'll put surveillance on both of them," he promised her.

They had one advantage here. If the strangler's next intended victim were Carly, for the first time, they'd at least know whom he was after. Sam decided to step up surveillance on her place without letting her know. He'd be with her himself every possible moment. He'd contact her friends and make sure she was never alone.

Luke's words came back to haunt him. "I stuck to her like glue. He almost got her anyhow." He wouldn't let anything happen to Carly, Sam vowed as he kissed the top of her head.

"I'm sorry." She drew back, swiping at the last of her tears. "I shouldn't take it out on you." She turned, her eyes fastening on the tree that looked so festive with the familiar ornaments, the bright lights. The stereo was on, a boys choir singing about peace and good will. "Maybe it's the holiday that's got me down. Facing a loss at Christmas seems to make things worse."

She'd taken to wearing his shirts occasionally over her jeans, saying it made her feel less alone when he was gone. Today, it was a pale yellow button-down collar version, the sleeves rolled up and still dangling at her wrists, the tail hanging to her knees. On her feet she wore a pair of silly Garfield-the-cat slippers he'd brought her last week just for laughs. How could she look sexy as hell in such a get-up? Sam wondered as he slipped out of his jacket and slid his arms along hers, drawing her back against his chest.

"You're right. Christmas brings our emotions to the surface." He buried his face in her hair, inhaling the clean, womanly scent of her. "You smell so good."

Carly snuggled back against him, willing her mind away from sad things and on to warm thoughts of Sam. "Mmm, you don't smell bad yourself, Detective. Kind of like snow and pine trees."

Sam turned her to face him and framed her face with his hands, wiping away her tears with his two thumbs, wishing he could erase her pain as easily. Since he couldn't, perhaps he could offer her a distraction or two. "I want us to try to put aside for a while all the rotten things happening out there. I want us to have a very special evening tonight."

She almost smiled. "Sounds intriguing. Go on."

"I brought you a surprise. Several actually." He kissed the end of her nose. "I'm amazed you haven't smelled one of them by now."

Carly sniffed the air, then smiled as she recognized an enticing aroma. "Doughnuts." Turning, she spotted the box among the bundles he'd hastily deposited on her chair. "What kind did you get?"

"The gooeyest I could find. I probably shouldn't be feeding your addiction." He saw her peer inside the box and lick her lips. "I wish you'd look at me like you look at doughnuts," he teased.

Carly already had one in her hand, a cream-filled, chocolate-covered confection, moving toward her mouth. "Smear on a little chocolate, and I just might."

"Don't think I won't, but don't be upset if the sheets get sticky."

"Might be worth it."

"It might at that." Sam gathered up the rest of his packages. "Now, you just orgy out right here while I go take care of a few things." He walked toward the hallway leading to her bedroom.

"What are you going to do?" she asked around a mouthful of cream.

"You'll see," he called over his shoulder.

She'd just finished and was wiping her hands when he returned, holding out one hand to her. "What's this?"

"Come with me." He led her slowly back, then paused at the doorway. "Now, close your eyes." When she did, he scooped her up into his arms and carried her into the bedroom. "Okay, open."

Carly did, and her eyes grew wide as she looked around. Candlelight danced along the walls and flickered in the corners. He'd placed thin tapers on her dresser, round ball-shaped candles on the desk, and a fat fragrant chunk on an end table. The blinds were drawn, blocking out the cold, wintry evening. The bed had been turned down, and a small bouquet of violets lay on one pillow. On the nightstand, incense burned, light and fragrant, adding a seductive scent. Alongside it sat a bottle of wine and two glasses, each half-filled with something clear and bubbly.

She smiled into his eyes. "Looks like a seduction in the making. Since when did we need all the trappings?"

"Oh, I just thought, for a change, it'd be nice to break from tradition. Instead of throwing you on the floor or ravishing you on the kitchen counter, I thought we'd try a little romance."

Her lips twitched. "Why, Detective English! A cynical cop with a romantic streak?" She leaned close, inhaling his minty scent. "I love it." She kissed him long and luxuriously.

He set her down and handed her a glass of wine, then picked up his own. "To happier days," he said, clinking his glass to hers.

206

Carly nodded, then sipped her wine. Sam handed her the violets, and she inhaled the sweet fragrance. "I think I like this," she confessed.

"There's more." Sam set aside their glasses, then tugged her back into his arms, his eyes on hers. "You're very beautiful, you know. I keep wondering why no man has made you his up to now."

"Because I gave no man permission to make me his. But then, no man has ever come barreling into my life like you have."

He let his mouth tease hers as he eased her onto her oversize brass bed. He let his fingers rediscover the softness of her cheeks, tracing the area around her eyes, chasing away the sadness that had lingered too long. He heard the wind outside whip against the bare tree limbs and heard Carly sigh as her arms reached up to welcome him.

He'd found great satisfaction in their previous wild matings, but now he would show her there was far more between them than frantic desire. He would show her that there could be a healing pleasure that would satisfy the body and restore the soul.

He understood how vulnerable she'd been feeling for weeks and knew that to be naked and open to him was another type of vulnerability. So he took her hands and coaxed them to rid him of his clothes, subtly telling her that he would allow himself to be exposed to her. He lay back as she undressed him, her fingers at first hesitant, then more bold, wordlessly communicating her pleasure at his allowing her to explore him at her leisure.

Sam felt his skin quiver as she threw aside his briefs, then ran her hands slowly over his chest and along his ribcage. She moved to his thighs then, her nails scraping along sensitive flesh, and he moaned aloud. His eyes locked with hers as she knelt on the bed and slowly unbuttoned his shirt and tossed it onto the floor. Angling, she shoved off her jeans. Her face became flushed as she removed the rest, but her gaze remained steady. She reached out then to draw him up to her.

Her hands crept around his waist as she lazily brushed her breasts against his chest. Unable to remain passive any longer, Sam thrust a hand into her thick hair and crushed his mouth to hers. The kiss went on and, knees weakening, they tumbled onto the bed, rolling and sighing in the tangled sheets. He tasted her hunger, felt her go limp with pleasure, heard the soft murmurings meant only for his ears.

This was what he'd been wanting with her, this deep awareness of one another, not just that wild race to completion. As good as that was, this was another way of making love — an exciting change. He hadn't craved this sharing of more than just his body with many lovers, but Sam knew he wanted this with Carly.

She was moving now beneath him, her hands reaching lower for him, but he evaded her as his tongue moved almost lazily over first one nipple, then the other. He heard her suck in a sharp breath, then arch toward his mouth.

"Are you trying to drive me mad?" she asked, her voice breathless with frustration.

"Yes, that's exactly what I plan to do." His mouth trailed hot fire along her shimmering flesh. He felt her shift restlessly, then cry out as his fingers moved inside her.

She rose to meet him, trying to capture the release he held just a breath away; but he moved out of reach, leaving her needy and anxious. Edgy with passion, she felt him trail kisses down her arching

208

body. Then his mouth settled on her as her hands curled around fistfuls of sheet.

The first heady climax surprised her with its intensity, leaving her weak and limp. Ragged breaths puffed from her as she finally looked up to see Sam watching her. Then, so swiftly she was dazed, he shifted and entered her, dragging her back into the eye of the storm. She had no time to think, to recover, but could only cling to him, her hands skimming restively over his sweat-slick back. In seconds she was racing desperately with him, seeking more and still more, embracing this unexpected bounty she'd been longing for.

Finally, a shimmering wave of pleasure slammed into her, and she was no longer aware of the room or the wintry night or much of anything else. There was only Sam and the marvelous sensations she was sharing with him.

And when it was over, Sam held her to him, cradling her. He hadn't been able to catch the killer stalking her yet. But he had been able to empty her mind of her fears, if only for a little while.

Replete, Carly snuggled into him. Here, like this, lethargic from his loving, she felt safe. Only with Sam. Here she could close her eyes and rest, and no one would harm her.

Drifting into a dream, Carly sighed. "I love you," she whispered.

In the darkness, Sam's eyes snapped open. Carly's breathing was already even, and he knew she probably wasn't aware she'd spoken aloud. But he'd heard, and the words left him shaken.

Don't love me, Carly, he silently told her. *I don't believe in love, not even with you. I'll only hurt you.*

* * *

209

The man read the article on the front page of the *Detroit News* a second time. The front page, yet. Judges obviously rated high in importance. But this judge would no longer be important to anyone.

Rogers had gotten what he deserved. The man smiled with satisfaction as he remembered the shocked expression on the judge's face when he'd looked up and discovered he wasn't alone. Then had come that spark of recognition, as with the others, followed by the quick flash of fear. The judge had nearly wet his pants as he realized his fate was sealed. The man had had the supreme pleasure of watching the bastard's eyes bulge as he'd squeezed the life from him.

Then, for good measure, he'd put a hole through him with his own gun. In death, the judge had resembled the man's mother when he'd found her dangling from a drapery cord wrapped around her neck, the other end attached to a cheap light fixture.

Yes, they were paying, one by one.

Love thy enemies, the Bible taught. But the man knew that needed to be changed. Avenge thy enemies, it should read.

Methodically, he picked up his list and crossed off number four.

Chapter Twelve

Someone had put up a Christmas tree in the squad room. Probably Megs, Sam thought as he draped his jacket over the back of his chair. It was a pitiful thing with scrawny silver branches and a hodgepodge of red and gold balls stuck here and there. Tiny blue lights winked on and off as it sat on a table in the corner. Homicide Division seemed an odd place for even that little bit of holiday cheer, almost a contradiction.

Rubbing his chilled hands together, Sam poured himself a cup of coffee from the urn set up on the same table and wandered over to the bank of windows. It would seem the Detroit area would have a white Christmas after all. Four days before the holiday, and the snow was falling steadily after an early morning start. Looking out, he decided that the pristine blanket gave a false illusion of purity to the grimy downtown location where the Beaubien station was located. Just as the Christmas tree gave a false all's-right-with-the-world feeling to a police department of men and women who dealt with murder and mayhem daily.

Still, outside these four walls, life went on pretty much as usual. Babies were born, people died, and the mortgage had to be paid. Yet somewhere out there was a solidly-built killer with huge, strong hands who'd killed four men and was probably laughing at the cops who hadn't come close to nabbing him in the four weeks since he'd begun his savage slaughtering. Sam sipped his coffee and tasted frustration.

They didn't have him yet, but they were getting closer.

Since Judge Rogers's death, he'd lost track of the number of hours he and Ray had put in on cross-checking names and cases that had involved three of the four men killed. They'd used the computer and compared written lists. Endless checking and rechecking. Doug Anderson was the one who didn't fit in and probably wouldn't until they narrowed their search down further.

They were down to six names, men who'd been represented by Homer Gentry, prosecuted by Will Weston, and been sentenced by Judge Rogers. Ray had driven out early this morning to confer with the warden at Jackson State Prison about the six men. Clark Abbott, Judge Rogers's assistant, was supposed to get back with them today about the two cases Mrs. Rogers had mentioned to them. Those were long shots, but they couldn't afford to bypass the smallest thing at this point. Unfortunately, Clark had taken off for a short trip right after the judge's funeral and had just returned.

Sam swallowed more coffee as he noticed Ray's station wagon pulling into the parking lot below. They'd both attended the judge's funeral last week, a sad and unproductive day. His widow and Isabel Weston had held up well, better than Carly, who'd broken down afterward, sobbing in his arms when they'd returned to her place. She wasn't as dispassionate as the older generation; and, oddly, he was pleased about that.

He'd grown up amidst people who'd taught him to

bury his feelings, to present a stiff-upper-lip detachment to the world. As a boy, he'd been unable to turn that teaching off when it came to private moments and therefore had been unable to acknowledge his feelings, to let them out. That kind of neutrality had served him well in his chosen line of work. But it had become such a habit that he'd blocked a majority of his human feelings, almost as if to deny them would be a show of strength, to give in to them a hint of weakness.

Sam well remembered his father's words as he'd been growing up. "Don't cry, Samuel. Men don't cry. Only babies cry. Be a man." Well, he'd done a fine job of it. And in so doing, he'd nearly dehumanized himself.

Until Carly.

With her, once they'd gotten past their initial animosity with one another, for some reason, he'd been able to drop his guard, to get past the barriers he'd erected, to let her in, to share his feelings. He wasn't sure why, but he knew it was so. She, too, had presented a cool, almost indifferent, dignified face to the world. Since being with him, she was more approachable, softer, unafraid to feel and to talk about her feelings.

Since spending so much time together, both of them unable to sleep, they'd talked about so much. Their pasts, their dreams, how they felt about everything from politics and religion to favorite foods and preferred pastimes. The only feelings they hadn't discussed were the feelings they had for each other.

That was a can of worms each of them was reluctant to open.

"Hey, buddy," Ray said as he sat down at his desk and brushed snow from his hair. "Come see what I've got."

Sam drained the last of his coffee and walked

over. "I've been waiting for you. What'd you find out?"

Ray slipped off his gloves, but kept his coat on. "We traced four of the six men." He handed Sam a slip of paper. "Three are still in prison and have been since way before these killings began. The fourth died last year. That leaves two: Vern Cummings and Ric Skelly. Both were clients of Gentry, prosecuted by Weston, and sentenced by Rogers. And both were serving time in Jackson when Doug Anderson was also in there, though none of them shared a cell, with him or each other. That connection, we still can't figure."

"Any clues as to where Cummings and Skelly might be?" Sam asked, glancing at his watch.

"Both were released from prison just weeks ago. Skelly doesn't appear to have any family around, but Cummings does. A mother and sister in Pontiac."

"Maybe you should check them out first. I've got to get in there with Frazer in a couple of minutes." Short-staffed as always, he and Ray hadn't been able to completely abandon their other cases while working to catch the strangler. Last night, the rapist had struck again, only this time, he'd run out of luck.

The female victim had screamed loud enough to attract a cruising police car's attention. The two patrolmen had captured him, and Sam was scheduled to interrogate at eleven. Ezra Frazer was an unlikely serial rapist, middle-aged and balding, but strong as an ox, a man who worked out regularly. He was also a family man with a wife and two teenagers, an eastside CPA who apparently got his jollies hurting women. The creep had called his attorney, who'd shown up almost before they'd booked Frazer. It wasn't going to be pleasant. All cops hated dealing with rapists.

"Yeah, I know. I don't envy your afternoon." Ray

214

glanced out at the heavy snowfall and shivered. "I'm not crazy about my agenda either. In this snow, it'll take me more than an hour to get to Pontiac." The suburban city was about thirty miles northwest of Detroit. "But I don't want to call and alert his family in case Vern Cummings is living with them."

"Right. We still haven't heard from Clark Abbott. I don't know what the hell's holding him up." This was nervous time, the point where they were closing in. Any small thing that went wrong could blow the whole case and put them back to square one. Sam felt the strain, and he knew Ray did, too.

"Want me to give Abbott a call?" Ray asked.

"Nah, I've already nagged him once this morning. It's his first day back after a week off, but I told him this was high priority." Sam checked his watch again. He was nervous about something else that had little to do with his work.

Carly was being picked up by her friend, Toni Garette, and they were going to The Glass Door where the two women were putting on a bridal shower for another friend, Amanda Stone, who was getting married after the first of the year. The luncheon had been planned for weeks, and he couldn't forbid her to go, though he'd liked to have. So instead, he'd called Toni and made sure she wouldn't let Carly out of her sight, not even to visit the ladies room. He'd also asked her to take along Amanda when they drove Carly home so the two of them could check out Carly's apartment before they left her alone. There was safety in numbers, Sam reasoned.

He knew that Carly might think his protection excessive, but he didn't feel it was enough. So he'd assigned a police officer to shadow the women to and from the restaurant. The regular surveillance squad car had also been alerted, and the phone monitor

215

was on. And still, Sam was uneasy. If only this rapist didn't require his attention right now, he'd have gone with her himself. Bridal showers weren't exactly his thing, but he'd have managed in order to keep Carly safe.

You got it bad, English, he admitted to himself ruefully.

"Well, I'm off," Ray said, picking up his gloves and rising. "You going to stick around most of the day then?"

"Yeah, till I finish with Frazer. Call me if you learn anything. If I'm not here, beep me." Maybe this session would go quickly. Damn, but he hoped so.

With a wave to Ray, he picked up the phone. He'd have just enough time to call Carly before she left for her luncheon.

"Did you see your mother's face when you opened that sheer black nightie, Amanda?" Toni asked with a laugh.

"Did I ever! I thought she was going to choke on her iced tea." Amanda joined in the laughter.

Smiling, Carly agreed. "I thought her remark was priceless." She lowered her voice, mimicking Mrs. Steven's well-modulated tones. "Surely you aren't going to wear that in front of anyone, Amanda." All three of them laughed.

Toni swung her Mercedes carefully onto Carly's street. The main roads had been plowed, but this side street was thick with the heavy snowfall. Slowly, she maneuvered around a parked car. "Does she just say those prudish things, or does she really feel like that?"

"My mother?" Amanda shook her head. "She should have lived in the Victorian era. She once confessed that my father's never seen her without her clothes, that he wouldn't dream of walking into their bedroom without knocking."

Carly raised a questioning brow. "You're joking?" She was aware that her own parents, about the same age as the Stevens, had mutually enjoyed their sex life. It wasn't anything she'd ever discussed with either of them, but rather something she could just tell from the way they had acted with each other, the small innuendos, the loving touches. "I can't imagine living like that, being so uptight about something so natural."

Amanda sighed. "Neither can I. Maybe that's one of the reasons I wasn't born until my mother was in her thirties."

"Wouldn't she flip if she knew you and Bob have been sleeping together for months?" Toni commented.

"Positively. Speaking of sleeping together, Carly, are you and this detective getting serious? I meant to ask you earlier, but there were so many people around."

"Serious? I don't know." It was difficult talking about her feelings when she wasn't sure exactly what they were. "I've been a bit distracted with this strangler thing." Her friends knew about the blouse, the rose, the notes, and calls. She hadn't been pleased when she'd learned that Sam had told them in order to explain the need for their help in policing her in his absence, although she'd understood his reasons. "He's very protective."

Toni sent a wink Carly's way. "Oh, I have a feeling he's a bit more than merely protective. He's all but lived with you night and day for two weeks now. Are you saying you haven't moved past the hand-holding stage yet? With a man that sexy?"

Much to her embarrassment, Carly found herself

217

blushing, then grinning at her friend. "Perhaps we have. You want details?"

Toni turned with exaggerated care into Carly's slippery drive and held the big car steady, stopping near her stairway. She looked at Carly as she turned the motor off, her eyes suddenly serious. "You can spare the details. What we want is for you to be happy. I've got a hunch this guy's nuts about you." Sam's voice on the phone today had been somewhat gruff, a man used to giving orders. But she'd heard the underlying concern he couldn't hide.

Carly lost her smile as she gazed down at her gloved hands. She'd been close all her life to both of these women. Maybe it would help if she talked to them. "Do you remember a while back when you told me that I'd probably never felt an attraction so strong that all else be damned?" She looked at Toni and saw her nod. "Well, I think I've met my match."

"It's about time," Toni said with enthusiasm.

"Right on," Amanda chimed in.

"However, Sam's thirty-five, and I don't believe he's ever had a serious relationship. He was raised in a very cold household, and he's seen no shining examples of happily-ever-after. I'm not even sure he believes there is such a thing."

"Then it's up to you to convince him," Toni said quietly. "Do you love him?"

Carly opted for an indirect answer. "I've been so preoccupied with thoughts of that madman that I haven't had much time to think about anything else. Sam's very different from anyone I've ever known."

"Bob's very different from the people I was raised with," Amanda interjected. "Frankly, that's one of the things that drew me to him. The guys we grew up with bore me. Same old, same old, you know. Bob's got character. He's not afraid to work hard to get what he wants, not just take over from daddy. He thinks for himself. He's not an echo of his family's opinions."

Carly angled toward the back seat to look at Amanda. "Is that why you fell in love with him?" She honestly wanted to know.

"That and the fact that he makes me feel things I've never felt before. Not just in bed, but whenever we talk. Even sometimes when we're quiet, he makes me feel at peace." She shook her head. "It's hard to explain."

"No," Carly said. "I think I understand. And you're right. That *is* the difference, and it's a big one." She turned to open her door, thinking she'd probably revealed enough. "Thanks for driving me home."

"Oh, no you don't," Toni said, climbing out. "Sam said we had to not only go in with you, but check the place out."

"Oh, please," Carly moaned, feeling more than a little foolish. As she stepped out, she saw the police surveillance car drive past slowly. Nice to know they were on the job.

"Yes, that's right," Amanda added, getting out.

"He called you, too?" Carly walked with them, shaking her head. "I can't believe him."

Toni linked her arm through Carly's. "That's what I mean. I think the man cares. I can't believe any cop does this for everyone he's assigned to watch, do you?"

Carly led the way up her stairs, stepping carefully on the wet wood. "I suppose not."

"Say, who shoveled your snow?" Amanda asked. "Your steps and porch are freshly cleaned."

"Probably Ted Masters. He lives in the front house and gets home from work about two. See, he's shoveled their walk and the drive as well. He always does. Nice guy." Carly slipped her key into the lock and opened the door.

"Let me go first," Toni insisted, moving Carly aside.

"Me, too." Amanda shoved past her.

"Honestly, you two." Carly followed them in.

"Stay right by the door," Toni told her. "Sam said to leave it open while we have a look around."

"Should we grab a weapon, like a kitchen knife?" Amanda asked with a nervous giggle.

"I think you've been watching too much television," Carly said. But she stayed put, listening to them clump through the hallway, checking both bedrooms, then the bath, finally returning to go through the kitchen and the darkroom. "Find anyone hiding under the bed or in the cupboards, Sherlock?" she asked Toni as her friend came back into the living room.

"All clear. Now, don't you feel better knowing no one's here?"

"Enormously." Despite the sarcasm, she hugged her friend. "Thanks. I really do appreciate everyone's concern." She turned to hug Amanda next.

"It was a wonderful shower. Thank you both." Amanda included Toni in her warm smile.

"Hey, it was fun." Toni watched Carly peel off her coat. "So what are you planning to do now?"

"Change clothes, maybe take a hot bath. Wait for—"

"Yes, we know. Wait for Sam to join you." Both women laughed as Toni opened the door. "Take care. I'll be in touch." Toni stepped outside.

"Thanks again, Carly." Amanda followed Toni down the steps.

Carly closed and locked the door, then sat down to pull off her boots. It had been a fun day, but she was weary nonetheless. Her lack of a steady eight hours of sleep over the past few weeks was beginning to take its toll.

She glanced at the phone machine and was relieved to see no light blinking. Sam would probably call soon. She shook back her hair and watched snowflakes fly off. It was still coming down out there, though it seemed to be letting up. Ted would probably have to shovel again later. She felt a shiver take her. A hot bath really would feel good. Yawning, she went to her bedroom.

Twenty minutes later, stretched out in a fragrant, steaming bath, Carly leaned her head back onto the rim and closed her eyes. She let the heat seep through her, concentrating on relaxing inch by inch. Lately, her muscles seemed bunched, tied up in tense knots. If only she could get her mind to float as loose as her limbs now were.

But the fear was always with her, always there, even when she was with others, talking, laughing. Like a heavy anchor, it lay in the back of her brain, never allowing her to forget that she wasn't free to walk about as she pleased, to come and go at will. She had to have people escort her everywhere, someone stay nights with her, surveillance cars, a phone monitor. Her privacy was gone, and she missed it sorely.

All because of a madman.

Carly sank lower into the water, wishing she could forget him. The only time she really did was when she and Sam were making love. She smiled. Now there was something to dwell on instead. The man really knew how to make her body sing. And she'd learned a thing or two about getting some pretty fierce responses from him as well. They were good together in bed. Millions of people probably were. But life wasn't lived in bed.

How would their relationship hold up, physical aspects aside? While it was true that they hadn't argued much, or even had too many differences of opinion, they also weren't living a natural existence right now. Stress heightened their attraction to one another. Fear had them excusing each other's sometimes bizarre behavior. Tension had them reaching out to one another for relief, for comfort.

When this was all over, what would happen between them? If, for instance, Sam captured the strangler tomorrow and she would no longer be at risk, would he then back away from what had been building between them? Did she want him to, or did she want something more to develop? Had she, who'd always been wary of opposites hanging together for the long haul, changed her mind? Was she drawn to Sam because he was different, as Amanda was to Bob?

She didn't think so. In a mellow mood after a passionate loving, she'd whispered those three important words to him and meant them. On sober reflection in broad daylight, she knew she still meant every word: She also knew she wasn't naive enough to believe that loving alone would make all the differences between them magically disappear.

Could she and Sam make it together in a forever situation like Stephanie and Luke seemed to be doing?

A tough question. And one she'd have to face one day soon. There would be — Carly's thoughts stopped cold. A sudden scraping noise sounded clearly in the silent apartment.

Carly eased up out of the water and straightened, cocking her head to listen. Heavy footsteps. They seemed some distance away, as if in the kitchen. It couldn't be Sam. He'd have called out to her by now. He was the only other person who had a key. *Dear God!*

222

Quickly, trying to be very quiet, Carly stepped out of the tub and moved to the bathroom door, firmly locking it. Her ear up against the wood, she couldn't hear anything else, or was it because her heart was thudding so loudly?

Grabbing a towel, she dried off hurriedly, then reached for her clothes. Thank goodness, she'd thought to bring them in. Her fingers were trembling so hard she could scarcely get the gold turtleneck sweater on over her head. It took two attempts before she could step into her brown corduroy slacks. She had only her Garfield slippers available, but she slid her feet into them.

Her hair was piled on top of her head to keep it out of the way, and she patted dry her damp nape as she again pressed her ear against the door. She heard the steps again, more clearly discernible this time.

Feeling frantic, Carly looked around the small bath. What could she defend herself with? Her fingers shook as she opened the medicine cabinet. A pair of manicure scissors was all she could find that could possibly be used as a weapon. A pitiful weapon, at that, but, though they were small, they were sharp. Grabbing them in a defensive hold, she leaned back to listen.

The footsteps were coming closer!

Sam closed the door to the interrogation room and crunched down on his mint with a vengeance. Damn attorneys constantly looking for a loophole. Bernard Ames was a cigar-smoking, rotund lawyer whose high-pitched voice was getting on Sam's nerves almost as much as his client's cocky confidence.

The two officers had caught Ezra Frazer practically in the act—at least running from the scene in the alley with the victim screaming—and still Ames was claiming mistaken identity. In the lineup earlier, the frightened young woman had identified Frazer unhesitatingly. Ames was questioning her eyesight and her morals, claiming that if a sex act had occurred, the lady had obviously consented.

Sure. She'd taken one look at middle-aged, balding Ezra and gotten so worked up that she'd undoubtedly coaxed him into that filthy alley, thrown him onto the slush-covered ground, and had at him. Another sex-crazed woman who couldn't wait to unzip a fly, according to Bernard. His client was a law-abiding, tax-paying, respected businessman who'd never so much as had a parking ticket. Right. Sam wanted to hit something hard, which was one reason why he'd left the room to take a break.

The other was Carly. At his desk, he picked up the phone and dialed her number. It was a little past three, and she'd said she'd be home by now. Sitting down, he knew he'd feel better once he heard her voice.

But no one answered. Frowning, Sam hung up. Carly must have turned off the answering machine. He knew how much she hated coming home to a blinking light ever since the calls had begun. He considered phoning The Glass Door, then decided he was overreacting. Toni and Amanda had promised they wouldn't leave her side, and he trusted her friends. They were probably driving Carly home right now, and it was taking longer because of the heavy snow.

Rising, Sam walked over to get a cup of coffee, then headed back to the interrogation room, a scowl on his face. He'd wait half-an-hour and call again.

Something peculiar was happening. Carly stood

back from the bathroom door, scissors still in her hand, listening.

She'd heard the footsteps come down the hallway and enter each bedroom, then come out to stop in front of the bathroom door. She couldn't be certain, but she thought she'd heard heavy breathing for long moments. Then, the footsteps had gone in the opposite direction.

Heart pounding, she'd listened again, trying to track the movements in the other part of the apartment. It seemed as if the intruder were rummaging through things. She heard drawers open and close and then something break, as if a glass had fallen on the kitchen floor or perhaps been knocked into the sink. Then, several minutes ago, she'd heard the front door open and shut with a bang.

Had her over-active imagination decided the intruder was the strangler? Could it have been someone intent on robbery instead? Had he come up her back stairs, which seemed more apt to be what a thief would do, broken in her back door somehow, stolen some items, and then left? Did the opening and closing of the door mean he'd really gone, or had he just intended she think so?

Carly wiped a trembling hand across her brow. Nerves and the steamy heat of the bathroom had her sweaty and shaking. She had no watch, but she felt as if the door shutting had occurred at least ten minutes ago. How long could she stay in the bath, cowering with a small pair of scissors her only defense?

Where had she left the gun Sam had given her? Breathing hard, she tried to remember. It had been in the bedroom nightstand, but she'd moved it to a kitchen drawer. With luck, she could creep out and get it, then look around. Swallowing hard, Carly gripped the scissors more tightly and unlocked the bathroom door.

Her slippered feet were almost soundless as she stole along the hallway. The building was old, but she knew where the hardwood flooring squeaked a little and avoided those spots. She stopped every few steps, but could hear nothing. She hadn't turned on any lights earlier which was probably a good thing. Cautiously, she peered around the arched doorway into the living room.

The blinds were slanted half-closed, and very little light was coming in from the one window because of the winter gloom outside. She was afraid to hit the switch for fear she'd reveal herself to someone if they were still inside. Straining her eyes, she could see no one and nothing moving in the eerie shadows of her familiar living room. Carefully, she made her way toward the kitchen.

She thought she remembered putting the gun in the first drawer past the doorway. Quickly, she eased around the corner and fumbled for the drawer knob. It was then she sensed something or someone behind her. Whirling, she raised the hand holding the scissors high.

A dark shadow separated from the kitchen side wall and came toward her. She heard the ugly laugh she now recognized from the phone calls. Her throat closed, and she couldn't scream, could only think to run. His hand shot out to grab her, but she angled out of reach and tore back into the living room, nearly stumbling into the Christmas tree in her haste.

He was right behind her. She could smell an unwashed body and bad breath, could hear his labored breathing as he again reached for her. Dodging the tree, she brought down her arm, the scissors poised to do harm. But he easily knocked the weapon from her hand and lunged for her.

Almost tripping backward, Carly's hands flew out

to catch herself. In doing so, her fingers closed on her camera on the side table. She had no defense except the one Jimmy Stewart had used in *Rear Window*. Raising the camera blindly, she clicked and watched the flash momentarily illuminate the room. For an instant, she saw a hulking figure outlined, his arms moving up to shield his eyes. She heard the man swear as she darted to the opposite side of the room.

She saw him move toward her and again aimed the camera in his direction and flashed, waited a moment, then flashed again.

"Come here, you bitch," the man snarled and staggered two steps forward. But when he opened his eyes, all he could see were white spots dancing, obstructing his vision.

No time to search for the gun, Carly decided as she raced back into the kitchen. She needed to get away from him. Hurriedly she ran into her darkroom, closed the door behind her, and shoved the lock home.

Thank God for Sam who'd insisted she have a lock put on all of her doors. *Sam, where are you when I need you the most?* Breathing hard, Carly stopped to catch her breath, then fumbled for the light switch. Amber light was better than none. But when she touched the switch, nothing happened. He must have turned off the power. Damn!

In the kitchen, she heard him cursing. His eyesight must have cleared for he'd apparently figured out where she was.

"You've got nowhere to run, you bitch." The man stood outside the door, his heavy hands hanging, his chest heaving as he tried to control his fury. "I've waited too long to go away now."

Standing utterly still, Carly tried to calculate her chances. Sam was questioning a rape suspect, she knew. She'd told him she'd be home around three, and she knew it was well past that. Maybe he'd call. When the machine answered instead, maybe he'd get worried and check with Toni at The Glass Door. Oh my God, she thought, with the power off the machine won't work. What would he think? Maybe he'd know something was wrong and race here.

But would he be in time?

The surveillance police car. Where had they been when this madman had been sneaking around and climbing up to her apartment on outside stairs? What good were they, anyhow? They could be driving past this very minute and nothing would look amiss from the street. All their planning, all their precautions, and he was still here on the other side of that suddenly frail-looking door.

Carly thought of the newspaper accounts of how this maniac had literally crushed the throats of four men, all larger than she. How could she possibly hold him off? she asked herself as she felt her lunch backing up into her throat. *Dear God, she didn't want to die.*

"Enough," the man called out. "Open that door, or I'll break it down."

She'd seen only a shadowy outline of the man, felt his meaty hand graze her arm, yet she knew if anyone could break down a door, he was probably the one.

The man had run out of patience. He threw his shoulder against the door and felt no give. Bracing himself, he hit it again, harder. He heard a satisfying crunch and felt the hinges protest.

Fighting panic, Carly turned, trying to see through the thick darkness. The only thing in the room she might be able to use against him would be some of the chemicals she kept to develop her prints. If he managed to break in the door, she would toss

228

the harmful liquids at him, hoping to disable him long enough for her to escape. Moving strictly by feel, she groped in the darkness for a couple of the jars.

Again, she heard something ram into the door. The splintering sound told her he was making headway. Carly opened one bottle and smelled the contents. Developing solution. She did the same with another and discovered her fixer chemical. She wasn't certain how much harm either would do, but Jim had warned her that breathing the chemicals in or working with them wearing contacts could do permanent damage. If she could aim the splash toward the man's face and perhaps hit his eyes, she guessed he'd have some adverse reaction.

The door was splitting. She could hear him breathing hard with his efforts. He had to be built like a bull elephant. She pressed her back against the wall alongside the door, holding a jar in each hand, waiting for him to come through. Waiting for her opportunity.

It came within seconds as the man hurled himself at the door one final time and came crashing through amidst the shattered wood pieces. The momentum sent him sprawling to the floor, his huge hands outstretched to break his fall. From the dim light drifting in through the kitchen windows, she saw him roll quickly onto his back.

Carly tossed the contents of first one bottle, then the other in the direction of his face. She heard him cry out, but didn't stick around to see what damage she'd inflicted. Stepping gingerly in the shadowy darkness over the splintered wood, she rushed out of the room. Behind her, she heard him cursing ripely.

She tore through the apartment, and with sweaty, trembling fingers, yanked open the front door.

Four o'clock, and there was still no answer at Carly's, not even the phone machine. Sam felt a prickle of fear race up his spine as he called dispatch to ask them to plug him through to the surveillance team. Impatiently, he waited for them to come on the line.

The captain had come in on the session with Ezra Frazer and, despite his attorney's best efforts, they'd finally managed to put the rapist behind bars minutes ago. Sam knew that Bernard Ames would be appearing with his client soon after filing papers, trying to get him out on bail. But he and Ray would be there, too; and, hopefully, the judge would deny bail. The problem was, though they had Frazer on this one, they couldn't tie him to the others at this time, nor could they prove he'd been the one who'd killed one of the victims.

But, with the creep off the streets, they'd have the time to bring in some of the other victims, get them to make a positive I.D., and nail the bastard. The biggest obstacle was that good old Ezra looked like a respectable, church-going, salt-of-the-earth type. A businessman with a house in the suburbs, a wife, and kiddies. Sam wondered if the general population ever guessed that many a rapist was just like that, not some filthy bum looking to get laid. They were sick men, violent men, mascarading as nice guys. He wished he could throw them all in the slammer and throw away the key.

"Yeah, Sam," the voice on the phone answered. "You looking for us?"

"Herb, where are you?"

"Over on Michigan Avenue. We were called to a B&E at a jewelry store. Sorry, but we didn't have time to check in with you."

Sam gritted his teeth. He knew it was unreasonable of him to expect the cruiser to keep constant watch on Carly's place. "How long since you've passed along Seminole?"

"About an hour. Why, is something wrong?"

"I don't know. Get over there as soon as you can, will you?"

"Sure thing." The patrolman signed off.

Sam flipped through his card index, found the number of The Glass Door. They answered on the second ring, but the polite maitre'd told him that Toni and the others had left the restaurant about two-thirty and Toni wasn't expected back today. Slamming down the phone, Sam leaped to his feet and grabbed his jacket.

Racing down the hall, he left word with the desk sergeant where he was going. Hurrying, he climbed into his Trans Am, turned on the motor, then picked up his snow brush. The damn car was covered.

Dusting off the windshield, he decided he'd try to reach the man he'd assigned to track Carly on his car phone. And he'd try Carly's number again. Maybe she'd fallen asleep or was taking one of her long baths. Finishing, he got behind the wheel and slammed it into gear, his nerves jumping.

He had a deep-down feeling that something was terribly wrong.

Chapter Thirteen

Were those footsteps behind her? Carly wasn't sure. The wind was whirling snow everywhere, and her heart was thudding in her ears. The porch was wet and slippery under the plastic soles of her slippers, and she nearly fell. She grabbed onto the handrailing as she took a few precious seconds to look around. She could see no one.

Desperate thoughts zipped through her mind. Why wasn't Ted coming out to shovel again? Why didn't one of her neighbors choose this moment to arrive home? Where the hell was the police car? If she could just make it to the big house, she'd be all right. She saw lights on in several windows. Even above the wind, they'd hear her pounding and let her in. It was dark and so very cold. Shivering, she started down, clutching the railing.

She'd only gone four or five steps when he came up behind her. Carly opened her mouth to scream, but he clamped a thick hand over the lower half of her face. Quickly he slipped his other arm around her waist and easily lifted her back against himself. She struggled, her arms striking out, but she might have been a child swatting at a giant.

"Hold still, bitch, or I'll break your neck," he snarled into her ear.

Carly tensed with fright, but stopped her ineffective movements. She knew he'd carry out his threat without a moment's hesitation.

Cautiously, the man backed up with Carly in tow, dragged her inside, and shut the door. Half-carrying her, he made his way to her bedroom and tossed her face down on the bed.

She clamped her jaws together to keep from begging him not to hurt her. Violent men were turned on by their victim's fear, she'd read. Hesitantly, she lifted her head to look back at him. She didn't know where he'd gotten the piece of rope, but suddenly he was tying her wrists together behind her back. His face was wet; but, from what she could see, the chemicals she'd thrown at him hadn't affected his vision. Grabbing her shackled hands, he yanked her viciously to her feet. She did cry out then as the cord dug deeply into her tender flesh.

He seemed not to hear or care as he shoved her down on the floor by the base of her bed. His hands where they touched her skin seemed greasy, slimy with some coating. Grunting as he worked, he tied the other end of the rope to the brass footboard, then tested it for security. She winced at his fetid odor as he leaned over her.

Straightening, the man stood looking down at her. A soft, spoiled, pampered woman who'd had everything go her way all her life, he thought. He'd taken note of her manicured hands as he'd bound her, unmarked, untouched by work. So unlike his mother's poor work-worn hands those last few years. This overindulged bitch had never scrubbed floors or cleaned toilets or worried over money. But where had her wealth gotten her in the end? Right here, in his clutches, under his control.

"Do you recognize me?" he asked, narrowing his eyes.

233

Carly had been studying his face and knew she didn't. "No. Should I?"

His beefy hand whipped out, and he slapped her across the face, hard. He couldn't help himself. She hadn't really looked at him all those years ago, hadn't met his eyes or noted his appearance. She'd merely looked *through* him, as if he were a piece of furniture. Why had he expected more?

Her cheek stung mightily, but she blinked back the quick rush of tears. She wouldn't cry in front of him. She wouldn't give him the satisfaction. Slowly, she turned to look up at him again. "Why are you doing this to me?"

He couldn't answer her. If he started, it would all spill out. Years of hating, of frustration, of pain. He had to go on with his plan. He had much work to do. It was getting late. He had to call Pete and then get moving.

"Don't make a sound. If you do, I'll come back and break your neck." The man left the room, lumbering down the hall.

Carly believed him. The rope was biting into her wrists. Silently, she struggled against the tight bindings, but the more she did, the more the cord dug into her flesh. She sagged back, limp with frustration.

She supposed she should be grateful he hadn't attacked her while he'd had her on the bed. But rape wasn't his game; murder was.

Her face was burning, and her feet were freezing. Somewhere along the way, she'd lost her slippers. Shifting uncomfortably within her narrow limits, she tried to tuck her bare feet under her legs in an effort to warm them. Her head snapped up when she heard a crash from the living room, as if a lamp had been overturned. What on earth was he doing? And more importantly, what was he planning to do with her?

234

Carly prayed he'd occupy himself out there for a long while. The longer the better, for Sam would surely come soon. She heard the phone ring, listening for the answering machine to pick it up. Heart pounding, she waited, then realized the machine wouldn't work without power. Finally, the caller hung up.

Next she heard the low rumble of her captor's voice, though she couldn't make out the words. Had someone come in? No, he was using the phone. Did he have an accomplice he was calling? She craned her neck, but couldn't see the clock. It was quite dark out so it had to be getting late.

Oh, God, where was Sam?

The Trans Am skidded around the corner onto Seminole, nearly careening into a snow-covered parked car. Sam swore as he clutched the wheel and straightened the car. Hurrying on, he reached Carly's drive and turned in.

He'd called her twice on the way over, but she hadn't answered her phone. Her Porsche was in its usual place, totally covered with snow, as if she hadn't moved it all day. And she likely hadn't, if Toni had picked her up for the shower and brought her home. But what had happened after that?

He'd talked with the detective who'd trailed them, only to learn that he'd seen them to the restaurant, had hung around drinking coffee, and had followed them back to Carly's. He'd watched Carly enter her front door and had stuck around a whole hour, but no one had come out except her two friends when they'd left. And no one had gone in. Figuring she was in for the night, the detective had radioed in to the station that he was leaving.

Glancing about, Sam frowned. There was no sign

of the patrol car that he'd hoped had doubled back here by now. Sam stepped out and closed the car door quietly. It was still snowing, but the drive and walk had been shoveled some time ago. Carly's windows were all dark. He prayed he'd find her in her bedroom asleep. But would she have slept through two phone calls?

Drawing his gun, he climbed the stairs slowly. Near the top, he saw footprints in a light covering of snow, both quite large, ending about the fourth step, and signs of a scuffle. On the porch, he reached out and curled his fingers around the doorknob. It turned easily and was slick to the touch. Petroleum jelly? Icy fear settled around him, for he knew Carly would never leave her door unlocked.

If that bastard touched Carly, he'd personally finish him off.

Sam pushed the door a crack, then swung it wide quickly, entering crouched in a shooting stance, his gun at the ready. He swung to the left first, but he wasn't fast enough. From his right, something fast and heavy came whooshing down at him, hitting him hard at the base of his neck.

Sam dropped to the floor with a heavy thunk.

Ray Vargas brushed the snow from the windshield of his station wagon and got inside. Shivering, he turned on the engine and then the heat, waiting for the car to warm up before starting the drive back. It had been an interesting afternoon.

Vern Cummings's family hadn't been exactly cooperative. They claimed not to know where Vern was and couldn't remember when they'd last heard from him. Leaving their home, Ray had passed a neighborhood saloon. Johnny's Joint looked like a gathering place for locals. On a hunch, he'd gone inside and found a talkative bartender.

236

Johnny wore a big white apron and a friendly smile as he polished glasses and told Ray exactly where to find Vern. He was shacked up with a waitress named Clara who worked at the Joint part-time. Johnny hadn't seen either of them in a week, but he knew they lived in an apartment on the seedy side of town. After scribbling down the address, Ray had gone to check it out.

He'd found Clara very much alone with her arm in a sling and a black eye that was only partially healed. Her boyfriend, Vern, it seemed, liked to knock women around. But this time she'd called the cops on him and they'd thrown him behind bars. She'd told Ray with disgust that the incident had occurred over a week ago and added that she hoped Vern Cummings would rot in jail.

Just to be sure, Ray had gone to the Pontiac jail and checked on old Vern. Sure enough, he'd been residing there exactly nine days, which would have made it impossible for him to be the strangler. That narrowed things down considerably.

To Ric Skelly.

The wagon had warmed up enough for Ray to remove his gloves. He picked up his car phone and dialed the station, asking for Sam.

"He checked out about an hour or so ago," the desk sergeant told Ray. "He can be reached at Carly Weston's place. You want that number?"

"No, thanks." Ray hung up. It was cold and dark, the snow still coming down. There was little more they could do tonight. He'd drive back to the city, then call Sam at Carly's, see what he felt they should do tomorrow to move in on finding Skelly.

It wouldn't be easy, Ray thought as he shifted into gear and left the Pontiac jail parking lot. Skelly had been out of prison for several weeks and, according to his file, had left a forwarding address with prison

237

officials as required. But when Ray had run a preliminary check of the address on Skelly's chart, it had turned out to be a cheap downtown rooming house that he'd left after the first few days. Not uncommon for ex-cons to move around a lot, and there had been no reason to keep Skelly under surveillance since he'd served out his full sentence. If he'd been paroled instead, it might have been easier to locate him.

Heading for the expressway, Ray frowned as he increased the speed of his windshield wipers. Damn snow. It had taken him an hour-and-a-half to get to Pontiac and would likely take him two to get back into the city with the increased downpour. He saw a salt truck lumbering along on the opposite side of the freeway. It was just too much snow falling in too short a period of time for them to keep up. Only one lane was open in each direction and, with the wind hampering visibility, driving was treacherous.

He and Sam would have to do some heavy digging tomorrow to track Skelly. His profile was sketchy, with few relatives listed, and those addresses probably not current. Vern Cummings had seemed a more likely suspect with a long history of violent episodes. They'd get Skelly, but it would take time. Ray swallowed a yawn, then gripped the wheel tighter. It was a foul night to be out.

He envied Sam who was probably snuggled up with Carly Weston this very minute.

He was waking up. Thank goodness, Carly thought as she reached her free hand to touch Sam's brow. She saw him shift painfully, then moan low in his throat.

"Sam," she whispered, "are you all right?" She'd been so worried when she'd seen that monster drag him in. His head had flopped onto his chest as the

238

man had dumped him alongside her. She'd been afraid Sam was already dead. But then the man had produced two pairs of handcuffs and bound the two of them together, removed the rope and hooked the second cuffs through theirs and onto the bedpost. With that, she'd realized Sam had to be alive for him to take such precautions.

She shook his arm gently. "Sam, talk to me."

Sam groaned, straightened his head and felt a pain shoot through him at the back of his neck. "Damn," he muttered, opening his eyes and reaching a hand to explore the injury. It was then he realized he was cuffed to Carly. He forgot his pain as his free hand reached to touch her instead. "You're alive. Thank God."

She put her hand over his, wincing as she brought it away from her bruised cheek. "Yes, we're both alive, at least for now."

Frowning, Sam checked her face. "He hurt you."

She could hear the rage in his voice, low and deadly. "Just a slap, really. He grew angry when I didn't recognize him."

"He didn't do anything else to you?" Sam let out a tense breath when she shook her head. "And you have no idea who he is?"

"Not a clue. Do you know him?"

Sam rubbed his neck gingerly. "I didn't even catch a glimpse of him. Some rescuer I am." He swallowed a bitter lump in his throat.

"Don't blame yourself. He's as strong as a bull. He's killed four men with his bare hands. I don't know why he's keeping us alive." She looked down at the handcuffs. "Where do you suppose he got these?"

"Police handcuffs, from the glove box in my car. Tell me what happened after you got home today." He listened carefully while she did.

"I think Luke was right," said Sam. "This guy's either a locksmith or knows how to jimmy them." He linked his cuffed hand with hers. "That was pretty clever, blinding him with the camera flashes. You're one gutsy lady, you know that? A lot of women would have passed out from fright or given up."

"Yeah, well, look where it's gotten me. Sam, what are we going to do?"

"We're going to have to outsmart him." With his free hand, Sam dug into his back pocket and brought out his wallet. "Let's hope he doesn't know much about handcuffs." He withdrew a small leather tool kit, flipped it open, and extracted a slim metal file. It was the same tool that enabled him to open locked doors. Holding up their cuffed hands, he inserted the file into a small hole at the base of the cuffs.

"What are you doing?"

"Most people don't know that there's a second way to open these cuffs without using a key, a bypass to the gears that mesh. It can only work if he didn't double-lock them." He worked the file carefully for several seconds, then withdrew it. "Damn him."

"He double-locked them?"

"Yes." Discouraged, Sam pocketed his tool kit and wallet, his mind searching for another way.

"I heard him talking on the phone before," Carly said. "I hope he doesn't have someone coming to help him with us."

"I think he works alone." The bedroom door swung open, and they both looked up.

Small wonder the man had had little trouble overpowering him, Sam thought looking him over. A big head on a thick neck, massive shoulders, muscular arms, and huge hands on an otherwise slight frame,

240

then a narrow waist and short, stocky legs. His eyes were small and mean-looking. And hanging from his belt loop was a large ring of keys. Sam was certain he'd have remembered meeting this guy.

The man was carrying Carly's jacket and tossed it onto the bed. "I'm going to unlock the cuffs so you can put that on," he told her. "We're going on a little trip, and you'll need it." He glanced at Sam. "Pull anything, and I'll kill you both right now."

Carly could feel the tension in Sam as they both struggled to their feet. "He means it Sam. Don't do anything." She was well aware he was feeling rotten that he'd been taken by surprise and was anxious to turn the tables.

"Yeah, listen to her, Sam." He found the key to the cuffs in his pocket and unlocked the one, but left Sam's on as he watched Carly squirm into her jacket.

"I don't have socks or shoes," she told him.

"Get some on," he ordered. "Move it."

Hurriedly, she got a pair of thick socks from her drawer, sat down to put them on, then reached for her boots and tugged them on.

"Get back over here," he told her. He quickly handcuffed the two of them together, leaving the second pair dangling from the bedpost. Stepping back, he pulled Sam's gun from the waistband of his pants and aimed it at them. "No funny stuff now. We're going to walk, nice and easy, down to your car, Sam. You're going to drive, and she's going to sit beside you. I'll be in the back seat with this gun pointed right at her head. One cute move, and she's history. You got that?"

"You won't get away with this," Sam said quietly. "The station knows where I am. If I don't check in periodically, they'll send a squad car out here." Where the hell was Herb and the surveillance car that should have been here by now after cleaning up that B&E at the jewelry store?

"Don't bullshit a bullshitter, Sammy," the man said, grinning humorlessly. "We all know you've been sleeping here nights. No one's coming looking for you. I've been monitoring you two playing house for two weeks. You don't call in regularly, and they don't check on you." Suddenly, his face turned grim. "Now, get going."

There was just enough slack in the cuffs for Sam to be able to grip Carly's hand in his. He led the way outside, down the slippery stairs toward the Trans Am. He didn't know whom he was more furious with, the madman behind them or himself for putting them in a position where his own gun was being held on him. At the car, he paused, hoping one of the neighbors would glance outside and see them. "What do you want us to do now?" he asked, feigning a cooperation he had no intention of giving.

"Open the passenger door. You crawl in over the console, I get in the back seat, then the woman. Hurry it up." He held the gun low, close to his body, so no one behind could see he had a weapon.

With a last glance at the lighted windows of the front house, Sam scooted over the passenger seat and sat down behind the wheel, holding his right hand in the air, stretched toward Carly and the cuffs that bound them.

The man grabbed Carly's hair and held the gun to her ear. "Now, Sammy boy, you hold the seat back so I can get in back. One false move, and I blow her away."

Grinding his teeth, Sam knew the man had him. He did as asked.

Once seated on the edge of the short back seat, the man motioned Carly inside. When the door closed, he handed the car keys to Sam. "I'm warning you again, don't pull anything. Back out nice and slow, take her out onto Jefferson, then drive toward the freeway heading north."

"Where are we going?" Carly dared ask.

"When I want you to know, I'll tell you."

Sam shoved the key into the ignition and turned on the lights. It was then that he saw that his police radio had been disconnected, the wires yanked out. His flashing light was missing as well. No, the bastard definitely wasn't stupid. Carefully, Sam backed the Trans Am out.

Carly's hand linked atop his had to move with him every time he shifted. He could feel her trembling. At Jefferson, waiting to turn out, he glanced at her and saw she was staring straight ahead. Her bruised cheek was facing him, and he felt the fury mount again.

He'd find a way to get this guy yet. He could take a chance, step on it, and whip out into traffic, causing an accident and hope for the best. But the gun was very close to Carly's head, and Sam knew this killer wouldn't hesitate to get off a shot before they hit. No, he'd have to wait. He'd stay alert and watchful, and he'd find a way.

Then he'd make him pay.

They were on the freeway the next time the man spoke. "Give me your beeper," he said to Sam.

"I think I lost it back at the house."

The man rammed the gun barrel into Sam's neck and smiled when he flinched. "Give it to me."

Sam reached into his pocket and handed it back.

"Get in the right lane," he commanded. He waited until they were on a fairly barren stretch of the highway. "Roll down your window," he told Carly. When she did, he tossed the beeper out.

The man sat back as she rolled the window up, but he kept his gun trained on her head. He removed

243

an apple from his pocket and began to chew on it. He could see in the rear-view mirror that the detective kept sweeping his eyes up to watch him. Let him, he thought.

He had the detective's gun and the keys to the cuffs. The radio was out, as was the flasher and siren. No beeper. Let them worry and wonder, he thought as he swallowed.

Sam drove carefully, gradually increasing his speed. Highway 53 leading north had been salted and wasn't too bad at this stretch just outside the city. But he wondered how far they were going and how well the roads would be maintained up farther. Where in hell was he taking them and why? He could have just as easily killed both of them back at Carly's place. Did he have more than murder on his mind? Ransom maybe, although that hadn't been his style so far. Torturing them, perhaps. Sam gripped the wheel and pressed down on the gas.

Then he felt the gun barrel ram into his sore neck again.

"I told you, no funny stuff. Stay under the speed limit. If you attract a cop car, I'll shoot you both before they stop us. I've already killed four. I've got nothing to lose."

Sam's hand resting on the gear shift felt Carly's fingers squeeze, wordlessly asking him to obey. Sam slowed down. He would try to be patient. He knew these roads going north well. An opportunity would present itself. It had to.

The man finished the apple and dropped the core on the floor. He'd been half-bluffing when he'd guessed that the detective didn't check in with the station once he left for the day. But he wasn't sure about that. He knew that Carly's place and Carly herself had been under surveillance for some weeks, cop cars patrolling at regular intervals. Maybe they would come looking for them both when they got no response at the apartment. No matter. They were well on their way now.

He could have finished them both back there, but he wasn't about to be robbed of his final pleasure. He needed Sam to drive. She'd have been much harder to control if he were the one driving. He'd have had to tie and bind her or knock her out. He hadn't meant to involve the cop, but he'd had no choice when Sammy had barged in like that. It had all worked out for the best though. He'd now have the added pleasure of having the cop watch him torture Carly before killing them both.

He'd take them to the secluded cabin where her father had been staying when he'd died. Deep in the woods—no one would trace them there. He could drag things out, have some fun, make her beg. And him, too.

Then, when he grew bored with that, he'd see that they joined the others in a most painful death before doubling back and picking up Pete. He'd told his brother to be ready and waiting. The cop's car would be faster than his old Volkswagen, and probably Sam's precinct wouldn't start looking for him for a day or so since they were used to his shacking up with Carly. Later, he'd abandon the Trans Am and hot-wire a different one until he and Pete settled somewhere safe.

Bracing his gun hand, the man kept his eyes trained on the two people in the front seat.

Half-an-hour into the drive, Sam saw they were coming to a decision point. Highway 53 would continue bearing to the east, running through the middle of the Thumb area. To the left, Highway 24 would veer more to the west and ultimately end up around Pigeon. Both roads would likely have only one lane open in each direction due to weather. As

245

they came to the fork, he glanced in the rearview mirror.

The man was sitting as he had been all the way, seemingly tireless as he crouched on the edge of the narrow back seat, the gun steady on Carly, his small eyes watchful. Only a strong man in good condition could maintain that position so long without stiffening.

"Which way are we going?" Sam asked.

"Turn onto 24, and watch your speed." The man swept his eyes along the highway. Very little traffic, which was good. The goddamn snow was a hindrance, but also a help. Few would be out tonight, and their tracks would be covered over quickly.

He saw that the next exit was Lapeer and decided that, even with the snowfall, they should be in the Owendale area in another hour. The dashboard clock read seven-thirty. Despite the weather, they should be in the cabin with a fire going by nine at the latest.

When he'd first gone to Owendale to track Will Weston, he'd let himself into the cabin while Will and his buddies had been hunting. It was called a hunting cabin, but it was nicer than the homes he'd lived in after his father had been taken from the family. After his mother had had to work to try to support two young boys. Dumps mostly they'd lived in, rental houses with leaky roofs and, later, dingy apartments with smelly hallways and rats scurrying around at night.

The Weston cabin had a large main room with a big Michigan fieldstone fireplace, a neat kitchen well stocked with canned goods and a freezer, and two big bedrooms. He'd chain them to one bed tonight and take the other for himself. There was a large propane gas tank out back, he remembered, and plenty of firewood. With the way it was coming down, they could hole up there for days without anyone knowing. There was a shed in the yard with an attached garage. He'd hide the cop's car in there.

Then, in the morning, the fun would begin. The man smiled in anticipation.

In the mirror, Sam saw the man's evil grin and felt his jaw clench. The sonofabitch was enjoying this. Or maybe he was thinking of all the things he was going to do to them. Or, more specifically, to Carly. *He's been fantasizing about her for years,* Clio McIntyre had said. Good God, could it be true? Since she hadn't recognized him, where would this slime ball know her from? Not a good time to ask, he decided.

The highway edged around several small lakes, clinging to the shoreline like a slippery snake as the winding road made its way north. The wind rocked the car as the snow whirled in from nearby Lake Huron, intensifying the storm at this point. As his hand gripped the wheel, a thought occurred to Sam. Was the bastard leading them to Will's cabin in Owendale?

He couldn't think of a single reason why, except that it was secluded and would be a difficult location to trace. If that were their destination, he'd better make his move soon. Searching the man's face in the mirror, Sam thought the bastard looked less alert, as if his mind were wandering a bit. If he were to catch him off guard, he'd have to use split-second timing.

There was an area just before Owendale that Sam knew was thickly overgrown. A ravine-like section, sparsely wooded and uninhabited, where the ground sloped down to a lake, a good three-hundred-yard slide from the road to the bottom. He'd watch the man carefully as they neared there, hoping the monotonous weather was mesmerizing him somewhat, causing him to ease his hold on the gun just a fraction. His hand tensed on the wheel as he went over his plan in his mind.

The only sounds Carly could hear were the frantic windshield wipers slapping back and forth and her own anxious breathing. The heater was on, and she was warm enough. Maybe too warm. Yet instead of making her drowsy, as it might have under other circumstances, her skittery nerves had her wide awake.

Her hand on Sam's strong one felt like a lifeline in an unreal world. She swallowed frequently, fighting the nausea as her stomach roiled, although she hadn't eaten in hours. She felt as if she were in the middle of a terrible dream and she had no idea if they would come out of it alive.

The man was leaning forward again, so close she could smell his rank body odor and his foul breath in the cloying intimacy of the car. She shifted to her right more, trying not to attract his attention, but not wanting to get sick in the car. She was certain he'd simply ignore her retching and order them to drive on. She felt Sam's hand turn and squeeze hers reassuringly. It was their only means of communication in this tense, silent ordeal.

Was it his imagination, or was the storm lessening? Sam wondered. The wipers didn't seem to be working as hard as before. He peered anxiously ahead. They were coming toward the wooded area. Another couple of minutes, and they'd be alongside the ravine. It would be then or never. Sam tensed, bracing himself, hoping that if Carly felt the change in him, she'd not let on.

So attuned was she to Sam that Carly felt his hand tighten on the gearshift lever, felt the tension move up his arm. He was planning something, she was certain. Oh, God, please let it work.

They were only a little way from the turnoff to the

248

cabin, the man decided. It was difficult to see with this damn snow everywhere. Though he'd only been there once, he had a good sense of direction. After they passed these woods, the exit to Owendale would be next. Then he'd direct them to the road that . . .

Suddenly, the Trans Am swerved off the highway, taking a sharp right and racing down a slippery embankment. The man in the back seat jolted sideways, then lost his balance and rammed to the floor, the gun flying from his hand. Carly stared out the windshield, her hand clutching Sam's as she let out a sharp cry. Sam gripped the steering wheel, holding on for dear life, trying to keep from hitting a tree.

The car careened downward at breakneck speed, helped along by the wet snow, hurling forward into the ravine. Near the bottom, the land leveled and the Trans Am slowed, then spun around and finally came to rest with its trunk lodged against a tree and the hood pointing up toward the road. An eerie silence settled over the crashed vehicle, with only the wind whipping about outside making a keening sound.

With a puzzled frown, Ray listened to Carly's phone ring and ring with no answer. Was something fishy going on? he wondered. He'd already beeped Sam and waited ten minutes, but Sam hadn't called back. That was odd.

He stretched his long legs toward the fire he'd finished building in his fireplace mere minutes ago and decided to try something else. He dialed the station and asked the dispatcher to plug his call through to the surveillance team patrolling Carly's place. In minutes, they were on the line.

"Herb, Ray Vargas here. You checked on Carly Weston's place lately?"

"We drove by about an hour-an-a-half ago like Sam asked us to,"Herb answered. "We haven't been back because her car was still parked where it's been all day and Sam's Trans Am was parked right by her stairs. We figured they're in for the night and that she's all right if Sam's there. Why, is there a problem?"

Ray was thoughtful a long moment. "No, probably not. I beeped him and he didn't phone back yet, so I got to wondering."

Herb's chuckle came over the wire in a burst of static. "Hey, man, you seen that Weston lady? Some looker. What would you be doing on a cold, snowy night if you were up there with her? Think you'd be answering the phone — or occupying yourself with *other* things?"

Ray gave him the expected laugh. "Yeah, I guess you're right. Still, I'd like you guys to swing by there the first chance you get and let me know if everything looks okay, will you?"

"Sure, sure. We're up on East Gratiot right now. Gonna grab a sandwich, then roll back over that way. Want me to call you after we check it out?"

"Yeah, I'd appreciate that. I'm at home, Herb."

"Gotcha."

Ray hung up just as Donna came in with a tray. Nearly five-ten with long blond hair and a firm body that he knew as intimately as his own, Donna was the only woman currently in his life. Behind her trotted Hamlet, his Great Dane, sniffing the air. He'd phoned Donna from his car and persuaded her to let him pick her up on his way home. This was no night to spend alone. "What've you got there, honey?" he asked as she set the tray down on the coffeetable.

"Just a couple of things I brought along. Brie, imported crackers, pâté. Food for the soul." She sat down beside him, curling her long legs beneath her, and spread liver on a cracker, then slipped it to the waiting dog. "You're spoiled rotten, Hamlet."

She had on the long, peach-colored satin robe that he kept in his closet for her visits. Ray knew that under it she wore nothing, which was exactly what he liked her in best. They would get to that later. "And in the cups?"

"Hot toddies, like my granddaddy taught me to make. Try some."

Ray did, welcoming the hot, smoky liquid trailing down his throat. "Mmm. Bless granddaddy." He leaned back and pulled her closer.

As he caressed Donna's arm, he thought that Herb probably was right. Sam was busy in the bedroom with Carly for, despite his comments to the contrary, Ray could see his partner was crazy about her. Okay, so they're not answering the phone. Ray would still call again in another half-an-hour. Maybe by then, Herb would be in the area. He couldn't really relax until he heard from Sam. Storm or not, partners had to be there for each other.

That decided, Ray touched his mouth to Donna's and was rewarded with her quick, hearty response. Hamlet put his long snout first on Donna's knee, then on Ray's lap, hoping for a second helping. A bit put out when he was totally ignored, he sighed heavily and lay down on the floor to wait.

Sam was the first to move. The dive had thrown him against the door, his left shoulder ramming into the unforgiving panel at first impact. Gingerly, he sat up and felt a quick, sharp pain shoot through, nearly numbing his left arm. But his concern was for Carly as he turned to her.

She was slumped low in her seat, her legs folded

251

oddly, her body held back by the seat belt. His right arm was still braceleted to her left. He reached to touch her and when she moaned, he let out a grateful breath.

"Carly, are you all right?" he asked.

She wiggled to right herself, but could barely do so because the car tilted backward at an odd angle that made it difficult to move. Rubbing her head, she opened her eyes, feeling dazed. "I think so."

"Nothing broken?" Sam stretched his own legs, glad to see they weren't damaged.

"No." She shook her head as if to clear it.

Sam stretched to peer into the back seat. He saw that their captor was slumped in a heap on the floor, his large shoulders squeezed into too small a place. His eyes were closed. Sam couldn't see the gun anywhere. Carefully he reached to press two fingers to the man's throat, searching for a pulse. He found it, faint but steady.

"I've got to find that gun," Sam said. Unlatching his seat belt, he twisted around, half-kneeling, moving the man's feet aside. At last, he found it and shoved it into his pocket. Next, he searched the man's jacket pockets for the handcuff keys. Nothing.

"Damn, where are those keys?" he muttered in frustration, trying to get his hands into the man's pants pocket.

"Please, Sam, let's just get out of here." Carly's voice was strained and quivery as she rid herself of her seat belt.

He supposed she was right. Their choices weren't many. He couldn't remove his own cuffs in order to handcuff the guy. He didn't think it wise to wait out the storm here in the car. They had to get somewhere safe and warm. The night would bring sub-freezing temperatures. "Do you know the way from here to your family's hunting cabin?"

"If we can make it up to the highway, I think I can find it." From where she sat, it seemed an impossible distance up, and everywhere she looked there was snow.

"We'll make it." Sam shoved at his door handle, then pushed at it. He winced as another slice of pain shot through his bruised left shoulder.

"You're hurt. Let me see." Carly was stretching to look at the injury.

"There's nothing we can do about it here. When we get to the cabin." Sam glanced to the back. The man hadn't moved. Using his foot for leverage, he shoved at the door, pushing against the drifted snow, harder this time. It gave some, but it took several more strong nudges before the opening was wide enough for them to crawl out. "We're going to have to do this together because of these damn cuffs," he told her. "You ready?"

"I guess so."

With no small amount of maneuvering, Sam crawled out, immediately sinking into snow nearly to his knees as Carly, poised on his seat with her shackled arm stretched toward him, waited. "Careful," he warned, as he helped her out, then watched her try to get her footing in the deep snow.

Sam gazed up at a dark sky and saw that the storm was letting up a bit. At least the white covering enabled them to see in the darkness more easily. Surprised that the electrical system hadn't shorted out, he decided to leave the car's lights on to give them additional illumination. He reached to pull Carly's collar up around her throat, then his own. Curling his fingers over hers, he forced a smile. "We can do this," he told her in his best reassuring manner.

"I know we can." She held on to him. She had to believe.

253

Sam started up out of the ravine, trudging toward the highway he could see faintly in the distance. It was slow going and difficult walking in knee-high snow, but he concentrated on one step at a time, then waiting for Carly to step into his tracks.

It seemed to take them forever to make progress, but, slowly, they were doing it. Halfway up, he stopped to let them catch their breath and looked back down. The car and its occupant were eerily silent.

"He's alive," Carly said, her breath puffing out. "He'll come after us when he wakes up."

"Let him." They had his gun back, and there'd likely be hunting rifles in the cabin. "Is there a phone?"

"Yes, but the power often goes out during storms up here."

"Still, we'll be inside where it's warm." He held her hand tighter. "Let's go."

But with the next step Sam took, the snow suddenly was much deeper. As he started tumbling forward, he realized that there was no solid ground beneath that particular pile.

Helpless to do anything but follow, bound to him as she was, Carly fell with him.

Head over heels, they plunged back down the incline.

Chapter Fourteen

Ray picked up the phone on the first ring. "Vargas here."

"Yeah, Ray, this is Herb. I think we've got a problem."

Ray shifted the afghan from his long legs and sat up on the couch as he clicked the television off with the remote. He'd been dozing, watching Katherine Hepburn and Spencer Tracy in a golden oldie, and yet he was now instantly alert. Danger always did that to him. "Where are you, Herb?"

"Parked in Carly Weston's drive. Sam's Trans Am's gone. Only one set of tire tracks leaving. Her car's undisturbed, still covered with snow."

Ray was already slipping his feet into his shoes. "What else can you tell me? Did you go upstairs? Can you get in?" Static rattled in his ear. "You, there, Herb?"

"Yeah. Looks like the drive and steps were shoveled a while back, and there are faint footprints leading down, lightly covered with recent snow. Clancy went up. Door's unlocked, electricity's off, and the place is empty. We checked the area and couldn't find anyone around."

Phone tucked under his chin, Ray hurriedly buttoned his shirt. "Any sign of a struggle?"

"Lamp overturned in the living room. Looks like she had a darkroom off the kitchen and someone broke the door in. The floor's all wet, but it's not blood. And there's one other thing that doesn't look good."

Ray stood, tucking the shirt in his pants. "What's that?"

"There's a pair of police-issue handcuffs dangling from the brass footboard in one of the bedrooms."

"Shit." Ray glanced at his watch. Not yet nine. "I'll be right there, Herb." Hanging up, he turned to Donna, who was sitting up and reaching for her robe. "Got to run, honey. Why don't you climb into my bed? I don't know how long I'll be." He was already at the closet, getting his jacket.

Donna heard the tension in his voice that he usually hid so well. "It's Sam, isn't it?"

"Yeah." Ray reached for the doorknob.

She went to him for a long kiss. She was accustomed to Ray having to leave at odd hours, but she'd never really get used to it. "Be careful."

He nodded. "I'll call you as soon as I can."

Donna watched through the window as he quickly got into his car and rushed off. She liked Ray Vargas very much and knew they enjoyed one another immensely. But this was exactly the reason she'd never marry him. She simply couldn't handle the thought of kissing her husband good-bye with the realization that he might never return.

Locking the door, Donna turned and went upstairs.

By the time they dug themselves out of the pile of snow and painstakingly made their way up the ravine to the highway, Carly wasn't sure she could feel

256

her toes. She was certain she couldn't feel her fingers, she was so cold and wet. And still the snow kept coming down, and the wind kept tossing clumps in her face. Her cheeks were damp, whether from the snow or her own tears she didn't know. She was ready to sit down and give up.

But Sam wouldn't let her.

He held her upright by their linked hands and sheer force of will, trudging along, keeping his steps slow and his stride short enough for her to stay abreast of him. He tugged, he supported, he encouraged. His voice was what she listened to above the howl of the wind, certain that he could lead them out of this quagmire of ice and snow.

When they reached the highway, she didn't know whether to cheer or collapse. There were no street lights along this section, and Carly could see no traffic coming in either direction. Small wonder, for who but the truly foolish or the desperate would be out on such a night?

"We need to stay on the shoulder here so a car doesn't hit us," Sam told her, "yet close enough to the road that a driver might pick us out in his headlights." He saw she was exhausted, yet he knew he couldn't carry her all the way. "How far ahead is the turnoff to the cabin?"

Weaving unsteadily, Carly narrowed her eyes and peered ahead. "It's there," she said, pointing with their joined hands, "just after this section of trees ends." She looked at him wearily. "But the cabin's another half-a-mile in off the road."

"I know it sounds far, but we'll make it." He raised a hand to brush snow from her collar, then tightened it around her neck. "Just focus on the cabin, a fire, a warm bed. We'll be there soon."

Nodding, Carly set out, plodding along beside

257

him, knowing they had no choice but to keep moving. To stop now would be to freeze to death. As it was, she was wondering if frostbite would take her fingers and toes.

Looking down, she saw that Sam was wearing ordinary shoes, not boots. She knew he had to be soaked through, yet his steps were firm, his hand on hers steady. She didn't know how he was managing. She'd thought of herself as in pretty good shape until this hike. Concentrating as he'd suggested, she shifted her thoughts to the stone fireplace in the cabin, picturing a roaring fire and the two of them getting warm by it.

A car whizzed by, apparently not seeing them, splashing slush onto them. Sam swore under his breath. Man against the elements was a worse situation than man against man, he thought. With training, quick-wittedness, and luck, you could defeat another man, but the elements were more unpredictable and always had time on their side. To even the odds, you had to keep going. Something else kept him going, Sam realized with no small touch of irony.

His father had accused him of being a quitter, saying that he'd quit college before giving higher education a chance to appeal to him, that he'd quit working for the Kingsley dealership before he'd given himself a chance to enjoy business administration, that he'd basically quit the family and all it represented because they didn't measure up to his expectations. Raymond Kingsley had been right; he had quit. But not for the reasons his father thought.

He'd quit a school he didn't fit into, a job he hated, and a family that didn't understand him or even try to. But he was far from being a quitter when something mattered to him. Police work and his commitment to it mattered to him. Saving his life mattered to him.

And Carly mattered to him.

He glanced at her again with no small measure of admiration. She was holding her own, marching along uncomplainingly, despite being almost frozen, soaked to the skin, and nearly spent. To say nothing of her frazzled nerves after having been held hostage for hours and knowing that that madman was still out there. And to think he'd once thought her soft and pampered.

She was soft, in all the right places, and at all the right times. Soft and loving and caring. Lately, he'd begun to think how lonely his days and nights were when she wasn't with him. Funny how that sort of thing sneaked up on a guy. He'd sort of drifted into caring for her without conscious thought.

But what about after all this was over? One vulnerable night she'd whispered that she loved him, but Sam had no idea whether her trust in him had to do with the man stalking her or her feelings for him. Did he even want her to love him, with all that love involved? Something to think about. But right now, he had to concentrate on getting them to the cabin.

Finally, they reached the road leading to the Weston place. Sam steadied Carly as they paused to rest a moment. "Not far now," he told her. She was beginning to worry him, her steps becoming more and more sluggish, her eyes a little unfocused. "You all right?"

Carly nodded. "Let's just get there."

They started out. Only one car had come along during their hike roadside. It had to be well past ten by now, Sam estimated. The private drive wound and twisted through the trees, wide enough to allow only one car at a time to pass. The snow was deeper

259

here than on the highway, the drifts higher. From this distance, he couldn't even make out the outline of the cabin. He hoped Carly was right, that her hazy mind hadn't confused the road with another.

When at last Sam caught sight of the cabin, he felt like cheering even though it was still far off. As he turned to point it out to Carly, he felt her slip and nearly fall. She'd about had it, he decided. Sliding his left hand around her waist, he steadied her. "I'm going to pick you up, but the only way I can carry you is over my shoulder because of these cuffs. Okay?"

"You don't have to. I can make it." She spoke slowly, as if each word took even more out of her.

He wasn't in the mood to debate. Bracing his feet, he hoisted her up somewhat awkwardly because of the handcuffs. Ordinarily, she was quite light, but with the heavy, soaked clothing, it was all he could do to keep upright himself and keep moving. His left shoulder hurt like hell, but he ignored it. A man who worked out frequently in the police gym, Sam had reason to be grateful he had as he slowly inched his way toward the outline of the cabin ahead.

As they neared, he saw huge icicles formed around the perimeter of the overhang. By the time he reached the porch, he almost dropped Carly as he eased her to her feet. She slipped from his grasp, her feet unable to hold her weight, probably numb with cold. Quickly, he grabbed her and held her to him for a moment. "Is there a key around outside somewhere?"

"Not that I know of. We'll have to break in." Carly clutched his jacket with frozen fingers.

"If you can manage to lean against the wall here, I'll get my tool kit out and pick the lock."

She did her best, slumping against the wooden

260

wall. A warm bed was just minutes away. Carly couldn't ever remember being so cold and tired.

Sam worked quickly and had them inside the door in minutes. Groping along the wall, he found the light switch and hit it. Nothing. "You were right. No power. Where would I find candles and matches?"

"Kitchen drawers, I think. And there's a kerosene lamp on the fireplace ledge."

He sent her an apologetic look. "You have to come with me, I'm afraid. These damn cuffs."

"I know. It's all right." She could scarcely feel her feet, but she shuffled after him as he found matches and two candles, lit them both and led her over to the fireplace where he lit the lamp.

Sam was grateful to find wood and kindling already stacked in the grate, and a generous supply in a copper container. "Sit here on the ledge while I light the fire. Then we'll get these wet things off."

Carly followed orders, too weary to protest or make decisions herself right now. In minutes, he had a wonderful blaze going, and she angled closer, reaching out to the most welcome heat. "I feel frozen all the way through." She looked at him in the light from the fire. "Sam, you've got to get out of those shoes."

Sam wiped his hands on his damp pant legs and slipped his shoes off, then turned to help her out of her boots. Next he tugged off her slacks and socks, then his own, laying them on the hearth to dry. He looked with annoyance at their shackled hands. "We can't take our coats off over these. Let's go into the kitchen and see if we can find something to break them with."

But a search of every drawer and cupboard yielded nothing strong enough to break the steel cuffs. Sam glanced out the kitchen window, frowning. It was

261

still snowing, lightly now but nevertheless coming down. He could see the faint outline of an outbuilding in the backyard. "Is that a garage?"

"Yes, and a shed with tools in it. But Sam, please, could we rest before we go out there. I don't know how much longer I can stand up."

If he weren't cuffed to her, he would explore more tonight, get oriented. The snow had drifted high against the garage and he'd have to plow through. But he couldn't risk Carly coming totally unglued on him. He had no way of knowing if and when the man slumped in the back seat of his car might climb out and set out after them. When he did, perhaps he'd surmise that they'd flagged down a passing motorist and were miles from here by now. If luck were with them, they'd be safe here for a little while and they could use that time to rest.

"Let me prop a chair under the knob or put something heavy by each door so if someone does come while we're asleep, we'll hear." Moving slowly to accommodate Carly, he secured each door and checked the windows. "There's a propane tank out back, right?" Sam knew they didn't have natural gas in this area so far back off the main roads.

"Yes."

He could see she was too whipped to go out tonight. "I'll turn it on in the morning. We can sleep by the fire tonight."

He stopped to check the phone, but it was out, too. "Where did Will keep his hunting rifles?" Sam had his revolver, but he'd feel more comfortable with additional weapons.

Carly released a listless sigh. "We're out of luck there. After Dad died, Mom and Mabel came up here, gathered all the guns and sold them. Mom hates guns."

262

Terrific. Tomorrow, he'd take a better look. Perhaps they'd overlooked one. "Let's find some towels and dry off."

It took them a while, but finally, they had towel-dried one another and fixed a makeshift bed in front of the fireplace on the thick rug. Sam spread a heavy quilt down first, added two large pillows and placed several blankets on top for cover. Nothing had ever looked so inviting, Carly thought.

"Let's strip off everything we can that's wet," Sam suggested, lowering himself to their bed and urging her down with him. He watched her struggle one-handed out of her underwear, as he did the same. Leaning over, he placed their wet things on the brick ledge to dry. They were down to their sweaters and damp jackets which they couldn't remove over their cuffed hands. Holding the edge of the covers back, he helped Carly slip beneath, then joined her.

Before laying down his head, Sam thrust his gun under his pillow. The movement caused him to groan aloud.

Carly rose up. "Your shoulder. Let me see."

"It'll be fine."

"Stop being the macho cop and *let me see it*."

Surprised at how strong her voice was despite her fatigue, he pulled up his sweater, checking the injury himself in the firelight. The skin around the shoulder joint was dark. "It's bruised, that's all."

Gingerly, Carly touched around the area. "It doesn't feel dislocated or broken, does it?" She doubted he could have carried her if his shoulder were badly injured.

Sam adjusted his sweater and eased her closer. "I'll live." He raised their braceleted hands above their heads to get the jackets out of the way, then stretched his free arm around Carly as she lay facing

263

him. Her hair, nearly dry, was fanned out on her pillow, but her cheeks looked red and chapped. Her eyes were already closed. "Are you feeling better?" he asked.

She snuggled closer, her bare legs twining with his. "Now I am."

Sam drew in a ragged breath. They were as safe as he could make them for now. Forcing himself to relax, he closed his eyes.

"You want me to call for a fingerprint crew?" Herb asked Ray as the detective stood looking around Carly's kitchen, a large flashlight in his hand. "It's kind of late, but we could probably get someone."

Ray turned and moved past the uniformed officer. "No, I don't think we need them." He had a gut feeling he knew the man's name. Ric Skelly. He hoped the hell he hadn't learned it too late to help Sam. He glanced up at Herb's big, redheaded partner standing by the door. "Clancy, I want you two to check the woods behind this place and see if you can find any tracks, a car hidden away, anything. I don't think the bastard took a bus here. Check the street, too. Knock on doors if you have to, and see if the neighbors can spot an unfamiliar car."

Herb strolled into the living room. "It's after ten. Maybe we—"

Ray whirled about, his face hardened by strain. "I don't give a damn. Wake 'em if you have to. Somebody might have seen them leaving or something suspicious."

"Right." Herb shot his partner a look. Everyone knew that Detective Vargas rarely raised his voice or lost his temper. Everyone in the department also

264

knew how close he and Sam were. "We'll find them, Ray," he said.

"Yeah." Ray fingered his mustache anxiously. "By the looks of the footprints on the steps and the diminishing snowfall, I'd guess they've been gone a couple of hours. But we don't know where or even which direction." He reached for the phone. "I'm putting an APB on the Trans Am. You guys get going."

After he'd made his call, Ray checked out the small apartment and could come up with nothing of any importance that the bastard had left behind. It looked as if someone, probably Carly, had hidden in her darkroom and Skelly had broken the door in to get at her. Had that been when Sam had arrived, surprising him? Who'd been handcuffed to the brass bed?

It was a full twenty minutes later that Herb returned, stomping snow from his boots. "Got something here, Ray. There's an old Volkswagen parked in a cluster of trees behind the carriage house. Driver must've come in along this almost hidden path into the woods. The closest neighbor says she remembers that it's been there since mid-afternoon, around two or three."

Ray swallowed hard. Had the strangler hidden awhile or been playing with Carly all this time? They'd determined that he'd picked the backdoor lock and gotten in through there. Ray shuddered to think what Sam would do to the man if he'd touched Carly in any way. "Did you get the license number?"

"Right here." Herb held out a slip of paper.

Glancing at it, Ray nodded. "Call from your cruiser, and run a check on it. Then let's secure this place. Nothing more we can do here tonight."

"Right away."

Turning aside as Herb left, Ray ran a shaky hand across his face. He'd seldom been so scared. Sam was like a brother to him, and he was out there somewhere with a maniac who had strangled four men with his bare hands. And he had Carly Weston, too. Choking down his impotent rage, Ray walked outside.

Sam slept for a while, then awoke suddenly. He opened his eyes and saw that neither of them had moved. Exhaustion could do that to you.

Lifting his head, he listened intently, but could hear nothing but the wind, which appeared to have died down. Where was that sonofabitch? Sam hoped he'd broken both legs in the crash and was stuck in the back seat of his Trans Am until morning. Maybe by then he could get to a phone and call the state police to get him out. But the bastard was so damn strong that he'd probably be able to walk with two shattered kneecaps.

Had the killer been leading them here? He probably knew the place since he'd strangled Carly's father not far from here. But why would he want to bring them to this cabin? Maybe he'd been headed elsewhere and was even now making his way there. At first daylight, he'd find a way to get the cuffs off, Sam decided, leave Carly his gun, and get out to the highway to flag down help.

Checking his watch, he saw it was three o'clock. That loneliest of nighttime hours. He gazed at the fire and wished he could get up without disturbing Carly to add another couple of logs. But she was sleeping so soundly that he hated to waken her just yet.

Her cheeks were still red, and the bruise on one from when that sonofabitch had struck her looked tender. Her face was without makeup. Studying her in the firelight, he saw a few freckles sprinkled across the bridge of her nose that he hadn't noticed before. They made her look young and vulnerable. Enormously appealing. Sexy.

He knew he should let her rest. But he'd been so damn scared on the drive to her place and later, seeing the gun aimed at her head. He had to touch her, to feel her warmth. He leaned closer to press his lips to hers lightly, experimentally, gently. He felt more than heard a sound come from her, the soft mewing sounds she often made when she was getting aroused. And he felt his body's swift reaction.

They were naked from the waist down, their legs tangled together. It would take a stronger man than he, Sam thought, to not react to Carly Weston naked and curled up close to him. Perhaps it was the aftermath of danger that wasn't yet over that heightened his need, the need to reassure both of them that they were alive. Whatever the cause, it was no longer sleep he craved.

He covered her mouth more possessively this time and felt her lips respond, then open to allow his tongue entry. Still half-asleep, Carly shifted closer. She wound her free arm around him, grunting in frustration when their linked wrists sheathed in their damp jackets inhibited her movements.

Not for the first time, Carly came awake in a rush, stunned at how swiftly Sam could take her from dreamy to demanding. Needs tangled with nerves, and she was suddenly reaching for him as she opened her eyes and looked into his.

He gave her a lazy smile as he took her free hand down to close around him and heard her breathless sigh. His hand left hers and slipped up inside her sweater. His fingers found her breasts warm and waiting for his touch. All the while, he kept his eyes locked with hers, saw hers darken with passion.

Carly tried to find the breath to speak his name, but found herself without a voice. Instead, she lifted her arms to urge him closer. She felt the power and the need, the strength that was so much a part of him, as he rose above then lowered into her. She took him inside and felt him spread his hands palm to palm with hers. His breath warm on her cheek, she watched him lead the climb.

Carly marveled at how quickly, how fiercely, she peaked—she who had more often than not been an also-ran. She shuddered her release and felt Sam tense, then give in to a satisfied moan. Utterly spent, she let her hands relax on the quilt beneath them.

Some time later, after Sam had dragged her with him while he stoked the fire, Carly lay half-sprawled over him, her cheek against his chest. She was very much aware that their nightmare wasn't over. But for just a few more hours, maybe she could pretend that they were out of harm's way.

Lazily, she ran the fingers of her free hand over his chest. "Do you ever pray, Sam?" she asked.

"No," Sam answered. "I cut deals with the Man Upstairs. Or try to."

"Maybe it's time to give that a try."

"I'm not sure He's listening. I'm not exactly over-burdened with redeeming qualities."

"I think you are."

He was silent several minutes. "We're good together, aren't we, Carly?"

What had brought that to mind? Carly wondered

as she angled back to look into Sam's dark eyes. The first time she'd seen him, she'd thought he looked dangerous with a stubborn slant to his strong chin. Now, with a day and night's growth of beard, he looked even more so. And he was wandering into dangerous conversational territory, one they'd so far avoided.

"Yes, we are." She would have to walk carefully in this possible minefield. "What made you think of that?"

He shrugged, his arm tightening around her. "Being marooned in this remote cabin in the middle of a snowstorm, maybe. If it weren't for that madman, it might be exactly what I'd wish for. You, here with me, with no one else in the world knowing where we are. All the time in the world to be together, in bed and out. One of my fantasies, making love with you day and night till neither of us can move."

"Oh, shit!" Carly squirmed into a sitting position.

Sam frowned. "What's wrong?"

"It just occurred to me that I didn't take a birth control pill last night, and I don't have any with me. And we just . . ." She propped an elbow on her knee and leaned her head in her hand. "Oh, damn, now we've done it."

Sam sat up slowly. "Could it happen that fast?"

She sent him an incredulous look. "Come on, Sam. You know it can."

A baby. Jesus. He remembered how Carly had looked the night she'd held Luke and Stephanie's baby. He'd never really considered having children, because he'd not considered marrying since his youthful fling with Marcy. He studied their linked hands. "Abortions are legal, you know," he said quietly, wondering why the suggestion bothered him. "I mean, if we were faced with the worst scenario."

269

Carly sank back into the pillow, feeling suddenly depressed. "Yes, I know they are."

She lay quietly a long while. Beside her, Sam wished she'd never remembered not taking the damn pill, wished they could go back to the warm feelings they'd been sharing after the loving. He wished he knew what to say to ease the tension, to make things right. "Or. . . . or you could keep the baby." He felt her head turn toward him, and he looked at her. "I mean, I'd help you, of course. Would that be so terrible?" Again, he thought of little Max Varner. A son. A brand new thought.

"Yes, Sam, it would be terrible. I'm not crazy about raising a child without two parents."

"Well, maybe you wouldn't have to."

She narrowed her gaze. "Are you saying you'd do the right thing, Sam? Marry me to give the baby a name?" She turned away. "No, thanks. A marriage for the sake of propriety has never been one of my fantasies."

His expression turned cloudy. "You're too good for me, is that it? On a much higher social scale. The rich heiress and the lowly cop."

Carly ran a hand through her hair. "Now, that's truly ridiculous. I don't give a damn about social scale or money, and you know it. It's just that I think you're way ahead of me on this. Just because we're good in bed doesn't mean that we could make a marriage work." She swallowed around a sudden quivery lump in her throat. *Tell me I'm wrong. Make me believe it.*

"Oh, so you used me, like some kind of sex machine, to satisfy your cravings. I'm only a fling to you, someone to keep you distracted during the long winter nights."

Carly almost laughed out loud. So he wanted to

lighten the conversation. Perhaps it was best. Her lips twitched as she looked at him. "A sex machine? I used you? Undoubtedly, I seduced you against your will, too, is that it?"

"As I recall, I think you did." Sam yanked the covers off and leaned down to her. "No one seduced anyone, Carly. We made love that first night like two people wild for each other. Every time I'm with you, it's like that. When I'm not with you, I'm thinking about what we're going to do when I am with you. And frankly, it scares the hell out of me."

She sighed shakily. "That makes two of us." She touched his face, trailing her fingers along his scratchy jaw. "You excite me like no other man ever has. But I know you don't trust women, especially monied women. And my past choices have shown me that I need to think long and hard about a man before I seriously discuss the M word." She was concerned and perhaps even a little frightened about marriage, but she would chance it because she loved him. She needed to hear those words from him, though. Needed badly to hear them.

Sam saw something in her eyes, something she wasn't letting him in on. Slowly, he brushed back her hair from her face. Like Carly herself, it resisted taming. "I do care about you."

Carly released a trembling breath. He cared about her. But that wasn't what she wanted, she realized with a frightening clarity. She wanted love from Sam English, the forever scene, the whole enchilada. "I care about you, too," she said, her voice soft. "Maybe it's the timing. I'm not sure I can deal with my feelings right now, plus that maniac out there wanting to kill me." She forced a smile. "But you have shaken up some of my lifelong convictions."

"Such as?"

"Such as opposites attract, but aren't compatible living together. Such as you have a better chance if you both grew up with the same experiences."

"We did. I just walked away from all that."

"Right, but —"

"We were raised about the same and, though we may be opposites, we still seem to have lived together the last couple of weeks quite compatibly under enormous pressure, wouldn't you say?"

"We seemed to."

"Maybe you still care a great deal more for Brett or Pierce than you're willing to admit."

Carly shook her head adamantly. "Brett's a good friend, but I never loved him as more than that. And Pierce, well, I could never love a man who lied, who used me. I feel a woman should believe in the man she loves, in what he is, what he does."

Sam couldn't resist asking. "How do you feel about what I do?"

She looked down at her hand resting on his heart. "I admire the work you do, and I know you're very good at it. The dangerous aspects of your job are scary, but I don't think you'd be happy doing anything else. Why'd you ask?"

"Because I admire what you do, too. I think you're very talented, that you could go far in photography. That you could work for a magazine, or free lance for several, or put together a book. Or open a studio. Whatever you like. As long as you believe in yourself."

"Well, well. The detective isn't a chauvinist then."

"Never have been, maybe because my father's a flaming chauvinist." Sam gathered her to him more comfortably. "You probably think I haven't married because of my experience with Marcy, but that's not all of it. See, I always thought of getting married as

272

being swallowed up whole. I don't know where my mother begins and my father ends. They parrot each other's thoughts until I used to feel like screaming." He angled his head to look at her. "I like being with you *because* we're different. I'd be bored to tears with someone who'd mimic my every thought. I don't think I ever have to worry about that with you."

She smiled. "I think you're right on that score."

A month ago, Sam couldn't have imagined himself having this conversation with anyone. With Carly, it felt right. His eyes grew serious. "I've often thought that when I was born, some important ingredient was left out, some chromosome or something. I don't think I'm capable of loving a woman the way she wants to be loved."

Nerves jumping, she held his gaze. "I suppose that depends a whole lot on the woman."

"You think a person can learn to love?"

"Yes, I do." Because she was afraid he'd see too much in her eyes, she glanced over her shoulder toward the window. Outside, it was still dark and eerily quiet. She shuddered to think what the morning would bring.

She was getting anxious again, Sam thought, worrying about that creep somewhere out there. He was, too, but there was no point in doing something foolish, charging out there in the middle of the night. There'd be time enough at first light to go for help.

He drew her closer, trapping her lower body with his two legs. "I know what you're thinking, but there isn't anything we can do about him right now. Why don't you kiss me?"

It was so easy to let him divert her attention, Carly thought, to allow him to draw a response from her body that was already craving more of him. Too

273

often lately, she'd come face to face with her own mortality, most recently just hours ago when a gun had been held to her head. No one knew how long anyone had. It would be foolish not to reach out for small snatches of happiness.

But long habit had a practical thought intruding. "I don't know, Sam. If only I'd taken the pill . . ."

Sam's arm tightened around her. "If it's going to happen, it probably already has."

He could probably talk the Eskimos into purchasing large quantities of ice cubes, Carly decided. Slowly, she inched closer, reaching for his kiss.

It was then that they heard a crash from the back of the house that shook the very foundation of the cabin.

Chapter Fifteen

"What the hell!" Sam scrambled to his feet, tugging Carly upright with him. The crash reverberated through the small cabin, then in moments, there was only silence.

"Oh, God," Carly whispered, "he's found us." She should have known their reprieve would be short-lived.

Sam pulled on his pants in record time, considering he could have full use of only one hand, while Carly struggled into her corduroy slacks. "Don't say anything more until we check it out," he whispered, grabbing his gun from under the pillow. Holding the weapon in his left hand, he released the catch and moved slowly toward the kitchen.

There wasn't a sound to be heard. Sam inched them to the back door, removed the chair propped against it, and peered out the small window into the moonlit night. From behind him, Carly stretched to see over his shoulder, her heart pounding. Outside, the snow was heaped in uneven piles covering a maze of boards and lumber and chunks of asbestos roofing. Jagged edges of bracing beams thrust upward into the night sky. A shower of snow lingered in the air, settling gently on the mess.

"The porch roof fell in," Carly commented.

"Probably from the weight of the heavy snowfall."

"It looks that way." Sam's cautious nature had him questioning the timing. "But why now? Up here, they must have plenty of storms every winter."

She was too relieved at not finding the strangler waiting for them with an axe to question much else. "The cabin's easily twenty years old. Maybe the support beams have weakened through the years. Do you think someone caused it to break?"

"Probably not." Straining his eyes, he could see no footprints around the perimeter, nor could he see a sign of an intruder trapped under the debris. If only they weren't handcuffed together, he'd feel better about going out there and checking. He knew he couldn't just lie down again without making certain. Yet he hated taking her out and exposing her to possible danger. Odds were in their favor since he'd taken the only gun. He *had* to make sure the man wasn't out there, he finally decided. "Do you feel up to going outside with me? I want to take a look around."

She'd rather have endured a swift kick, but Carly knew neither of them could relax until they checked the yard. "I'm fine."

In minutes, they were dressed and ready to go. Sam had to push hard on the back door to shove it past the fallen timber made heavier by the drifted snow. Still cautious, he drew his gun as they stepped outside.

The night sky was clear, the snow no longer falling, and the wind was reduced to mere swirls rearranging the accumulation. Gripping Carly's hand, Sam urged her along behind the protection of his body. They were getting thoroughly soaked again walking through nearly knee-high snow, even maneuvering around the higher banks, but there was no preventing it. Carefully, they trailed around the

276

cabin all the way to the front porch and found no trace of footsteps of uninvited guests. Their own prints from last night were totally covered on the front path.

"I don't see anything suspicious, do you?" Carly asked, praying he didn't either.

"No." He turned them around, pocketing his weapon. "While we're out here and already wet, let's see if we can get into the shed and find something to break these cuffs with."

Carly shivered involuntarily, casting a wary look behind her. When would she be able to stop glancing over her shoulder? "And maybe you could turn on the propane tank so we could have some heat inside."

Agreeing, Sam retraced his steps. At the shed, he had to use his bare hands to clear the snow from the door. When he saw a large lock dangling from the bracket, he swore inventively.

"Oh, no. Now what?"

"I hate to waste a bullet, but I see no other way. I don't want to take the time to go back inside to search for a key." Shielding her, he took aim and shot. The lock shattered, and parts of the door splintered. Sam hoped the killer wasn't wandering around close enough to hear the shot. Of course, the caving in of the porch roof could have been heard all the way to the road. He yanked open the door and went inside.

"Damn, but I wish the electricity were working." By feel, he found a couple of tools hanging on the wall behind a wooden workbench.

Carly shoved the door open wider so that the moon's light could spill inside. "Is that better?"

"A little." The handsaw wouldn't work, he knew. It was small and probably rusty. No hammer in sight. He found a vise, a wrench, a couple of screwdrivers, and a large rock. "Why would Will have kept a rock in here?" he wondered aloud.

"Maybe to prop open the door while he was doing something."

That was logical. Sam looked around in the dim light and could see nothing else he could use, so he picked up the rock. He gathered up the tools he'd set aside, grabbed a shovel leaning against the side wall, and left the small shed.

Sam's gaze swept along the back of the cabin and spotted the propane tank, covered with snow. He dumped the tools at the door and moved to the tank, using the shovel to bat snow away from its base. It was slow going with Carly of necessity close beside him, her arm dragged along with each of his movements. Finally, he uncovered the valve. He turned it on with chilled fingers and straightened. "That should do it."

Inside, Sam turned on the corresponding valve, then turned up the thermostat.

With immense relief, Carly heard the furnace go on. "Thank goodness Dad was good at maintaining this place. I was afraid we might be out of propane." She glanced around the large front room, remembering. "He sure loved it up here."

Sam slipped off his soaked shoes. "Let's go into the kitchen and see if we can break these cuffs."

Sam frowned in concentration as he attached the vise to the solid kitchen table. Next he braced the chainlink section that held the two cuffs joined together onto the smooth lip. Standing awkwardly, her arm at an odd angle, she tried to stay out of his way.

"I'm going to have to do this with my left hand, so I'll need your help." He positioned the largest of the screwdrivers so that the business end rested on a portion of the chain. "Can you hold this here very steady?"

278

"I'll try."

"You have to grasp it by the stem so I can hit it at the top." He waited until he felt she had a firm grip, then hefted the rock and brought it down on the top of the handle. The screwdriver flew out of Carly's hand.

"I'm sorry."

"It's okay." He retrieved and repositioned. It took another half-a-dozen tries before the metal links finally broke apart. Both of them sighed with relief and tenderly touched their sore wrists. "I wish we could take the bracelets off as well, but at least we're not glued together any longer." Feeling relieved, he reached to touch her face. "Of course, under other circumstances, I might enjoy being handcuffed to you."

She smiled at what was probably a compliment as she slipped off her jacket. "Is that right? Into the kinky stuff, are you?"

"That's not kinky. It's just making sure you're close by when I need you."

Need you. The trouble was that he didn't need her, Carly thought. Strong, indepcndent, self-reliant, Sam English didn't need his family or his family's money. And he certainly didn't need her. Carly turned aside from a sudden rush of sadness. "I don't know about you, but I'm heading for the bathroom."

"It shouldn't be too long before we have hot water," Sam said, removing the vise from the table. "I'll check the hot water heater."

"There're probably some clothes in the bedroom closets. Some of Dad's things might fit you."

"I'll take a look." Sam rummaged around in the kitchen drawers as she left the room. The candles had burned down to mere nubs, but he found replacements. And on the high shelf of a cupboard, he discovered a flashlight that worked.

Back in the main room, he added more logs onto the fire, even though he could feel the heat finally flowing from the vents. Then he went to the largest bedroom, flashlight in hand.

In the bathroom, Carly washed up in water still quite cold. Holding up the chunky candle she'd brought in with her, she checked her mirror image and nearly groaned aloud. Her face was strained, her eyes tired-looking, her cheeks red and wind-burned—the left one discolored from the killer's hard slap. Her hair was in wild disarray.

She felt like crying.

Sitting down on the covered seat, she almost gave in to tears. Delayed reaction to being held hostage with a gun rammed to the back of her neck, she supposed. Who wouldn't look like hell and feel like weeping? How could Sam have wanted to make love with her when she was such a frightful sight?

Perhaps she was still disturbed by the mixed signals she was receiving from Sam. All that pillow talk earlier about a baby and marriage and caring was just that—late night ramblings, a lover made mellow by the afterglow of sex. She didn't believe he felt any differently about serious relationships and involvements than he did the day he'd walked into her life.

The way she was feeling, this let-down, was all her own fault, Carly chided herself with painful honesty. She'd told him she wasn't going to fall for him and warned herself over and over not to fall in love with him. Then she'd ignored all that sage advice and done it anyway.

Sighing, she rose to open the medicine chest. A comb and brush, thank goodness. She may have to wait for a while to bathe, but at least she could neaten up a bit. Pulling the comb through the tangles, she grimaced.

Here she was miles from home without even her purse; there was a maniac on the loose probably searching for her; her left wrist was raw and aching; she badly needed a bath as well as clean clothes; and her stomach was growling noisily. And if that weren't enough, she was in love with a man who just a short time ago had told her that he liked being with her because she was different, yet suggested abortion in case she were pregnant, and then casually confided that he didn't think he was capable of loving. Shit!

Tossing down the comb, Carly picked up the candle and left the bathroom.

"I'm in the bedroom, Carly," Sam called out. "Come look at these." He'd found a pair of her father's heavy pants that he could substitute for his sodden jeans and some thick socks. Not great, but beggars couldn't be choosers, and at least he'd be clean and dry.

He looked up as she walked into the room, on her face an odd expression. "Is something wrong?"

Hell, no, everything was peachy. "The water's not hot yet," she answered evasively. "Good, you found some clothes."

Something was bothering her. Not that he could blame her. Maybe it was all just now registering, the impact of her ordeal. "I couldn't find any women's clothes anywhere."

"I didn't think so. My mother rarely comes up here." She turned to her father's closet. "I'll put on one of Dad's shirts after my shower. I'm anxious to get out of this turtleneck."

Sam came up behind her. "I could help take it off."

She wasn't in the mood, but she didn't want to anger him. They'd managed to come through a lot without a temper flare up, and she wanted to keep it that way. So she turned and put on a smile. "Nice thought, but I'm really hungry. Why don't we see if we can heat something in the fireplace?"

Her smile had an edge to it, Sam noticed. He'd let it go for now. Probably stress. "Good idea."

By the time they had heated a can of soup and ate it with some stale crackers, the water was warm enough for showers. Carly took hers first, then dressed while Sam cleaned up. Wearing one of her father's very large plaid shirts that trailed down to her knees, she spread her own clothes and Sam's jeans on the hearth to dry again.

She checked his watch and saw that it was nearly six. They'd had a mere four hours rest, but she wasn't sleepy. Tired perhaps, but not sleepy. Too keyed up, she supposed as she gathered up the bedding they'd spread on the floor. Restlessly, she wandered the cabin as she heard Sam turn off the shower. She peered through all the windows and saw the sky turning pale, the accumulated snow making it appear lighter than it should be at this early hour.

Then she curled up in a large chair facing the fire to wait for Sam to finish, her dismal thoughts racing around like mice in a maze.

Ray Vargas poured himself another cup of coffee from the pot on the corner table of the squad room, took a sip and made a face. Not quite dawn, and he was on perhaps his fifth cup of coffee, having spent most of the night at his desk making calls in between his nervous pacing.

And still no word of where Sam was.

He frowned at the false gaiety of the artificial Christmas tree. Christmas in two days. Where had the month gone? The holiday frenzy, something he

282

wasn't much into in the best of years, he faced now with a chilling fear.

Every good cop knew that the longer a missing person was gone, the less chance there was of finding them alive.

Slugging down another swallow, he returned to his desk to stare at the name he'd scrawled on his note pad. Ric Skelly, the DMV had finally revealed to them. Yeah, he was the one, all right. A day late and a dollar short. Where would that bastard have taken Sam and Carly? What was an ex-con's connection to the Weston family and the other victims? Idly, he ran through possibilities.

One scenario: Ric Skelly had been defended by Homer Gentry and been convicted. Prosecutor Will Weston had nailed him. Judge Nathan Rogers had sentenced him. That much was logical and probable and enough to make an unstable man look for serious revenge once he's out of prison. The connection to Doug Anderson was more iffy. Someone he'd met in prison, a buddy who'd let him down, perhaps in a fight? Or maybe someone from Skelly's earlier past.

On that thought, Ray picked up the phone and punched in Juvenile. Maybe Skelly and Anderson had had a record that went back to their teens together. It was worth a shot. He had to try something rather than sit here worrying.

It took Ray only a few minutes to explain what he wanted to the officer in Juvenile. He was told his request would take a while. Hanging up, he leaned back, picking up his thoughts where he'd left off.

The big question: Why was Skelly after Carly Weston? The psychic had said something about the killer having fantasized about her for years, that she was the one he really wanted. But Ray couldn't picture a woman like Carly even knowing a man such as Ric Skelly.

Leaning forward, Ray opened the file and stared at the prison photo of the strangler. Dark shaggy hair, average features, a thick neck. His eyes were guarded, giving very little away. A man most people wouldn't notice in a crowd. The only man Skelly had killed out of the Detroit area was Weston, and that had been up in the Thumb area around Pigeon. He'd probably had opportunities to kill the prosecutor in and around his home or office. Why had he followed him all that way to that remote location?

Again, Ray picked up the phone and dialed the State Police. A really long shot. Maybe Skelly was heading back up that way. He'd alert the State Police to be on the lookout for Sam's Trans Am up around that area. The snow would be deeper up there, and cars harder to spot, but it was worth a try.

As he was hanging up from that call, the clerk from the back room came walking toward him. "Did the phone company come through?" Ray asked.

The young man nodded. "Here's a list of all the numbers that were dialed from Carly Weston's apartment yesterday and the times the calls were made."

"Terrific. Thanks." Ray skimmed the short list carefully. Only one call after three in the afternoon. Lapeer, Michigan. Not quite up in the Thumb, but about an hour's drive north of Detroit. He dialed the number.

Twenty minutes later, Ray hung up, his expression thoughtful. The number he'd reached was a state-run institution in Lapeer for severely disabled or mentally retarded children. Ray didn't think that Carly had phoned there, so, on a hunch, he'd asked if any resident by the name of Skelly lived or worked there.

Jackpot. Peter Skelly had resided in the Lapeer home for years, the sleepy-voiced administrator had told him. His only known relative was a brother,

Richard Skelly, whose address was unknown. But Ric sent packages to Pete and called him frequently. The puzzle pieces were beginning to fall into place.

Ray remembered Judge Rogers's widow mentioning one of the cases involving children that had worried the judge. His assistant, Clark Abbott, was supposed to have gotten back with them about that case and another. Why the hell hadn't he? If he'd called earlier, they might have had Skelly's name yesterday or the day before and Sam would be sitting in the chair opposite him right this minute.

Angrily, Ray called the courthouse and left word to have Clark Abbott call him the minute he got in. Like pulling teeth, he thought, getting some of these people to get on the stick. He was about to get another cup of coffee when his phone rang again.

The desk sergeant was apologetic. "Ray, I've got a woman on the line who's quite upset. She wants to talk with Sam. Her daughter's missing. Name of Weston."

Ray closed his eyes, thinking he didn't need this right now. "Put her through, Sarge."

"Detective Vargas, this is Isabel Weston. I'm terribly sorry to bother you, but I can't get a hold of Carly and now they tell me that they don't know when Detective English will be in. Might you know where they are?"

She didn't sound hysterical, Ray realized with a grateful sigh. But then, from what he'd seen of Isabel Weston, she was too classy a lady to scream into phones. However, he didn't know just how fragile she was beneath that dignified veneer. She'd lost her husband weeks ago, and now her only child was missing. He decided to buy a little time, to tell her just enough of the truth to satisfy her without alarming her. "Actually, I don't know exactly where they are," Ray answered honestly.

"I see. I received a call from one of the men who lives in the front house by Carly's apartment. He said there'd been policemen at her place last night for some time. Detective, I. . . . I need to know what's going on."

"At this point, the most I can tell you is that apparently Sam felt Carly was in additional danger and he's taken her to another location, for her safety."

"What sort of danger?" Her voice was suddenly quivery.

"I'm not sure."

"Where do you think he's taken her?"

"I don't know. We're waiting to hear from him any moment." Matter of fact, he'd give a month's pay to have the phone ring with Sam on the other end. He could feel Isabel Weston's tense uncertainty through the wires. "I assure you that as soon as I hear, I'll let you know."

"But isn't there anything we can do in the meantime?"

"We're doing everything that can be done. You're going to have to trust me on this, Mrs. Weston."

"Trust you. Yes, I suppose so." She made a small, fluttery sound. "Carly. . . . Carly's all I have, you know."

Ray heard the muffled sob. "I know. Sam's pretty important to me, too. We'll find them, I promise you."

"Detective, is that . . . that strangler involved in this?"

Damn. Ray tried to keep his voice even. "We have no way of knowing that for certain." The truth, as far as it went.

"All right." She sounded defeated, frightened. "You will phone as soon as you know *anything*."

"Absolutely. I have your number right here."

"Thank you, Detective Vargas."

286

Ray dropped the phone into the cradle. There were days when this job sucked, big time.

Sam stood at the front window looking out at a pale sun trying to lighten the winter sky. He couldn't see out to the road, couldn't tell whether the highway half-a-mile away had been cleared or if the salt trucks had been out yet. Even so, there'd probably be some traffic already. He needed to go out there, to hail someone and catch a ride to a phone that worked.

Turning, he saw that Carly was sitting much as he'd found her when he'd finished with his shower. She was staring into the fire, lost in her thoughts. He hated to leave her, worried that maniac might be watching for a chance to catch her alone, doubling back through the surrounding trees and sneaking up on the cabin. It seemed unlikely since they hadn't heard from him yet. But he couldn't put off going for help any longer.

"I'm going to leave you my gun, Carly," he said, picking up his .38 and placing it on the table next to her. "I need to get to the highway and call for help."

She swung tired eyes toward him. "All right."

"Do you remember how to use it?"

"Yes." She saw him frowning, saw he looked worried, which caused her own anxiety to increase. She'd been lulled these past few hours into feeling safe; but, in the light of morning, she knew they weren't home free yet. The strangler was still out there. She couldn't really draw an easy breath until he was caught and behind bars. This waiting was terrible. "Why don't I just go with you?"

"There's no point in both of us trekking around in waist-deep snow. It may take me some time to flag down a car. As soon as I do, I'll send them for help

287

and come back to wait with you." He didn't mention that making their way out to the road on a path obscured by snow, they'd be unable to run away quickly if the strangler happened to be out there waiting. Instead he reached for her hand and drew her to her feet. In her father's shirt, she looked small, fragile even. "Will you be all right?" Staring up at him, she nodded. "Are you afraid?"

Carly didn't feel like lying. "Yes." Closing her eyes, she leaned her cheek on his chest, her trembling hands settling at his waist as she breathed in his clean, masculine scent. He didn't love her, but she knew he cared in his own way. She longed to say the words to him, but they were words he didn't want to hear.

"I've checked all the rooms, made sure all the windows are locked. The front door is bolted, and I'll leave the back way so you can lock it from the inside. Take the gun with you even as you walk around room to room, all right?"

"Do you expect him to come here?" She hated the uneasiness she heard in her voice, but was helpless to hide it. The feelings she'd had, the fear she'd experienced during that dreadful car ride with that vile man right behind her, came rushing back in vivid detail.

"No." There was no point in alarming her with all the possibilities she hadn't thought of herself. "I have a feeling he's hurt and probably still in the Trans Am. I doubt he'd have had the strength to make it up out of that gully in a storm, especially if his legs were injured. But since we can't be sure, I want you to take every precaution."

Carly leaned back from him, catching the concern in his eyes. The possibility of Sam encountering the killer on his way to the highway was also a worry, one that had her heart racing. "Please be careful."

"I will." He bent to kiss her, to hold her close, to inhale the female scent of her. "Carly, when all this is over—"

She pressed two fingers to his lips, stopping the rest. "Shh. Not now." She wanted no promises given under stress, no pledges made under duress, no false vows to hang her hopes on. "When it *is* over, we'll talk."

He knew she was right. That was the smart thing to do. Yet it left him feeling oddly empty. He hugged her to him a long moment, then shrugged into his jacket and went out the back way. She followed, locking the door, watching him hunch into a light wind and start off in the vague direction of the path leading to the highway.

Back in the chair by the fire, Carly studied the gun, wondering if she'd really be able to shoot at a real person, if push came to shove. Target practice was one thing, but reality was quite another. Leaning her head back, she resumed staring into the flames, praying that Sam would be safe, that he'd find help, that this nightmare would soon be over.

"Sergeant Cooper, are you there? A lot of static on the line. I can barely hear you." Ray frowned as he strained to listen to the Michigan State Police officer on the other end of the phone.

"Yeah, I'm here. Can you hear me now?"

"That's better. So, what've you got?"

"The Trans Am you guys called about earlier. We found it."

Sliding back his chair, Ray stood. "Great. Where?"

"Down in this wooded section in Owendale. Driver must have lost control in the storm. Car swiveled around and ended up with the trunk rammed against the tree and the hood pointing up toward the

289

road. Lights were still on, and somebody passing by spotted them. Pretty faint and barely glowing, but still on."

Ray cleared his throat. "Anyone in the car?"

"Nope. Couldn't find tracks leading up either, but it had probably been snowing when the accident happened. We're trying to get the car up now, but it's the one you're looking for all right. Plates match."

His hunch had paid off, Ray thought. Skelly had to have been headed for the Weston cabin. "Tell me exactly where this wooded area is, please." Ray listened, leaning over and taking notes. "Thanks, Sergeant Cooper. I'll be in touch." Hanging up, Ray opened a file, looked up a number, and dialed it. In moments, a message came on telling him that the circuits were busy and to try again later. As soon as he hung up, the phone rang. "Vargas."

"Detective, this is Clark Abbott. I apologize for not getting back with you sooner. It's been so hectic since the judge died, and—"

Ray was fresh out of patience. "Did you get the information I asked for?"

"Yes." Clark shuffled papers, then began. "Here it is. The case involving the two young boys was the more recent of the two. The father's name was Tom Skelly, the wife was Martha Skelly and the two sons are Richard and Peter. You see—"

"That's all I need to know. Thanks."

"But what about the other case you asked about?"

"I no longer need that info. Thanks, again." Ray hung up. He didn't have time to waste. Grabbing his map, he hurried to Captain Renwick's office, knocked once, and went inside. "Got a minute, Captain?"

Renwick sipped his first cup of coffee of the morning. "Sit down, Ray. You're here awfully early."

Impatiently, Ray briefed him on what had happened since he'd left the precinct yesterday and during the long night.

"You're sure this Ric Skelly's the strangler?"

"Yes, I am." Ray spread out the map he'd brought in. "This is the area where Sam's Trans Am apparently went down," he said, pointing to the circled area. "Over here's where Prosecutor Weston's body was found. And this X is the location of the Weston hunting cabin. I believe that's where they were headed."

"What makes you think so?" Renwick asked.

He updated the captain on the phone call he'd had with the administrator at Lapeer. "Evidently Ric Skelly is attached to his retarded brother, Peter, who lives there. He called from Carly Weston's apartment yesterday and talked with the kid, trying to get Peter to get someone to give him a ride to Owendale. But the storm had already started, and no one would. So he told his kid brother he'd be back to pick him up tomorrow or the next day. Peter's all excited, has his clothes packed, and has told everyone he's leaving today, the administrator told me."

Renwick removed a cigar from his pocket and slid it along his nostrils, inhaling the tobacco scent. "So what do you think Skelly's plan is?"

"For some reason, he planned to take Carly up there, and my guess is that Sam interrupted them and got taken along. Maybe he was planning to take his sweet time killing both of them in Will's cabin. Who knows for sure what he had in mind? Sam must have seen his chance and sent the Trans Am down the hill. Or maybe he really did lose control, although I doubt that. Sam drives like Knievel, but he's damn good. At any rate, the State Police found the car empty so they all three got out somehow."

"And you think they're in Weston's cabin?"

291

"Yeah. I just called there, and they say the circuits are busy—which probably means the storm's knocked out the phone lines. I think it's worth checking out in person. I need the chopper. Sam and the Weston girl could be in deep shit. We can't sit it out while the State Police get around to it."

The captain knew exactly what it was like when a cop's partner was in danger. "You got it." Renwick picked up the phone to order the police helicopter readied. He wanted this case solved badly.

Ray let out an anxious breath. "Thanks, Captain." Turning, he headed for the elevators.

Carly awoke with a start. Swiveling her head around, she checked out the room, then exhaled shakily. How could she have fallen asleep? she wondered, brushing back her hair. It was the warmth of the fire as well as the heat pouring out of the register. She got up to turn down the thermostat.

The warmth and only a couple of hours sleep in the last thirty-six, she reminded herself with an expansive yawn. Moving to the window, she peered out, but could see nothing different from when she'd looked earlier. She'd wound the old mantel clock and set it to the time on Sam's watch. Nearly seven. He'd been gone only twenty minutes. Already, it seemed like forever.

At the fireplace ledge, she checked and found her slacks dry again. She pulled them on, arranging her father's shirt to hang down over them. It was too warm inside to put the turtleneck back on. She needed something to keep her awake and alert. First, she put on her heavy socks, somewhat stiff from being wet and dried twice now, then padded into the kitchen.

In the cupboard, she found a jar of instant coffee

292

and put water on to boil. While waiting, she squinted out the back window. Everything looked as before, except for Sam's deep prints leading away from the cabin. Maybe luck was with them and the strangler had been hurt in the car crash and was still stuck in the back seat of the Trans Am. She fervently prayed he was.

Oh, Lord, she'd forgotten to carry Sam's gun with her. She hurried to get it, toting it into the kitchen. The safety was on so it wouldn't accidentally discharge. She tried to cram it into a pocket of her slacks, but there simply wasn't enough room. Annoyed, she set it on the counter before fixing her coffee. Carrying both steaming cup and gun, she went back to curl up in the fireside chair.

She'd never been good at waiting. Even as a child, she'd had an impatient nature. She sent Sam a mental message, wishing he'd hurry, frantic to have all this end.

Was he at the road yet? Surely, in the light of morning, the first passing car would stop for him. She'd read newspaper stories where people seeking help were often ignored by passersby who were afraid to get involved. But they were in the country here, in a small town where residents were kinder. At least, she hoped they were.

But the occupants of passing cars along the highway weren't necessarily residents of rural Owendale. They might be heading way up north or back down toward Detroit. But also, there'd be street crews to clear the roads and police cars checking damage. Someone. Please, God, send someone.

Carly sipped her coffee. Hot, strong, almost bitter, but it would do the job. She heard a sound and jerked her head in the direction of the front door. Then through the window, she saw that a gust of wind had blown a clump of snow onto the porch where it was breaking up, particles showering down slowly.

Jumpy. She was downright jumpy. Who wouldn't be?

Focus on something positive, she ordered herself as she took a bracing swallow of the bitter brew. She tried to picture herself back in her apartment, safe and warm, on her own couch watching the Christmas tree she and Sam had put up. Tomorrow was Christmas Eve. Carly felt her eyes fill.

She'd had so many wonderful Christmases with her family and friends. Within the boundaries of her protected neighborhood, her small world, she hadn't ever been exposed to the frightening side of life. Until recently. She'd been oblivious, even though she'd read of murders in the papers and seen killers and their victims on the television news. Never once had she thought any of it would touch her, not even having grown up with a father whose job was prosecuting such criminals.

What a Pollyanna she'd been, Carly thought with no small measure of self-criticism. As Will Weston had said, no one was immune from violence today. A sad truth.

Again, she heard a sound. She cocked her head, but there was only silence following. Probably more snow being shifted about. Still, she took the gun from the end table and settled it in her lap.

Christmas. It would be so hard this year without her father. Her mother would have a very difficult holiday. She wondered if Isabel Weston had tried to call last night or this morning and found her gone. Was she worried, even frightened? Carly sighed. She couldn't do much to reassure anyone until help arrived and they were rescued.

What would it be like when this all ended and she was back home again? She'd have to put her apartment in order after that maniac broke down her darkroom door, clean the place up, take a long bath. She'd give a lot to be able to spend tonight in her own bed.

With Sam.

Back to that, she thought as she finished her coffee and set the cup aside. Would he come around and realize he loved her, too? Probably not, if she were to be painfully honest with herself. He didn't know how to love, he'd confessed. Bull!

He would turn away from commitment, from being tied down. He'd been on his own for fifteen years, happy with his freedom and not about to change it. Well, fine. She certainly didn't want a man who didn't want her.

Liar. She wanted him, all right. But it would be no good unless Sam wanted her, too. Maybe he'd walk away, then miss her so much he'd come running back. The day pigs fly, she thought with a disgusted groan. Still, there was no point in letting negative thoughts rule her because . . .

Now she definitely heard a sound coming from the area of the back door. Sam had returned. She jumped up, and the gun slipped from her lap. Picking it up, she hurried toward the kitchen. In the archway, she came to a screeching halt, frozen in mid-step.

The man who'd killed four people with his bare hands was standing inside the kitchen door holding a hunting rifle aimed at her heart.

Carly let out a scream and dropped the .38.

Chapter Sixteen

Ric Skelly backhanded Carly across her face to stop the scream, then shoved her into the kitchen chair against the wall. He kept his eyes on her as he picked up the gun she'd dropped, then tossed aside the rifle he'd been holding. Taking a deep breath, he gave her a sinister smile. "Thanks for the gun, bitch. The rifle isn't loaded."

Carly recognized the ugly laugh. Recoiling, she shook her head to clear it and blinked to ward off the tears that had sprung to her eyes at the force of the blow. Though her face throbbed with renewed pain, she didn't want to cry. She couldn't break apart now. Surely any minute, Sam would return.

"How did you know where to find me?" she asked.

Again, the evil chuckle. "You and that cop think I'm stupid, don't you? I was going to bring you both here anyway. Have a little fun with you." His face turned hard, angry. "But your boyfriend changed my plans."

She thought she'd try a bluff. "Sam's in the bathroom. He'll hear you and—"

Ric's heavy hand shot out, catching her with a glancing blow to the head. Ears ringing, Carly cowered in her chair, unable to prevent a whimper from escaping.

"Don't you lie to me again, you hear? I was hiding in the woods and saw him walking to the road. It'll take him quite a while to make it out, then flag down a car and go for help. Meanwhile, I thought I'd pay you a little visit." Turning, he shut the back door and looked around the kitchen. "Nice place to have a cozy chat."

Carly sucked in air, fighting panic. She had to keep him talking, but she'd have to be careful what she said. She didn't know how many more of these blows she could take without passing out. Warily, she watched him as he removed his heavy jacket, tossing it aside before he stuck the .38 in the waistband of his pants.

Spotting the box of crackers next to the stove, Skelly walked over and helped himself to several. As he ate, he leaned against the counter and studied his hostage. "Bet you and the cop thought I'd bought the farm in that crash, didn't you?" He shook his head. "Takes a whole lot more than a slide down a snowbank to do me in."

"You weren't hurt at all?" she asked hesitantly.

He glanced down at his left foot. "A sprained ankle. You think that would stop me? Haven't you figured it out yet? Nothing's going to stop me from watching you die."

Chewing on her lower lip, Carly tried to keep her shuddering reaction from showing. His heavy work pants were soaked and crusted with snow, as were his thick-soled shoes. His face was dirty and unshaven, his hair unruly and matted. There was no question that he looked menacing. "You haven't been out there all night, have you?" Surely, even this oxen-like man couldn't have survived overnight in the cold and snow.

"Nah. I couldn't remember which road this cabin was on when I climbed up the hill. So I took a wrong turn and wound up at another cottage, all closed up for the winter. I broke in and spent the night there." He opened the refrigerator, then frowned in annoyance when he saw that there wasn't much inside. "Trouble was they didn't have any food and no shells for that stinking rifle." He laughed at her naïveté. "Fooled you, though, didn't it? You damn near wet your pants when you looked into the barrel of that rifle." Removing a bottle of beer, he screwed off the top, tipped back his head, and drank deeply.

Oh, swell. Now he was drinking. Next, he'd be drunk and vicious instead of just plain vicious. She struggled to think of something, anything, to occupy him, to delay him long enough for Sam to return. "How did you get here?"

"I hot-wired an old tractor they had in the garage." He belched noisily.

Carly hid her repulsion. "You must be hungry. There're cans of soup in the cupboard." Maybe food would distract him.

Ric wiped his mouth with the back of his hand and eyed her. "What do you care if I eat or not? You turning Good Samaritan on me? Ha! That'll be the day." He took another long swallow before shifting his narrowed gaze back. "You go to church?"

"Yes, sometimes."

He saluted her with the half-empty bottle. " 'Let us eat and drink, for tomorrow we die.' " he quoted. "Old Testament." He chuckled. "One of us will die, that is, but not tomorrow. Today. Yes, indeed, little lady. Today. 'The Lord giveth, and the Lord taketh away.' The Lord gave you a lot, but you didn't appreciate it. So today, I'm going to take it all away." Upending the bottle, he drained the rest of the beer.

"What is it I didn't appreciate? How could you think that when you don't even know me?" *Keep him talking, but be careful.*

"I know you, all right." Ric opened a cupboard,

saw a jar of peanuts, and took it down. He screwed off the lid and shook out a handful, cramming them into his mouth before getting another beer. "You and me, we go back a long way."

"I. . . I must have a bad memory. Tell me where we met." Trying to keep from reaching to soothe her aching cheek, Carly kept her eyes on him. There was a sugar bowl and a set of salt and pepper shakers on the table alongside her about a dozen inches from her hand. If only she could divert him, maybe she could throw the bowl at him or toss pepper into his eyes. But she'd have to be really sure of her aim, for he had the loaded gun. And she hadn't forgotten what those powerful hands could do.

Chewing thoughtfully, he studied her almost lazily. She was too scrawny and too pale for his taste. The trouble was he hadn't had sex in so long he'd probably embarrass himself. If she laughed at him, he wouldn't be able to bear it. Besides, he'd found that squeezing the life out of someone was far more satisfying than sex.

And toying with her made him feel powerful, mostly because he could see she felt powerless. Good. It was about time the power shifted from the *haves* to the *have-nots*.

Ric took another pull on his beer, set down the second bottle, and yanked the gun from his waistband. "In time, little lady, I'll tell you everything." He walked close to her and watched her eyes widen as she swallowed on a dry throat, then leaned within inches of her. "You *sure* you don't remember me?"

Carly felt the blood drain from her face. She wasn't about to try another bluff. "I'm sorry, but I don't."

"You're going to be a lot sorrier." With a quick movement, he stuck the point of the gun into her left ear and held it there. "How's it feel to be scared shitless, Carly? To know your life is over?"

* * *

Breathing hard from walking in knee-deep snow, Sam reached the road and stomped his feet, shaking off as much of the clinging snow as possible. He squinted against the pale sun reflecting on so much whiteness and saw that the salt trucks hadn't been by but one lane in each direction had been plowed not long ago. He could see no cars coming in either direction at the moment. There *had* to be traffic along soon.

Rubbing his hands together, he glanced along the row of trees on either side. Something unfamiliar was parked to the left, and he started walking toward it. Closer, he saw that it was an old tractor. What on earth was it doing here at the edge of the woods? It hadn't been here last night when they'd passed by.

A sudden thought hit him, and he touched the rusty hood. Warm. Someone had driven it here — and very recently. He saw footprints from the tractor disappearing into the trees. The strangler. *Dear God!*

Racing back toward the path, Sam heard a car coming from behind. Like a madman, he dashed out into the middle of the road, turning to face the oncoming car, waving his arms frantically. An older Chevrolet, moving slowly due to the weather conditions, skidded to a stop a mere foot-and-a-half from him. Sam hurried around to the driver's side as the puzzled man rolled down his window.

"Police officer," Sam said, reaching into his pocket for his ID and flipping it open. "I need you to stop at the nearest phone and call the State Police for me and give them a message."

The driver appeared to be a retired rancher, his skin permanently bronzed from the sun, his hair white as the snow piled on either side of the highway. "Sure, okay," he said.

300

The woman beside him wearing a thick head scarf searched around in her purse. "I'll write down the message, Officer."

"I'm Detective Sergeant Sam English. Tell the State Police to get a car over here right away." Sam pointed down the path he'd just left. "To the Weston hunting cabin, about half-a-mile through those trees. And have them call Detective Ray Vargas, Detroit Police Headquarters, and tell him I've got the strangler here. He'll know what to do."

The woman's voice was high-pitched, suddenly nervous. "A strangler, here?"

"Yes, ma'am. And tell them to hurry. Thanks." He nearly slipped on the wet soles of his shoes as he raced around the hood of the Chevy and rushed back down the path toward the cabin.

Please let me be in time, Sam prayed.

"I want to hear you beg," Skelly said, his eyes boring into hers. "Beg me not to kill you, Carly."

She felt the cold sweat slither down her back and heard her heart hammering in her ears. She prayed she wouldn't pass out, yet something deep inside wouldn't allow her to beg. "Did you kill my father?" she asked instead, hoping she hadn't earned another whack to her head.

She wanted to talk, did she? He would accommodate her, see if he could break that uppity composure with some gruesome details, maybe jog her memory as to who he was. She looked a little nervous, but not panicky. He wanted her sobbing, begging, desperate. He removed the gun from her and stepped back.

"Yeah, I killed him. He was sitting down resting next to a tree in the woods not far from here. I walked up slow-like and made sure he recognized me. Then I put my hands around his throat and squeezed until he made this funny, wheezing sound. Did you know that when you strangle someone, Carly, they make this odd gasping noise?" When she didn't react, he went on. "I let go of him, and he slumped over like a rag doll. Sure I killed Will Weston. Just like he killed my father."

Carly swallowed hard, fighting the nausea backing up in her throat. "How. . . how do you mean?" She took a deep breath, trying to clear her nose of the stench of him as he'd leaned over her, trying not to think of the mind-pictures he was painting. "My father was a fair man, a compassionate prosecutor."

"You think so, eh?" He tossed down another swallow of beer, then wiped his damp neck. It was damn hot in here, or was it just that he'd been so cold all night that it felt hotter to him than it really was? "Let me tell you a little story, sweetheart. Then you decide how *fair* and *compassionate* your daddy was."

Holding the gun in one hand and his beer bottle in the other, he paced the length of the kitchen, turning to swing his eyes back to her. "*My* father was the good man. Good to my mother and me and my little brother. A family man who worked hard to support us. He took us fishing in the summer and sledding in the winter. You know the kind of guy I mean?"

She had to humor him, keep him focused on telling his story. She kept watching him, looking for her chance, wishing she could risk a glance out the window to see if she could spot Sam. "Yes, I know the kind of man you mean."

He wiped beads of sweat from his forehead with the back of his hand. "He had a good job in a big corporation. Company CPA, you know. In charge of the books. Then suddenly, he was accused of embezzlement."

Carly could guess where this was leading. "And he

302

didn't do it." She didn't say it as a question, not wanting to rile him. He was sweating profusely, and she wondered if he were ill since it wasn't that warm in the cabin.

"Hell, no, he didn't do it. My father was honest as the day is long. I was only twelve years old and he sat me down and swore to me that he was innocent, that someone in the company had set him up."

"Did he have an attorney? Did the case go to trial?"

"Oh, yeah, it went to trial, all right." Ric took another slug of beer and made a face when he found it lukewarm. He set the bottle in the sink and turned back to her. "Good old Homer Gentry defended him."

His story was beginning to make sense. "And Gentry didn't get your father off?"

"Right as rain. Your old man was the hotshot new prosecutor, trying to make a name for himself. He had a big crusade going against white-collar crimes, and he nailed my dad, but good. Then Weston's friend, Judge Rogers, threw the book at Dad. I read the articles in the paper later, when I was older. My mother kept all of them in a shoebox in the closet."

"I'm sorry," Carly said quietly. And she meant it. She *was* sorry for the twelve-year-old boy he'd been. His father going to prison had apparently warped his entire outlook on life.

"Sorry doesn't cut it, lady." Ric resumed his pacing, waving the gun he held, remembering the humiliation. "Everyone was sorry, but no one could do a damn thing. You know what it's like for a kid to go to school and have his friends make fun of him because his father's a jailbird? You know how I felt, watching my mother have to go to work cleaning other people's houses 'cause she didn't have any other training to get a better job and she had two young boys to raise all alone?"

He stared into her eyes so long that Carly felt she should answer. "I can only imagine how hard that must have been for all of you."

"Yeah, hard. Worse than hard. But not as hard as the day I came home from school and found my mother hanging from the light fixture, a drapery cord wrapped around her neck."

Carly sucked in a startled breath. "Oh, God."

"God? My mother believed in God. She used to read the Bible to Pete and me. Until they locked up my father. She didn't open the Bible again after they took him away." He took another swing around the kitchen, needing to get rid of the building tension. "Why is it so goddamn hot in here?"

She watched him unbutton his heavy shirt, peel it off, and toss it aside. A large ring of keys hung from his belted pants. He had on a dark green tee shirt, sweat-stained under the armpits. His chest hair curled over the neckline, and his thick arms were corded and hairy, giving him an ape-like appearance. Carly struggled to repress a shudder. "The thermostat's in the other room. You could turn it down."

He ignored her, caught up in making her understand. "You want to hear the rest? You got the stomach for it, rich lady?"

She had to face him down. "Yes, tell me the rest."

Ric straightened, drawing in air, his powerful chest expanding. Maybe this was the hardest part of all. "They took him away, my baby brother, to a state home in Lapeer. He's mentally retarded, and he didn't understand what was happening or why. He still doesn't. And they put me in one foster home after another, 'cause I kept running away. I used to get good grades; but after I lost my whole family, I didn't give a damn any more. I kept flunking out, disrupting class. Incorrigible, they called me. When I turned sixteen, I cut out on my own. I'd had enough of the state trying to jack me around."

304

She watched him silently, not knowing what to say. By anyone's yardstick, he'd had a very rough childhood. That didn't give him license to kill, but Carly was at least beginning to understand why his thinking had gotten so twisted.

"I bummed around a couple of years like that, living with this friend and that, working nothing jobs for minimum wage. I didn't have trouble finding jobs. I'm real strong. I like working with my hands. Construction bosses really like me." He sounded prideful for the first time.

"I'll bet they did," she commented, glad she could find a word of praise to lighten his mood. She had to buy enough time for Sam to make his way back.

"Around the time I turned eighteen, I found a permanent job with this builder, rented a room in this old man's house, and borrowed his car so I could go visit my dad in prison." He shook his head and closed his eyes tightly for a long moment. "I was too late. They told me my dad had died the year before. They hadn't known where to contact me."

Carly waited, worrying her lip between her teeth, wondering where this agonizing story was going.

Ric ran a hand over his smudged and unshaven face. "That was the last straw, you know. The system had beaten a strong man like my dad. I decided, screw the system. It's every man for himself. I knew this guy, Doug Anderson. He had a gun and a plan to make some quick money. He'd already robbed two convenience stores and gotten away with it. Doug figured the two of us could do it faster, better." He stared off, remembering.

That was the man who'd been killed in the alley, the one Sam couldn't connect to the other three deaths, Carly realized.

After a moment, Ric brought himself back to the present. "Doug felt I was bigger, tougher, so I should go in with the gun while he waited in the car. Only

305

something went wrong. The clerk must have pushed a silent alarm. Just as I ran outside with the money, a cop car pulled up, sirens screaming. The cops jumped out, both with guns drawn. Shit!" He brushed back his damp hair with his thick hand.

"It was your first robbery?"

"Yeah."

"Usually, the courts go easy on first offenders."

He let out a disgusted grunt. "Maybe they would have, if Doug hadn't turned state's evidence and lied, telling them the robbery was my idea and I'd forced him to go along. Maybe if my court-appointed attorney hadn't been good old Homer Gentry."

How ironic, Carly thought, but she kept silent.

"So Gentry takes me in to see your dear old daddy. Says he's going to try a plea bargain, 'cause of my age and it being my first offense. He got me a haircut, cleaned me up, and walked me into Weston's office." Ric moved closer to Carly, close enough that he could see the fear leap into her eyes. "Now do you remember me?"

With all of her being, Carly wished she did because, maybe then, he'd back off. But if she lied, he'd figure it out and probably hit her again. Or worse. Bracing herself, she returned his look. "No, I'm sorry, but I don't."

Ric felt the anger rising in him, felt the heat spreading. The bitch still didn't remember. "Let me refresh your memory," he said through gritted teeth. "Homer and I were sitting across the desk from your father. You came breezing in, all smiles, wearing this little yellow suit and smelling like a spring garden, telling him you were a little early in picking him up for lunch. You barely glanced at us."

Carly tried to remember, but couldn't recall the exact incident. She'd often gone to her dad's office and picked him up for lunch. It was something they'd both enjoyed. There was nothing she could say to ease his anger, so she kept quiet.

"I knew what you were like," Ric said, his voice low and menacing. "A rich man's daughter, pampered all your life, spoiled rotten. You'd had every advantage I'd never had. A great house in the suburbs, the best schools, nice clothes. It wasn't my fault my father wound up in jail or that my mother killed herself or even that Pete's not quite right. But here I was, only eighteen, with one small mistake on my record, and facing two-to-five years, hard time for armed robbery. And there you were, not good enough to even look at me, anxious to be off to lunch in some fancy place."

"You're judging me unfairly. I had no idea who you were when I stopped in Dad's office. I wasn't looking down on you or—"

"Oh, no? Then why didn't your daddy introduce us? Isn't that what you polite society types do when you meet someone new? Only we weren't good enough for that. We weren't important enough to meet his sweet-smelling daughter."

"Perhaps he didn't introduce us, but surely Dad considered your request before leaving?" It was a loaded question, but she had to say something. He was staring at her with eyes that shone brightly with a hatred she could almost reach out and touch.

"He considered it, all right. For about ten seconds. Then you said something like . . ." His voice mimicked a high falsetto. ". . . 'I didn't mean to interrupt, but Mom's waiting downstairs.' " He resumed glaring. "And Weston hopped to his feet, denied Homer's plea bargain, and walked off with his arm around you. Your fair, compassionate daddy left us both sitting there like so much garbage."

Carly felt certain he had twisted the facts somewhere along the way. She never would have inter-

307

rupted a meeting in progress, certainly not one determining a man's fate. Perhaps her father's secretary hadn't been there and she'd stuck her head in. There had to be some reasonable explanation, but she was sure the man before her was in no mood to hear it. Her father had never been casual or callous with people no matter the crime they'd committed. She withdrew further, until the back of her head was touching the kitchen wall. "I don't know what else to say except I'm terribly sorry."

"Sorry." He gave that same mirthless chuckle. "You want to know the name of the judge I got? Judge Rogers. How's that for history repeating itself? The judge's memory was no better than yours. He didn't figure that Ric Skelly was Tom Skelly's son, the same Tom Skelly who'd died in the prison he'd sentenced him to rot in years before. He gave me two-to-five years."

"Usually, you can get out earlier for good behavior." She really couldn't imagine that this desperate man had behaved well enough to be paroled, but she took a chance.

His voice sounded tired, defeated. "I could have been out in eighteen months, but this one dude kept hassling me. One day I took care of him, and they nailed me for it, made me serve out the whole five."

"You killed him?"

"Nah, just beat the hell out of him. He didn't mess with me again, and most everyone else stayed away, too." Ric took another long breath, then braced his feet as he stood in front of her. "I spent five long years thinking about getting even. For my dad, my mom, and for Pete. Killing all those bastards who ruined my life. And most of all, getting you."

"But what did I do?" she asked, honestly puzzled.

"Don't you get it? You had everything I didn't. I used to lay in my bunk at night and remember how you smelled passing my chair. Maybe, if all that embezzlement shit hadn't happened, one day my dad might have met your dad at some business function. Our families could have become friends. And a guy like me could actually have been invited to eat with someone like you, to visit your home. You would have *noticed* me instead of walking past me like I was a piece of furniture."

What could she possibly say to ease his thinking? "You're right. You got a raw deal. You were orphaned, and none of that was your fault. The robbery was a mistake, but one you could have overcome. When you got out of prison, if you'd started over, rebuilt your life, then maybe you would have still been okay. But to start killing innocent people—"

"Innocent?" Ric almost roared his outrage. 'Haven't you heard a word I've said? All of them deserved to die, every last one. And so do you." He raised the gun. "I wanted you to know most of all how the people who *aren't* so privileged feel. I followed you, ripped up your blouse, sent you the butchered rose. I wanted you to know you couldn't run far enough or fast enough, that there was no place you could hide from me. I wanted you to know what it was to be afraid, to be helpless, to be a victim. Like my mother was, and my dad. And me."

Carly's pulse was pounding as she stared at the gun aimed at her heart. "Please, what will killing me accomplish?"

Ric Skelly bared his stained teeth in an ugly smile. "It'll make me feel a lot better. It's your turn to pay. Say good-bye, Carly." Slowly, his index finger squeezed the trigger.

When nothing happened, he realized that the safety was on. As he checked the gun to remove the safety, in his peripheral vision he saw Carly dart from her chair and into the living room. Cursing, he

309

rushed after her.

She almost made it down the hall, but her stock-inged feet slipped on the bare wood floor and she fell. As she tried to scramble up, she felt her arm grabbed in a steely grip. He yanked her upright, his arm circling her waist, pulling her against his sweaty body. Carly moaned in frustration.

Barely breathing hard, Ric returned her to the kitchen and dropped her back into the chair. Standing in the arch, he watched her cower in fright, which was exactly what he'd wanted her to do. "Now, then," he said, "where were we?" Again, he raised the gun and pointed it at Carly.

At that moment, the back door slammed open as Sam all but fell inside. "Stop!" he yelled.

Ric swiveled, narrowing his eye at Sam now. "All right, you first, then," he snarled and took aim.

"No!" Carly screamed and leaped to her feet, trying to deflect the shot away from Sam. But her movement fell just short of her target, and the gun went off. The bullet slammed into Carly's right chest. With a small sound, she dropped to the floor.

Sam's horrified gaze rose from Carly's fallen form to the man still holding the gun. Enraged, he lunged toward Ric Skelly, tackling him, sending the gun flying, then skittering across the slick floor. He knew he couldn't take the time to check on Carly until he had this maniac subdued. His injured shoulder took the brunt of the hit, but he paid no mind to the pain. Adrenaline pumping, Sam rose to his knees and got in two good body punches before Ric recovered enough to hit back.

Ric was by far the stronger man and quickly landed two stunning blows to Sam's head, sending him reeling. He'd seen the gun go flying under the stove. Swearing ripely, Ric turned back to Sam, who was dazed but trying to sit up. He reached toward

310

his throat, trying to get his hands around the cop's neck, but Sam's knee came up and connected with his ribs.

Furious now, Ric hit him in the stomach and heard a whoosh of air puff out. Quickly, he brought his other fist up, landing a hard uppercut on the cop's chin. As Sam fell back, Ric raised his head at a distant sound.

Sirens, coming closer.

Damn. Ric glanced at Carly, crumpled on the floor, blood oozing out of a chest wound. She was a goner. At least, the thing he'd set out to do was done. She knew why he'd needed to kill her, and now he had. To hell with the cop, Ric thought as he scrambled for the door. He'd never been a part of the plan. He'd hightail it through the woods. They'd never catch him. Didn't they know? He was unbeatable. He'd have to hurry. Pete was waiting for him.

Grabbing his jacket, Ric yanked open the back door.

Following the highway, the officer flying the police helicopter spotted the State Police car heading toward their destination. "Looks like we'll beat them there by minutes," he told Ray who was seated beside him, peering down.

"See that cabin over to the right there?" Ray asked. "That's got to be Weston's."

"Yeah, I think so, too."

"Can you set this thing down in all that snow?"

"We're equipped with snow shoes. Besides . . ." The pilot grinned. ". . . I can set this baby down damn near on the head of a dime."

"Okay, hotshot. Do it." As he spoke, Ray saw a man running out the back door of the cabin. They were too far away for him to identify the man. "Hurry. I think we've got trouble."

The pilot pulled back on the cyclic to cushion the

landing, then pulled up on the collective stick, adding a push on the anti-torque pedal to keep the nose straight. "Hold tight," he told Ray. "There's going to be a white-out when we land, with the snow spraying up at us."

The mists were heavy, trying to drag him back down, but Sam fought like he'd never fought before. He made it to a sitting position and swiped at his mouth. His hand came away bloody, but he couldn't take the time to think about that. With waning strength, he made it to his feet and hurried through the door. He had to get that bastard.

Ric had just rounded the debris when Sam caught him with another flying tackle. He scarcely felt something in his shoulder snap. In the snow, the two men rolled over and over, fists trying to find purchase and getting in only minimal licks. Finally, Ric managed to pin Sam to his back.

"You sonofabitch," Ric grunted as he hit Sam another powerful blow.

But Sam had some fight left in him and got in several good punches. Then suddenly, he felt the man straddle him and begin a pummeling to his head, one blow after another. He heard a ringing in his ears and his vision blurred.

An experienced street fighter, Ric was ruthless, battering at Sam, whose punches were becoming more defensive than aggressive. His hands were almost ineffectual as Ric opened up a cut on his eye and another at the corner of his mouth, his defense just enough to keep those strong hands from closing around his throat.

He was sinking fast, Sam thought. It would all be over in moments if he didn't do something. He simply didn't have enough left to push the man off him and reverse their positions. His graying vision was turning black around the edges. He couldn't give in, couldn't let Carly down.

Arms outstretched in the snow beneath them, his fingers groped for something, *anything*. At last, his right hand settled on something wet, slick and smooth. A thick icicle that must have fallen from the roof. Gripping the heavy end, Sam raised his arm.

Another searing blow to his jaw, but Sam absorbed it, then opened his eyes. He saw a double image of a man leaning over him. He smelled the blood from all the blows to his head. But his grip on the icicle was steady.

Slowly, carefully, Sam lifted his arm and paused a moment, then aimed the point of the icicle into the area of the man's lower left side in the vicinity of his kidneys, thrusting with all the force left in him. The blade-like ice plunged deeply into hard flesh, not in the least hampered by the soft cotton of his green tee shirt.

The man let out a howling scream, bucked fiercely, crying out again, then he collapsed onto Sam.

With a strength he didn't know he possessed, Sam rolled the man from him. Eyes wide open stared back at him as the killer's weight settled farther down into the deep snow. Sam wasted little time on pity.

Climbing up on his knees, aware his face was bleeding and his fists were badly bruised and battered and possibly bones were broken, he refused to acknowledge the pain. He had to get to Carly.

Overhead, he heard a loud noise and glanced up to see a police chopper maneuvering to land. They'd gotten ahold of Ray, he thought as he lunged around the porch debris. In the distance, a police siren could be heard as he opened the door and stumbled inside.

She lay as she'd fallen on the kitchen floor. Sam

313

pressed experienced fingers to the pulse in her throat and found it faint but still beating. *Thank you, God,* he offered up as he slid his arms around her, cradling her body to his.

"I love you, Carly," he whispered into her ear as he held her, knowing help was on the away. "Please don't die."

No one, not a living soul, had ever done for him what she'd done. She'd taken the bullet meant for him. Without a moment's hesitation, she'd thrown herself into the path of that bullet. No one had ever cared that much, not for him.

He rocked her as he waited. He'd been fooling himself all these weeks, in love with her and denying it. He'd never dreamed he could love like this, could have someone love *him* like this. But she did and she'd proven it tonight.

He and God weren't on the best of terms. But he would make a rusty attempt, beg if he had to. Anything. He'd do anything, but Carly had to live. *Had to.*

Harper Hospital was one of the best in the state. Sam knew that. And Dr. Andrew Simmons was one of the best surgeons in the Midwest. He was certain of that. Yet he was still worried.

In the waiting room alcove, he leaned forward in the fake leather chair, propped his elbows on his knees, and studied his hands. They were a mess. Knuckles swollen, cuts that had been swabbed with some orange stuff, the small finger of his right hand broken and set in an awkward splint. They hurt like hell. They'd offered him pain pills after they'd snapped back his dislocated shoulder and put him in a figure-eight bandage to keep it as immobile as possible, but he'd refused to take them.

He wanted to be alert not groggy. He wanted to

talk to Dr. Simmons the moment he stepped out of the operating room just across the hall. He wanted to know how Carly was doing.

"Detective English," Isabel Weston said from the couch to his left, "you look as if you might topple over any moment. Why don't you go lie down and rest for a bit? I'll come get you as soon as the doctor comes out."

"Thanks, Mrs. Weston, but I need to be here." She was a nice woman, Sam thought, but she didn't understand. He'd told her as soon as she'd arrived, needing to share his pain, that the bullet that had just missed Carly's lung and embedded itself in the wall of her chest had been meant for him. He should be the one in there struggling for life, not Carly. Never Carly.

Isabel Weston had stared into his burning eyes for a long moment after his confession, and then she'd nodded. "I didn't know that you were in love with Carly," she'd said, calm as you please. Then she'd led him over to the chair and insisted he stop pacing and sit down.

Ice had to flow in her veins; she was like his own mother. These women didn't feel, they just sashayed through life *handling* things. No blow too large or too small for them to handle and handle well. Her only daughter in there under the knife, and she was serenely seeing to his needs. Amazing.

Sam leaned his head back and took a breath, almost moaning out loud at the swift pain slicing through his chest. They'd taken X rays and told him no bones were broken, but many were badly bruised. They'd taped his ribs, yet every breath he took hurt. And then there was his face.

He wasn't sure Carly would recognize him when she awakened. One eye was nearly swollen shut; there were scrapes and cuts aplenty, and his lips were puffy and raw. Quite a sight. He hoped he wouldn't frighten her.

"What the hell is taking so long?" Sam asked, hardly aware he'd spoken aloud.

"It's delicate surgery," Isabel answered. Waiting was so very difficult, and she was no less concerned than Sam English. But she'd trust Andrew Simmons with her life, and certainly Carly's life was far more important to her. She'd grown up with Andrew and knew what a remarkable surgeon he was. As they'd wheeled Carly into operating, Andrew had assured her he would get the bullet out and her daughter would be fine. She believed him.

Unobtrusively, she studied the man opposite her. There was scarcely a section of skin unbruised or unbroken on his face or arms. She knew he was in pain, yet he refused to acknowledge it. Perhaps if she distracted him, the waiting would be easier. "I want to thank you for what you did. Detective Vargas told me you killed the man who strangled my husband. It couldn't have been easy."

Easy? No, it hadn't been easy. Opening his eyes, Sam wished to hell he'd have returned to the cabin a couple of minutes sooner. Just a minute earlier even, and maybe Carly wouldn't have gotten shot.

Ray and the State Police had loaded Carly and him into the chopper and flown them here to Harper, leaving the boys up north to deal with the dead man. By now, the body was probably on the way to Detroit's morgue. Ray had stayed with him awhile, then gone to Headquarters to brief Captain Renwick, to let him know it was over.

But was it? No, not until Carly was all right.

Unsteadily, Sam got to his feet. "You don't owe me thanks," he told Mrs. Weston. "I was just doing my job." Walking with difficulty, he paused in the archway to stare at the double doors to the operating room, willing them to open and the doctor to come rushing out with good news. "I'm the reason your daughter's in there fighting for her life."

"She'll make it," Isabel said with quiet conviction. "Carly's always been stronger than most people think. And a fighter. A real fighter."

Sam nodded, remembering how well she'd held up on that long drive north with a gun held to her head and for however long that monster had held her captive in the cabin. "Yeah, that she is."

"She must care a great deal for you to have done what she did." He'd explained just how Carly'd been shot, though Isabel felt he'd given her his own dramatic version. People in pain had a tendency to do that, exaggerate their guilt.

She knew her daughter well, knew the passion inside Carly. If she'd tried to save this man's life, it was because she loved him more than her own life. Isabel had hoped that one day Carly would feel that strongly about someone—the way she had for Will. It had been a while coming and had hit fast and furious. Isabel felt pity for people who would never know such a love.

"Have you told her how much you care?" she asked him, knowing it was none of her business. Yet sharing a life-or-death situation often allowed an uncommon kinship to develop.

Sam turned, uncomfortable with talking about his feelings—the ones he'd only just acknowledged he had—with a woman he barely knew, even if she were Carly's mother.

Isabel saw the answer on his face. "I thought not." That was another reason he felt so bereft. "I'm sure that hearing the words will help her recover more quickly."

Her concern for her daughter finally came through to him. Not ice cold at all. Just a woman who'd learned to cover her feelings, much as he had. Until Carly had shown him that, with her, he could let himself be vulnerable, for she'd never hurt him.

317

Understanding Isabel Weston finally, he gave her a crooked smile. "I mean to tell her the minute she opens her eyes."

Isabel smiled. "Good. Best medicine in the world, knowing someone loves you."

He hadn't thought so, not until recently. But now . . . Hearing the doors behind him open, Sam turned around anxiously.

The doctor was smiling.

Carly was floating, weightless, through a heavy fog. She felt disoriented, wandering through unfamiliar territory. She tried to open her eyes, but her lids were heavy, so very heavy.

Perhaps she was dreaming. Sweet dreams of Sam holding her, Sam whispering in her ear. "I love you," he said softly. Yes, she had to be dreaming. Sam didn't need anyone.

Giving in, Carly slept.

The floaty feeling was easing, lifting. This try, she was able to open her eyes.

A hospital bed in a hospital room. An IV was hooked up to her right arm, and she could hear machines behind her bed making small blipping noises. She blinked, seeing the slanted blinds on the window revealing a dark night sky. A dim light cast shadows on the pale walls. She had no idea which night it was, nor which hospital she was in. Her heart picked up its rhythm as the questions piled up.

There was no pain, yet she felt weak, drained. She could make out heavy bandages across her chest beneath the light sheet and the hospital gown. Frowning, she struggled to remember what had happened. Then it all came rushing back.

Ric Skelly in the hunting cabin, his pathetic story,

his gun aimed at her, Sam crashing in, and Ric turning toward Sam. No, she couldn't let anything happen to Sam. She loved him too much. She'd tried to hit Ric's arm, but she'd miscalculated. She'd felt the searing pain, felt herself falling. Then there'd been only the blackness.

Oh, God. What had happened to Sam?

Very slowly, she turned her head, and felt the panic subside. He'd pulled the armchair up close to her bed and was asleep in it, his head tilted at an awkward angle. His face—that wonderful face—was a mass of bruises and cuts. And his poor hands! But he was breathing. Thank God, he was breathing.

Hesitantly, she moved her left hand and touched his arm.

Instantly, Sam came awake and saw Carly looking at him. In her eyes, he saw all he needed to see. Sitting up a little awkwardly, he took her hand in his. "I love you," he said quietly. The rest could wait until later, until they were both healed.

Carly smiled. Maybe she hadn't been dreaming after all.